The Edge of Darkness Trilogy

RESTITUTION

Book 3

LEIGH RIVERS

Art designed by Zoe Maxwell (@kowai_girl_tattoo on IG)
Cover Design By: Ashlee O'Brien at Ashes and Vellichor Designs
Formatting by Charly Jade *of* Designs By Charlyy

Edited by Laura at Ten Thousand Editing
Proofread by Lauren at PSR Editing

Distributed by Zando

First Edition: September 2026

978-1-63893-548-3 (trade paperback)
978-1-63893-608-4 (BAM signed edition)

10 9 8 7 6 5 4 3 2 1
Manufactured in the United States of America
LAK

PLAYLIST

Cities – Toby Mai & Two Feet
Hearing Damage – Thom Yorke
REAR LIGHT – SAKUREYE
Dead Man – David Kushner
Meet you at the Graveyard – Cleffy
Chokehold – Sleep Token
Calm Down – Rema
medicine – onte
The Woods – Hollow Coves
with u – lucidbeatz
Change (In the House of Flies) – Deftones
From Now On – The Greatest Showman

The Edge of Darkness Trilogy playlist can be found on Spotify.

CONTENT WARNING

As this is a continuation of Insatiable and Voracious, I highly recommend reading those first to avoid any major confusion.

This story deals with dark themes that some readers may find uncomfortable. If any of the below listed subjects trigger you, please put yourself first and think of your mental health before deciding to read the final instalment of The Edge of Darkness Trilogy.

Dissociation, drug use and withdrawals, attempted suicide, accidental somnophilia, forced cannibalism, violence and detailed gore, torture, character death, psychogenic non-epileptic seizures, mentioned but not detailed CSA, destruction of mind, extreme trauma and its mental responses, sexual and physical assault.

1

KADE

The warm blood of my best friend seeps through my fingers as I keep pressure on the gunshot wound in his chest. His back arches, and he grits his teeth through the pain, pupils still fully blown from the drugs they forced into him. Into us. I can't fucking see properly, but I can see all the blood and his pale face as he gasps.

None of the guards are helping me. They won't. They aren't allowed to. They all watch as I lean over him and try to slow the bleeding. He's not dead – yet – so the shot didn't hit his heart. But there's so much goddamn blood. If Dez was here, he'd pass out from the sight.

My other best friend is sunning it up on vacation with his girlfriend while we're all fighting for our lives. It was always best to keep as many people out of it as possible. Good for him for having the normality we can only dream of.

The fact Base got dragged into it all and is now lying in a pool of crimson fucking enrages me. I'm a protective dickhead – Bernadette knows this and used it against me. She just had to mess with my friends and family. If Base dies and I don't find my sister and Stacey, Bernadette better hide on a different fucking planet, because nothing, and I mean nothing, will stop me from ripping that rotten bitch to shreds.

Regrettably, or not so regrettably, I snapped the neck of the wanker who shot Base and hit someone else repeatedly with a chair until they were dead. Their bodies are in a heap beside me. And for some reason, despite the excess of drugs in my system melting my fucking brain, I'm fine and unharmed.

The eyelids of the Russian beneath me fall shut, and my chest caves. "No." I grip his chin. "Don't you fucking dare close your eyes, Base."

He doesn't open them, and my heartbeat accelerates. "Look at me. Fucking look at me."

I slap him across the face, staining his cheek crimson, and he blinks his eyes open. Groggily, his words broken, he mumbles, "Did you… just… fucking *slap* me?"

Words coming from him are a good sign. Relief rushes through me, and I sag against him, pressing my forehead to his while keeping my hand over his bleeding wound. "You need to help me find the girls," I say, whispering, emotional – I can't think straight. The room is fucking spinning still, and everything is glitching. Is this even real? "Stay with me. Please."

They have Stacey. My sister too. Sold them.

Bile rises in my throat – I try and fail to control the harsh breaths through my nostrils.

Base's hand reaches up, snatching at my collar feebly. "Lu-Luciciella."

My jaw tightens. "I'll find her. I promise."

Guards fill the room, two medics follow behind, and I move to the side to let them work on him while keeping his attention with a hand on his face – keeping him awake while they assess the damage. The bullet has an exit wound in his back, which is another good sign, but he's still weak and losing quite a bit of blood.

Nothing they can't treat, as long as he gets urgent care *now*.

I hear them talking among themselves about whether to take him to a hospital or to one of Bernadette's dodgy doctors who works under her belt here in London. Someone injects him with morphine, sticking shit to him to check his obs, and his eyes fall shut as the pain meds take effect.

I sit back on my haunches and look up at where the nightmare rolled out before me only minutes ago. The fear in their eyes... That fucking sinking feeling in my gut repeats in my mind. I need to get there before it gets worse. I need to get the fuck away from these assholes and find my sister and my girl.

We aren't together – haven't been for a while – but Stacey is my girl.

Mine.

And people don't fuck with what's mine. I gave in to Bernadette, gave up my control and my life when she found out who Stacey was, so why is she now going back on her word? I've done everything she's asked. Every-fucking-thing.

I can't even think straight to figure out what I did wrong.

In Bernadette's ballroom, they auctioned off people. Me and Base too. But going by the state he's in, I doubt he'll be fulfilling any duties with his buyer anytime soon. Mine, annoyingly, will summon me in a matter of days. That's fine. I'll kill him like the last person who bought my time – right after I hang Bernadette's husband and make her watch.

I'm finally hitting my limit.

"Where did they take the girls?" I ask one of the guards I know hates his job. I point at the blank screen with a shaky, blood-covered finger. "The last two before the feed cut."

I have a feeling – I was never taken to initiation since I'm technically classed as "trained" to take orders and fuck on demand. But I've heard horror stories about the process.

His eyes flit to his colleagues, then he lowers his voice. "They'll go to the loading floor for induction. They stay there for about five days with their new owners before they leave."

The intense need to snap his neck like I did his colleague's is almost too much to handle, so I fist my hands at my sides.

"Why was the auction at the Sawyers' property and not in Edinburgh like it usually is?"

His gaze floats around the room again, to the guys lifting one of their dead friends, then back to me. "Stop asking questions," he grits.

My right eye twitches as their head of security enters the room. "We've got orders to lock you up, kid," he says, and I imagine him dead on the floor like the other two. "You're not to be released until the induction is over."

Base is lifted onto a stretcher and carried out while my eyes go between him and the guards. They won't let me go with him – they have guns pointing at me now, but I know he's not going to die.

Since I don't have my phone, I glance at the guard I just spoke to. "I want Bernadette on the line. I'll go to the cells, but I want to speak with her first."

We're in one of Archie's houses on the outskirts of London – somewhere they like to go when things get too heated and want to lay low.

The main guard huffs, and he pulls his phone out, taps the screen then puts it to his ear. "It's Polner. Yeah, everything is fine down here. Is the boss there?" He straps his gun away and turns his back to me while the others keep their aim on me. "The mouthy one wants to talk to her. No, not the Russian. Tobias Mitchell's son."

There's a pause, then the faint sound of the voice I despise.

"Good evening, Mrs Sawyer. I have Kade here. No, sorry, he isn't in the cells yet, but he said he'd go willingly if he speaks with you. Yes, the Russian is alive – he'll survive his injury."

He turns, his face red as he hands me the phone, and I snatch it from his grip. My body trembles with a mixture of everything I'm feeling. "Call off their deals," I demand when Bernadette stays silent, yet the sound of her nails pianoing on her desk echoes through the line. "My sister and Stacey. Call it off. Or I'll pay for them and let them go. Do *something*."

She hums, and I can tell she's smiling. "And why would I do that?"

"The only thing you hold over me is the people I care about. The only thing you ever held over me was those I loved. You fucked with my dad for years, and now you're fucking with my sister and my—" I stop, gripping the phone tighter. "You're playing a dangerous game here."

She laughs. "Is that a threat, Kade?"

"It's a promise. If they're inducted and leave with whoever fucking bought them, I will fuck you up. You'll no longer have anything to blackmail me with. You sell them, and I will make sure the last day of your life is a nightmare. Your daughter? I'll record her screams while I skin her alive and send you her fucking bones. I'll make you watch Archie suffer, and I'll leave you for last. If anything fucking happens to those girls, you better hide, you piece of shit."

"So feisty, my dear boy."

Then the line cuts out, and I throw the phone at the wall, smashing it to pieces.

"Nice one, asshole. You owe me a new phone. Now do as you're told and get in the cuffs."

Glancing up, I see the mouthy one – the main guard, head of security – unsheathing his gun. He's much larger than me and built like a fucking tank. I drive my fist into his face so hard, I hear a snap. I'm so blinded by rage that I think the snapping sound might have come from my hand, but when I look down at him on his knees, his broken jaw hangs as he cries in pain. I sigh and let them shackle me then drag me to the cells.

2

STACEY

The room is dark and cold – icy air licks at my exposed skin. Compared to the elegance of upstairs, down here looks like one of those *Saw* movies.

Am I about to die? Where's Luciella?

The elevator dings behind me as it starts ascending, leaving me to tremble in fear and terror. There's a shadow of a guard standing by the door, his gun strapped to his chest, and I can hear light sobs coming from somewhere. Through the air vent?

"We have another one!" he calls out, and I flinch. "Should I send her through yet? Is the other one sorted?"

I have no idea what the person says in response. It's a mumble. Faint. An echo. The sobbing through the vent stops, or maybe it just gets quieter, or maybe I'm just imagining it in my state of shock.

I need to find Luciella. We need to get out of this.

"Stacey Fields," I whisper, shaking uncontrollably, a lone tear slipping down my cheek. "Pl-ease."

Then I flatten my lips and pause as the guard briefly shines a torch in my face before turning around again. "She's young, maybe early twenties. Appears unharmed," he says and then laughs. "Well, for now. How much did she go for?"

He whistles and laughs again. Glancing over his shoulder to me, frozen in place, he sneers. "She's tainted with ink though. It's a disgusting sight. Are you ready for her yet? Should I strip this one too?"

Strip...

Oh God.

My punishment might be even worse if they find an earpiece on me, a wire attached to my body, hidden between my breasts. While the guard has his head down, trying to hear what his colleague is saying, I tug out the earpiece and try to pull at the wire – the glue sticks to my skin, and I silently sob as I rip it off and drop it on the ground.

The guard glances up at me through the darkness, finishing his conversation – I kick the wire behind a box and hug myself as he approaches me. He towers over me, the gun making me nervous as he chuckles at spotting Bernadette's blood on me.

"Heard you messed up the boss's face. She'll make you pay for that. Are you going to fight me like little blondie?"

My chin trembles. "Did you hurt her?"

"She's lucky I didn't," he says, grabbing my arm and pulling me towards the door. "Don't worry about her – you won't be seeing her again anyway." He shoves me out the room, into a corridor with pipes lining the ceiling and flickering lights that hurt my eyes. "Take her to room six."

I'm grabbed again, dragged down the corridor by another guard. I can already feel bruises forming on my skin from their deadly grips. I try to pull away, but he presses something hard and cold to the base of my spine. A gun?

"Walk, or I'll make sure you never use those pretty legs again."

As I pass doors, I can hear crying, screaming, and... moaning.

Not the good kind either. Like forced moans – moans that indicate their bodies are betraying them in the middle of screaming for help. Both men and women are begging for help – for their attacker to stop.

My stomach twists.

I think I might be sick. Is Lu in one of those rooms?

"Is my friend okay?" I ask, using a pleading tone. "Please just tell me she's okay."

We stop at a door at the end of the corridor. "You should be more worried about yourself."

He swipes a card against the scanner, and the door beeps – a red light above it changes to green. I'm shoved inside, the lights automatically turning on, and my eyes widen at the sight before me.

"I suggest you shower. Your new master might not enjoy the sight of someone else's blood on his pet. Leave your dress by the door."

I turn to look at him. "He's coming here?"

"You thought you'd leave so easily? No, you need to be initiated. You'll stay in this room together until he's happy with your submissiveness."

The guard closes the door with a slam, leaving me in the torture chamber by myself. A four-poster bed sits in the middle of the room, leather cuffs at each post. There's a shelf filled with... My gut twists when I see the ball gag attached to a chained leash. There are loads of tubes of lube, other sex devices and a rack of different sizes of blades, the edges facing out.

I rush to them and freeze, my hand outstretched to the smallest. Instead, I grab the biggest one, like a mini machete, and hold it behind my back. Then I press myself into the wall opposite the door. When the person comes, I won't let him touch me. I used a smaller blade once, when Chris sold me to his friends, and I won't hesitate to do it again.

Even if the person who won my auction is a giant.

He won't be getting anywhere near me.

I swallow down a lump growing in my throat as I wait.

And wait and wait and wait. Until my legs are shaking and sweat lines my face and chest. I think an hour passes with me being in my head, worrying about Luciella. Will Kade make sure Bernadette gets her back? Yes. He'll do anything for his sister, so I know he'll do what he can to save her. And Base was shot. He was shot in the chest and... and he might be dead.

My eyes water. How did my life come to this?

Where the fuck is Chris? He's a psychopath, but right now I wouldn't mind if the insane bastard got me out of this.

Voices pause my thoughts, and my hand tightens around the handle of the blade. The door beeps, and two guards walk in, a large presence behind them. In a white, faceless mask, taller than the others, with wide shoulders, my *master* walks in in only his white shirt, the jacket he previously wore discarded somewhere.

My breathing stalls as he walks between the guards and stands in the middle of the room – his eyes are the only things I can see as he watches me. Then his head tilts to the side. No words. No actions. Nothing.

"We will provide you with a key card that only you can use to come in and out of the room. The loading floor is the only one you have authorisation to walk freely. Your meals will be brought to this room three times a day. She's only to wear the white dresses provided in the dresser, but you are welcome to use our laundry system. Do you have any questions, sir?"

He doesn't respond, just stares at me, his hands in his pockets.

The guards glance at each other before one of them narrows his eyes on me. "We'll take your dress."

The blade's coldness is pressing against my spine thanks to my open-backed dress. Maybe I should just cut my own throat instead of trying to get out of this. Maybe it'll be easier than actually being fully awake while being raped this time.

One step forward from the large presence is all it takes for my heart to stop, and I lunge forward and try to stab him in the chest – but he captures my wrist before the guards can react, squeezes until I drop the weapon and tuts at me as he shakes his head.

"Little psycho bitch," one guard says.

The eyeholes of the mask are mesh, so I can't see his eyes that well. I know they're blue. The only detail of my attacker that I know. If he never shows me his face, how can I identify him to report him if I ever get free?

I shiver as I feel my dress torn from the back, cut from my body and pulled away as I stand before this man in only the underwear Chris made me wear. No bra.

Not that the man even looks at my body. His eyes are burning into my soul.

"First test, sir. Then we'll be out of your way."

"You're a bad girl," he whispers, his deep, gravelly voice muffled by his mask. He releases my wrist and snatches my jaw as the guards step away. "Kneel."

I stay still, standing my ground, refusing to drop to my knees. The guards stare, waiting to see if I'll successfully pass my first test of induction. If I refuse, they might make my stay here longer. They want me to be compliant – to be a good, submissive pet to my master.

But I'm dead already anyway.

I try to drive my knee between his legs, but he dodges it and forcefully shoves me down, so my knees crash into the floor, pulling a cry from me.

His hold on my jaw moves to my hair, and he tugs it, so I look up at him. "Take his belt off," one of the guards says. "Now."

I close my eyes as more tears slip free, and I try to control my breathing as I reach up to the buckle. My fingers tremble as I fail to pull it free twice before finally tugging the leather from the loops. The man snatches the belt before I can drop it, and I gasp as he wraps it around my neck, slots the leather through the buckle then tightens it till it settles against my throat.

He pulls tighter, and my air shuts off, burning my lungs, my eyes pressured.

The guards seem to be happy, so they pat his shoulder and tell him to enjoy his first night. The door opens and closes, then I hear a beep. I let out a choked, strangled sound as he lets go of the belt so I can breathe.

I bend forward, my hand pressing to the carpet as I cough and cry, wishing I hadn't let Chris force me to come to this stupid fake party-turned-auction. But when the mask drops to the carpet and

I see the man lowering to his knees, I freeze waiting for a blow or an order.

Hands grab at my face, forcing me to look up into the eyes of my new master.

Tobias Mitchell.

My lips part, all my fear washing away as I manage, "To-Tobias?"

Kade's father grabs the blanket right next to us, wraps it around me, then pulls me in for a hug I didn't realise I needed.

"I'm sorry. I'm sorry. You're okay. You're safe with me," he says softly as he strokes my hair, letting me cry into his chest. "I found you, little one."

3

STACEY

Tobias pulls back, his eyes searching my face, refusing to let them drop lower even with the blanket covering me. "Are you hurt?"

I shake my head. "You were the one to win my auction?"

"Yes. Barry found out Bernadette's plan when she sent your insufferable asshole of a stepbrother the invitation and deal. We were halfway to London to find Kade but turned back. Are you sure you're not hurt?"

My eyes are burning given how hard I'm holding back a waterfall of tears. If I start bawling my eyes out, I don't think I'll be able to stop. "Barry's okay?"

He nods. "As annoying as he is, he's kept me hidden. His wife and child are in a safe house in Aberdeen."

A tear slips down my cheek, and he notices, wiping it with his thumb. "I'm going to get you out of here."

"What about Luci—"

"Sebastian Prince's uncle won her auction. They're going to take her to Moscow and keep her under the radar until Bernadette is dealt with. It was the deal I made with the grandfather to get his help – I told him I'd kill his grandson's abuser in exchange for him protecting my daughter. There are Russians surrounding this building as we speak."

"They know about Bernadette having Base?"

"The underworld is a ruthless place. A war between the Scottish law enforcement and whoever else she has under her belt against the mafia would be a mess. A lot of lives would be lost. I offered to kill her and her husband."

I go to speak, but he cuts me off. "We need to get you out of here before they tell me to start the next task. They'll shoot me on the spot, and someone else will get you."

He turns, swipes the key card on the sensor pad, and when the door beeps and opens, he leans his head out but pulls back in quickly. He mutters a "fuck" then fishes a mobile from his pocket and puts it to his ear.

Pacing the room, Tobias huffs as it rings and rings and rings, until I hear someone answer.

"When I call, you asshole, you fucking answer right away. I have her. Yes, she's fine and unscathed. There are four guards outside. Can you see on the footage the safest way for me to get her out of here without risking her life?"

I nibble my bottom lip as Tobias turns and fixes his gaze on me, his eyes burning into me. He goes to the dresser and pulls out white material. It's a dress. Short. Thin straps on the shoulders. Silky and actually really pretty, if I wasn't in the middle of a sex ring's hideout and trying to escape with my boyf— ex-boyfriend's father who's just broken out of prison.

"How did you escape?" I ask as I take the dress. "I'm mad at you for that, just so you know."

He scoffs as he turns round, letting me drop the blanket and pull on the dress. "You didn't come for visitation, and I got bored."

"Bored..."

"I'm a little irrational and impulsive. Plus, I had a feeling something was wrong – call it a sixth sense."

The dress sits mid-thigh, and I hate it. I hate everything about this day.

"Kade and Base were auctioned off too," I say as I find a hair tie in the dresser and pull my hair into a bun on top of my head. "Are you going to help him?"

He turns around. "As soon as I know you're safe, yes."

I stand in the middle of the room, taking a deep breath. I still feel so overwhelmed. Only a matter of minutes ago, I thought I was going to be attacked and forced upon. I thought I'd end up dead, but no.

"Thank you," I say quietly.

He frowns, leaning against the dresser, crossing his arms and ankles while he waits for Barry to call back and tell him it's clear to go. "Why are you thanking me?"

I throw my arms out. "I accepted that I was going to die. I thought I was—" I stop, nearly choking. "Just accept my gratitude. I know your children are your priority, but I appreciate that you're here for me."

"You are also my priority. I would have always hunted for you to the ends of the fucking earth, little one. I know you didn't have the best relationship with your father, your brothers are useless pricks, and my son is shackled to a bitch on an insane power trip, but you have me."

The force of my body catapulting into his knocks him back a step, but he catches me.

My dad never protected me. He loved me, but as soon as Nora came into the picture, I was a second thought to him. As much as I miss him, as much as I love him, Tobias treats me better. And I never thought I'd say this, and forgive me, Aria Miller, but to be safe and sound in Tobias Mitchell's hold is a dream I never want to wake up from. I don't want to let go.

What if I pull away and he vanishes? What happens if this is a dream and I'm drugged? What if I'm imagining this entire scenario and I'm shackled to the bed with an old, overweight and sweating man claiming me?

"Don't hold it in," Tobias whispers. "If you need to cry, then you fucking cry, little one. Get it all out right here and now."

This *is* reality, and I have Kade's father's arms around me, reassuring me with slow strokes of my hair and tightening his hold as I tremble and let my emotional state loose.

Although I should be going crazy at him for breaking out of his institution and causing a worldwide fugitive hunt that's taken over the news and radio, all I can do is hug him, inhaling his scent. Not an old sweaty man. No. Cinnamon. A spiced cologne Kade's clothes always smelled like.

I used to stick his hoodie under my nose and inhale as I lay in bed, waiting for my stepbrother's next blow. I'd always take longer to get home, because I knew what was to come.

I was alive when I was around Kade. And now I'm alive because of his father.

And all Tobias is doing is hugging me back, his grip on my nape keeping me firmly to his chest. "I've got you," he assures me in his deep tone.

Those three words have my body shaking against his, tears of both joy and exhaustion making me sob uncontrollably until he's taking all of my weight.

"Shhh. I've got you."

He grips my shoulders and pushes me back enough to study my face. "Tell me you're okay, because we need to leave as soon as Barry gives us the go-ahead. Can you keep your emotions in check until we get out of here?"

"You told me to let it all out."

The slight tilt of his head shows his confusion. "There's more?"

I huff out a laugh and wipe my eyes. "Sometimes I forget you're an unfeeling idiot."

Smirking, he steps away. "You didn't answer my question."

I raise an unsteady shoulder. "I'm okay."

Apparently, I must still have tears running down my numb face, because he raises a brow at me and wipes my cheeks. "Don't cry any more tears because of them. You've got it all out. Dry your eyes and keep your chin up. They don't deserve your tears." He gives me a tight smile, which makes his dimple dent in. "No one does."

I take in a deep breath through my nose and exhale through my mouth. "Right. Okay. I'm okay. Really. I still can't believe you're here. You escaped and—"

His phone rings, cutting me off. Tobias silences it as he says, "You can yell at me later. I did what I had to do for my family, and you" – he flicks my nose – "you are part of it."

Smiling, I hug myself. I've not been part of a real family in years.

It feels good.

He leans down and grabs his mask, a gun peeking from inside his suit jacket.

Gone are the images of Tobias playing board games and reading historical literature while baby Eva sits on his chest and grabs at his face.

The door behind him beeps just as he fixes the mask in place, and we both freeze as the same guards who left only fifteen minutes ago enter.

"We have orders to remove the girl. You will have your payment refunded within twenty-four hours, but you are welcome to take your pick of any of the others left over from the auction to keep you company in a different room for the night."

They both step to the side, giving Tobias a clear path to walk out. "Please follow us."

It takes Kade's father all of two seconds to snatch his gun from his jacket and put a bullet in one of their heads. The abruptness of the bang has me wincing and backing away just as the other guard knocks Tobias's gun from his hand and proceeds to punch him across the face.

With the size of the man's hand, I would be on the ground and screaming with a broken jaw. Tobias just laughs and headbutts him, then grabs him by the nape with a deadly grip while he's dizzied from the broken nose. I watch in horror as Tobias drags the man towards the rack of blades and starts smashing his face into them so fast, blood splatters everywhere, cutting himself in the process.

The man squeals like an animal until the blades cut into his throat, then the sound turns to choking, twisted gasping, and then nothing.

Tobias lets go of the guard and watches his body slump on the ground in a pool of blood. He grits his teeth at the small slashes on his hand and fingers, flicking his hand out to get rid of the blood.

"What a waste of life," he sighs, rolling up each of his white sleeves to the elbow. "We can't wait any longer. Fuck Barry's plan."

I nod and rub my hands up and down my exposed arms; my white dress has little splashes of blood down the front.

"I'd offer you my jacket, but I need to pretend I'm a piece of shit who just paid millions for a pet. Some of them will be flaunting their prizes. Because I was a new bidder with no history in this fucked-up world, I had to agree to the five-day induction trial to get past security. But if we're out there, I cannot draw attention. We need to blend in. We're completely outnumbered, even with the people we have surrounding the manor."

"I understand." I chew my lip. "Kyle and Chris were outside. Did anyone catch them?"

"No. Why were they here? No. Fuck that. Can we focus on you first?" But yet again, his phone rings and cuts us off.

"Now?" Tobias answers. "Fucking *listen* to me, Barry, you motherfucker, I have two dead guards here, and it's only a matter of minutes before more come. Either you find a safe way, or I'll find one myself. I. Need. To. Get. Her. Out."

I hug myself, nearly tripping over one of the dead guards as I step back. I slip on a puddle of crimson liquid, shaking the blood from my foot while Tobias discusses the new escape plan quickly – the route we'll take and how many guards we'll pass on the way.

He hangs up the phone and takes my hand, pulling me out of the room without another thought. "We need to go. When we see someone, act scared. I need to hold you like I plan to fuck you in every position possible without your consent."

"Jesus, Tobias."

4

STACEY

As soon as we round the corner and go up a floor, we hear whimpers. Moans. He swears and pulls me to the side when I falter in my steps. "You can't run if you get scared. You need to be an obedient prize and stay by my side, okay?"

I straighten my spine and nod up at him. "Yeah."

"I'll need to treat you terribly."

"I know," I reply, my eyes flicking to the side when I hear a man laughing.

"I apologise in advance."

He genuinely sounds terrified, so I soften my voice. "Tobias, it's okay – just hurry up."

He grips my arm and pulls me along the corridor, and I try to keep up.

We round another corner, and my back hits the wall before I

can even let out a gasp. Tobias plasters himself against my front and lowers his head to the hollow of my throat.

"Sorry," he whispers, a soft breath through the hole at the mouth of the mask. "I'm sorry. I'm sorry. I'm sorry," he breathes repeatedly as he grabs my thigh and pulls it up to his side, playing the part. "Forgive me."

Archie walks past with three guards. He's talking on the phone and not giving us any attention. He's yelling at someone to get someone under control.

Once they're out of sight, he drops my leg and flinches back like I've burned him. "Sorry." He straightens me up and turns his head.

"Do you think he was talking about Kade?"

Tobias trembles a little, and I know he's vibrating with rage he's struggling to control. "Probably," he grits, glancing in the direction Archie went. "It's taking me everything not to snap the bastard's neck, but I can't risk you. Come on. I'll make sure he burns along with the manor."

He takes my wrist and pulls me along the corridor once more. Annoyingly, a man with a cigar is walking towards us with one of the auction paddles in his hand. Tobias lowers his hand to my hip and greets the man, trying to blend in.

The hand burns.

Once the man is gone, his touch snaps away.

I accept his hand in mine, his thumb rubbing over my skin to remind me that I'm safe as I follow him into another corridor, cold and clammy, doors lining one side of the wall, the rooms locked and filled with more moaning.

I whimper and lower my head when a door opens and I see a girl waiting inside, her hands obediently resting in her lap. "What about the rest of them?"

"Once I get you out safely, Barry, his men and the Russians will storm the place. They'll get the rest out before they burn it to the ground. The latter wanted to storm it right away, but I couldn't risk you getting hurt. This is the safest way."

My hand is in his once again as we ascend the staircase, the music slowly filling my ears. Orchestral music – Alexandre Desplat. I usually enjoy his music while dancing or reading, but right now, it's making this entire situation worse. It grows louder as we get to the top, the stairs opening to the main foyer as the melody merges into "Statues".

In the open, he lets go of my hand and takes my arm again, dragging and pushing me around corners. I know he's hating treating me this way, but we can't let anyone recognise him or what we're doing.

Some of the other buyers are walking around, showcasing their new pets, all in white dresses identical to mine. Some look a little younger than me, some older, and some are downright terrified and sobbing.

Instead of going through the entranceway doors, we take a right, bypassing the auction room, which is filled with workers cleaning up. He walks slowly, so I can keep up in my bare feet. No one blinks in my direction, despite the splatters of crimson dotted all over my dress and face.

As if this is normal to them.

A guard stands to the side with a gun strapped to his chest. He nods to Tobias. "Are you enjoying your prize, sir? Is she to your liking?"

My body goes stiff as Tobias yanks me to stand in front of him, pretending to whisper in my ear words of assault, his hand just under my breast, while actually telling me not to give him eye contact and that he's once again sorry. "Oh, she's more than to my liking. Beautiful, isn't she?"

"You'll join the others in the conference room?"

"Maybe next time," he says, then grabs a fistful of my hair and drags me into the next corridor.

I elbow him when we're out of view. "You did not need to pull my hair."

"I like pulling hair."

I roll my eyes. "Of course you do."

He winks and pulls his phone out. "We're approaching. Have your men ready." He hangs up and looks at me. "There are no guards on this floor. Nearly there, little one."

We stop in a small alcove in the lobby, and he throws aside the mask, his brows furrowing. He slips off his suit jacket, removing a blade and a gun and tucking them into his waistband.

"Here," he says, sliding the jacket over me, helping me get my arms into each side and buttoning up the front to hide more of my exposed skin. "Well, that could've gone a lot worse. It was rather easy, to be honest. Other than having to touch you. No offence, but that made me want to vomit all over you."

I want to call him a psychopath for thinking that was anything but terrifying, but he is one, so I'd just be stating the obvious. He doesn't feel the same way I feel; his emotions are learned, altered and altogether different from mine.

"I think you enjoyed throwing me around a little too much. Payback for all those times I beat you at chess?"

He scoffs. "Do not delude yourself into thinking that was even slightly enjoyable. I'd rather be throwing Aria around, preferably while she's wearing—"

"Stop! Some things are best kept in a locked box, you idiot. And if this doesn't kill you, Aria will for escaping," I say. "Have you seen her?"

"I've watched her, but I don't have the balls to go see her. Fuck, no. She'd send my ass back to the States. I think she might cut me off completely after this."

"I think she'll understand," I say, letting out a confused *uhh* as he tugs at the suit jacket around me, so I'm glued to his chest, his face dropping to my throat as he pulls my head back by the hair, pretending to bite me just as a guard walks by.

Then he pushes me away like I'm poisonous. "Barry is supposed to be good at his fucking job, the motherfucker. And again, no offence, but if one more person comes, I might need to let us get caught."

"Why?" I ask.

"I'm... very uncomfortable acting this out," he says, looking away and shoving his hands into his pockets. "I feel like I'm betraying my son and Aria."

"It's not real."

"I'm aware," he hisses. "It still makes me uncomfortable."

His phone rings again, and after Tobias goes nuts for a solid minute, Barry tells him they're nearly ready and in position. He gives directions to the window we've to jump from, and we'll escape out the back of the grounds since no one is there.

"I don't think Aria will forgive me for this one, if I'm honest. I've probably lost her. She'll hate me like the rest of the world." He sighs again and pinches his nose. "But I had no other option; you didn't show up for visitation. I had to escape."

With something close to a disbelieving laugh, I stare at Kade's dad, at the tiredness in his eyes from constantly fighting with himself. "The world really has no idea who you are. You are a little bit nutty, but you care a lot about your family. You taught yourself to love – in your own way, yes – but that alone goes against everyone's opinion of you. You aren't heartless, Tobias. Who cares what the world thinks?"

He grimaces; he hates compliments and softness. "Shut up or I'll take you back."

I giggle. "I missed you."

"Are you done?"

I roll my eyes, and he takes my hand and leads me through the corridor again. We turn left and pause in our steps.

A girl is pressed up against the wall, crying for two men to stop. They aren't guards. They're in suits. Bidders. One is trying to pull up her dress while the other grabs her face and tries to shove his fingers into her mouth.

I can't see his face, but I feel the energy crashing into a dark void as Tobias pulls me behind him slowly, sliding the blade from his waistband at the same time.

The girl turns her face to dodge a tongue, and I almost step forward when I see it's Cassie Sawyer, Bernadette's daughter.

His fingers flex over the handle, and in a silent flash that has me backing away until I hit the opposite wall, he grabs the closest man's hair, yanks his head back and slices the knife along his throat.

Animalistic noises fill the corridor, gurgling chokes, crimson splattering Tobias's face as he punctures his victim's skull with the blade for good measure. The blade stays impaled as the body drops to the floor, lifeless, sightless, his unseeing eyes on me.

His beastly friend lets go of the sobbing Cassie, now covered in blood. She slowly falls to the floor in a huddle, her eyes glazed over, her lips chewed from her biting them. One of her nails is pulled up, the skin butchered, as if she'd been trying to claw herself free of their clutches.

I rush to her, dropping to my knees and pulling her away from them as the remaining guy tries to swing his fist at Tobias, failing when he captures his wrist, breaks it with a quick snap then headbutts him.

The man's nose cracks.

Tobias shoves his arm away and punches him in the face, hard enough that he crashes into the wall – the man unable to retaliate as he smashes his face again and again. It's a vicious, continuous beating that has more crimson spraying around us like a fountain until the vile human is unrecognisable.

Tobias has caved his face in completely.

Cassie is conscious but slurring her words, blood drying into her cheeks. Her dress clings to her sweating body, and there's a large puncture hole in her arm. She glances up at me, barely seeing me – then her eyes roll to the back of her head and she collapses into my arms.

Tobias's lips flatten. "Well, this is unfortunate. She's the enemy." He helps me up and tosses her over his shoulder. "Good thing we're nearly out of here. Grab her phone – it's on the floor over there."

I pick it up and give it to him, and he slides it into his pocket. "Where are we taking her?"

"She's the bait. Or blackmail. One child in exchange for the other. That's if they don't all perish when this place burns down."

He links our hands again, keeping an unconscious Cassie on his shoulder as he leads us to the end of the lobby and slides open a window. I let out a relieved breath as Barry's face pops up.

He grins at me when I smile. "Good evening, miss."

I chuckle. "Stop calling me that."

Kade's father grunts. "You both shut up. Take this." He practically tosses Cassie at him. Barry catches her limp body then hands her to one of his men, ordering them to take her to his car.

Tobias helps me up to the window ledge, and one of Barry's men helps me down. As soon as my feet press into the soft grass, Barry pulls me into him – another hug I had no idea I needed. I wrap my arms around him just as tightly.

"I'm glad you're okay. I was worried about you. I wouldn't have ever forgiven myself if something happened to you, Miss— Stacey."

Tobias scowls at us and narrows his eyes at Barry. "Let go of her and move. Before someone sees us."

Barry walks with us as we sneak through the grounds and into a small area of trees. My feet hurt, and I wince a little, but I don't say anything. We have more things to worry about than my bare feet.

I accidentally forget to hold a branch, and it slaps Tobias in the face.

I cringe and glance over my shoulder, mouthing an *oops*.

He looks like he wants to stab me.

We hurry through trees, and the music dies out as we pass by stables. There are no horses. I can't imagine Bernadette even caring for one.

We walk out of the grounds' unused back entrance, the metal gate harshly creaking, yet not loud enough to draw attention to us in the dark.

I'm too scared to feel relief yet, because something always goes wrong.

Barry offers me a low nod and opens the door to one of the cars for me. "It's good to see you again," I say. "I hope Eva and Lisa are okay?"

"They're safe and hidden. And it's really good to see you too. However, it's been rather peaceful without you."

I shake my head. "Your cheeks turn red when you lie."

When the car pulls out, Barry tells us that the Russians are readying themselves to storm the manor; that within the hour, it'll be up in flames.

Hopefully the Sawyers burn.

Even if their daughter is in the trunk.

When we reach the lodge, the sun is already starting to rise, and I'm exhausted. I'd nearly fallen asleep on Tobias's shoulder, but he shrugged me off while he tapped away on the iPad, hunting for Kade's location through the security feed Barry had hacked into.

I keep watching how much Tobias is trying to hold himself together – a shell as he turns the tablet screen off and blankly stares out the window, blinking more than usual, before checking the screen to see if there's any change then going back to staring.

His shell shatters when we get out of the car. The door of the lodge is thrown open, and Aria rushes out, her eyes red as her body slams into Tobias and she lets loose a string of sobs.

"Our babies," she cries. "We need to help them. Please help them."

He strokes the back of her hair, his arm around the small of her back. "We will. I promise we'll get our kids back."

The door opens again, and my eyes land on Jason.

5

STACEY

My head is fuzzy as I pry my eyes open, wincing from both the sunlight shining through the window and the ache in my muscles.

I curl into Kade's embrace and freeze all over, like ice-cold water has doused my naked body when I realise the chest has no tattoos. The hand resting on my hip belongs to someone who isn't my boyfriend. And when I lift my eyes to see the person's face, my stomach curdles.

It's Jason.

Kade's big brother.

I'm in my boyfriend's brother's bed. With no clothes on.

I feel like dying when between my legs throbs with the worst pain imaginable.

"No," I blurt in a croaky, dry voice and pull away from him – my heart instantly racing and shattering to pieces. I inwardly wince from

how stiff my body is. "No. No, no, no. Please no."

He groans and tries to reach for me. His eyes are closed, a frown line between his brows as he tries to pull me to him. "Go back to sleep, Giana. We'll go buy tests later."

The breath I let out catches halfway, and everywhere tenses as his hand lowers to my ass.

I launch myself away from him with a scream and hide my naked body with the duvet, pulling it completely off his. I close my eyes and beg myself to wake up – to rise from this nightmare as I back into a desk chair and drop into it.

I open them to slits when I hear the bed shift. I keep my hand up to hide his lower region.

Bile rises in my throat.

All I can think of is how Kade is never going to forgive me – I've broken his trust and ruined our future together. I'm not like this. I love Kade more than anything in the world. He was the only person who kept me breathing. He was the air to my starved lungs.

And going by the indents on my chest, the bite marks all over my breasts and the cut on my nipple, not to mention the bruising and dried blood on my hips and inner thighs, I know I've screwed everything up.

Jason sits straight on the mattress, one eye still shut. "Baby, what are you—" His voice stops, and he tilts his head at me – looks back down at the bed then back to me, completely lost. "What are you...? Who...? Stacey?"

He grabs a pillow and holds it against himself, his hand shaking as he brushes it through his sweaty hair. "What the fuck?"

A tear slips down my cheek as I shake and look at the wall. I'm trying so hard not to sob, to drop to the ground and curl up into a ball and scream for forgiveness.

I've betrayed Kade. I... cheated on him. With Jason.

Why would I do that?

I wouldn't. Kade is everything to me. He's my person. The one I'll have a big family with – grow old with.

I don't blink, my body trembling as I rise from the chair, keeping the covers against my chest as I put as much distance between me and the bed as possible. If my body allowed me, I would run, but I can barely stand.

My ribs are still cracked. From Chris finding the ultrasound picture in my room and throwing me around in utter rage, kicking me repeatedly in the stomach until my baby girl died.

I barely recognise my own voice as I stand and somehow ask, "Did you touch me?" I already know the answer as my words break. "Did we...? Did you...?"

Jason's eyes bulge. "Wait. Hold the fuck on a minute. We fucked? I fucked you? I thought you were Giana." His mouth hangs open, and he looks down at the dried blood all over his lower abdomen. "Is this your blood?"

I try to gulp and fail, nodding. "I think so."

"Fuck, I didn't... We wouldn't..." He stops, shaking his head and dropping it. "This is not happening. Please tell me this is not fucking happening. I have a goddamn fiancée! You're my little brother's girlfriend!"

I try to swallow again, but my throat is swollen. "Why am I here, Jason?"

He glances up, his hair a mess, eyes red. "I don't fucking know. Why are you here? Why were you in my bed?"

I flinch as I step back, and there's a horrible stinging sensation between my legs. My knees buckle – my spine is close to snapping from the pressure of my body trying to stay upright.

Flashes come to me, and my chest caves inward, seeing different faces above me. Bodies. In and around me.

I remember different smells. Grunts. Being bitten.

Someone pressing his large hand against my face, forcing my head into the mattress, hard enough that I thought my skull would crack.

Being strangled until my vision faded.

Someone slapping me, or was it a headbutt?

My stepbrother's voice.

The need to run and scream but not being in control of my body. My mind was barely there, but I remember parts. The feeling of being lost. Empty. How much I wanted my boyfriend or my other brother to burst in the door and put a stop to it.

I remember the terror. I remember more than one person being... And they...

My heart sinks as an image of Jason comes to the forefront of my brain, and my eyes burn as I remember that he was with them. He was on top of me and beneath me. My hand covers my mouth, and I back into the corner of the room, far away from him. "Did you rape me?"

He pulls on a pair of boxers and stands. "What? No. I wouldn't... I would never... I... Wait, some guy got me shit-faced and... Fuck, I think we..." He bites his lip and stares at me desperately. "What age are you? Same age as Kade?"

"Nineteen," I reply, my jaw jittering as I grip the duvet until it hurts more than my body.

"I didn't rape you. Please fucking believe me. I would never do that."

I chew my already swollen and cut lip. "I was raped. I remember being raped. I screamed for it to stop and tried to fight back. I remember you."

He looks at the bed, the fluid stains there, and his chest rises and falls heavier. "I think we just... I didn't rape you, Stacey. I promise you. I'm not a rapist."

My cheeks are soaked. "But you were on top of me," I say with a sob, sinking my nails into my palm. "You were on top of me. I didn't want to. I love Kade."

Jason looks over at me, his face pale. A part of me believes that he's innocent. "Did we really...?" he asks, his eyes glazing over.

"I think so." I wet my dry lips and glance away. "I think we did. I'm... I'm really sore."

His face falls when I lift my eyes back to him. "You're sore?"

I nod. "And I have deep bite marks on my chest and thighs. I'm bruised." I don't mention the pain in and around my behind. I'm distraught as it is.

He paces, pulling at his hair, muttering to himself about his partner, how Kade will kill him, and questioning himself on whether or not we actually had sex. Wondering if it might be a bad dream.

"I'm sorry," I sob. "I'm so sorry. I need to go. I need to go." I try to walk, but my lungs seize, and I gasp from the combined pain all over me and hunch over.

I flinch as Jason tries to help me, a terrified sound escaping my lips. He steps back, raising both hands.

"I'll get you something." Jason rubs his face with his palm and yanks open the drawers of his dresser, pulling clothes out. "Put these on." He drops the pile in my lap and opens his bedside unit while I slide them on. While his back is turned, I drop the duvet and pull on the top as he hurries into the bathroom and pours me a glass of water. "Take these. If you're sore, they'll help."

I stare at his hand, at the two white pills, and I shake my head. "No."

"I promise you," he says, slowly kneeling in front of me but still keeping his distance. "I didn't know it was you. I... don't remember much, but I... I thought you were Giana. I'm sorry. I'm truly sorry. I'll fix this."

I flinch as he takes my hand and puts the pills into it.

"Do you want to go to the hospital? To Kade? If you... If you think I slept with you without your consent, do you want to report me? I'll explain what I can to Kade and hand myself in."

Pressure builds behind my eyes. I believe him. "It wasn't your fault. I think my brother brought me here as punishment."

Thinking back to last night, my head hurts. I was at the club with Chris and his friends, and he forced me to swallow a pill, then another and another. He held my jaw and yelled at me to drink to flush down the drugs.

He made me dance.

Someone's fingers were... I said no.

And then it all went blank.

Jason... where did he come from?

I remember seeing him in the club. It was brief, when Chris tried to manhandle me onto the dance floor, or was it off it?

I drop my head to my hands. "I'm so sorry," I say. Chris brought him into this. And not only has he ruined my relationship, but he's also ruined Jason and Giana's. "It's my brother. He's a monster. He would have set this up. He's like that. He's evil and manipulative. He... he would have made me do this to get back at me for being with Kade."

I hiccough, and a lump of sick climbs up my throat.

"I... I came off my pill because me and Kade were trying for another baby. What if? What if we—" I struggle to finish the sentence, the forbidden question that makes me ill. "I love Kade. I thought you were Kade when I woke up. I need to tell him. I can't keep this from him."

"I don't remember anyone else being in here. I think... I think we just came here. I don't know. We'll both tell Kade. We'll explain ourselves. The last thing I said to my brother was to keep you safe and keep his chin up." He lets out a disgusted snort, his own eyes red as they water. "And this *happens."*

"What about your fiancée?"

Jason stares at me. "I don't think she'll ever forgive me for this.

Regardless of the circumstances. She's at work." He glances at the clock. "She'll be home in a few hours." He stands. "I'm going to take you to hospital."

"No!" I reach up and grab his arm. "I just want to go home."

"I'll pick you up once I speak to Gi. We'll talk to Kade." He wipes his cheek, sniffs and nods. "I'm sorry, Stacey."

My lip trembles. "I'm sorry too."

By the time he drops me off at home, barely able to walk into my house without cringing in pain, I feel a heaviness on my chest. Both physically and mentally.

I'm waiting for my world to end.

Chris is playing music in his room. Nora is at a charity event with my dad. And Kyle is at college.

I slowly make my way up the stairs, crawling the last flight, and locking my room door behind me. The shower is boiling, turning my skin red, and I sob until I can't anymore as I wash away all the mess.

The water goes from red to a light pink to clear, and I stay here, even after it turns cold. I'm not sure how long it takes me to get out and dress, then I lie in bed, staring at the ceiling as I think of a million ways to make Kade not hate me forever.

I'm going to lose him.

A knock at the door doesn't faze me. Even when it opens thanks to my stepbrother's annoying ability to unlock it from the outside. He chuckles and faintly, I hear him ask, "Rough night?"

My eyes don't leave the ceiling.

"You left this in the club," he says, dropping my phone on my chest. "You really shouldn't drink. You were quite the mess last night."

When he gets no response, he kisses my cheek and leaves.

A tear slides down the side of my face, past my ear, and soaks my pillow.

An hour goes by. And the pain gets worse. Jason will pick me up soon, and we'll go to Kade.

At some point, I check my phone, and my heart twists in my chest when I see all the messages from Kade. Some from my friends. Tylar asking me to go over plans for the studio Ewan is building in the manor. Luciella telling me I need to visit because she's always bored and Base keeps pestering her.

My dad telling me him and Nora will be home in the morning.

Chris asking if I'm alive yet.

And one from Jason, asking if I'm okay and saying he can't face Kade yet. He's sorry. He tells me that Giana had to take on an extra few hours at work and is due later tonight.

He apologises again.

Kade's final message comes through.

My Person: I'm having withdrawals, Freckles. Want me to come to your house and nurse you back to health?

Me: No!

Me: I'm okay, just really tired. Me and Tylar are coming over later to go over plans with Ewan for the surprise studio he wants to build Luciella. We're just going to stay over. I can come and see you once Ty is asleep? I need to talk to you.

My eyes water for the hundredth time, my throat tight as I type another message.

Me: I miss you.

My Person: Sure. I miss you too, Freckles.

I swallow more pain meds and force my legs to work so I can meet with Tylar. I wear a turtleneck and jeans, hiding all the evidence from last night. She asks if I'm okay, notes that I'm pale and tells me to get a good sleep when we're done with Ewan.

Jason looks like Ewan.

I can barely look at him.

When I meet with Kade, he receives a clip of me and Jason, and everything falls apart.

He yells at me. He hates me. He says I'm dead to him. He leaves me.

He doesn't answer me when I call or text, and when I try to call Jason, he declines.

Everything is just... slow, sore, an ache in my head as darkness drapes me. A bubble forms in my mind, and my chest is so heavy that I need it to end.

All of it just needs to end.

An hour later, the wind whips my hair around as I stand at the Erskine Bridge. I stare into the mist, the drop beneath me deadly but effective. All I need to do is step forward, and it all goes away.

Chris can't get me, because I'll be dead.

You're fucking dead to me.

I'm dead to me too.

I'm not scared.

It'll make it all stop.

I won't be scared to go home.

I can be with my baby girl.

A car screeches behind me, but I keep my empty gaze forward. Each breath counts down to my last as my grip on the railing slowly lessens, but movement in my peripheral vision stops me from letting go.

"Please don't do this," Jason says, and I can see from a sideways glance that his face is burst open. Kade must have got him. "Don't jump."

I have nothing left. It's all just pain and dark and a bunch of nothingness. I want to tell him this, but I can't. I keep my eyes forward.

"Killing yourself isn't going to make it all go away. If you jump, then it might be done for you, but everyone who cares for you will suffer. Do you know why? Because you are loved, Stacey."

I want to shake my head. No one loves me. I'm dead to everyone.

"Stacey..." He inches forward, and my jaw trembles. "We can fix this. We can talk to him. I'm sorry I got scared. We can fix it. We can find out what happened last night."

The wind is heavier, and I should be cold in just my T-shirt, but I don't feel anything. I don't feel anything at all. I don't want to jump because Kade left me. I want to do it because I want to die.

"Look at me," he says, his voice closer. "Please, Stacey. I lost everything too."

I turn my head to him slowly.

His face is a mess. His nose is bleeding, his eyebrow cut, and his bottom lip is swollen. "I lost my fiancée, who's probably already pregnant. I lost my brother. And I've most likely lost the rest of my family. If you jump, then you're leaving me to do this on my own."

My voice betrays me as it croaks, my face cramping, "But it hurts." Inside and outside. I have plasters all over my chest and thighs. The bruising is only getting worse, and inside me is ripped to shreds.

He raises his hands as he inches forward, until he's right beside me, on the opposite side of the railing.

He's got a grip on my top from behind.

"I lost my baby girl, and now I've lost him."

Carefully, Jason moves closer. "I'm sorry this has happened to you. But death is not the answer, Stacey. You'll leave so much heartbreak behind, when we can all help you. You jumping off this bridge will not make it stop."

"Maybe not," I say, looking out into the mist again, my voice monotone. "But it's the only way I think I can stop it from hurting so much."

Jason sighs. "What's your favourite movie?"

I stay quiet, confused by his question.

"Mine is Fight Club. *I think I've watched it over a thousand times. What's yours?"*

I wet my lips, and as I go to reply, images of me and Kade lying in bed, watching The Greatest Showman *flash before me, Milo and Hopper jumping around with me as I dance, and my gut drops.*

Jason keeps going. "Tell me about your family. What do they do?"

I frown, but instead of staring into the abyss and letting go of the railing, I say, "My dad is an engineer. Nora, my stepmother, stopped working when she married him." I blink, unsure why I'm even responding to him. "She has two sons. One is fine, but the other is the reincarnation of Satan."

"My dad is an engineer too."

I turn to face him. "What kind?"

"Structural. He built his business over the years. What kind of engineer is your dad?"

I remember the day he got his big break and was picked up by a well-known company. "Chemical."

He hums, and his grip tightens on my top as I lessen my hold on the railing. "The good brother, what's he like?"

"Bossy," I say, my lip quirking at the corner. "He's the way all brothers should be. He loves me like I'm his real sister. He... he didn't want to go to college, because that would leave me with Chris. He knows Chris is possessive of me and controlling, but he doesn't know just how far he takes things. He deserves to go over this bridge."

He nods. "Then let's throw him over instead."

I turn my face to him again, tears running down my cheeks then blowing away with the wind. "Promise?"

"Come down, and I promise."

Little did I know, when he helped me off the bridge and drove me home, that would be the last time I'd see him.

He broke his promise and, along with Kade, vanished from my life in the process.

6

KADE

My trigger finger has a permanent indent. I never really noticed it until now. Strange to think that will always be there. That if I ever escape my position, it'll be a constant reminder of the people I've killed.

The skin is rough and dry. I rub it with the pad of my thumb and study it while Base hums a Taylor Swift song to himself.

There's a tremor in my fingers too; they shake absentmindedly, but at least Ewan will stop asking me to work with him, since I probably can't use a screwdriver or a spirit level for shit. I doubt I'll be able to shoot with any sort of precision now either.

I fist my hand to stop the annoying memento of my torture.

If Stacey ever lets me hold her hand again, will she feel all the death I've caused?

She'd be disgusted with who I am now. Especially when she sees the scar from the corner of my mouth to the middle of my chest. If she ever asks me how many people I've killed, do I lie? Do I admit that I've lost count? That I enjoyed most of the killings?

I'll never have her looking at me the way she did when we were teenagers.

When my mind is blank, it's her voice I hear. A giggle. Singing. Crying. Screaming. Begging. When my hands are wrapped around someone else's throat, my psyche likes to fuck with me and show me her face – Stacey struggling beneath me as she clings on to the final breath trapped within her lungs.

I'll never feel her lips on mine again. Feel her fingers interlacing with my own while we hide our linked hands under the blanket. Kiss her during a game of dares. Laugh with her while she belts out songs from *The Greatest Showman.*

Stacey won't in a million years give me another chance, no matter how much I beg.

And why would she? I'm a fucking mess. I ruined her too. I treated her like shit and walked away when she needed me. Plus I'm shaking like a junkie looking for their next hit, aching for it with a deep hunger – a need to feel that high to escape reality and lose my fucking mind. It could also be the fact that I *am* having withdrawals. I haven't felt this ill in... ever.

Is she even still alive?

Did whoever buy her make it quick for her? Not that I'd grant the fucker the same courtesy – when I find out the person's name and where they live, not even my mother could stop what I'll be unleashing.

I screw my eyes shut in the darkness and sit up.

Thinking makes me emotional, and when I'm emotional, I lose focus. I do things wrong. I make mistakes in my work. And when I make mistakes, I end up with a punishment. Or Bernadette takes it out on Base.

He shouldn't even be here – he should be in America chasing my sister around while she pretends not to be interested. He should be partying, getting drunk, being his usual wild and dickish self and loving his life, not here, with me, forced to do messed-up shit.

Fuck. We've even been forced to beat the crap out of each other.

Probably Bernadette trying to turn my best friend against me. But no matter what she makes us do, whether that be fighting or... other things, we've kept strong. We told each other that we'd both get out of this together. One goes, we both go. We got stronger. We fought for our sanities.

We still do.

He said his family would interfere, but it's been a year since he promised they'd come for him, for us, yet we haven't seen or heard from them. Hope is slowly fucking fading away.

I close my eyes and lie down once more in my cell and try to picture my bedroom back home, instead of this shithole. I try to pretend there's a dip in the mattress at my feet, where my dogs Milo and Hopper are asleep, an arm slung over my waist, with a leg between mine, my fingers buried in thick hair.

I try to think of a time when I had everything. It used to make me feel better, to think of her and what we had together; to think of the feelings that rushed through me when I was falling madly in love with Stacey Rhodes.

It doesn't have the same effect it used to. It doesn't give me a sense of comfort. If anything, thinking about her now makes all of this worse. It makes me angry. Frustrated. Lost. And worst of all, it makes me want to kill more people.

They were sold. Gone.

Bernadette set up and sold two of the three most important women in my life. I practically begged her to get them back, but it was too late. They were already gone – their buyers decided to escape and burn her manor to the ground three days ago.

Sadly, Bernadette and her husband and daughter got out. Not so sadly, a lot of her guards died. When she showed up here the following day, her face was messed up. Stacey got her – hit her.

My girl. Even when faced with the worst kind of horror, she fucking fought. I didn't think it was possible to love her more than I already do, but I do.

Archie had ordered that I be tied to a chair, then his fucking asshole guards made me watch the recording of Stacey being raped. Every second of it was replayed and replayed. Me and four of their guys watched her be abused over and over while Archie made comments that resulted in me biting his ear off.

One-eared Archie, the prick.

Which is why I'm here and suffering from hunger and withdrawal pains. A cell. A cold prison. A small room with no windows and stone walls, one lined with bars so I can see into Base's cell. Underground. In the dark. And it's the most peace I've had in months.

Apparently, our buyers have agreed to wait until next month to take our services.

Hopefully someone cuts my cock off before then, or I'll have yet another death on my hands for Stacey to be even more disgusted by.

I should be punching against the door and hunting for Stacey. But I'm not – I don't think I'd even manage ten steps without passing out. My energy is depleted entirely, and I keep falling in and out of consciousness.

Don't get me wrong, I'd love to go look for her. I'm livid. I want to rip these walls down and blow the entire world up for her, to snap the neck of the guy who has her.

I'd burn him first but keep him alive enough to feel every agonising second. I'd carve the name of every victim who's fallen by my hands into his skin – the ones I remember anyway. I'd cut his eyeballs out, snap each finger then pull up each nail. I'd drill into each thigh and nail him to a chair.

So many scenarios have played out in my head. It's a little concerning how detailed each one is.

They're nothing compared to what I'll do to Christopher Fields when I get my fucking hands on him though.

Base listened to one of my descriptions before he passed out this morning, and he asked if I needed a hug.

I definitely do not.

I pick up one of the pieces of brick that's broken off the old wall and chuck it through the bars, hitting Base on the head. I do that a lot to pass time while we're down here. He's grown used to it and ignores me.

I look over at my friend. "You awake?"

"Nope," he says.

I can just make out his arm over his eyes, a bloody bandage over his naked chest. The wound's probably infected since it's not had any of the dressings changed in forty-eight hours.

"I think I'm dying again. I can't see."

"That's because there's hardly any light in here," I say, snorting. "Does it still hurt?"

"You mean the hole in my chest that I got three days ago? Nah, I'm sound," he replies sarcastically, his voice echoing over to me. "It is a little throbby and feels swollen, which can't be good signs." He's silent for a beat. "Does your scar still get itchy?"

I trace the raised skin lightly with my fingertips. "Yeah, a little."

"I was always the handsome one of our group, but I think people will be more attracted to you because of the belting scar. They'll feel sorry for you. Just remember, baby Tobias, when you're getting all the attention, I'm the naturally handsome one."

I roll my eyes. "Sometimes I wonder why the fuck we're friends."

"Because I'm funny." He snorts at himself. "Hey, do you have any smokes left?"

I sit up and check the packet under my bed, the lighter stuffed inside it. "Yeah."

They were thrown at us yesterday. A gift from Bernadette to keep us sweet – not food or water or something healthy. I move to lean against the bars separating us, and Base groans as he sits up, holding his chest with a wince, then comes down to lean against the bars with me.

"Do you think they're okay?" he asks, taking a cigarette from me and lighting it up. "The girls."

"I don't know."

"Please tell me we're going to teach those fuckers a lesson."

"We will. I promise." I light my own smoke, blowing a cloud above us. "Do you think they'll bring Dez into this?"

"Nah. Dez is probably married to Tylar by now, with three or more bairns chained to them. Do you think they're travelling?"

"Last I knew, they were in Thailand."

"Better staying there," he says, inhaling and exhaling. "No doubt Berna-bitch will use him against us."

We're silent for a beat, the smell of cigarette smoke filling the cells. The only sounds are the dripping taps from our sinks and the rumble of a car driving over the gravel road above us.

"I need to find Luciella before I die."

I lower my head, nodding. "We need to find them both before we die."

"You die, I die."

"You die, I die," I say back, taking a draw to stop the uncontrollable twitching in my hands and face. I blink a few times, fighting the uncomfortable feeling, and blow out another smoke cloud. "Just try to get better and we'll figure out a plan."

I move back to my bed because the cell is spinning – Base stays in position, probably too weak to move, with the cigarette between his lips. "Trying to keep people safe is so exhausting," he says. "I don't know how to get rid of all the threats."

"By killing. Everything I've been doing for the last three years has been to keep everyone safe. And I fucking miss Stacey more than I can explain. But if I show that? More ammunition for Bernadette. I simply cannot show it anymore. I trained myself not to, so you need to do the same. If you make my sister more of a target, then I'll need to kill you too."

He's quiet, smoking the rest of his cigarette before flicking the butt across his cell. "Tell me about her."

"You know who Stacey is," I grumble. "Don't make me talk about her."

"We have fuck all else to do," he replies, the mattress squeaking as he lies down again. "Come on. I've sucked your dick, for fuck's sake. You can at least appease me by telling me who actually made you hard."

I grimace. "If you ever speak of that again, or any of the other times, I'll put a bullet in your heart."

We were forced. It's always forced between us. Entertainment for Bernadette. We just don't let it break us. Base has an awful and dark sense of humour and likes to bring it up whenever he's bored to death. It pisses me off more than anything.

"You have to admit, it'll make for awkward dinner-table chat when I'm married to your sister. Do you think your dad will snap me in half when he finds out I've made both his offspring come?"

My eyes close. "Please stop saying your thoughts out loud. And talk about my sister like that again and I'll break through those bars and hit you."

Base halts the images of me murdering him by scoffing and saying, "Talk to me about Stacey, and I won't mention it ever, ever again. I know you can't see, but I'm holding up my hand, swearing to the Lord that I shan't ever discuss those nights with your sister, nor will I ever speak about your sister's orgasms out loud."

I shake my head. He's fucking insane. A ruthless killer when we're working together, usually getting jobs done a lot faster than me, but then he's a goofy prick that has heart eyes for my sister.

He's like the sun shining into a ditch full of dead bodies.

Bernadette likes his work ethic and firing precision, and often tells me to be more like him. In a fistfight, I'll kick the shit out of Base, but in a shoot-out, he'd blow my brains out before I could even pull the trigger.

Not that I ever would shoot my friend.

"The night we all played dares when we were younger. That was the first time I kissed her – the first time I kissed anyone."

He hums. "I remember. The best night of my life. I was seriously rooting for you to at least kiss someone. Were you quick off the mark when you fucked her? You were only in there less than five minutes."

I roll my eyes for what feels like the millionth time since we got locked in here. "I only kissed her."

"Ah. I forgot you were a virgin for a bit longer. Was she your first?"

I make a noise of acknowledgement. "Yeah."

"The night in London? You were strangely cheery after that."

"Yeah."

"I still can't believe you were in a relationship with Rhodes and told no one."

"Yeah."

"Mate, if you keep giving me one-word answers, I might peel off this bandage and hit you with it." He chuckles at himself, then it cuts off with a wince. "No, but seriously. Stop being fucking vague. Tell me about your relationship with her. You never answer me when I ask shit. Stacey was pregnant, was raped, and you left her. Her dad died a few months later, right? How can you lie there and declare war on the world when you treated her like that?"

"Base, shut up."

Fuck. My chest caves in at the memory of me yelling that she was dead to me. I believed my girlfriend had fucked my brother, but she didn't. They were both drugged, and therefore, it wasn't sex. It was fabricated. It was rape.

And I disowned them both because of a lie.

I screw my eyes shut to banish the threatening pressure. "I was sent a video of her fucking Jason. It was edited to make it look like she was willingly cheating on me with my brother. We lost our daughter a few weeks before, so I thought she was doing it because she blamed me."

"And you didn't let her explain?" His voice is low, and I know he's disgusted with me right now. "Or Jason?"

"I was going to," I say, swallowing and nearly choking on the lump in my throat. "I drove to her house and… and… his car was outside her place. She tried to kill herself, and he was helping her out of it, but I didn't know that at the time. It just looked like they were finally able to be together without sneaking around. I snapped and left."

I sit up dizzily and lean my elbows on my thighs.

"Bernadette chained me to a chair and made me watch hours of footage of Stacey being raped by multiple guys, her stepbrother included. Chris fucking Fields. I didn't know about him. She kept him a secret from me because he was abusive and manipulative, and she was scared." I feel my body tense at the thought of him anywhere near her. "He's abused her since she was young. He killed our daughter."

"That's brutal, man. If anyone deserves to be tortured to death, it's him."

"Yeah. And instead of being there for her, I shoved her out of my life." I drop my head, blanking out the pain of my cramping stomach. "I beat up Jason, told her to stay the fuck away from me, and the day you dropped me off after we went to America? That's when Bernadette found me. I didn't even reach out to Stacey when her dad died. I've been trapped ever since."

Base doesn't speak for a few minutes.

My eyes are burning.

"I take it you loved her."

Loved. Past tense. The way he says the word almost makes me flinch. We've been split up for three years now, and I don't think I've ever stopped loving her. I don't know how to not love her. Not a day goes by that I don't despise myself for leaving her.

We'd probably be married with kids by now.

The idea that my life should be the total opposite of what it is, that I'd be a dad and husband and an engineer if I'd ever made it to uni, makes me want to take a line to numb it all.

"She was everything to me. I think she still is," I say quietly, frowning to myself at how honest I'm being. Then I hate myself for saying *think*. "No, she *is* still everything to me."

"Deep."

Scoffing, I give him the finger through the shadows. "Fuck you."

Base chuckles. "If it makes you feel any better, I love someone who's never once loved me back, and I'd still die for her. Your sister, by the way." He sighs into the darkness. "And when I find her, because I will, I'm not going to let her out of my sight. She'll love me one day. She has to. Even if she just fucking told me she liked me, it would be enough."

"She does like you – she used to ask me a lot about you," I say.

"Well, she can tell me that when I save her."

He's being serious, and to be honest, I couldn't think of anyone better for my sister. Even if he is a walking headache on happy pills. "Just hold on. She'll eventually come round. She's just scared of the way she feels."

"She did mention once that she would break my heart because she doesn't know how to love someone properly, but I guess we'll see."

I nod, even though he can't really see me.

He then says, "The next time you see Stacey, you better apologise and promise never to be a cunt again."

"No shit," I retort, my voice hollow. "I'll fall to my knees and beg for forgiveness the next time I see her."

7

KADE

I'm not sure how much longer we've been here – a week, a few days, fucking years, but we hear heels clicking, growing closer, the sound grating on my nerves while me and Base share the last cigarette, our stomachs rumbling, both weaker than we've ever been.

Aside from the sound of shoes, I hear a manly cough. Great. Archie is here. Can't wait for him to throw a few comments at me, knowing I'm in no state to punch him like I usually do. His wife walks in first, and guards flood the cell.

"Are we going to behave, boys?" she asks, hand on her popped-out hip as she taps her foot. "Or will I leave you both to fester in your own stench a little longer?"

"I'd rather die of an infection in my chest than behave for you. Wait, did you get even uglier? Unlucky, Archie-pops. I find shoving a bag over her face helpful when she's being a greedy whore for my cock. You're not very good at pleasing her, are you?"

As much as his words are cutting, I know Base hates himself whenever he's sent to her room or when she slithers into his. I know the sickening feeling well. If she didn't have a fail-safe in place that would see our families and loved ones killed upon her death, we would have strangled her by now.

Her eyes cast to Base, narrowing, the lights from the corridor shining in. "Careful, Prince, or I might need to tell your family you tragically succumbed to your injuries."

We both look at each other. His brows furrow. "What?"

She sighs. "It seems your grandfather, someone I've successfully avoided this far, isn't very happy that you're in my care."

Care isn't the word I'd use.

Base stands and strides to the bars, grabbing them with one hand. He sneers. "Keep talking."

She glares at him. But I think she's used to his forwardness and attitude towards her. "We've come to an agreement. You will return to them tonight."

My friend stands back, glancing between me and the woman who's been terrorising him for the past year. He doesn't seem even slightly pleased. "Kade goes with me, or I'm staying with him."

She smiles wickedly. "I don't think so. Kade is mine. The deal was – you for two hundred. *Only* you."

She arches a brow when we both stay silent. Base seems on the edge of exploding though. "I won't pass up on two hundred million. You will leave tonight. This isn't up for discussion."

Two hundred million? Fuck, Base said his family was rich, but *that* rich? Damn. They must be like kings and queens over that side of the world.

Yet – they know where he is and instead of blowing the world up to get him back, they offer a deal? It makes no sense.

"No," Base says through gritted teeth.

"I'll destroy all the evidence I have on you. A clean slate. It's part of the deal. You will go, Sebastian."

"I'm not leaving Kade behind."

I give a long sigh. "Stop being dramatic and take the deal. I'll be fine."

"I'm not leaving you," he refuses. "Not fucking happening. You die, I die, remember?"

Bernadette moves forward, pulling Base's phone out of her purse. "I wonder if you'll still say the same when you hear this. From a contact called *Princess...*"

Base straightens.

She inputs the password only she knows and places it on loudspeaker, his voicemail playing. Base is gripping the bars again, with both hands now, as if he's ignoring the pain in his chest.

I sit up in my squeaky, metal bed as soon as my sister's voice fills the deadly silence.

"Sebastian," Luciella sobs, her voice muffled, the sound of a car engine humming around her. "I... Oh God. I... I was only there because I got your text, and then – and then – and then..." She cries out and starts hyperventilating. It causes me to stand up, rage injecting strength into me once more. "I'm so scared. They... they locked me in a trunk." The way her voice changes, I know she's covering her mouth as the engine cuts off and a door opens. "I think they're going to kill me. I never got the chance to tell you how I really feel. I... I'm so sorry... for pushing you away."

A deep, unintelligible voice sounds in the background, and it's obvious they're about to open the trunk.

"Please find me... please, please, please."

She gasps as the trunk opens, screams and warns them not to touch her. One of them yells in pain and tells someone she bit his cheek. She must grab the phone back, because her voice is once again close. "Sebastian, they traded me for blackmail!" She cries even more, fighting against them. "Your grandfather sold—"

She's silenced abruptly, and it curdles my empty stomach.

The call ends.

A guard grips my arm as I step forward, but I tug it out of his grasp. "Fucking let go of me."

Bernadette crosses her arms and smiles at Base. "I'm sure you probably already know who has her. It's quite bizarre that your own family would buy you from me yet easily traded the woman you care for – I wonder why? Maybe they saw that she was significant to you. You are sickeningly obsessed with her, and it got her recognised by someone even I wouldn't like to stand in front of."

I narrow my eyes at her, looking over at a very silent and pale Base, then back at Bernadette. "Who?"

"Shut up. You're not involved in this."

I take a step forward with clenched fists, but I'm stopped by a gun to my head. "She's my fucking sister. Who has her?"

"Blood is just that... blood. Meaningless. My daughter decided to fight for you and hit her father the night of the auction – even though you were only sleeping with her because you wanted me to pay you less attention and not because you cared for her. Poor little lamb is probably in a worse position than your whore of an ex." She chuckles dryly, her eyes on me. "I guess there's no wedding on the cards now. Don't be too disappointed – you'll still be mine."

I flinch away as she tries to tap my cheek with her palm.

"You're insane," Base says blankly.

"And impatient. We have an important matter to attend to. Take him to the medical wing and have his injury seen to. I can smell the infection from here."

"I'll find her," Base says to me as someone grabs him. "I'll need to go back to my gramps and agree to whatever his terms are. I'll... take up my position and find her." Then my friend scowls at Bernie. "*Togda ya ub'yu tebya.*"

Her eyes light up as she translates his words. She knows some Russian.

"I'm sure you will try to kill me. So, before the Prince family causes me any more trouble and gets in my way, you will leave tonight, after we have dinner. We'll send you to Moscow on the jet Kade oh so nicely gave us, and if I ever see you again, I'll kill you."

Base doesn't respond – he's staring at me, his eyes wide as he's slowly taken out of his cell. "Fuck. I'm sorry, man."

"Don't be sorry," I say, shrugging away from a guard who attempts to take my arm again and walking out of my own cell on shaky legs, trying my best not to appear weak and on the brink of passing out. "Just find my fucking sister."

Once we wash, sharing the shower room while guards watch

us, they hand us clothes. I wait in the medical wing for Base to get treated, downing bottle after bottle of water before we're led to the main dining area. I glance out the window on the way instead of taking in the fancy decorations – it's just trees upon trees upon trees.

We're in one of Bernadette's many properties.

But not far from my apartment – I could escape here and run there within half an hour, once I get my strength back. I could get on my bike and start searching for Stacey. Fuck the consequences.

It's around midday, going by the height of the sun, and my eyes struggle to adjust to the daylight after being locked away for days in darkness. Minimal compared to past punishments.

One time, Bernadette buried Base in her yard and I had to find him. If I was even a minute later dragging him out of the soil, he would be dead now.

I beat Archie up for that. I think Bernadette gets off on seeing him bruised and bloodied. She gave Base a week off because he was so fucking traumatised and put all his duties on me. I think I killed more than my usual body count that week.

They're sitting in front of us, workers and guards standing along the walls as servers bring in food in silver dishes. All fancy and ridiculous. Just the way Bernadette likes it.

She was born into wealth, a silver spoon in her mouth. So was Base.

Fuck, so was I, in a way. But my mother never let us be brats about it and made me and Luciella work if we wanted something.

A waiter lifts the lid of a dish in front of me and my stomach growls painfully.

I'm past caring about being drugged through ingesting food or drinking poisoned water. My stomach aches just looking at the steak and mashed potatoes – everyone can probably hear it growling. I devour it all, Base doing the same – we're like fucking animals after being starved so long.

The first time she starved us and locked us up, I thought I was dying by day three. Eventually, I just got used to it. But right now, as I swallow each bite and down more of the water, all I can think about is what's for dessert.

I've lost a lot of weight over the past few months. My muscle mass is still decent, but I'm not anywhere near the same shape. More lean than bulky, I'm not working out as much as I was, since she refuses to let us half the time, and of course, our eating habits have been fucked up. Not to mention the drug use.

I doubt Stacey would even be able to look at me and feel the same way. I'm trash, tarnished, and my mind is broken – why would she like me anymore?

Bernadette smiles at me when I look up. I know that smile. I've become haunted by it. As soon as I finish, she'll order me to go to her bedroom, Archie will probably follow and Base will be sent to Russia to his family.

At least he'll be safe. I think.

If Luciella is with the Russians, then where is Stacey?

I straighten my spine and drop my cutlery. "Do you know where Stacey is?"

She stares at me, her smile slowly turning faker and more demonic. "Why would you like to know?"

"Just cut the bullshit and tell me."

"She was seen on CCTV being taken out of the manor by her buyer before the fire started. I don't currently know her location, but my team is on it."

I lose my appetite instantly.

Base nudges me with his knee. A sign to tell me he's here without her seeing. We always do it, letting the other know they aren't alone when we're being forced into a void or when we're so fucked up we can't think straight.

She clicks her fingers, and a server brings in three files. He lowers them in front of Bernie. "This is the fun part. I'm going to refund your bidder's money and send you on a little... adventure."

I blink once, twice, three times. I haven't done a kill contract in a few weeks.

Taking someone else's life has become so normal to me, I almost missed the power of seeing the light go out of their eyes, especially if they're bad people. Which most are.

The first contract I was ever given, I had no idea what to do. I mean, I wanted to run, to ask for help or just say no, but no one said no to Bernadette Sawyer. I held the file in my hand and tried to set fire to it, to hand it in to the nearest station, to fucking beg the person to run and hide.

But I killed the guy. In cold blood.

I pulled the trigger, my entire body jolting with the kickback from the gun, and I ran. Bernadette gave me hell for leaving so much of a mess. Then she handed me another file. Then another. Then training. More contracts. It became endless. Familiar.

Three Manilla folders are sitting on the dining table between us. From the deprivation of my senses the last few days, my vision is still unclear and not properly adjusting, so I can't read the names on them.

"I think it's time to make a decision. You're distracted. Massively. And I don't like it. You lack focus on me and don't give your all to your missions. So I've decided to do something about those distractions."

She crosses her arms, lounges back and smirks. I raise a brow when she doesn't elaborate on what the fuck she's on about. "Meaning?"

Base is still eating beside me, but his eyes are on Bernadette.

"You need to assassinate one of them, Kade." She opens the first one and pushes the file towards me.

It opens, and my eyes widen as she says, "Your father."

She does the same with the next. A picture of Base. "Your best friend."

My eyes lift to her, and I glare as she opens the third. "Or your lover."

I glance down, and my teeth grind together when I see numerous images paperclipped at the corner. They're screen grabs from CCTV. Stacey being pinned to the wall by her buyer, her thigh up his side, his masked face buried in her neck.

The image beside it is them in a lobby.

Holding hands.

He isn't short, or an overweight, sweaty man like Bernadette threw in my face. He's... built, muscular, and my height. He doesn't have grey hair; it's brown, and she almost seems comfortable with him. In the second image, she looks like she's half-smiling.

Some of my panic subsides.

I know exactly who that is, but I'm not going to give Bernadette ammunition by telling her my father has Stacey. I look back up. "Hmm."

"Hmm? That's all?"

I shrug.

I won't look back down at the pictures, because they're fake. My dad would never do that to me or my mother. He's putting on a facade to try to get her out of there.

My lips almost curl at the corner. He burned the manor down too.

Fucking psychotic genius.

I keep my stare blank. Base is still eating – he probably thinks I'll choose him since he isn't my father or the woman I love.

"I'm waiting, Kade." She strums her acrylic nails on the table, impatient. "Who?"

I lean forward. "Why is Base here?" I point at his file. "If you struck a deal, why is he here?"

"He's a disruption. You kill him, that's not on me. As long as I have proof he left here and his death isn't on my hands, then I'm not responsible – you are."

"And you think I'd kill my own father?" I sneer at her. "How sick are you?"

Not to mention, my dad is a fucking tank. He'd beat my ass to the ground without even blinking.

"Blood is just blood," she says again, shrugging. "Choose, or I'll order them all to be killed."

I sit up straight. She's serious. She's horrific that way. If I don't choose one, she'll definitely take them all out and make a show of it too. She'll order high-value hits on them all that no assassin will refuse. If I reject this, they'll all die anyway.

I look back down at the three files, chewing my lip nervously, hating myself as I reach for one and stop, reaching for the other and pulling my hand back.

Fuck, I can't. If I choose one and don't complete it, they'll send someone else to finish the job.

But she'll kill them all if I fail.

Archie releases a dragged-out sigh. "Just fucking pick, boy."

I want to stab him. I *will* stab him one day. I'll rip his jaw clean off.

I itch the scar as I stare at each file. Whoever I choose, it'll be my last kill for her. If I pick my dad, he could help me. He could hide me and Stacey and deal with Bernadette. He's Tobias Mitchell, for fuck's sake.

If I choose Base, he won't be able to save my sister. Plus, he's my best friend.

"I do this, I want my freedom."

Bernadette smirks, and part of me knows she's lying as she says, "Deal."

I take a deep breath, and Base spits out his water as I grab one of the files.

While Base waits for his flight to Russia, I sit on the bed, my elbows on my knees. In sixty minutes, my best friend will leave for the jet. He'll find my sister, and I'll start my hunt.

He asks if I'm okay, but I keep staring at the carpet between my feet, my knees bouncing, fingers twitching, eyes blinking.

I can't stop the blinking. It's new – and constant.

"I'll do what I can to get you out of this, alright?"

I don't reply. There's nothing that will make Bernadette release me from this hellhole.

"I… How do I contact you?" he asks, crouching in front of me to grab my attention. "There's not a chance I'm going over there without knowing what's happening with you."

"I know your number," I say in a whisper. I'm still not looking at him – in fact, I'm looking straight through him as my mind races. "I'll call from another phone."

"Do you know where you're going first?"

I shake my head. "I'll go get my motorbike. It's parked at my apartment."

"And you're actually going to kill…" He trails off, not wanting to say it.

Nodding, I lace my fingers together to stop them from trembling. "I have no choice. I can make it quick. If I don't do this, Bernadette will drag it out."

I lift my eyes to his, and he drops to his haunches. "I don't want to leave you, man. I... We're a team, you know? There's no me without you or you without me. How do I... How do I just go away and not fucking worry?"

I grab the back of his neck and press my forehead to his. "I need you to forget about my situation and focus on finding my sister." I shake him. "Please find her."

His bottom lip trembles. "Fuck, man. Fuck."

"Maybe I'll be standing by your side as the best man at your wedding," I lie, talking shit to make him laugh. "Get my sister, marry her, fucking give her the life you both deserve, even if she's a bitch to you half the time."

I won't be there – once I do this, there'll be no reason for me to live.

He snorts. "More than half the time." A tear slides down his cheek.

There's a knock at the door, and he grabs my shoulder. Squeezes. "I hope you know what you're doing," he says in a low tone. "Because I sure as fuck don't."

I yank him into an embrace, slapping his back. "Who the fuck knew you'd be worth two hundred million though?" I laugh, and so does he. "You kept me slightly sane, Base. Thank you."

He pulls back and wipes his eyes with his good hand. "I'm worth a lot more, just saying."

We both stand and grab our bags as the guards knock again, heavier and impatient. We step towards the door, and I grab Base once more, hugging my best friend tighter but being careful not to hurt the wound in his chest. I hug him like it'll be the last time.

"You die, I die," he whispers.

I can't say it back.

I pull away and yank the new black material up and over my mouth, concealing the scar that makes everyone flinch. The fabric covers my neck too.

"Can you see it?" I ask Base, and when he shakes his head, I sigh in relief. "Good."

8

STACEY

What was once Nora's holiday lodge, where she and Dad used to disappear to for some peace from the hectic combined family, is now what Barry keeps calling the "safe house".

Technically, it's mine. Or should be. My parents owned this long before he met Nora. But when he died, she took everything.

A perimeter has been set up around the lodge. Some of Barry's men, who were once Kade's, drive around the place, send out drones into the sky and patrol on foot to keep everyone out.

Although Tobias is still a heavily wanted man, still dominating headlines and social media, given all the fake sightings, he couldn't be any calmer about his situation.

He's a psychopath. An actual one – not just a madman with crazy, obsessive tendencies that people label as a psycho. He thinks differently. He's been watching us for the past two days like he's learning the way we greet each other in the morning and how we start conversations. He listens like he's studying each and every one of us.

When Aria is talking to him, it's obvious he's taking in every word like it might be the last time he hears her voice. When she giggles, his eyes light up. He always needs to be beside her too. Always looking at her. Always keeping her the centre of his attention.

A man full of regret for his past mistakes, loving the woman he can never have.

And when she falls asleep on the couch, he stays close before carrying her to her allocated room, across from his.

For someone who doesn't feel love the way romance novels portray it, he certainly makes her swoon and blush like a teenage crush by just smiling at her. When he laughs at something Ewan says, she beams. And when he starts to blink uncontrollably and knows to remove himself from the room to find a way to hold on to control, she sits with him, silent, just there.

He's trying so hard to fit in with the rest of us, but all of his meds suddenly gone from his system has brought on paranoia and sleep disturbance.

The guy is about to hit his fifties, yet he works out like he's in his twenties with insane stamina. He's forced Ewan to go for a run with him the past two mornings while he also tracks the area, plotting potential escape routes if a situation arises and we need to run. He has muscles on muscles, and his eyes are blue, but not the same shade as his son's.

Kade has his mother's eyes. From being so close to him on multiple occasions that play out in my mind when the nights are dark, I remember the flecks of silver in them, iridescent shades of the ocean looking back at me as he tells me we'll have a family together.

On screen at the auction, those same eyes were empty. He was there but wasn't. My heart breaks for him. I need him to be okay.

The safe house is in the middle of the woods, surrounded by vast blankets of treetops and beautiful little streams. It's raining, but everything is a bright, verdant green. When Chris brought me here, I couldn't properly enjoy the sight, but now, I give myself a few minutes at a time to stare at the vastness of the world and breathe.

It's cold, but Tobias and Ewan make sure the fire is kept lit all day and night. Aria cooks with what she can find in the cupboards, and Cassie complains on the sofa while we all pretend she doesn't exist. Aria looked after her when we got here – she'd been drugged, probably by her own mother, and not once has someone looked for her.

Sad, but I don't care. I hate Cassie. Though not as much as Tobias does – he's only tolerating her presence in case he can use her at some point to get to Bernadette.

I push up from the couch to go to my bedroom, stopping when I see Jason standing on the patio, his hands in his pockets, watching me.

He's so thin, his face drawn, his hair longer. His eyes are empty, as if the weight of the world is on him. I barely recognise him.

"Are you okay?" he asks me, his voice deep but hesitant. He's dodged me for the last forty-eight hours. If I entered a room, he left it. I tried to say hi when we got here, but he looked like he was going to vomit and vanished.

Aria told me he just needs time.

I nod and cross my arms. "Are *you* okay?"

He stares at me then looks down. "Yeah." He shifts on his feet, rubs his face and looks at me again. "I'm sorry."

"What for?"

"I broke my promise. I said I'd be there for you. Your dad died, and I was gone. Kade was gone. If I'd stayed and helped you, maybe none of this would be happening."

"You did what you had to do. People respond differently to situations."

He lets out a huff of air and shakes his head. "I didn't fight for my relationship with Giana or try to get my brother back – I couldn't even face looking at him to explain my side. I sold my house and blew every penny on drugs. I didn't do what I had to do; I did the total opposite."

With the sound of the breeze outside, I swallow. "I'm sorry."

He shrugs. "My own fault, not yours."

"Are you clean now?"

"Three months. My dad put me into rehab, and Giana told me I needed to get sober." He drops his gaze to the ground. "It took me two and a half years to get a text back from her. I got to see her for the first time a few weeks back, and we've talked about trying again, but she doesn't trust me. I'm a cheat after all."

"I have all the footage from that night," I tell him. "Chris, my stepbrother, he drugged us both. He made us do it. Neither of us were in our right mind or even fully conscious. You aren't a cheat, Jason; you're a victim."

Jason's brows furrow. "He drugged us?"

I hug myself and step onto the patio with him. "Kade was sent an edited clip of us. It looked like we were willingly..." I pause, shaking my head.

"Even if I try telling her, she's not going to believe me. Why would she?"

"Then make her believe you," I say, stepping forward again, seeing the tiredness in his eyes. "We were attacked. It's clear as day in the full recording. You could show her it as proof."

His eyes are red as he looks away. "I'm not going to show her me fucking a teenager."

"It wasn't consensual, Jason."

After a minute, he looks at me again. "I'm sorry I shut you out," he says. "I shouldn't have blocked you and ran. I just needed to... get out. Escape. I lost my job a few days later and couldn't handle it all. It's no excuse. I failed you. I'm sorry I broke my promise," he says again.

"You don't need to apologise to me."

"Do you always do that?" he asks.

I tilt my head. "Do what?"

"Ignore your own demons to cater to everyone else's? From what I've witnessed, you seem to run after those around you, be there for them, centre yourself in their trauma, and no one seems to do the same for you."

I shrug and give a tight smile. "I'm fine."

But his comment hits hard. Do I ignore my own pain and focus on others?

"Things will get easier," I say. "I'll help you with Giana if you want? Maybe I can explain what really happened?"

He closes his eyes and sniffs, wiping his face with his sleeve. "I don't deserve your help."

"Well, I'm giving you it. Come on – I can hear the kettle boiling." I grab his thin wrist and pull him into the house as Aria leans out of the kitchen and asks if any of us want a cup of tea.

For the next week, Barry keeps himself busy with securing the perimeter and hunting for Chris. Him and Kyle went back to the Fields manor and packed. But they lost his trail when my stepbrother infiltrated the signal following him. He's also trying to track Luciella, as per her father's orders.

She's in Russia the last we heard. Tobias made a deal with Base's grandfather, but now, he won't reply to any emails or phone calls. All the Russian guards have been ordered home by their boss, and all communications have been cut.

Tobias is losing his mind about it.

He's paying more attention to Aria than anything else now, probably to keep his mind from deteriorating. She walks to the bathroom, he follows. She hangs up the laundry, he helps. She cooks, he cleans. She goes for a walk through the woods, Tobias goes with her.

Strangely, Ewan doesn't seem to mind; he's completely unbothered by the sight of his wife and the father of her kids being so close and touchy. Even when they're on the sofa, she's between them while one holds her hand and the other plays with her hair.

Imagine having that much attention? I would blow up.

Maybe what Kade thought when we were younger was true, and they are messing around. All three of them.

On day eight, Barry and Ewan are scanning Bernadette's database for any trace on where Kade is, or if she's tracking my brothers, when Sebastian's grandfather calls back.

Tobias is restless as the man speaks in his thick Russian accent and tells him to get to the fucking point as Aria laces their fingers together.

Luciella is still in Russia.

The older man informs us that Base has been released from Bernadette's clutches. He tells Tobias that Luciella was taken but is with them again, that she's safe and will be on a jet home soon.

But only because Base gave up his entire life to save her.

I can see the relief on her parents' faces when they hang up. Ewan holds Aria's hand as she happily sobs into Tobias's chest. I smile, because my best friend is okay and coming home. Even Jason looks a little more alive after the news.

"Do we know where the stepbrothers are?" Tobias asks Barry. "Or are you still being an incompetent dickhead?"

Barry narrows his eyes. "You're not exactly doing much, are you? You're too busy staring at your ex-wife."

"We were never married," Aria says, completely unfazed by the bickering. It's all they've been doing since we got here.

"We'll catch him and kill him – don't worry," Barry assures him.

Tobias steps forward, closing some of the distance between them. "When I find that piece of shit, I'll be the one to skin him alive and make him eat his own flesh."

"That's a bit inhumane, don't you think?" Cassie's voice goes right through me, and I glare at her. "No one deserves that." Her lip curls in disgust. "Monsters, all of you."

I grit my teeth. Ignoring her existence is way easier when she's silent. "That's a little rich coming from you."

She's been annoying me the past few days, bragging that Kade and her parents will come for her. Kade this, Kade that. Marriage this, marriage that. I even contemplated cutting off her wedding finger so she'd never wear a ring there.

Barry sets up the big TV in the sitting room and plays footage he found from the manor. This time to look for clues – on what, I have no idea.

Tobias is sitting beside me, his arms on the back of the couch, his finger twirling a strand of Aria's hair. Ewan holds her hand. Cassie hugs her knees across from me as we watch Luciella being dragged through the corridor by a bulky man.

She doesn't go to a room like I did – a bag is put over her head, her hands cuffed behind her as she's taken to a car that rushes out of one of the many garages that Bernadette had.

"Did anyone report seeing this car speeding out?" Barry asks one of the guards standing around the room.

They shake their head, and he huffs. "I want more information on this. Since the Princes won't elaborate on who took Luciella from them during the auction, I want to know everything about the people who took her in this clip."

One man nods and vanishes from the room with his phone to his ear.

Jason is smoking out on the patio again. He's always smoking, barely talks and sleeps maybe an hour a night. He doesn't want to watch.

I swallow and train my gaze on the screen.

Tobias has the white, faceless mask on as he stabs a blade into someone's chest and drags him into a room. He does it three more times before he reaches four guards, two of which lead him to the room I'm in.

The footage skips to Tobias pulling me out of the room.

My cheeks go bright red. It's embarrassing watching it all back in front of everyone. I'm in the shortest white dress ever pretending to be his obedient pet.

This is very awkward for me. It's an act, obviously, but we can all see Tobias pressing me to the wall with my thigh up to his hip. Us holding hands as he drags me through the lobby. He needed the spectators to think I was his.

From the corner of my eye, I see Tobias kissing Aria's shoulder and whispering something. An apology. He's pale, pain written across his face as she assures him it's okay. That he didn't do anything wrong.

The footage cuts to a different scene, and I straighten my spine at the sight of Kyle punching Chris across the face and yelling at him. We don't know what's being said, but my brother looks panicked, raging, grabbing Chris's collar and pushing him to the ground.

He scurries after him as Kyle walks away, running his hands through his hair. Turning, he stares at the manor again, and when Chris tries to say something, his arm swings, his fist smashing Chris in the nose so hard, he drops onto his ass.

Another cut, and the CCTV footage is grainy, smoke filling the corridor we snuck through, bodies strewn across the floor in the auction room, main foyer and yard.

The manor blows, and the footage stops.

Tobias whistles in the silence.

When I wake up hours later, the lodge is in darkness aside from the glow and crackle of the fire. I try not to make too much noise as I creak open my door and tiptoe into the kitchen for a glass of water.

I freeze when I hear a song playing – "Medicine" by Daughter. I remember it from one of the times me and Kade watched a home movie of Tobias and the twins spending Christmas together in the institution. That song was playing in the background of each clip. Glancing up at the clock above the entrance of the sitting room, I see it's two in the morning.

When I slowly walk across the landing, holding the doorframe, I look in to see Tobias and Aria… slow dancing?

His hand is on the small of her back, his head lowered to her shoulder as she leans into him, their laced fingers held out to their side. They barely move, but they don't need to.

In another life, they would make the perfect couple, but in this one, they love each other so dangerously there's no chance of ever being together. This version of Tobias is already cracking around the edges. He doesn't have any of his meds, and adjusting to reality when he's spent over twenty years locked up and controlled is hard for him.

Aria cries softly as she holds on to him tighter while he kisses her forehead. His gaze lifts to clash with mine, and I give him a soft smile before backing away.

I go back to my room, noticing I have a missed call from a

random number. I sit on the bed and call it back, thinking it might be Luciella. The person answers on the first ring, but they don't speak.

"Um, hello?"

"Ah, Freckles. It's been a while since I heard your voice."

My lungs stop working, and I'm not certain I'm even blinking as my hand grabs at the bed sheets beneath me. "K- Kade?"

For a split second, things start to brighten. Even a smile pulls at my lips. "Are you okay?" I ask when he says nothing. "Where are you?"

I gulp as he remains silent, and my voice betrays me as it breaks. "Kade?"

"Stand up."

Frowning, I look around the room. "What?"

"I said..." He pauses as I hear metal clanking. A gun loading? "Stand the fuck up."

My legs fail me, and so does my voice.

My entire body stiffens when I see the red dot shining against the door. He's aiming into the room? What is he doing? My lips move, but no sound comes out.

"Stand up," he snaps. "I won't tell you again."

"No," I croak, my face twisting. Is this really happening?

"Are you scared?" he whispers, amusement in his voice.

But I don't reply. I can't.

"You know the best part about accepting kill contracts? It's the chase. The adrenaline that comes from knowing someone is terrified, running, hoping they see the next day. I'm going to make *you* run. And I don't mean the way I did before you whored yourself for me at the party." He inhales deeply, taking a drag of his smoke. "I'm giving you a day to run. Make it exciting for me. Because once I find you, I'm not going to bury my cock inside you – I'm not going to kiss you until we can't breathe."

I go pale as he deeply chuckles, inhaling smoke. "I'm going to fucking kill you, Freckles."

I close my eyes, my heart sinking. Maybe all the drugs he's consumed, the deaths he's brought about and the abuse he's endured have finally destroyed the Kade we all once knew.

"You don't mean any of that," I say quietly, standing and reaching for the door handle. I need to get to Barry or Tobias. "I want to help you, Kade. Please let me help you."

"Don't fucking move," he snaps. "Stay exactly where you are."

I go ramrod straight, my eyes wide as I turn around, looking down to see the red dot on my chest. "You won't hurt me."

"Even from a distance, I can still see how much of a bitch you are." He laughs, amusing himself as he takes another draw of his smoke. "Play a little game with me. Keep your eyes open until they burn. Blink, and Barry dies." The red dot vanishes from my chest. "Got a clean shot on him too. Ready, get set, go."

"Kade..." I stop, my eyes flicking over the small hill to the side, the woods and the grass verge near the river. I still don't blink. "I know it's hard, but we just want to help you. We can get you away from them."

"Yeah, you can. You just need to die in the process. That was the deal we settled on. I had to choose between you, my dad and Base to win my freedom. You were the obvious choice. Oh, did I see you blink?"

I shake my head. "You're bluffing."

The window smashes as he pulls the trigger, and a searing burn rips across my cheek as a bullet grazes me before I drop to the ground.

The blast of the gunshot echoes outside and in. He chuckles through the phone, loud enough that I can hear it lying beside my head. "Don't underestimate me, Stacey. I'm not the stupid little boy who fell in love with you. Run, and I'll come find you. This is my final warning. Stay, and I'll kill them all. That's a promise."

The call cuts out as the door bursts open, and someone picks me up off the floor. It's Tobias. I can tell. His fingers touch my painful cheek as warm liquid trickles down my face to my neck. Someone yells to get Aria. Barry rushes to the window, his shoes crushing the shattered glass on the carpet.

"Jason ran out," I hear Cassie say. "Is she okay?"

My lip trembles as Tobias lifts me from the ground and carries me to his room. Aria is trying to safely pull a small fragment of glass from my thigh before cleaning my cheek while I blankly stare at the ceiling.

I think I might be in shock.

I was in love with Kade Mitchell, and now he's going to kill me.

9

KADE

My heavy boots and bursts of breath are drowned out by the harsh, erratic beating of my heart as I run through the woodland. Branches snap beneath me as I put as much distance between me and the lodge as humanly possible.

I abruptly stop, pull down the material covering my face and vomit all over the forest floor. It burns my insides. Makes my eyes sting and feel pressured, and I stagger sideways and bang into a tree.

I fucking deserve this.

Pulling that trigger and the way I spoke to her… she's never going to forgive me.

All I want is her forgiveness.

After heaving until my eyes feel like they're going to pop out, I spit, breathe and wipe my mouth with the back of my hand, gasping for air as I rest my head against a tree trunk.

There's a crackling in my ear, and I tense my jaw when her voice comes.

"You missed," she tuts at me, her voice fucking grating on my nerves. "I'm disappointed."

I close my eyes and shake my head, as if it will get rid of the devil's voice. I have a fucking migraine. "I did," I reply into the earpiece as Bernadette huffs. "It won't happen again."

Lie.

Although my insides still twist at the sight of her fear burned into me. The way her eyes widened when she realised I pulled the trigger.

I just need Bernadette to think I'm serious about killing my ex, even if it means scaring the shit out of Stacey in the meantime. It worked, I'm sure of it. She was terrified, and I can still hear the tremor in her voice that fucking broke me.

I told her vile shit while mentally memorising everything about her through the scope, as if I don't already remember every inch of her, every conversation we've ever had.

She'll run. After the threat I made about killing everyone, she'll run. That girl will never risk everyone's safety. She's insufferable like that – always putting others before herself.

And when she does leave the lodge, I'll find her. I'll message with a location and time, and I'll make the minutes of peace we grab worth it.

All she needs to hear is my apology. Whether she chooses to accept it or not is up to her. Regardless, it all ends the same for me.

At least it'll be close to being over. I'll force Stacey to listen, then I'll hunt down and slowly kill her stepbrother. By then, Bernadette will have her army looking for me. She'll want me to watch her kill everyone I care about. I'll take me, Bernadette and her shitty husband out with one of my home-made bombs.

And I'll need to just fucking pray her team don't realise it was me and retaliate.

If I don't end it all soon, it'll keep going, and I'm so fucking tired.

"You never miss," she says, tsking. "We need to get those shakes of yours under control. They're hindering your work." She sighs, and I look behind me when I hear a branch snap, but nothing's there. "You have quite the team on foot looking for you. I suggest you stop fucking around and get back to your bike. Your assignment is still ongoing."

Screwing my eyes shut, I stand up straight. "I left the sniper rifle back there. I can't run with it."

"You evidently can't walk either. Why are you stationary?"

My stomach churns as I look down at my vomit and back up. I can hear faint voices at the bottom of the hill. If there wasn't a canopy of trees above me, one of the drones would find me.

Bernadette speaks again. "Don't get yourself caught, Kade. That's an order. If you do, kill as many of them as possible. You have your blade in your boot?"

I nod, even though I know she can't see me. I'm just a dot on a digital map on her screen. "I do."

"There's a team of five near you. Move it."

Sliding the cover back over my mouth, I take a few quiet breaths before I get moving again, slapping branches out of the way until I reach a small stream. I splash through it, the icy water filling my boots and soaking my black trousers.

I'm exhausted, but with adrenaline coursing through my body, and the uppers Bernadette made me take before I left my apartment, I'm able to ignore the stinging pain from the cold. I focus on getting to my bike as quickly as possible. It's hidden below a grass verge, with branches and scrub covering it.

Bernadette's order was plain and simple: go to the lodge and shoot Stacey.

All I could think about on the way here was how to tell Stacey I meant none of it without Bernadette hearing me.

I intentionally aimed to the side last minute, but then my finger spasmed as I added pressure to the trigger and fired. My heart stopped for what felt like hours until I heard her gut-wrenching scream. The one sign that I hadn't shot her in the head.

My dad threw the door open, and my eyes widened at the sight of him rushing to my girl's side. He cares for her, that much is obvious. Barry had run in too, and I'd known I had to get the fuck away from there.

But I hit her. I fucking hit Stacey.

She needs to live.

I'm not going to kill the only person that's kept me alive this long. If it wasn't for her, I would have ended it years ago. Ever since I found out what her cunt of a brother did to her, to our daughter, I've done everything to keep myself in line, to not lose myself, so I can be strong enough to ruin him.

That doesn't mean she'll ever forgive me. But as long as she's alive and he isn't, that's fine.

The contract changes everything. It's her, or me, and I know who the fuck I choose.

"You have someone—"

Her voice cuts off as someone tackles me from the right, winding me and sending shocks of pain through my cracked ribs. We skid across the muddy grass and roll down a small hill until I land on my back, groaning at the tightness in my chest.

A hand grasps my collar and shoves me into the long grass when I try to get up and defend myself. I'm weaker than usual. I've not slept, and I've hardly been able to hold my food down most of the time.

Plus, I'm high as fuck.

A fist smashes me across the cheek, and I glare at the person above me.

But then my lungs seize.

Jason.

Before I can say a word, he snatches my jaw and grips me hard enough that I can feel my teeth nearly cracking. "What the fuck, Kade?"

Then he hits me again.

"You fucking shot at her!" he yells. "What the fuck are you playing at?"

This is not how I wanted my night to go. Bernadette's going to get him killed if I don't deal with him.

I grab his throat and headbutt my brother. "Get the fuck off me."

Jason falls back with a bleeding lip, wiping it with the back of his hand as he comes for me again. This time, I kick him in the chest and get to my feet while he falls back once more.

I roll my jaw. "Stay in your lane, Jason. Stay the fuck out of this."

He looks fucking terrible. Thin, pale, his eyes sunken – he looks like he needs a year of sleep.

What happened to my big brother?

"Kill him," Bernadette snarls in my ear.

Everything goes quiet at those two words.

Kill him.

Kill your brother.

Kill the brother you beat up and left behind.

The brother who lost everything the same night Stacey did.

I roll my jaw again and throw my fist at his face as he pushes to his feet. Once, twice, three times, until my knuckles are red and split open. Jason doesn't even try to block the blows, his head snapping back with each one.

He falls to the ground.

When I try to climb on top of him to stop him from fighting back, to *make* him fucking stop, he knees me in the ribs again, and I nearly burst into tears at the ripping pain cracking my bones.

When I got to my apartment in Stirling, Bernadette had every guard nearby waiting for me in my front yard. They beat me to a pulp and left me lying in the mud.

Rough him up, Bernadette had said. *Make sure he remembers his task.*

Now Jason is throwing me aside and punching me again. "Stop fighting me!" he yells. "Fucking stop it!" The next smash to the face stops me from retaliating, and I let him keep going – I just lie there and take it. "Why would you do this?" My eyebrow splits. "Why?"

He's shouting over Bernadette's voice. She's telling me to use my blade and kill him.

"Stacey didn't cheat on you," he says, stopping his attack and grabbing my chin with a solid grip. "She was raped. *We* were fucking raped, Kade."

Bernadette huffs. "I swear, if I hear this girl's name one more time, I'll go there and kill the bitch myself."

I ignore her, even though I want to tell her to shut her fucking mouth.

Jason's hold on me slackens. "She has a stepbrother. Christopher Fields. He kicked the shit out of her when he found out she was pregnant." He slaps me when I stare at him. "Do you fucking hear me?"

He shakes me and slaps me again. "Are you listening to me?"

Another smack.

"Help me find that piece of shit," he cries. "Fucking please."

"Stop," I say quietly.

But Bernadette hears me. "Stop what?"

I close my eyes, gritting my teeth until they hurt before I shove Jason away. "Go back," I say. "Turn around and go fucking back."

"I ordered you to kill him."

I shake my head, trying to communicate with Jason to leave without speaking. I point behind him, stepping into his personal space, mouthing, *Go back – please.* I beg him with my eyes, fucking pleading for him to get the fuck away from me.

Frowning, he looks at me in confusion. "What?"

I sigh and hope the world forgives me as I clench my fist and smack him as hard as I can in the side of the head, knocking him clean out. He drops at my feet, and something cracks in my chest.

I'm so sorry.

I search for his phone and send Ewan his location. I want to say something else in the message, but I can't risk them discussing it and Bernadette overhearing them, since they've already hacked the lodge's system.

"Are you deaf?"

I roll my jaw a third time and shake my hand. It throbs from hitting Jason too hard. "For once in your life, stop fucking talking, Bernadette."

I'll regret that later.

The text to my new phone comes twelve hours later.

StaceyNew: *Where?*

I lie on the couch in my apartment, half asleep, half buzzed from taking a line. The word is jumbled in random letters for a second, but when I focus, I can see it properly.

I glance up at the camera in the corner of the room with one eye screwed shut. As I sit up, the bag of ice slips from my ribs, my skin red from the coldness. I have bruises all over my face from Jason belting me with his fists.

Shirtless, I stand up straight and crack my neck from left to right, yawning as I stretch my arms above me. I didn't mean to sleep – I knew the message would come, so I was icing my injuries while I waited.

Must've dozed off.

My place is bare. No decorations, no pictures hanging on the wall. If it weren't for the dog bowls in the kitchen and the toys strewn across the living-room floor from the last time I had Milo and Hopper up here, someone would think it was unoccupied.

I miss the dogs. My mother's been looking after them, but since she left to go to the lodge, the staff at the manor have been watching them. Milo seems lost, and Hopper keeps searching the grounds. Either for me or Stacey.

I hope the latter takes them when I die.

I lean on my kitchen counter, set a line out to calm my nerves and try to type back as I sniff it. It takes me ten attempts to spell the message correctly.

***Me:** Knew you'd come to your senses, Freckles.*

Although I'd rather tell her I'm sorry and that I didn't mean a fucking word I said, or to goddamn shoot at her, my messages are also being monitored. Bernadette thinks I'm actually going to kill Stacey to save my dad and Base.

A quick death. The ultimate sacrifice.

Stupid bitch.

She's at a meeting with some group from the underworld – she pissed off the wrong people and now she's trying to fix it while Archie stands by her side like a shadow.

StaceyNew: Where?

Sighing, and a little nervous, I call her, holding the phone to my ear and listening to each ring as I make my way to my bedroom. When she doesn't pick up, I toss my phone on the bed and rake my hand through my hair. It badly needs cut – the black waves are tickling my neck and nearly covering my eyes.

What's the point?

Sitting on the foot of the bed, I lean on my thighs and wait for her to call back.

I wait. And wait. And wait some more.

I eventually accept she's not going to call back and decide to grab a shower. The water is too hot, scalding my skin as I step under the spray, instantly drenching my hair.

My forehead stays against the tiles as I close my eyes, trying to rid the image of her through the scope from my mind. The terror. The betrayal. The sound of her scream after I pulled the trigger.

Fuck. I shot at Stacey.

Regardless of the reasons, I shot at her.

It takes me nearly an hour to leave the shower, and I dry my hair with a towel after wrapping another around my slim waist. The weight I've lost has me looking like I did when I was eighteen, when I first started working out properly and getting into shape.

I pull open my dresser drawer to get a pair of shorts, pausing when I see the box I shoved in there when I first bought this place years ago. I didn't want it in the manor, and I barely stayed here, so it seemed best to keep it here.

Settling back on the bed, I place the box down beside me. A shaky hand lifts the lid to reveal the pair of pink booties and a drawing of Stacey, and I quickly slam the lid back down, screwing my eyes shut.

My heart races so fucking fast, and the idiotic part of me opens my eyes as I lift the lid once more, letting it drop to the floor.

I gulp, reaching for one of the ultrasound photos. The first time seeing one of these, Stacey's first scan, feels like a lifetime ago. The delicate paper between my fingers holds the image of the daughter that was taken from me – murdered.

Something cracks within me then. Something harsh and painful that has me shaking as I run my thumb over the distorted image.

A nearly four-year-old should be cuddling up to me and Stacey in bed right now while we read her a bedtime story. She'd fall asleep on my chest, and I'd carry her to her own bed, only for her to sneak back in when me and her mother are sleeping.

I let go of the picture and the box, launching it across the room, the contents smashing into the wall and cracking the mirror hanging there. I tip the dresser over in a fit of rage and grab the lamp, throwing it, destroying anything I can get my hands on as I blindly lose my shit.

Staring at myself in the cracked mirror, I'm disgusted with who I've become. A murderer. A sex slave. A scarred, sick, mentally deranged motherfucker who can't go a day without drugs.

When I reach for my gun, I don't stop to think before putting the barrel to my head and pulling the trigger.

Click.

My back hits the wall, and I slide down it until I'm on my ass. I let the gun fall from my hand, and my body goes limp as a tear slips down my cheek.

My heartbeats are all I can hear. They're strong. Hard. Fast. Proof that I'm somehow alive after my loaded gun failed to fire.

Proof that I'm not ready to die.

I glance down at the material under my hand – the pink princess dress I bought years ago still has the tags on it; it's still unworn, still fresh. I grasp the fabric in a fist and lift it my chest, hugging it as more tears fall.

"I'm sorry," I whisper, the two words broken. "I'm so sorry I couldn't save you."

How different our lives would be if she'd survived. She would have been so loved by everyone. She'd be spoiled and adored and wild like her mother.

My phone rings from the bed – somehow it survived the rage-induced spiral of destruction my room suffered. I lean forward, not daring to let go of the dress, and grab my phone to see Stacey is calling me back.

I answer but don't say a word as I shift and lie on the floor, the dress still clasped to my chest.

"Kade?"

Fuck. Her voice. She has no idea how much she soothes the darkness within me. It's like the fragments of my heart slowly join back together – until I hear the soft whimper of her trying to hold in her tears, and everything comes crashing down again, because I caused those tears.

"Kade? Are you there?"

Can she hear how uneven my breathing is?

If I talk, I'll fuck this up. She'll know I'm upset.

She's met with my silence. "I don't know what's happening with you, but if you need to do this assignment for your freedom, I'm willing to let you do it. I..." Her voice breaks, and so does my heart. "I don't have anything to live for, but you do."

Swallowing, I close my eyes, still refusing to speak.

Her voice is so soothing without her even realising.

Stacey Rhodes. My girl. My anchor that sank to the bottom of the ocean without me.

"Send me the location and I'll come. Just... get this over with."

The line cuts out, and the phone slips from my ear.

10

STACEY

Everyone sits around the table, talking, bickering, trying to figure out how to help Kade. All I can do is stare at my fingers fidgeting in my lap.

"I've been working with him for years, and I've never seen him like this."

Aria wipes her eyes and leans forward. "He's having withdrawals. Has my son always been on drugs?"

Barry looks at Tobias, then at me and Aria. "Not willingly. Kade didn't want any involvement in these activities. But I noticed closer to his departure to Russia a year ago that he was losing weight, wasn't eating or working out like he used to, and his body spasmed a lot. I put it down to trauma, but I later found out that Bernadette's husband had been injecting him daily before..." He trails off, not wanting to continue.

"Before what?" Tobias pushes.

"I'm not comfortable disclosing any further details," Barry says, crossing his arms. "If Kade knew I'd told you half the stuff I already have, he'd kill me."

Jason, still bruised from earlier, speaks up. "What did Archie do to my brother?"

Barry stays silent.

But it clicks.

Archie abuses Kade too.

I feel like I'm going to be sick.

Except for Cassie arguing her father wouldn't sexually assault a man, silence fills the room, and my heart slowly shatters into millions of fragments that only Kade can mend.

Tobias stands. "I'm not sitting around here any longer. I'm going to find them both and make it fucking painful. You" – he points at Cassie – "get out of my sight before I blow your fucking brains out."

Barry, bold as brass, stands in front of him as he heads straight for Cassie. "Going after the Sawyers isn't a good idea. Trust me, I've been trying to get Kade away from this from the start. You'll only put a target on his back if you insert yourself."

He scoffs. "You expect me to do nothing while my son is being fucking drugged and raped?"

Everyone flinches at his truthful words.

"I'm asking you to work with me and your son's team to get him out alive, not go in and cause a riot and get everyone killed in the process. Your daughter might be safe from the Russians thanks to Prince, but with the control the Sawyers have over everything, Luciella's flight won't land in Edinburgh tomorrow. You'll never see your son again, and Aria will be next. Are you willing to risk them all?"

"He chose her over me," Tobias says, stepping right up to Barry, ignoring one of the guards shifting his gun from his waistband. But I see Aria moving forward, blocking the path between them so he can't shoot. "He should have picked *me*. Because if he even attempted to come after me, I would've taken him away from all of this and helped him."

The arguing goes on and on, and I eventually get to my feet and join Jason, who's headed outside to the patio once more. I slip the cigarette from behind his ear, and he lights it for me. I fill my lungs with deadly smoke and blow it out into the distance.

I haven't told them that I've been in contact with Kade.

When none of them pays attention, I'll sneak out. Once I get a message with the location, it all ends. Everything.

I stare at Kade's older brother. He has bruising on his cheek and a split lip.

The moon is peeking out from behind a hill far away, and it's in the calmness that I let my eyes water. "I hate this," I whisper. "I hate it all."

Jason doesn't speak, but he shuffles closer to me as we lean our elbows on the wooden railing.

I inhale, exhale and allow the burning nicotine to fill my lungs once more. The debate inside stops, and we watch Aria and Cassie walk out onto the patio, standing in front of the small river.

She's crying. Aria's trying to calm her, always the neutraliser, even though Cassie's a bitch and the daughter of her son's abusers.

Eventually, Jason clears his throat and says, "If we really have lost my brother, I won't let him hurt you, even if that means taking a bullet for you."

"You think we've lost him?"

"He shot at you, Stacey."

I close my eyes, the cigarette slipping from my fingers. Because I think he might be right. And the idea of losing Kade forever hurts me to my very core.

How did we all get here? Why? One glorious minute, I'm on a flight back from Greece with Kade's hand gripping my thigh, ready to tell the world he's mine, and now we're here. Hiding in my family lodge, unsure where my abusive brother is, waiting for Luciella, and Kade just shot me and beat his brother up.

I don't blame him for choosing his life over mine. He deserves freedom.

He has a file, one that requires a password to get into it. One night, while I was drinking coffee and browsing on the laptop Barry had given me while Eva slept in her crib, I typed in *Freckles0907* – the date we first kissed in the tent – and it opened.

I'd spent hours browsing the images and video clips, the recording of him laughing while I tried to sing every song from *The Greatest Showman.* Me running on the manor grounds with the dogs chasing after me. Him kissing my cheek while we had a picnic at Lunderston Bay beach.

He'd recorded me dancing a lot. Moving around a hoop, a pole, and blushing when I notice him.

Us both drunk in Greece, singing "Kings and Queens" with sweaty faces and big smiles.

Kade zoomed in on my smile a lot. And my ass.

There were clips he'd deleted. Intimate videos and images that I would have shamefully watched again and again if I had the chance, yet he kept everything else.

Now he's accepting kill contracts with my name on them.

"He might have a plan," Barry says, appearing next to me, and I flinch as Aria rests a hand on my shoulder, comforting me. Tobias stands behind her.

Seems the arguing has stopped and everyone has followed us outside.

Ewan is leaning against the wall behind us, and Cassie is shaking, her eyes welling with tears. "My mother is a monster. I knew she wasn't a good person, but..." She covers her mouth on a choked sob. "My dad..."

"How old are you?" Tobias asks.

"Twenty-two," she replies. "Why?"

"It took you twenty-two years to realise your parents are a pair of assholes who deserve to die?"

Her crocodile tears quickly vanish. "I didn't say that," she retorts.

"No, I did. I don't give a fuck about you. When I next see your mother, I'll kill her, right after I force her to watch her husband being tortured. Nothing you say will stop me. If you try to intervene, you'll be subjected to the same fate. I've been patient having you anywhere near my family."

Aria rolls her eyes. "Tobias. Behave."

"With all due respect, sweetheart, I behave for no one when it comes to our children."

She throws her hands up and starts pacing around. "Fine. But you don't need to threaten a little girl."

His eyes darken. "She's not little. She's also not oblivious to how evil her parents are. She knew Bernadette was drugging our son, and she still went after him. She witnessed his mistreatment and still demanded he marry her. She's as much the devil as her bitch of a fucking mother and deserves the same treatment. And when I see Archie? Not even a gunshot to the head will fucking stop me."

Cassie wipes her face. "Kade loves me."

I flinch and turn away from them as Tobias laughs. "You might be more delusional than your mother."

I glance over my shoulder at the silence. She's narrowing her eyes at Tobias. "And I'll still become your daughter-in-law someday. Now stop threatening me."

I stare at my fingers for a second. They're shaking like fragile leaves in a heavy wind. I glance back up and fist my hands, sitting on them. I want to hit her.

"You're not fucking marrying my son." Deadly and cold, Tobias looks at her, a snarl on his lips. "I promise you, and everyone in this room, if you get in my way, me threatening you will be the least of your worries. You're lucky to still be fucking breathing as it is."

"My mother will come for me. She will come, and you'll be thrown back in jail where you belong, you psycho!"

"If your mother ever comes, you'll get front-row tickets to her demise, and you'll follow." He blinks twice, harshly. "Don't fuck with me."

Aria stands between the two of them before grabbing her ex's hand. "Come with me, Tobias."

Ewan shifts on his feet, Jason whistles and heads round the side of the house for another smoke, and Cassie excuses herself and escapes to her designated room.

As soon as she's gone, a twinkle appears in Tobias's eyes, and he winks at me as Aria stomps out into the garden. He follows, messing my hair as he passes.

Ewan stares at me, noticing my puffy red eyes. "For the record, with everything you've gone through in your life, I think you're strong. I just wanted you to know that."

I look down. "I don't feel it."

"You are. This, all of this, isn't what we wanted for the twins. Me and Aria raised all three kids to have respect for others, and I believe Kade is still innocent. He... cared about you. He went to considerable lengths to deny it at the beginning, because he thought he was going to break your heart, but he cared about you a lot. I believe he still does."

"I hope you're right," I reply, and his eyes flicker over my head, to the pair talking across the garden. I glance over my shoulder, and Aria is crying into Tobias's chest again. "Forgive me for saying this, and tell me to stop if you think I'm out of line, but... those two, the way they still are..." I bite my lip. "You deserve better."

He chuckles, as if he's heard it a thousand times.

"She tells me that. Often. I love her too much to accept it. We've been important to one another since we were eighteen. I... I cheated on her when we first got together. I was such a dick back then. It was one time, and it's still my biggest regret. Jason was only a few months old when we got together, and when she fell pregnant, during our break, to Tobias, we stayed active in each other's lives. I could never leave her, even if she still loves him."

I give him a warm smile. "It doesn't bother you?"

"Nah. She's happy, and so am I. At the start, I would have probably left, but their connection, it's... I don't know. It's hard to explain. It helps them both. But thank you," he replies. "Everything will work out in the end. I feel it. He'll come back. We'll get Kade back, and Luciella will be home soon. Then all I need to do is find Jason somewhere in that shell."

"I'm going to speak with Giana. When this is all over."

He smiles at me briefly, then he walks back inside, out of sight.

Everyone's busy. I could easily sneak away now and wait for Kade's message.

Maybe it's idiotic to think this'll work, but if giving up my life means Kade gets his freedom, then I'll do it. I have nothing. No real family. No job. No reason to keep going, but look at what Kade has. He has everything.

I make my way to my own room quickly, noticing the time. It takes me a few minutes of breathing and hyping myself up, but I manage to pull on clothes and brush my teeth.

My phone vibrates.

He's sent a screenshot of the Maps app, with a pinpoint on where we've to meet. A small parking place at the bottom of a hill walk in the middle of nowhere. I guess he needs privacy – no witnesses while he puts a bullet in my skull.

11

KADE

When I bought this place and realised I had too much money that could get swallowed up by the system if I died, I made a will. When my untimely passing happens, I'll split half my money between my family. They can argue among them who gets what amount.

The other half will go to Stacey, along with the ownership of the dogs, my Stirling apartment, and my bike and car. She already has a few of my accounts that Barry gave her when they moved to America.

My savings – all thirty million dollars hidden in a separate bank account – goes to Barry. It means college fully paid for his daughter and any future kids, and he'll have full control of my business and all guards.

Base is basically richer than royalty, and Dez is probably going to marry Tylar, who's also filthy rich from her parents owning an architecture empire. They don't need my shit.

I sit at the kitchen counter, "Cities" by Toby Mai (featuring Two Feet) echoing through the surround-sound speakers all over the house, and watch my phone screen – the dogs are running wild in the backyard, and the manor workers are trying to catch them. They look happy, barking and rolling around with each other.

I miss them.

A message pops up, and I sigh.

Bernadette: *Kill her this time, do you understand? I can see through CCTV and track you with the bug in your phone and hear you through the earpiece – you can't try any funny business.*

Bernadette: *A deal is a deal. I will clear your files of any criminal activity, and you'll be free. Just get rid of her.*

You'd think she'd want me to ask about her daughter – why does my family have Cassie in the lodge and why is she still breathing? My dad is there, so I'm shocked Cassie isn't buried in a shallow grave by now given his impatience and lack of medication.

Stacey messages me, and it shifts my mood completely. My heart races in my ears. All she's sent is her location. A little blue dot on a map, moving down the A9. I keep the app open and grab a glass of water, downing some of it and rushing to my bathroom to check my face and hair.

There's no fixing the latter; it's too long and wavy, and my face is ripped apart with bruises, little cuts from Jason hitting me and the hideous scar that'll probably scare her.

I don't want to scare her.

The instant twisting in my gut has me vomiting into the toilet bowl – my eighth time being sick today, I think. It's been happening for a while, but it goes away after a bit or I push through the nausea.

Before I leave, I brush my teeth then settle at my kitchen counter again with a pen and paper. It's addressed to everyone, I guess. I scribble down words that have me pausing every few paragraphs, and when I write to Stacey, the ink runs out.

Must be fate.

I don't have time to find another pen, since Stacey is close to the location.

She won't be interested in what I was going to say anyway.

I leave the note sitting on the counter and turn out the lights, fixing my phone onto the handlebars of my bike and pulling my gloves on. Material over my mouth, I shove the helmet on and press the button on my app to open my garage door.

As I drive off, I watch her little blue dot draw closer to me.

It shouldn't make me more nervous, but it does. Anxiety is clawing at my chest, begging to rip me to shreds. I slow down, speed up, wind between cars, the cracked skin of my knuckles rubbing against my gloves.

Twenty minutes later, she pulls into a gas station not far from me. I speed up to catch her, pulling in and stopping beside one of the tanks to fill up.

A black SUV sits alone in the station. One of mine. She must've snuck off under everyone's noses, because if they knew she was here, I'd be toast by now.

Remembering the look on their faces when they rushed to Stacey after I took that shot, they truly believe I want to kill her, that I've gone off the deep end. Even my own brother beat me up for it.

They no longer trust me.

I fix my leather jacket and keep my helmet on as I head into the building to pay. My pulse pounds when I see her. Like my teenage crush from back in the day returns and I'm unable to even form a word in front of her – to look her in the eye without imagining us spending the rest of our lives together. My hands shake, and I fist them.

For over a year, I've imagined the conversation we'd have. Twelve months of waiting, finding different ways to get to her. Fifty-two weeks of torture while Barry and my team kept her safe. It all boils down to this moment, when she glances over her shoulder and gives me a tight smile out of friendliness, not knowing it's me.

The one who shot at her.

The ex-boyfriend who would burn the world down for her.

The piece of shit who could never fall out of love with her.

I nearly drop to my fucking knees, staring at her little dimple and the freckles dusting her cheeks and nose. She's truly a work of art. A masterpiece. And I'm proud to say that I was her first love.

She turns away from me to speak to the cashier, exchanging pleasantries while she pays. I flex my fingers, roll my jaw to hype myself up to close the distance and walk towards her.

Regretfully, I need to scare Stacey again and make her hurry up and get to our meeting place. It won't be long until Barry realises she's gone and hunts her down. We need privacy. We need a few fucking minutes for me to get everything off my chest.

The closer I get, the more I want to drown in her. All of her. I want to wrap my arms around her and hide from this fucked-up world. I want to say I'm sorry for everything and beg her to run away with me.

As soon as I'm behind her, I pause. Even through my helmet, I can smell her shampoo. The top of her head reaches just under my chin, and all the memories of me holding her from behind flash before my eyes.

"Thank you," she says to the cashier, taking her change.

Fuck. Her voice sounds even better than it did on the phone. Am I so far gone that hearing her speak makes me feel like a pubescent teen? I have goosebumps, for fuck's sake.

"Anything else?" the cashier asks, her eyes skimming me then moving back to Stacey.

"No. Thank you."

I push myself forward despite my nerves shattering, keeping my visor down as I lean my elbows on the desk beside her. She bumps into me when she pockets the change, and my heart stops from the contact.

"Oh, sorry."

With a deadly slowness, I turn my head to look at her. She can't see me, but I can see her.

I can see the winter wonderland within a forest in her eyes, her long lashes touched with mascara, the lip balm coating her lips, her hair falling down her back in soft waves that make me want to brush my fingers through them.

Her skin has always had a slight tan, freckles scattered across every inch, and her lips, those full fucking lips, part as she stares at her reflection in the blacked-out visor.

My hands bunch on the counter, the leather gloves crunching, aching to push a lock of hair behind her ear, to flip up my visor and force her to accept an apology right here and now.

Not that an apology is even close to being enough, but at this point, it's all I've got. I don't have the privilege of time to do everything I can to win her back. I can't grovel at her feet for months, years, a lifetime.

I won't kiss her. I can't even imagine kissing her without breaking her. The thought of touching her, making her unravel beneath me, is unrealistic. Bernadette and her team have well and truly fucked that all out of me.

I'm so sorry, Freckles, I want to say. *For everything you've been through. By my hand and others'.*

But everything I do, Bernadette can hear and see right now.

Instead, I tilt my head at her as the cashier asks me if she can help me. My stomach twists, the dire need to vomit making me dizzy, but I ignore it. Ignore the layer of sweat in my hair, the double vision. The intense feeling of needing to sit the fuck down.

Shit.

Stacey blinks with realisation, trying to take careful steps as she backs away without causing any alarm. The cashier asks me again, but I twist and lean my elbows on the counter and watch my girl turn the whitest shade of white.

She's taken three steps from me. I can clear that distance in one.

I want her to stay, even if she's unsure of who I am or what my true intentions might be when she meets me. Having her so close makes me want to fucking live.

I haven't wanted to live for such a long, shitty time.

When I left for Russia a year ago, all I could think about was her. In fact, since I met her at fifteen, I've not had one day where she hasn't been on my mind.

I let my impulsiveness win, and I reach forward to tuck a loose curl behind her ear, but she pulls back on a rushed breath before I make contact. Her eyes widen, and she turns and runs to the car, not bothering to pick up the shelf of fruit she knocks over in the process.

After setting notes on the counter to pay for my fuel, I follow her out with slow steps, ignoring the cashier asking if there's a problem. Stacey hurriedly opens and locks the car door, steps on the gas and speeds out of the station.

Good girl.

It takes me less than three minutes to catch up to her on my motorbike.

While she goes as fast as she can, I stay on her tail. I need her terrified enough that Bernadette believes all of this until the very last minute. I need as much time as possible before she realises I'm aborting the mission.

My breathing halts when she nearly misses a turn on the road.

Fucking hell, Freckles. Drive carefully.

I speed up, approaching her right side. For dramatic effect, because she's only doing fifty on a road with a limit of fucking seventy, I pull out my gun and keep it in view as I slide up beside her window and aim right at her.

She looks to the side, and her eyes widen.

She abruptly takes the next turn.

Good. We were supposed to meet on this road anyway.

She's still as terrible a driver as ever. But no matter how fast she goes, I match the speed, mocking her every time I turn my head to look at her. She keeps her eyes forward, gripping the steering wheel for dear life.

Finally, she slows down, and we both pull over at our meeting place, before she's opening the car door without pausing. Instead of a hello, she slams the door behind her. "Get this over with."

I swallow and turn off the bike's engine, my eyes finding the cameras Bernadette set up trained on the car park for a split second before I look back at her.

She crosses her arms, and it kills me that she's holding back tears. She's trembling. I can see the quake in her knees and how stiff her entire body is.

I pull up the visor, and she doesn't give me any eye contact; she just stares at my hands as one lifts to aim the gun at her, the other pushing into the space of my helmet to press the button in my ear.

Fuck, forgive me.

Fucking please forgive me, Stacey.

"I have her," I say in a firm tone. The uncontrollable blinking starts, a layer of sweat forming on my face. "She's right in front of me."

12

KADE

Stacey shakes her head and tightens her arms around herself, looking off into the distance now, waiting for me to pull the trigger again. To put an end to her life. Waiting to give up everything to win me my freedom.

Bernadette's sadistic laugh comes through my earpiece, loud enough for Stacey to hear. "Are you intentionally playing with your food?"

"You know I like the chase," I say, removing my finger from the trigger as it spasms.

Accidentally shooting her in the head is one of my biggest fears. Especially after my fuck-up earlier. She has a gash on her cheek from where I hit her, and I feel ill that I hurt her.

"I'm not in the mood for games, Kade. You have a job to do. And I'm busy."

My eye twitches, my jaw ticking, and I swallow hard. "I do this, and you'll cut all ties with me?"

Stacey closes her eyes and takes a deep breath, before opening them again to glare at me. A tear slides down her cheek.

"If that's Bernadette, tell her that her days are limited. When they find the old bitch, she won't last a day. That evil, vile, disgusting *rapist* of a woman."

Damn.

"She's feisty. I understand her appeal to you before. Pretty, spunky, with a little bit of attitude," Bernadette says. "Well, give us a show then, Kade. Shoot her. Shoot the slut who cheated on you with your brother."

"She didn't cheat on me," I snap.

Stacey frowns as I add, "Watch your fucking mouth."

"Excuse me?" Bernadette replies in confusion.

I lower my aim from Stacey and walk to my bike, grabbing my phone and smashing it onto the ground until it's in pieces. I pull the earpiece out and detach the wire, tossing it into a nearby bush.

Stacey stares at me like I'm a lunatic. "What are you doing?"

I don't respond as I shoot the cameras, getting both the first time and breaking the last connection Bernadette has to where I am, what I'm saying and what the fuck happens next.

The sound is deafening, the gunshots still echoing far in the distance, and I turn to see Stacey's shoulders tensed as she stares at me in shock.

My ears ring as I drop my arm to my side, the weapon dangling from my twitching fingers until it hits the ground. I lose my breath for a long minute, just staring at her.

This is it.

This is the moment I've been playing in my head since I crashed my car trying to get to her a year ago. My first fucking chance to actually speak to her face to face.

"Did you get my voicemail?"

She stands as still as a statue, unsure what to say as confusion fills her. Her hand moves behind her back, feeling for the handle of the car door. She's scared. She's scared of me.

I've broken the last piece of us that was left hanging by a thread.

But I had to. I had to make Bernadette believe I would hurt her, so I could get this moment right now.

Tear trails stain her cheeks, and I want so badly to wipe them away.

But she'll probably slap me – or scream. Either would be a nightmare.

What the fuck do you expect?

"Did you get my voicemail?" I ask her again, desperate as I step forward, causing her to back into the car, and I freeze. "A year ago. I crashed the car trying to get to you. I called. I left a voicemail. Did you listen to it? I meant every word."

My hair is a mess as I pull off the helmet and throw it aside, fixing my mouth covering before raising both my hands to show I don't have anything on me.

"Freckles..."

"Don't you dare call me that! Don't you dare!" Her face contorts as she fights tears, her chin trembling as she points a finger at me. "You tried to *shoot* me."

My voice is low, quiet. "I intentionally missed."

She steps forward, and I flinch back. "You hit me." My eyes lift to the cut on her cheek. It's quite deep. It'll likely scar. "Why?"

"I had to make it look real," I reply quietly.

"Make it look real?" she retorts. "Were you performing the entire time? Everything you were saying to me? When you beat up Jason *again?*"

"Freckles," I say again, my chest tight. I'm running out of time. "Please. Just tell me if you heard my voicemail."

"No. Was it another threat? Another deal to kill me to save yourself? I feel sorry for you, Kade. I really do. I want you out of the mess you're in, and I'm willing to give up my life to give you your freedom, but don't you dare try and call me that name."

She gets closer, and my insides shrink to nothing at her red, swollen eyes and the look of disgust on her face. "Stac—"

The slap knocks my face to the side. "I tried to tell you before you ran off and left me on my knees on your bedroom floor. You won't silence me again. You wouldn't listen before, but I'm fucking talking now. I was raped. I was raped by my own stepbrother and all his friends. Jason was drugged, and he was raped too! And you..." She covers her mouth and steps back once. "You left me when I needed you. My dad died, and I was alone and scared."

"I know," I say quietly, stepping forward and trying to take her hands, but she pulls away. "I saw the full footage of that night. That's when I tried to find you and crashed my car. I called you. I left you a voicemail."

She doesn't pull away again as I snatch her hands in mine. With my gloves on, I can't feel how soft her hands are.

"I'm sorry," I say, my voice breaking. "I'm so sorry, Stacey. I'm sorry I left. I'm sorry I didn't realise you were being abused at home. He was hitting you, controlling you, and I had no idea. He—" I swallow. "That motherfucker took our daughter from us, and I left. And then I walked away from you a year ago. I'm just so fucking sorry, and I have no idea how to make it up to you."

Her forehead lowers to my chest; she must be able to feel how fast and hard my heart is beating. "Please just shoot me and get your freedom, Kade. I can't hear this – not when I'm ready to give up. Please don't give me something to live for."

I shake my head and lift my hand to her hair. "I'm not going to shoot you. I wanted to speak to you where she couldn't hear me," I say, wetting my lips. "Everything I've been doing since that contract, she's been there. In my head – and watching me. I couldn't stand the chance of her finding out—" I stop, and it's then I taste my own salty tear on my lips, soaking through the material. "She couldn't find out that I..."

She backs away from me. She's pale and looks exhausted. "Find out what?"

I swallow a lump threatening to suffocate me and force out the words, even though they're muffled through the material covering my mouth. "That I'm still in love with you."

"You're not," she replies, her cheeks soaked. "If you were still in love with me, we wouldn't have just spent years in hell, Kade. If you were in love with me, you would have stayed by my side when I tried to tell you the truth a year ago. You don't love me – I'm just someone you used to have in your life when it was normal, so you hold on to the thought of me."

"That's not even slightly true. If I could go back, I'd go back to the very beginning with you. I'd protect you and our daughter and hide you both from the ugliness of the world."

"There is no going back," she replies, her voice shaking from both the coldness around us and the terror I've put her through. "Our girl is dead, and so is our relationship."

"I'm sorry," I whisper. "I love you."

"Please stop saying that, Kade," she says, sniffing, her jaw shaking. "I want you free from the Sawyers – can you just hurry up and complete your contract? I have nothing left, but you have a family waiting for you to come home. Please. Please let me give you this."

Carefully, my boots move forward again, carrying me towards her until her back presses to the SUV. "I would rather kill myself. I did what I had to do to get us here. I had to apologise to you. I'm not going to complete the contract."

Stacey shakes her head. "Then she'll kill you."

"I'm aware."

She flinches as I tuck a curl behind her ear.

"I'll deal with Bernadette. I just needed to apologise. You don't have to ever forgive me, but I want you to know that if I had all the time in the world, I would spend it trying to win you back. I'd prove myself worthy of you, Stacey. Because there hasn't been a day that's passed where you haven't kept me going. My love might not be enough for you, but it's all I have left. I love you. I love you so fucking much that I want to live."

She doesn't pull her hand away. "Then live. Finish your assignment." Her breaths are uneven as she shakes. "Please live for me."

I close my eyes. "I can't."

Tyres screech in the distance, and we both snap our heads in the direction of the cars heading straight for us.

"Finish the task, Kade," she demands, stepping out of my hold. "We have no future together, but you can have one. Love isn't enough to fix us. Even your kind of love." Her head turns to look at the SUVs speeding towards us, then her pleading expression is back on me. "Please shoot me. Please. Before she reaches us."

I narrow my eyes. "That's not Bernadette. Barry must've tracked your phone." I turn and head for my bike, snatching up my gun from the ground. "Motherfucker."

When I grab my helmet and throw my leg over the bike, Stacey takes my arm. "Please stay. You don't need to do this alone." Her eyes are desperate. "Please." She tugs. "They can help you. You can still finish your assignment. I'll be okay. I promise I'm okay with dying to save you."

I shrug my arm free, fixing the covering over my mouth when it slips. "I'm not fucking shooting you, Stacey. And them helping will only get everyone killed."

Stacey grabs one of the bike's handles. "Tell me what you said in the voicemail."

I stop trying to twist the key, dropping my head. "It's a bit pointless now, don't you think?" I look up at her and pull down my visor. "Like you said, we're done. We didn't have a chance anyway. It was always going to be me or you who died today, and I would never let anything happen to you. I just needed time to say I was sorry before it was too late."

Her hand snaps out to grab my gloved fingers, the other pulling up my visor. "I want to know what you said in the voicemail."

The doors fly open in the distance. Boots hit the ground – people are running towards us – but my eyes are on Stacey.

She moves closer, gripping my hand like I'll vanish on the spot. Her forehead is nearly touching the helmet. "What did you say in the voicemail?"

I lift my free hand to her face, my fingers spasming over the gash on her cheek. Instead of telling her what I said, I smile, even though she can't see my mouth. "The first time I saw you, I was yours. I'll always be yours, Freckles. Our girl will be proud of the woman you've become. You'll both always be my girls."

Before she can respond, I lift my gaze over her shoulder to see Barry coming towards us, his gun raised, pointing straight at me. "Get the fuck away from her," he warns. "I don't give a fuck who you are, sir. Stacey is my priority."

I raise a brow and glance at Stacey, who shakes her head, raising her voice enough for him to hear. "No, don't shoot! He's okay!"

Barry stops, his eyes flickering between the two of us, realising I'm not trying to kill her – and lowers his aim. Before he can say anything, my dad grabs him by the nape, ordering him never to point a gun at his son again before shoving him aside.

Mum is crying. Jason and Ewan are holding her hands to comfort her while my dad marches towards me looking more than pissed off.

I feel ill, like a sudden dizziness has taken over me – I'm going to vomit.

It's the same feeling I get when Bernadette makes me go cold turkey – the stomach cramps and sweats and everything else. I end up blacking out and waking up covered in vomit – not knowing what the fuck happened. I'd put it down to withdrawal symptoms, but I've had a few lines of coke today, so it can't be that.

Stacey leans down to me – I didn't know I'd folded forward – our eyes clashing as she grabs my helmet and pulls my head up. "Are you okay?"

I huff and force myself to straighten, my eyes flickering to Stacey and my parents. I pull my hand free, but Stacey tries to grab me again. "Let me go," I snap. "This is dangerous for all of you. Do you have any idea what Bernadette will do to get me back?"

"Then she can go through all of us. Please, Kade. Please don't go," she whispers, begging me. "I need you."

Everything relaxes. Fuck, I stop fighting her. How can I leave her again?

There's no chance I'm getting away from them now. And their stupidity in trying to save me will get them all killed. I give them a day before they're six feet under. Barry better have a plan – he's been running the show since I left a year ago, taking care of missions and assignments and all the guards.

But he just had a baby girl. And he's still here? Fuck.

None of them are going to understand that I was trying to keep them all safe all these years, and now they're fucking up my plan.

But then Stacey's face screws up when a squealing voice fills the air, and every single one of my nerve endings shrivel. Jason tries to grab the annoyance, but she slinks under his arms.

"Kade!" Cassie yells. "Oh my God! I missed you so much! Tell them we're getting married and to stop bullying me! Oh and get your filthy hands off him, you whore!"

"Fuck off," I mutter through the material covering my mouth.

Stacey scowls, her hand clenching into a fist as if she's going to punch her. And as much as I'd love to see it, I won't put Stacey under any stress.

Cassie comes running straight for us, but I roll my eyes and put a bullet in her skull before she can reach me.

Stacey flinches and turns away in revulsion as Cassie's body drops to the ground like a sack of potatoes. Gone. Dead. Good-fucking-bye.

Dad steps over her body and shakes his head at me. "Stop being a fucking asshole and get in the car."

13

STACEY

Kade looks like he's going to pass out as he pulls himself off his bike, shaking his head. "You're all fucking idiots."

Tobias grabs his son by the helmet and drags him forward, smashing their heads together. "What the fuck do you think you're playing at? You could have killed Stacey."

"I wasn't going to hurt her. I just needed time with her to explain shit," he replies, pulling himself away before he scowls at Barry. "You should know better than to get my family involved in this."

His assistant doesn't back down. "With all due respect, sir, I was here to protect Miss Rhodes. We should leave. I reckon we only have a few minutes before this place is swarming."

"Give me the gun," Tobias says, noticing he's still gripping it harshly, his finger resting on the trigger.

Kade's fingers twitch around the gun, but his eyes slide to me, and he gives in. Resting the weapon in Tobias's palm, Kade lowers his head, not pushing away as his father pulls him by the helmet again and pats his back harshly.

"It's you and me, son," Tobias says, low enough that it's a whisper, but I'm close enough to hear. "You're not doing this by yourself anymore. I'm here. I'm not letting you do this alone. You and me, you hear me?"

Kade doesn't reply.

Tobias shakes him. "Do you fucking hear me?"

"All I can hear is you asking for death," Kade replies. "They'll kill you."

His dad chuckles and grips his shoulder. "Maybe, but not before every single one of them pays. Getting revenge, son, is what we are going to be fucking doing. I have a list, and Christopher Fields is at the very top. Help me hurt the motherfucker."

Kade lifts his head on hearing that name. "You know where he is?"

"We already have guys on their way to his location," Barry says, glancing at me when I frown. They must've got the information before I snuck away. "Can we leave now?"

Tobias looks at me. "You're a terrible driver. Never get behind a wheel again."

I roll my eyes.

Aria walks to her son, sniffling. "Are you okay?" she asks him, her chin dimpling as it trembles, looking at the dead girl on the ground. "Oh, my boy, are you okay?"

He doesn't say anything, just pulls off his helmet, tosses aside his helmet and walks to her.

I never thought that watching Kade hug his mother would make me cry, but here I am.

She's sobbing, hugging him, begging him to get in the car while Tobias leads them to the door. The older version of Kade huffs and stands by the door, holding it open. He glances over at me just as I wipe mascara from under my eyes.

"You good?" Tobias asks.

I nod back and rub my arm, trying not to look down at the river of blood currently sliding towards me. "I'm okay."

Barry crouches down to Cassie's corpse and checks her pulse. "She's dead."

Tobias frowns like a child just kicked his shin. "Of course she's dead. Are your eyes working? Her brain is splattered on the ground, you fucking idiot."

Barry mutters to himself then looks up at Kade's dad. "I was just stating a fact."

"A useless fact," he counters. "Any others? You want to tell me the sky is blue while you're at it?"

Aria tells them both to stop arguing, because it's all they've been doing. Anything one says, the other challenges it, then they get into a pissing contest until Barry backs down or Tobias gets bored.

Tobias tells Barry to leave the body for Bernadette to find. He refuses, and they argue some more before, ultimately, Barry agrees to leave her body on the ground so it can be found and reported. Apparently, it'll put a spotlight on Bernadette, and right now, that's not what she needs. The public will feel sorry for her, they'll hunt for the murder suspect, and hopefully, they'll find some dirty little secrets about her underworld dealings.

I don't climb into the same car as Kade – I follow Barry to another, and Jason sits in the passenger seat as we follow everyone else. My leg bounces, and I lift my eyes to find Kade's big brother staring at me.

"That was risky," he says. "What if he really did kill you?"

I shrug. All I can do is shrug.

I lower my head and lean it against the car window, silence filling the car all the way back to the lodge. When we stop, Jason climbs out, and Barry locks the doors before I can open mine. "Don't ever do that again, do you understand?"

"I was trying to help him."

"By risking your life?"

"He said that if he completed the contra—"

"I don't give a fuck, Stacey. If you ever sneak away from me and risk getting yourself killed, I'll kill you myself."

I narrow my eyes. "I'll tell Lisa you're threatening me."

He scoffs and unclips his seat belt.

When I get out of the car, I pause on seeing Kade climb out

the one in front. He pauses too, staring at me as he pulls up the fabric to cover his mouth, but I already see the purple line from the corner of his mouth, travelling down. He looks like he wants to speak. Aria says something to him, and he nods, not taking his eyes off me.

Even when he looks completely exhausted and drained of life, he's handsome. His hair is longer, wavy, and his usual clean-shaven face is covered in stubble.

I like it.

I love him.

I'm still dizzy from the turn of events. We're only a few footsteps from one another, with everything out in the open. No more secrets. No more lies. Nothing but the looming threat of Bernadette.

Him severing his connection with the bitch to get a few minutes alone with me was a shock, and I'm still processing it. I thought I'd be dead by now.

Wanting to kiss someone, to hold them and beg them to forget the last few years and go back to the way things were has got to be one of the hardest things I've ever experienced.

I'm not mad at Kade; I'm... lost. I know none of it was his fault. I could have just yelled from the treetops that I was attacked, that my brother was a lunatic, so I'm not innocent in all of this.

I could have asked for help when I found out Kade was in trouble with Bernadette the night we fucked next to a dead body outside that club. I should have. I went to Tobias because I thought he'd be able to give me advice; I never thought he'd break out and try to deal with him himself.

But he did escape. Is that my fault too?

If I'd just spoken up about my abuse, would we be in this position?

Would my baby girl be here?

Kade shifts on his feet. His fingers are spasming, and he's blinking a lot. "Do you think you could ever forgive me?" he asks, and I can tell the drugs he'd taken are starting to wear off – he's fidgety and sweating and his knees are bouncing. "I need you to forgive me. I'll do anything. Just tell me – I'll do it."

I flatten my lips to hold in a sob. "I don't think this is about forgiveness. I could have said something years ago about my brother, but I didn't."

"You were scared."

"And why didn't you tell anyone about Bernadette?"

Kade stays silent.

"Because you were scared, like me. This isn't about forgiving one another, Kade. This is about surviving."

"But I don't feel like I'm surviving," he says quietly, almost feebly.

I hate myself for believing he would actually hurt me, but how could I not? He shot at me and spoke to me like I was nothing but shit on the bottom of his shoe. He was violent in the way he said each word.

In a way, he is violent, because as annoying as Cassie was, I didn't expect him to shoot her in the head with no emotion.

Tobias puts his arm over Kade's shoulders, pulling him towards the lodge, and I follow beside Aria, who's still sniffing and wiping under her eyes.

"I'm going to need a lot of help with this one. He's on something, I can tell."

"I'll help," I say without hesitation.

"All we need is Luciella home, and we can work on fixing the family. Maybe we can come to an agreement with a judge for Tobias not to get a harsh punishment for escaping. I think... if they knew the reasons why, they'd understand."

It's impossible. Tobias is a murderer and not fit to be in public. He's not safe – a danger to everyone and himself. The second they find out where he is, if they don't shoot on sight, Tobias will never see a visitation or the light of day again.

"I don't think he has any intentions of returning," I say honestly. "He's not been in public in over twenty years, and I can tell he's assessing every detail. Going back would be mental suicide for him."

She turns to me as we stop at the porch. "What else am I to do? He can't stay on the run forever. He'll get sick again. He... The version of him we have now is after years of therapy and medication and training. I'll need to try to sneak his meds, and even then, I'll eventually be caught too. You didn't see what he was like before. I was afraid of him."

I lower my chin in understanding. "It's a horrible situation to be in. I know you care for him."

She snorts a little laugh, looking through the window to see Tobias pouring Kade a glass of water and Kade shaking his head, pulling down the fabric hiding his neck and mouth while Barry inspects him – shining a light in his eyes and checking his blood pressure.

Jason stands aside, looking nervous. The last two times he's been around his little brother, he's been beaten up. But he looks like he wants to talk to him, and I'm glad he does.

"I love Tobias more than words will ever explain," Aria says. "But I also know he doesn't belong out here. It's just a matter of time before he snaps."

The man in question glances towards us, giving Aria a soft smile. He mouths, *He'll be okay,* and goes back to holding a glass out to Kade.

They remind me of a couple in their twenties. They're goofy and hot-headed, yet the love between them is unbeatable. It's a shame for Ewan, even if he is okay with it.

Ewan, Barry and Tobias come outside to talk to the guards, seeking news on whether Chris has been caught. Nothing yet, but they know where he is. They talk about Cassie too, then discuss the drugs in Kade's system and how we're going to need to lock him in a room and make him go cold turkey.

I shiver at the thought and head inside. I find Kade standing in the kitchen now, leaning against the counter, watching me. He tilts his head towards the stairs, a silent request to speak to me again in private. He still has the material over his mouth, refusing to remove it.

Such a bad time to find him hot, but I do. Even if his eyes are bloodshot and he can't stand still for more than a second.

I nod slightly, and when he realises I'm not going to go first, he sets towards the stairs and goes up them. I go to move, but I notice Jason pushing off the wall and following his little brother.

It doesn't matter though, because as soon as Jason reaches the top, he's yelling out for help.

When we rush upstairs, Kade is seizing on the floor. Aria tells everyone to give him space, but I reach for his hand, holding it tightly until the seizure stops. I don't let go of it while Tobias carries him to the bedroom across from mine, or when I sit beside his bed while Ewan and Aria discuss the type of seizures Tobias used to have.

He's sweaty, pale, and he keeps flinching in his sleep.

"Kade's only ever had a seizure once," Aria says, hugging herself. "He was eight, and doctors had no idea what caused it. Said it could've been due to his high level of anxiety. We were to monitor him and record the next time it happened." She glances at her son. "He'll be okay. He's gone through a lot, so I think he's mentally exhausted."

"Or it's the drugs," Barry adds. "Bernadette forced a lot into his system over the years."

We all stay silent.

Twelve hours I stay sitting beside his bed. He hasn't once budged or shifted or awoken. Kade's completely drained – out cold, asleep, resting as he should. It'll get worse before it gets better, Aria had told everyone.

But we'll be here for him this time. He doesn't need to do any of this alone.

I don't register the cars pulling up outside until Jason walks over to the window. "Shit. They got them."

I sigh as I stroke my thumb over Kade's clammy hand.

My stepbrothers are here.

14

STACEY

I cringe as another splatter of Chris's blood nearly hits my shoes.

"Stop fucking hitting me."

Chris spits on the ground, his face stained red, his nose crooked. He's strapped to a chair in the middle of the basement, and his eyes follow Tobias as he flexes the fingers on both hands, slowly walking around him. Stalking his prey like a starved animal.

"Tell me again why you think you own her."

I gulp as Chris looks at me before replying, "Um, *duh.* Have you seen her?"

Even as a captive, he needs to be a sarcastic knob.

"Yes." Another punch, and his head snaps to the side, a tooth rolling across the dirty floor. "Now, let's try this again. You think you own her. Give me a valid reason why."

Kyle is sitting beside me, his knees bouncing, head down. He'd tried to talk us out of this, but when Tobias told him he would tie him to a chair too, Kyle baulked and gave in. They were staying in a hotel, trying to figure out a way to rescue me, not knowing I'd already been saved.

He knows why we're doing this, but he's insistent that Chris is sick and should be sectioned, not tortured by none other than Tobias Mitchell. That'll never happen though.

Tobias offered Jason a clean hit, but he's been sitting with Kade ever since they arrived. Ewan is aware of the situation between Kade and Jason, so he's waiting patiently for the chance to beat Chris to a pulp too.

My head snaps over to Ewan as he stands, fed up. "Why did you involve my son?" he asks, rage in his eyes. "Why?"

Chris grins. "Does it matter? It worked."

Tobias kicks him hard in the chest, knocking the chair back. A gust of air pushes from his mouth, and he grits his teeth. We're more than happy to let Kade's dad mess around with him – Chris is terrified of Tobias. I can still see the look on his face when the bag was taken off his head and he spotted the older Mitchell.

His arms and fingers, tied behind his back, are crushed between the ground and chair. His shoulder pops out as Ewan slams his boot on him. "Fuck!"

Barry huffs and pulls the chair up before going back to his corner.

Chris moves his head from side to side, cracking his neck, then glares. "Do you really need to keep hitting me? What are you getting out of being violent?"

"Joy," Tobias replies, crossing his arms. "I like watching you bleed. I'll enjoy it a whole lot more when I kill you."

Chris pales and looks over at me desperately. "Are you letting this happen?" His eyes find Kyle. "And you? You're my fucking brother."

"I'm out," is all Kyle says, leaving as Tobias pulls a gun from his waistband and points it at Chris.

He cocks it. "What information did you have on Bernadette Sawyer that she wanted?"

"I don't know what you're talking about."

Tobias forces the muzzle of the gun into his cheek, pressing hard. "The USB you made Stacey give to her as a trade. What was on it?"

When Chris stays silent, Barry steps forward. "You broke into her system?"

"Maybe."

"How?" Tobias pushes. "How did you break in?"

"Because, unlike you, you fucking psycho, I have a brain."

The insult doesn't faze Tobias. "Are you still in her system?"

"Yes." He raises a brow. "Why? You want to trade information?" He grins. "I must admit, I wouldn't mind giving you some codes if it meant seeing Luciella and getting between her legs again."

My eyes widen. *Again?*

For the first time in forever, Tobias has no immediate response. His anger slips just enough to reveal his shock. Then: "What did you just say?"

"Your daughter moans like a fucking angel."

Tobias smacks the side of his head with the gun.

Chris screws his eyes shut, a trickle of blood trailing down his neck from the gash on his head. "That wasn't very nice. I was good to her, I promise. Just like I was good to Stacey. You know what my sister feels like, don't you? Have you been inside her? Warm. Soft. Fucking *used*. Luciella was the same."

Tobias goes to step forward, but Ewan gets there first.

He grabs him by the throat, cutting off his air supply. "Stop fucking talking about my daughter like that, you piece of shit!"

Barry tries to pry him off Chris and fails. They need him alive for a little longer – information about the Sawyers at this point could change everything.

Then we can kill him.

Ewan releases him when his eyes begin to bulge, and he gasps before chuckling at Tobias. "I thought she was *your* daughter? Man, you are all a bunch of inbred fucks. But you didn't answer my question, big guy. Are you or are you not fucking Stacey?"

Aria is upstairs cleaning the kitchen, or she'd be as mortified as I am right now.

Tobias glances at me. "This is what you've had to deal with all these years? He's annoying."

"Yep."

"I knew it," Chris says, blood trickling from his mouth, his teeth red. He licks them. "You've been fucking my sister."

Tobias grimaces. "Don't call her your sister."

"You didn't deny it."

Tobias leans in, gripping the arms of the chair. "What if I have been? What the fuck are you going to do about it?"

I want to tell Tobias to shut up, that baiting him won't help, but the rage in his eyes makes it all worth it.

"I'll kill you if you have. She's mine."

"She doesn't belong to anyone," Tobias says. "Are you done? Your voice is going through me."

Chris scowls. "I *will* kill you."

Kade's father chuckles and flexes his fingers, fisting his hand again. "You can certainly try." He looks at Barry. "Have you gone through his phone?"

"Yeah. He created a program that automatically wipes the phone. He broke his laptop when the guys got there, but he'll have backup files somewhere." Then Kade's assistant looks at Chris. "We're trying to take them down, just like you were planning. Where can we get those files?"

When Ewan and Tobias start punching him again, I decide to take my leave. I walk upstairs to the kitchen and find Aria erratically scrubbing her hands. I walk over, and she pauses when she sees me. "Oh, sweetheart. Are you okay?"

She's trying to scrub blood from her hand. Her eyes are wet, and she looks on the verge of a breakdown. "Are *you* okay?" I ask instead.

"I want to go home," she says, her lip wobbling. "I want Tobias to be well, for Kade to get better, and for my daughter to be with me. I want to go home."

Her ex comes up from the basement, red stains on his hands and clothes. "He's asleep."

No, he's knocked out.

"Are you crying?" Tobias asks Aria. She tries to hide her face, but he's already approaching her and taking it in his hands. "I'll make it right. I promise I will."

She forces a smile but ultimately falls apart in his arms, hugging into his chest.

15

STACEY

Kade is still out cold by the time night falls again. Tobias and Aria have gone for a walk through the woods, and Barry and Ewan are eating at the dining table. Some of the guards are sleeping while the others take over their duties, and the silence in the lodge is making me uneasy.

Kyle sits on the kitchen counter while I make us coffee. "I'm sorry I didn't get to you sooner. I left the house as soon as you yelled that you were here."

I give him a soft smile. "You have nothing to apologise for. I'm okay. You're okay. Chris is locked downstairs. Nothing much worse can happen."

"Bernadette Sawyer might know where we are."

"She does," I reply. "I'm not sure why she hasn't stormed in here for Kade though. I think she might have a plan."

"Is there anyone we can call? Police? Can we take to social media? Anything?"

"Too risky." I hand him his mug. "Have you spoken to Nora?"

"She thinks I'm still looking for Chris. Told her he'd lost his mind and was trying to kill you." He sighs, taking a sip of his hot drink. "She sends her best wishes."

I snort. Nora won't care about me. All she wants is her son back in her arms – she'll cocoon him in bubble wrap like he's a fragile piece of glass.

"I'm going to head to bed. Get some sleep," I tell him, noting the bags under his eyes and the dishevelled hair. "And shower. You stink."

"You're one to talk." He fakes a sniff in my direction and screws his face up.

I slap his arm and walk upstairs, stopping outside Kade's room, listening to Jason talking. I'm not sure what he's saying, but I know Kade is still unconscious. I hear a sniff, an "I'm sorry I couldn't protect you from them" and I back away from the door to give him privacy.

I'm not sure how I manage to sleep. The room is cold, and the blankets are thin. Maybe it's because I'm mentally and physically shattered.

I wake just a couple of hours later though. I know I won't sleep any more, so I sit up, stretch and turn on the shower. While I'm pulling off my clothes, I hear the door of my bedroom open, so I quickly grab my PJs from the floor and hold them to my naked body.

From the outline, I know it's Kade leaning against my door, his head dropping back against the wood. He's breathing unevenly, running his hand through his hair.

I take slow, careful steps, still hiding myself. "Kade?"

His eyes flicker to me, but he doesn't move.

He doesn't have the material covering the lower part of his face either. If anything, he looks a little out of it – as if his mind isn't here, but his body is.

I move forward and go to turn on the light, but he snatches my wrist. "No."

"Why?"

"No."

I blink and swallow, nodding.

"Christopher Fields," he says in a quiet tone. "Where is he?"

My breathing halts. "Why?"

"Is he here?"

Slowly, in the darkness, I pull my PJs back on. "He's tied up in the basement. We wanted you to get—"

He's out the door before I can finish, obviously fuelled by adrenaline.

I swear under my breath and run after him.

"Woah!" Barry jumps out of his chair and drops the gadget he was holding on the floor when he sees Kade abruptly kicking open the door to the basement. "No, boss. Wait!"

Tobias, Aria, Ewan and Kyle stream into the kitchen, and we all follow him as he hammers downstairs and heads straight to Chris, slamming his fist into his face; he comes to with a pained cry.

"Wake up, motherfucker."

The fear sinks in the second he registers who's towering above him, and he begins thrashing in his seat, kicking his legs out and getting nowhere.

We all stand at the wall near the stairs, watching Kade blinking uncontrollably and screwing his face up like he's trying to rid voices from his mind. "You have no fucking idea how long I've waited for this. Do you know who I am?" He points at himself. "I'm the father of the child you killed."

Kade snatches a blade from a nearby table, flips it in his hand to catch it by the handle and plunges it into Chris's shoulder.

He screams so loud my ears ring.

"You fucking—"

Kade covers his mouth and leans in, yanking the blade out. Chris looses a harrowing gasp against his palm then silently screams as he sinks it into his other shoulder and twists it.

"How does it feel? Huh? How does it feel to be helpless? To not be able to control your pain? To receive and not give." He pushes the blade further, and Tobias chuckles while Kyle turns away. "This, right here, is for my daughter, you piece of shit."

Aria covers her mouth on a whimper and runs upstairs. For once, Tobias and Ewan don't chase after her.

Kade pulls the blade out again and slaps him across the face, wiping the bloodied knife on his trousers.

"You were full of words in that little recording you took. Why so silent now? Because you don't have my girlfriend or my brother drugged and at your mercy?"

Chris doesn't respond, hunching over as far as he can in his restraints, the two stab wounds gushing down his top and onto the dirty floor.

We once sat in this very basement and played *Twister*. I got into a position where he could touch my boob without anyone noticing. From then, he was obsessed with touching them. Always looking, trying to grab them. I was never allowed to wear a bra around him.

Hours after that game, he dragged me down here, young and helpless, and made me strip while he touched himself. He took pictures of me. Told me I was his, even as I cried for my dad and took punches to the face until I removed my underwear.

I was fifteen.

I'm hauled from the memory when Kade pulls away and heads to the table filled with devices. Tobias set up when we first got here. He grabs the hammer, flips it in his hand like he did the blade then grabs some nails and strides towards Chris like a panther stalking its prey.

"You see her?" He grabs his head with one hand, his fingers and thumb at his temples, and turns him to look at me. "This will be the last time you see her."

Chris must think that means figuratively as he laughs through his pain, but Tobias moves behind him and pries his eyeball open. I quickly turn away as Kade hammers a nail into it.

The scream – it'll be burned into me forever.

He deserves it. He deserves it. He deserves it.

I keep my back turned as they do the same with the other eye, blinding him. I can tell he's shaking from the rapid gasps he lets out, and when I turn to face him once more, bile rises in my throat. He's crying tears of blood, and it's a horrifying sight.

Kade doesn't fuck around with words, and Tobias crosses his

arms, waiting for his son's next move. Kade paces between me and Chris. Blinking fast. Tugging at the hair behind his head – agitated.

Chris is chittering, trembling with pain and fear, shock consuming him as his fingernails sink into the arms of the wooden chair.

Kade stops pacing and looks at me. "Go upstairs."

I tilt my head. "What? No."

"You know he's going to suffer – I'll make it painful – so go upstairs. You don't need to see this."

"I do need to see this," I retort. "He took everything from me."

Kade stares at me, snarling and blinking. So much blinking and pacing and muttering under his breath. I'm more concerned about his mental state than taking revenge on my abuser.

Then he grabs a small hacksaw and stops in front of me again. "The first time he touched you, what did he do?"

I try to speak, my voice breaking. "I… was unconscious." Chris told me about it at breakfast the next morning.

Kade's eyes darken even more, something I thought would be impossible.

"Never mind – I have a better idea."

I frown as Kade turns to his dad. "Hold his hand still. The left one first."

Tobias doesn't seem to enjoy taking orders, let alone from his chaotic son, but he obeys anyway. Chris is thrashing again as Tobias holds his wrist to the wood, and Kade saws off four of his fingers.

The digits drop to the floor like bullet casings, and I nearly vomit everywhere.

Chris sounds like an animal being slaughtered.

"Now you won't be able to look at her or fucking touch her."

"He just pissed himself," Barry states.

"I can see that," Tobias snipes, flicking his boot out to banish the minuscule drop of piss that touched it. "Just stand there, you useless prick."

Barry shrugs. "I don't want his dirty blood on me."

Blood squirts all over Kade, but he keeps going with the other hand, yanking at the digits he hasn't managed to fully detach while Chris lets off more harrowing screams.

"I won't kill you," he tells him in a bored tone. "I want you to live and know you can never see her beauty or touch her perfection. I want you to be helpless and unable to walk." On the last word, he puts a bullet in Chris's knee, and I close my eyes at the sound that comes from him. "I'll leave your hearing, so I can tell you when I win her back, so you can hear her moaning my fucking name. When I marry her. When she births my fucking children. And guess what? I'll have all of that. You won't. Because Stacey Rhodes has been mine since the day I fucking met her."

He shoots Chris's other knee as Tobias whistles.

Chris has saliva dripping from his mouth, his face red with pain and rage. "She. Mine."

"Yours?" Kade wipes blood from his eyes with the back of his hand. "Everyone, get out."

Tobias grunts and grabs Barry by the collar to pull him out, but he shrugs him off and scowls. "I'm able to take myself out, you barbaric wanker."

Ewan goes upstairs first, and I chew my lip and watch Kade run his hand through his hair, smudging blood everywhere, little trickles going down his nape.

Barry gestures for me to follow, and when I take a step, Kade says, "Not you."

For a second, I hesitate. So does Barry. He's hesitant around Kade after he shot at me, like a bit of trust has vanished, but finally he nods and goes upstairs, leaving me and Kade with Chris.

"I almost feel sorry for you," Kade says to Chris when the door at the top of the stairs closes. "No, in fact, I do feel sorry for you."

"Why?" Chris replies, the word broken, weak and slurred. I'm surprised he's even answering back, considering he's bleeding from multiple places.

Not to mention the nails stopping his eyelids from fully closing.

Kade grabs another chair, settling it in front of Chris before sitting down on it, his eyes flickering over to me. He holds out his hand. "Come here."

I hug myself and step forward, and my breathing pauses when Kade pulls me into his lap. My nerves come alive from his touch, at feeling his thighs beneath me, at the way he wraps one arm around me while he settles the gun by our side.

"Do you trust me?" Kade whispers in my ear.

I give a slight nod.

The arm wrapped around me slackens at the same time his lips press to my nape. His hand slides up my bare legs to my PJ shorts, not stopping as he reaches my inner thigh and keeps going.

My heart races from his touch, a tingling sensation working its way to my core just as his fingertips brush over my underwear. Maybe it's because I haven't been touched in so long, or maybe it's because it's Kade, but I instantly part my legs to give him better access while I watch blood trailing from Chris's eyes and hands.

Kade's lips lightly graze across my nape to my ear. "I'm going to make you come in front of this piece of shit."

I don't have a chance to respond. My teeth bite into my bottom lip on a moan as he shoves aside my underwear and sinks two fingers inside me. "Oh God."

My mouth opens, my eyelids closing slightly as I feel him going slow and deep.

"You hear that?" Kade taunts as he works his fingers in and out in a rhythm. My body reacts the only way it can, and I rock my hips; feel him growing hard against my ass. "You hear the noises I can pull from her pretty mouth?"

Chris pulls at his restraints. "Don't fucking touch her."

I moan as he pushes a third finger in, fucking me with them while he alternates between sucking on my skin with his blood-covered lips and teasing my abuser.

He curls his fingers, and I whimper, parting my legs wider as my head drops back onto his shoulder. "K-Kade," I moan, moving against his hand. My hand grips the hair at the back of his head, using it as leverage to grind into his hand and push my ass against his cock.

More. I want more.

But this isn't romantic or anything other than Kade claiming me for Chris to witness – showing him that no matter what, I've always been his. Not Chris's, not the men he made rape me – two of whom are still walking around freely. Though Tobias has already said he'll deal with them if his son doesn't.

Teeth sink into my neck, and he sucks my skin harshly, causing me to cry out. "Tell him who you belong to," Kade orders. "Tell him."

"You," I breathe.

"Don't fucking say that!" Chris yells. "Leave her alone. Stop fucking touching her!"

Kade lets out a deep chuckle against my skin. "You want me to touch you, don't you?"

"Uh-huh," I moan as he rubs his thumb on my clit. "I want you, Kade, not him. Never him."

"Stacey, please," Chris sobs, blood still pissing from his eyes. "Please stop. Please."

"He killed our daughter," Kade says as he slips a blade into my hand. "Hurt him."

My eyes close momentarily, my high building, and I grit my teeth, remembering everything he ever did to me, to us, while Kade keeps touching me, his other hand sliding up my chest, between my breasts, until he's holding my throat.

"Hurt him with me, Freckles. Make him pay for ruining our lives."

I barely register the blade lodging in Chris's thigh, or Kade's fingers wrapped around mine, both of us holding the blade's handle now. My stepbrother cries out then grits his bloody teeth, unable to move from his restraints.

I breathe, pulling the blade out and doing it again, but Kade lets go, dragging his hand up my thigh and circling my clit while his other fingers keep fucking me.

Each time I stab Chris's thighs, he cries a little louder, his voice croaky and dry, begging me to stop, but I keep going and going and going, until my arm gets tired. I drop the blade on the ground and wrap my blood-covered hand around Chris's throat instead, cutting off his air.

I'm not strong enough to kill him with one hand, but the pressure building in his face brings me joy while Kade grinds his cock up against me through his trousers, dropping a "fuck" and a "keep going".

My hand cramps, so I let go of Chris's throat. He gasps for air, his entire body trembling as his blood pools beneath the chair.

I yelp as Kade pulls his fingers out, grabs my nape and bends me forward, my head dangerously close to Chris's knee. He's tugging at my shorts again, and I tense with euphoria as he finger-fucks me from behind then leans forward to circle my clit.

"She's such a good girl for me, Christopher," Kade teases. "Such a good, good girl."

He goes harder, and I need to grab the arms of the chair, careful not to touch Chris as my vision blurs and warmth gathers at my core, which is clutching at the fingers pummelling into me now.

"So," Kade continues, "back to what I was saying because we got distracted."

He thrusts his fingers faster, and I cry out as a wave of pleasure hits me. It happens again, and again, until my orgasm overtakes the feeling, and I'm seeing stars and moaning.

"Fuck, she's soaking and tightening around my fingers, Christopher. I bet you wish you were me. I bet you always wished you could be me. She's fucking drenched for *me*. Do you know what it feels like to be loved by her? To see a future with her? To watch her grow your child, only to lose it because of a piece-of-shit jealous cunt?"

Chris is trembling, yanking at his restraints still – fighting against them to try to... what? Stop Kade from touching me? To take over himself?

No one ever knows when it comes to Chris.

"F-Fuck you," he spits.

I gasp and tense all over when it finally gets too much. Kade pulls his fingers out and tugs me up by the hair to sit on him again as I try to catch my breath.

"You good?"

Tears sting my eyes, my lips trembling. "Can I go now?"

I'm scared. For the first time in a while, I'm scared of Kade. Not because he touched me, even if it was only to take revenge against Chris, but there's something different about him. Like he's fallen into a deep, dark hole and is trying to get himself out of it.

He stares at me, searching my face with a confused look. Then he lets go of me, and I don't wait a second to run.

I hear the door opening – Tobias and Barry are standing there – then Chris starts calling out my name, stopping me at the stairs, but he's silenced when Kade smashes a hammer into the side of his face.

I should be basking in his pain, but with all the blood, the thumb rolling near my feet and the other fingers on the floor... I try not to gag as Kade lifts another tool. The small hacksaw again.

Barry watches Kade lift one of Chris's fingers and toss it aside – he glances sideways at an impassive Tobias and sighs.

Then his eyes drop to me.

"Are you okay?" Barry asks me, his gaze flickering between the blood coating my hand and Kade. "Are you hurt?"

"I'm okay," I say quietly. "I'm going to my room."

Barry nods and steps aside just as Tobias goes to the table filled with blades and grabs the largest one.

Kade watches me take the stairs two at a time, and he honestly looks terrifying. He has a saw in one hand and a hammer in the other, and his face is red with blood, the whites of his eyes the only light present.

"Don't be afraid of me, Freckles," he calls, spitting out blood that's leaked into his mouth. "This is for us."

16

STACEY

I don't stop until I reach the upstairs bathroom, vomiting up my guts. Chris's blood is on my hands, now staining the toilet lid. I stabbed him. Multiple times. I stabbed him, and I liked it. I wanted to stab him again, to hurt him, but I couldn't focus.

Am I a monster?

I can hear Tobias laughing. I've never noticed how evil his laugh sounds.

I blink through my tears, wiping my mouth and pulling away from the toilet to lean against the wall. Blood on my skin, the aftermath of my orgasm on my underwear, the feeling of Kade's fingers inside me...

I gulp and close my eyes, trying to stay calm. There's a knock at the door, but I ignore it. Another knock, and I croak, "Come in."

Jason pokes his head in. "I heard you— What the fuck happened?" He rushes in and drops in front of me, inspecting the blood. "This isn't yours."

I shake my head. "No."

"Is he dead?"

I shrug. "I don't know."

He grabs a towel and soaks it, cleaning my hand and arm. "Tobias told Aria to keep him alive. He wants him to suffer."

"I want him dead," I whisper. "I want all of this to be over with."

"Me too," he replies, rubbing blood from my cheek. "Barry thinks Bernadette is planning to attack here. We should leave – find somewhere else to hide."

I nod, unfazed. "You don't want to go down?"

"No." Jason sighs, sitting against the bathtub in front of me. "Does it make me weak? Not being able to go down there?"

"No. Not everyone enjoys watching people suffer."

"I want him to suffer," he says. "But knowing it's my brother that's doing it makes me uneasy. He should be in university like he was supposed to be."

I hum. "Yeah. All our lives would be a lot different if it wasn't for Chris. I should have told Kade back when we were eighteen. Maybe we'd all be safe."

"Bernadette didn't target Kade because of Christopher. I hope you aren't putting the blame on yourself for this mess."

A tear slides down my cheek. "I don't know how to feel differently. Chris only came for you because of me. I didn't only ruin my own relationship; I ruined yours."

Jason leans forward and grabs my hand. "Stop. Stop blaming yourself."

"Promise me you'll win her back."

He nods. "I promise. I'll stay clean and get my shit together. I need to— She was—" He stops. "I need to get better for them both. Getting my brother back is more important."

"You're a good person, Jason. I'm sorry life handed us such a horrible hand. You both need to sit down and talk. Preferably when you're both in the right headspace. Kade loves you; he was always talking about you when we were together. He looked up to you."

Jason gives me a tight smile. "I'll try. I couldn't before because… because I was a coward."

"I was too."

He helps me up and hands me the towel to try to get the blood from my hair, but I give up. He goes to bed, and I pull on a hoodie and trainers.

When I walk back into the kitchen, the room is in darkness, and the screams downstairs have stopped, but I can see a strip of light running along the bottom of the basement door. I tiptoe down to see Kyle sitting in front of Chris, Aria beside him, Tobias in the corner.

There's blood everywhere. I don't think there's one part of Chris that's not red. His skin is slit open all over. They all look up at me as I reach halfway down the steps.

"He's upstairs," Aria says, white as a ghost. "Please go and see him. He… he's not in a good place."

Her eyes drop to Chris's mangled face, his fingerless hands, the slashes all over his body, as if Kade and Tobias had gone nuts and started throwing blades around blindly.

He has holes in his knees, and a foot is lying off to the side.

With this much blood loss, I don't think Chris will survive. His chest is rising and falling rapidly. How is he still alive?

The table full of weapons is overturned, and Tobias sits in the corner, nursing his hand with a bloody cloth.

"What happened?" I ask him, nodding to his hand.

Tobias uncovers the small gash on his palm. "I tried to make him stop. He lost himself, and we needed to ground him."

"He hurt you?"

"Not on purpose. Go see him," he tells me. "He's not armed."

My brows knit together as I glance back at Aria. She looks pale.

"I didn't want this for my son. I have no idea what to do," she says, stitching the holes where Chris's fingers once were.

"I'll go and see him," I tell her, glancing once more at Chris then walking up the creaky steps.

Barry and two of the guards are now standing around the dining table with an iPad, papers and a laptop, discussing Bernadette's whereabouts and ways to get her here without her own team of suited-up bodyguards behind her.

They want to kill her and her husband.

Cassie's body was discovered. We'll hear from her mother soon. I'm certain of it.

Was all this blood on the floor when I came down? The lights were off, but they're on now. My foot slips on it, and Barry's head snaps up. "There's a trail going all the way up to the rooms," he says, as if it's normal. "Watch your step."

There's a puddle of vomit at the bottom of the stairs and crimson stains on the banister, as if he's grabbed it while heaving.

I step over it and stop when I see a crack in the plaster on the wall. An obvious punch hole, dots of blood surrounding it.

The ruby-red boot prints take me up the rest of the stairs; there's the outline of a hand against the wall, as if he was trying to keep himself upright. Down the hallway to the right, across from my room, the door is closed, but I can hear him.

He's not crying, but he sounds like he's in pain, as if he's gritting his teeth and trying to hold back a gut-wrenching sob that's threatening to strangle him.

I push the door open slowly, quietly, to see Kade in the corner of the room, his head bowed and between his legs, rocking back and forth with blood soaking him. His hands fist at his hair, gripping it hard enough that I know it must hurt.

"Kade," I say as I close the door behind me, stepping into the middle of the room. "Kade."

He flinches but doesn't stop rocking back and forth, tugging his dark, bloodstained strands harder.

I say his name again, as gently as I possibly can. I lower myself in front of him. My fingers curl around his wrists, and he freezes his rocking, but his eyes stay down.

"Thank you," I say, settling between his parted legs, still holding his wrists to stop him from yanking at his hair. "Chris can never touch me again. He won't even be able to *look* at me again."

For minutes, maybe hours, we stay like this. Me in front of him, holding him carefully, letting him hear my soft voice as I praise him for sticking up for me. He doesn't give me a response, or lift his eyes to me, but I know he's listening.

His fingers spasm uncontrollably – his body tenses, and he braces himself.

I let go of his wrists and move closer, sitting on my haunches as I take his cheeks in my palms and caress under his eyes with my thumbs. Some of the blood on his face is still wet, some parts dried.

He trembles, twitching like he's close to seizing, and he's so, so cold. He shivers.

"Look at me, Kade," I say softly. "Please look at me and tell me you're okay."

Nothing.

I keep speaking. "I'm going to turn on the shower. You don't need to talk, but let me look after you. Please."

Slowly, Kade drops his hands from his hair, his head still bowed. He slips the face covering up to cover his top lip with shaky fingers and closes his eyes. I think he might be oblivious to the fact he just ruined Chris without hiding his face.

I don't want him to hide.

He stays sitting in the corner of the room while I walk into the adjoining bathroom and hunt for a towel, some soap and a scrubber, and turn on the shower. I wait for it to get hot, and when I turn around, Kade is back to rocking again, muttering under his breath.

He's whispering in Russian, I think. I can't understand a word he's saying.

I drop the towel on the sink and inch closer, trying to hear his words. The shower drowns out most of the noise, belting against the glass panel, and there's a clicking coming from the slightly ajar window.

Kade's shoulders shake, and he glances at me like I'm a ghost haunting him, like I'm stalking him and ready to pounce with a knife in my hand. Terror. Fear. The look of someone who's given up and is begging for mercy.

Then the words he's whispering are English again, and they get more distorted with his spasming body.

I stop moving when what he's saying becomes as clear as a summer's day.

"She's not there. She's not there. She's not fucking there." They're uneven, his face red as he forces each one out. "Stop looking. She's not there. She's never there. Not there. No. She's not there."

This is a massive flip from the way he was while I was in that room with him, while he whispered in my ear, fingers deep inside me. Until it all got too much and I had to leave. He was in control of himself, semi-sane, but now it's like his bubble has burst and the entire world is on his shoulders.

I sit on the bed, keeping my distance. "Kade..."

He flinches and curls in on himself, hiding in the corner some more. As if a dark shadow is pulling over him, he does everything he can to put distance between us, and I chew my lip, not sure what to do.

I'm not going to force him to look at me, but I need him to know he's safe. I'm not Bernadette. I'm not Archie. Nor am I any of the clients who took from him when he didn't want to give. I'm not asking him to kill anyone or to take drugs, or injecting him with substances that made him this way. I just want him to know he's safe.

He looks like a scared little boy, and I refuse to leave him like this.

"I'm here. It's me, Stacey. I'm not going to hurt you."

He slaps the side of his head, his mutters growing louder, and my eyes burn while I watch my first and only love try not to destroy himself. The eighteen-year-old who was nervous to kiss me during a game of dares – who shook nervously when he pressed me into the couch and kissed me – who shared all my firsts and treated me like a princess.

My voice cracks. "I'm your Freckles, remember?"

The hand beating against the side of his head stops, and his fingers curl into his palm as he drops it so he can hold his knees with both arms.

"We have two dogs. Milo and Hopper." They're with the manor staff, waiting patiently for their master to return. "Do you remember when we used to walk them on the grounds, and they'd get us all muddy when they dragged us through the woods? You always held the leads because I let them go when they ran, and you'd need to chase them through the manor."

He doesn't need to give me a response, but I know he's listening.

So I continue, kicking off my shoes and crossing my legs on his bed. I smile as I think of the times we've had.

"You always loved my singing voice, even though you said you didn't. It made you laugh. We laughed a lot. When we were drunk and singing karaoke in Greece, or even when we were just lying in bed and talking. We always had that, you know? We kept each other smiling. You gave me a reason to live when I felt like I was already dead inside."

I gulp, fresh tears already sliding down my cheeks.

"You still make me smile. When I think of you, I feel alive. I think of our first date a lot. London. Dinner. Hotel rooms and more firsts. They're *ours.* All of those memories are ours. Kade and Stacey. Stacey and Kade. What we had was special."

Kade stops shaking like a leaf, his head still lowered.

I study him. "I haven't been able to watch *The Greatest Showman* without crying. I don't even sing during 'From Now On' – can you believe that?"

The shower is still running, steam building in the room and causing the window to mist up. I stare at the blood on the floor, a slide mark showing that he slipped and stayed where he landed.

"I'm glad you designed some tattoos for me. I still have them," I say, standing up slightly, but the movement still makes him flinch like I've hit him. I step back to give him space and pull my hoodie down at the back, showing him our initials warped together with the design he made. "I'll never cover this one. It's my favourite."

Still not giving me his eyes, he flexes his fingers and tilts his head, so he's looking at the wall. "She's not there. Don't talk to her. She's not there. You aren't crazy. We aren't crazy. Because she's not there."

I chew the inside of my cheek.

"The first time we met, we shared a cigarette. I told you my name, and you just stared at me. I was looking for you and gave up when I reached the pool house. Jason dropped Luciella off at the studio when I first got there, and you were in the truck."

I smile at myself, remember how I aimlessly wandered the manor during Luciella's birthday party, hunting for her twin brother.

"Lu talked about you in class a lot. It was good to hear what it was supposed to be like having a brother – it made me like you before I even knew you, knowing you were good to your sister. I wanted to meet you." I glance at him. "And then I did."

I may have gone home that night, locked myself in the bathroom, and giggled as if he'd flirted with me and called me pretty. Maybe the fact he was rude had made me like him more.

"And when we got dared to kiss, I got butterflies. I fancied you, and I really didn't want to embarrass myself during my first kiss." I sit on the edge of the bed again, our feet close to touching. "But I was your first kiss too, so I was comfortable. You made those times I was in hell feel like heaven. I wanted to die so many times, wanted it all to end, but I had you, so it was worth it. Living was worth it. I trusted you with all my firsts, just like you trusted me."

I swallow a lump and look to the side, hiding my tears.

I'm trying to erase the way our last night together panned out. The footage he was sent on his phone; neglecting to tell him about Chris our entire relationship and how abused I was in that house.

If I'd told him, we might not be in this position.

If I'd told him, we might have our daughter with us.

Ultimately, this is my fault.

But I was scared. Chris had instilled absolute terror into me and made me feel like I was alone, even though I had Kade. He made me feel like I was small, useless and his.

I once tried to tell my dad, but it ruined my relationship with him. He chose Chris – I was a liar.

That night, he shared my bed for the first time, and I cried until the morning while Chris wrapped himself around me, his disgusting cock hard against me. But I couldn't tell Dad. He wouldn't believe me. I couldn't tell anyone if the one person who was supposed to protect me said I was a liar.

Trauma made me a shell, but I've slowly cracked free from it, and Chris can no longer touch me or even look at me.

But I lost Kade in the process.

I fight the wave of sadness and twist my fingers together nervously. "Despite our ending, we always had great trust. I'm sorry you got a distorted view of what happened that night, and I'm sorry I didn't tell you sooner about Chris. I was scared that he'd do something to you, or whisk me far, far away. I didn't want to lose you, so I kept the abuse to myself."

I glance at him, and the breath leaving my lips stutters when I see he's looking up at me through his messy, wavy hair, his blue eyes burning into me. As if he's trying to merge my fractured soul with his own.

"You feel alone," I say, my voice breaking. "So do I." When he doesn't look away, I press further, sliding off the bed and onto the floor. "You feel broken." A beat, and I add, "So do I."

I drag myself closer and settle against the wall beside him, making sure we don't touch. He smells like copper and death and all things Kade, but I focus on the powerful presence of being near him.

"I wish we could go back to the day we found out I was pregnant. Sometimes, I picture what she would look like. Blue eyes like yours, hair like mine, and an attitude and personality like your dad." I snort at myself. "She'd have definitely been a heathen. A three-year-old heathen that we loved infinitely."

Slowly, shakily, he drops his hand between us, fingers spasming, his skin pale beneath the blood, tattoos and scars, most of his nails bruised. There is no way to describe how I feel right now. I stare at that hand like it's the present I wanted for Christmas at age six.

I lower my own hand, sitting it close to his on the carpet between us, our pinkies slightly grazing. I'm thrown back to a time four years ago, a blanket over our laps while we watched a movie with his family, our touch electric. But now it's like a trillion bolts of lightning straight to my heart.

"Can I hold your hand?" I ask him just as his pinkie spasms next to mine. His body is still curled away from me, his arms still hugging his knees, his head down and angling away. "If you want to, you can take my hand."

The door opens, and my eyes lift to see Tobias. He glances at his son then at me and slips back away again. Hopefully he tells everyone else to stay away. Kade needs space – he'd hate it if everyone saw him this vulnerable. I shouldn't even be here. But I don't want him to be alone either.

For minutes – ten, I think – we stay silent, the shower still running, steam billowing from the bathroom, water droplets sliding down the window.

Kade's entire body tenses with a spasm, and he grabs my hand in an iron grip, squeezing until my fingertips are tight and tingling, his own turning white with how hard he's holding me.

I gasp, biting my lip and ignoring the pain of his grip.

Trembling once more, Kade tries to slap the side of his head, but I stop it by covering the targeted area with my free hand. He hits my hand instead, but when he realises, he freezes, and his head snaps up. He's still gripping my other hand.

Red, swollen eyes stare at me in horror, like I'm a demon haunting his dreams, the monster under his bed that whispers to him about nightmares and torture.

"I'm here," I say, gulping as I brush my fingers through his hair. I'm still holding his hand tightly with the other, our fingers interlaced. "Do what you need to do, but I'm here. We don't need to talk or do anything."

The material hangs off his chin, but I don't make it obvious or look at the deep purple line from the corner of his mouth. I just keep stroking his hair, my fingers getting caught in the dry blood.

Kade breaks my heart as he slowly lowers his head to my shoulder. His hair tickles my nose. It's sticky and tangled in places from Chris's blood – some of it dried in completely, some still wet from mixing with his sweat – and I run my fingers down and back up, separating the hard clumps while his breathing turns less heavy.

"You hate me," he manages to say, his throat dry and rough. "You're always going to hate me."

"I could never hate you, Kade."

The dam explodes, and he grips my wrist to stop me from removing the dried blood from his hair, his shoulders tensing as he lets out a deep sob that will be ingrained in my mind forever.

The last time I heard him like this was when we saw the blood on the bed sheets – the moment we knew we'd lost our daughter. And even then, he controlled himself. He isn't strong enough anymore.

"Forgive me? Please. Please forgive me." His words are broken, but I understand each one, muffled as he pulls away from my shoulder and drops his head into my lap, hugging the back of my knees. "I'll do anything. I know we can't get back what we had, and I'll never be that eighteen-year-old kid again, but please don't hate me. Please forgive me. I didn't want to be like this, Stacey. I didn't want this. I didn't... I... Stacey."

He drops his head again, unable to speak as he sobs and sobs and sobs until he's barely able to take a breath without it shattering like glass.

I can't speak. I'm struggling to keep it together as I hug him back, holding him.

Finally, he falls asleep, but I wake him enough to get him into the shower and stand outside the cubicle while he washes, giving him his space. Then I help him onto the bed, where we lie on our backs, side by side, hand in hand, listening to the silent night.

We don't cuddle, don't get close, nor do we kiss each other goodnight. I understand why. We aren't ready for that, despite him claiming me in front of Chris. Kade's mind, body and soul have gone through a lot over the past three years. Even holding his hand is making him flinch.

When he falls back to sleep, I watch him. I watch the way his chest rises and falls, the tension on his face, his dreams obviously causing him stress, even though he's passed out.

Once I'm certain he'll stay asleep, I lift his hand and kiss his knuckles. "I won't leave you," I promise. "And don't you dare leave me."

Barry reckons his PTSD will be severe, and he's abruptly stopped drugs after being on them for years, so it'll be a messy road ahead. He fears Kade may have dissociated a few times during his abuse, but he hasn't shown any signs of it until tonight.

That version of him was terrifying, in all honesty.

And I knew he hated seeing me afraid of him. Not from the fake threats or the gun to my head. I saw the version of him that was created through extreme manipulation.

I only last a couple of hours beside him before he wakes thinking I'm a client.

When he shouts at me to get out in a terrified voice, I do. I sit outside the room with Tobias, leaning against the door, both of us waiting for him to calm down.

In the space of an hour, he wakes up four times yelling.

I want the real Kade back.

This Kade Mitchell is a glitch in the universe. But he's *my* glitch, not Bernadette's, not Archie's, not the men and women who paid for his forced services and punctured him with needles to dope him up.

Under the skin of the devil they created, buried in the fucking void of the darkness he's trapped in, I will find a glimmer of his humanity.

Why?

Because he's mine.

17

STACEY

The first time I walked into Fields manor, a large pink suitcase trailing behind me, I was excited for a new start. My mother was dead, and Dad had met a woman named Nora, with two sons who couldn't wait to have me live with them.

Kyle, my new twenty-two-year-old brother, had walked me to my room, helped me decorate it the way I wanted and started driving me to my dance classes. We always got fast food on the way home, and he made sure I always had the newest technology. He bought me an aerial hoop to put in their basement, but Nora refused to let him drill into the ceiling.

He was the good big brother. One I always wanted.

Chris was the worst.

When he first laid eyes on me, he shook my hand, squeezed it too hard, then let his eyes drop, lingering on my flat chest.

We were halfway through lunch when I realised he'd been staring at me the entire time. He kept kicking my foot, pressing his thigh up against mine, and when we got home, he walked me to my room and asked if I needed help out of my dress.

I remember the revulsion I felt as I told him to get out, and it was at that moment I realised who I lived with.

He barged into my shower that night. Ordered me to strip while he dealt with himself, watching, staring, forcing me to wash my body and hair.

I was innocent and young, yet he made me feel dirty without even touching me. He put thoughts in my head that shouldn't have been there at that age. Praying wasn't something I ever did, but at night, when he would sneak into my room, I'd pray that he died.

I'd pray for him to meet his end.

I needed someone to help me. Someone to listen.

My dad was all I had, and he didn't believe me, so I had nothing. Nora became his number one, and Kyle just thought Chris was obsessed with having a little sister. Why would he believe me when my own father wouldn't?

I knew he would eventually go too far.

From the age of fourteen, I waited in fear every single fucking day for that monster to land his hardest blow. And when I turned nineteen, he did it twice in the same month.

He killed my unborn child then drugged me, raped me, and destroyed the only good thing I had left in life.

After Kade moved away and my dad passed, the violence got worse. I have a scar between my breasts from him dragging a key down my chest to deter others from touching what he thought was his, and multiple mental bruises from the memories of fists flying at me – always in places others wouldn't see.

Let's not forget the time we went on a family holiday and he held my head underwater until I nearly passed out, only to then "save me" from drowning to look like a good big brother.

The look my dad gave me when I told him about Chris still haunts me – a look that said, *You really want me to believe he sexually assaults you?*

Chris was sick. Deluded. Monstrous. Brutal. The thorn I

couldn't remove from my side.

I was terrified of him.

Now I'm staring at the piece of shit while Aria stands back, her hands covered in blood from trying to stop the bleeding.

She managed to stitch some of his wounds using what she could find in the lodge, but then again, she's a scientist not a medical doctor.

It's no use. The evidence of Kade's rage is all over the room. A severed foot, slashes everywhere and an evident stab wound to the groin. My own stab wounds are in his thighs, still leaking dark blood.

"He's lost too much blood," Aria says, wiping her hands on a cloth. "I'm not sure how he's still alive. But he won't be for long."

She's ghostly pale as she watches me, her tired eyes flickering to Chris.

She's seen death. Tobias made sure of that.

He might well be insane, but at least he's on our side.

So much trauma in our lives, yet we're still here, fighting.

Aria's hands shake as she rests one on my shoulder, squeezing. "Luciella will be home tomorrow, and I think when she is, we should all go home. Barry can put on extra security around the manor. We... we'll figure out what to do for Tobias. Kade needs to be home."

I chew my lip. "Bernadette will come for him."

"She's busy dealing with the media frenzy and the death of her daughter."

True. Within hours of Kade putting a bullet in her head, Cassie's picture has started circulating news channels and social media. *The Sawyers are grieving a terrible loss*, the reports say.

In the nicest way possible, the girl is better off dead.

And as much as the idea of Chris being kept alive and forced to suffer as Kade described is tempting, I meant what I said to Jason. I want him gone. Knowing he isn't walking the same world as me would make me far more comfortable.

I pat Aria's hand on my shoulder. "I'm sorry," I say. "For all of this. If I'd told Kade about Chris when we were together, then we wouldn't be standing in puddles of my stepbrother's mess." I gulp and lower my head. "Maybe our kid would be here too."

"You can't blame yourself for any of this, Stacey. He's the monster. He's the one who took from you. And, therefore, he's the one at fault. Survivors deal with abuse differently, and not everyone can speak up. I don't want to hear that from you again."

"After my dad didn't believe that Chris was abusing me, I didn't feel like I could speak to anyone. I thought he would target Kade. I wanted to keep him safe," I admit, wetting my lips, remembering how innocent and full of life Kade was when we were eighteen. "I fell in love with him so fast, and the thought of Chris ruining that made me stay silent."

I know Chris, in his slowly dying body, can hear me.

"Chris wanted me to love him, but it was always Kade."

The corner of Aria's mouth curls slightly with a look of exhaustion, the lines at the side of her eyes tightening. "I know, sweetheart."

I slowly turn, walking towards Chris. "Can you give me a minute?" I ask her, and she smiles with a nod and walks up the stairs, leaving me alone with my stepbrother.

I kick the chair he's strapped to, but he doesn't budge. "Kade didn't touch your ears, so I assume you can hear me."

Nothing, not even a twitch.

I kick the chair again as I circle him, and he lets out a low, pained groan.

"Do you remember my twentieth birthday?" I walk around the chair, not caring that my shoes are getting covered in sticky blood. "When your mum went to Italy, and Kyle was away at college, and you forced me to wear a short dress and dance for you?"

He doesn't reply. Not that he's strong enough to do so.

"You invited two of your friends to watch me too. Do you remember what you did when I refused to have sex with all three of you?"

My anger is spiking. I can feel blood roaring in my ears as I circle the chair once more. I snatch his hair and pull his head back.

"You made me swallow pills, nearly broke my jaw, and I woke up in your bed hours later. You said you didn't touch me, but did they?"

I have so many memories that are broken from him drugging me, and now that I know he raped me multiple times, I'm trying to figure out when. I blacked out more times than I can count.

For some reason, before I saw the video of him sliding inside me, I believed he hadn't touched me. I thought he would've boasted about it; yelled in my face, but he kept it to himself.

"Or the time we went on the cruise and Kyle had to shove his fingers down my throat when he found me nearly drowning naked in the pool? I had bite marks on my inner thighs, remember?"

Thankfully, Kyle didn't see much, since he'd launched a towel over my body. My dad had been dead three months, so they decided me getting wasted was my way of dealing with his death.

The more I think, the angrier I get.

My foot hits metal, and I pick up the blade Kade dropped after mutilating him. I twist it in my hand, the point of the knife against the pad of my pointer finger as I keep walking around him, reeling off all the times he screwed with me.

The pain he caused me.

Mentally fucking me.

Physically too.

He was never brave enough to do it without me being drugged. I would have fought until my dying breath if I'd been conscious.

"You should know, you look hideous right now. And I think death is far too kind for you. You should suffer. You should see what my life is going to be like without you. But you don't deserve to breathe the same air as my future children."

The door at the top of the steps opens, and Tobias walks down, his eyes trained on me. I stop behind Chris, watching as Barry walks down too.

"Kade's asleep again," Tobias says, his lip cut at the corner. I know his son didn't mean to hurt him. "We were coming to take his body away. Is he still alive?"

"For now," I say blankly, turning back to Chris, seeing every single thing he ever did to me.

I see myself. Innocent. Quiet. The teenager who fell in love – happy with her boyfriend. She doesn't have bruises or fears or monsters under her bed. I see Chris smiling down at me when he told me my dad was dead. Sudden. Unexplained. Out of the blue.

I see a blue-eyed little girl with dark hair and a smile that could've lit up the world, a giggle that would've made the stars shine brighter and a future that was ripped away from her before she reached a single milestone.

I see Kade holding her hand while she wears the princess dress he bought her when I was pregnant.

And as my mind messes with me some more, I hear my daughter screaming as Chris grabs her. She's crying for me, for her daddy. Until her sobs are cut off, and darkness falls.

Everything quietens in my head. There's a dull throb in my ears as I stare at him.

The blade is in my grasp, but I don't feel it. I don't feel anything but loss.

Little princess, this is for you.

My eyes well as I tip his chin up with the blade, making the hammered-in nails he now has for eyes look up at me, his eyelids unable to close. His throat bobs slowly, tears of crimson sliding down his cheeks.

His lips try to move, but nothing comes out.

Maybe because his jaw is crushed.

With bared teeth, I shake my head. "You don't get to speak now. You've done enough damage." My voice is shaky as I say the words, grabbing his hair to hold his head back, readjusting the blade to press the point to his throat.

Tobias and Barry don't say anything, but I can feel them in the room with me. Two men who are like family.

They're here and I'm not alone. Not anymore.

"I want you to know that it'll be me who kills you. Kade might have caused you all the pain you deserved, but it will be *me* who ends your life." I harshly slice to the right, the sharp edge of the blade cutting through skin, flesh and muscle. Blood hits my face, mixing with my tears. "I hate you, Chris. And if by some miracle you make it to heaven, I hope my mother kicks your ass. If not..." I lean forward to whisper in his ear as the gurgling stops. "I'll see you in hell."

I stand up and let go of the blade. It clatters to the ground, my jaw trembling, as I watch Chris's head drop, even more blood puddling beneath the chair he's tied to.

For the longest moment, I stand in silence, waiting for the relief to set in, the weight on my shoulders and chest to vanish, the sickness in my stomach to go away, the breath that makes me feel at ease.

It doesn't come. None of it does.

Everything he caused is still there.

Tobias walks up beside me and throws his arm across my shoulders. "Come on. You need a shower and a good sleep. We'll clean up here. He can't get you anymore, little one."

Barry looks around the room. "This is going to be horrible to clean up."

"What can I say? My son is an artist."

We all grimace.

Tobias leans down and picks up the severed foot. "Think fast," he says as he throws it at Barry's face.

He catches it automatically, then jumps back and drops it on the ground. "*What the shit?*"

I bite my lip as Tobias winks at me, and I know he was just trying to cheer me up.

He's so goofy sometimes. Aria said he was never like this before, but after years and years of therapy and meds and other resources, he found himself.

It's his way of coping with all the change, I guess.

Apparently, this is what Tobias is like without that darkness having taken hold. But it's there. Looming. Waiting to claim him once more.

The door opens, and I spin around to see Kyle slowly walking down the stairs. He stops when he sees me, his eyes sliding to the chair in the middle of the basement and Chris's slit throat.

Before he can speak, I step forward. "I was fourteen, Kyle. Fourteen and terrified. If you understood how much he made my life hell and took everything from me…" I cover my mouth with the back of my hand. "I had to. I had to kill him. I had to end it."

I have no idea why panic is suddenly wrapping around my heart like a fist, but I care about Kyle. He was always the good brother.

And I've just killed his real, blood-related sibling.

Kyle narrows his brows as if his response is obvious. "I know you had to. I'm not mad at you. I just… wish he didn't turn out the way he did."

"Please don't hate me."

He looks confused for a second, glancing between us all. "My little brother abused you for years. Why would I hate you for dealing with him?"

"Because he was *your brother*," I say, my bottom lip wobbling. "And he's dead. You didn't want him dead."

"Of course I didn't. But look at the damage he's caused. I loved Chris but not what he turned into. He wasn't the kid I taught to ride a bike or helped with his homework because our dad was a lazy wanker. I taught him everything, and I tried to make sure he grew up to be good, not this…" He gestures to the body. "He turned out a lot like our dad."

Tobias rolls his eyes. "Was your dad a rapist, murderer and an abusive asshole?" He steps forward. "Did your dad groom a fourteen-year-old girl?"

Kyle shakes his head, turning white. "No. But he did beat us."

He tuts and tilts his head. "No comparison, kid."

I stare at Chris again then back at his brother. "Chris made his own bed; he can die in it." I walk past him on the steps. "I'm going to see Kade." I stop halfway. "You should go home. Nora will be worried. They'll dispose of the body."

"What about you?" he asks. "You aren't coming with me? You're my sister. The Fields manor is your home."

"I'm where I belong. You'll always be my brother, and I love you, but I never want to set foot in that house again."

Before I can reach the top, he says, "Wait. I can't take him?"

"Ask Barry," I say, opening the door. "I'm done."

18

STACEY

No one speaks to me as I hurry to my room, covered in blood, and I stop at Kade's door opposite mine, opening it slightly to pop my head in. He's asleep on his back, arm slung over his eyes, his other hand resting on his chest. A glistening layer of sweat coats his skin, and his brows are drawn together.

Tobias locked the windows, just in case he tried to jump out.

I've witnessed withdrawal before, but Kade's situation is different. He's mainly traumatised from everything he's endured over the past three years. He doesn't believe he's safe and with his family.

I think that's the scariest part. Watching the light vanish in his eyes as he dissociates and goes elsewhere in his mind. He throws up a wall and closes himself off from the real world.

A cracked shell.

The drugs are just the tip of the iceberg.

Tobias and Aria found thirty-six scars on his body; four injuries that have gone untreated. He has tattoos covering most of them, but some are still visible.

I close his door and go to my room, turning on the shower and freezing when I stare at my hands. Blood is dried under my nails.

When I get under the spray, I scrub until my skin is raw, washing my hair three times until I feel clean enough. I brush my teeth and spend nearly an hour drying my hair.

By the time I walk back over to Kade's room, he's awake. His eyes are fixed on the ceiling. Dazed. He doesn't look at me as I gently close the door behind me with a soft click.

The mattress dips beneath me as I sit down, still keeping my distance. A glow from the lamp is the only light in the room; it casts a shadow down the side of his face, making the muscles on his body more defined.

Yes, he has lost weight and is paler than usual, but he's still lean, attractive, and I want so badly to lie my head on his chest and stay there forever.

Hell, I've lost a lot of my muscle mass. I haven't danced, trained or worked out in so long. I've been going for a short jog around the lodge, Tobias usually joining me and telling me to slow down, but that's all.

Our lives have just kind of… stalled.

Unsure where the boundaries are for him at the moment, I lie down on my side to face him. "Is this okay?"

His chin dips in acknowledgment, but he barely blinks, still staring at the ceiling. Another person may think he's tapping his chest, but I know it's a spasm. Sometimes they're not so bad, and other times, it seems he can barely move without trembling.

It's only been two days. And all I keep thinking is that Bernadette will come for him. She's going to torture him all over again. Archie too.

I don't want to lose him again. I'm so fed up of losing him.

Ten minutes pass, then Kade, who's been still as a statue, fists his hand against his chest, stopping the sudden tremor that's affected his fingers.

Suddenly realising I'm here, he pulls the face covering up, as if trying to do it without me noticing. The black material sits at his top lip, below his nose, and stops at his chest.

I wish he didn't feel like he needed to hide from me.

"We're going to go back to the manor as soon as Luciella is here and it's safe," I tell him. "I was going to come too, since I don't really have anywhere else to go."

That last part stings worse than expected. I can't go back with Kyle, so I really do have nowhere to go. Nowhere to call home.

"We could walk the dogs together."

Fidgeting with the corner of the pillow, I settle my head on it again. I know he won't speak to me, and that's fine. He knows I'm here, and I always will be.

"I can stream *The Greatest Showman* on Barry's laptop. Do you want to watch it? I can't promise not to sing."

My heart restarts as his head turns to the side, his eyes on me. His chin dips again, but before I can sit up to go get the laptop, he croakily says, "Stay."

"Okay," I reply in a soft voice, taking his hand from his chest and bringing it to my lips. I press a kiss to his knuckles, waiting to see his reaction. "I'm not going anywhere."

His body strains a few times, and he blinks rapidly before asking, "Why?"

I frown. "Why what?"

He wets his lips, running his hand through his hair, messing it. His words are slurred, his eyes unfocused. "I don't know why you're here. Is it… Is it because you f-feel bad? Am I imagining you here? Does Stacey know you're here? Did you pay me? Have I lost you?"

"Kade. I *am* Stacey." I tighten my grip on his hand as the questions keep mindlessly falling from his lips. "I'm your forever, remember?"

Shaking his head, he tries to pull out of my grasp, repeatedly muttering a *no*. His sweaty hand slips from mine, and he quickly gets to his feet.

He backs up until he hits the wall then slides down it and stares right through me. Tobias said when this happens to just remain calm, to remind him that he isn't alone. But when I try to talk, my voice cracks in my throat. "Kade, I… I'm here."

He's silent, and as I crawl off the bed and get closer to him, I see tears track down his cheeks, his face contorted in pain. "Make it stop," he says, begs, pleads with me. "Please make it stop. Please, please, please. Do you have my gun? Can I have it? I need to kill them."

He's hallucinating, flinching like someone threw something at him.

I wish I could make it stop. If I could take it all away from him, all the demons and the bad memories, I would. I'd take them all to my grave and keep them buried with me, so he'd never suffer again.

We barely make it to the toilet before he vomits. I rub his back in small circles, and he warns me not to look at his face as I try to wipe his mouth. With the material a bundle on the floor, he covers his chin and neck with his arm.

"I have scars too. Look," I say as I pull the nightdress down at the front, showing him the one Chris made with the key. "You don't need to hide from me, because I'm the same."

I show him my thigh, behind my ear and my scalp.

When we were together, I never had any scars. Chris was careful to keep his abuse to bruises only. I think I have about nine altogether now.

Kade shakily raises his finger and pulls down the front of my nightdress again. Any other person would see it as sexual, but I know it's not. He isn't looking at my naked breasts; he isn't even paying attention to them as he runs his finger down the purple line.

"Did your brother do that?"

"All of them are from him," I reply.

"I'll kill him," he says, as if he can't remember he ripped him apart already. "Did Barry locate him?"

My heart breaks for Kade. "I think you should rest. He can't get me anymore."

His glazed eyes lift to my face, his other hand still hiding his chin. "Because you're with me? I can keep you safe?"

"Yeah. He'll never be able to hurt me again. I promise."

Kade's eyes darken, and he drops both hands to his parted knees. His grey sweats are the only clothing he's wearing. "I'm going to kill him when I see him."

I gulp and nod, helping him to his feet and out of the bathroom. The room is in darkness aside from the light glow of the moon outside.

Frantic fingers wrap around my wrist when I try to sneak out once he's in bed. I want to go and ask Aria if the delusional stage is usually as extreme and sudden, or if it's a trauma response to shut out memories.

How can he have forgotten what he did to Chris?

"Stacey isn't going to forgive me," he says as he tightens his grip on my wrist. "She's going to think I'm disgusting."

"I don't."

"I had to do a lot," he says. His pupils are dilated as he stares through me again. "If she knew what Archie did to me, she'd never go near me again."

"No, that's not true." My bottom lip quivers, and I catch it between my teeth, a painful rushing sound in my ears. "I… Stacey loves you."

"Do you think so?"

I'm catapulted back to that night in America, where I had to take Kade to the hotel room. He was drugged and thought I was a client. He had no idea I was Stacey and spoke about me. Maybe it wasn't the drugs; maybe it was his mind playing tricks on him.

Déjà vu is kicking my ass right now.

Do I think Stacey loves Kade? Infinity times yes.

I asked myself on his private jet, minutes after he whisked me away to protect me from Bernadette, if I was in love with him. I said I wasn't sure.

But I've never not been in love with Kade.

This rough patch he's in, we'll get through it together. Even if it takes years until I get a glimpse of my Kade back. I know he'd do the same for me.

A tear slides down my cheek as I lie on the pillow beside Kade, facing him. "Yeah, she loves you so, so much. She thinks you're strong and brave, and all she—" My voice breaks. "All she wants to do is cuddle you."

He hums then goes silent as his face contorts, another spasm vibrating through his body. He grabs his stomach and winces, then settles as he tries to control each breath.

Still as stone, his exposed chest rises and falls as he stares at nothing. The only clue that he's even breathing. I want to reach over and trace the new scars on his side, a large indent against his ribs that isn't fresh.

There's a tattoo over it, and something in my chest twists as I make out what it is.

A bunch of dead roses have been inked across his ribs to hide an injury. I have ones that look the exact same on my back.

"What happened to your side?" I ask, hoping he doesn't recoil from my question.

His middle finger trails over the indent. "I crashed my car before I went to Russia. I... I was trying to get to her. But I was too late."

After a few minutes of silence, he looks over at me, and his glazed eyes brighten a touch. Confused, he asks, "Is that you, Freckles?"

I fist the duvet and pull it over me, tucking it under my chin. "Yeah," I breathe into the dark. "It's me."

He sighs, and as he takes in my face, his bloodshot eyes studying me, I feel content. Enough so that I fall asleep with his hand on my cheek, faintly feeling his thumb stroking under my eye.

The last thing I hear are whispered words in Russian.

"Moya vechnost."

19

STACEY

"If you fart in my face, I'll tell Kade."

I scoff as Tobias pushes me further up the tree with a camera strapped around my neck. "Kade has heard me fart plenty of times, thank you very much."

When I look down, he's shaking his head then smiling. "Aria accidentally farted once, and she was mortified. It smelled terrible, and she walked out of the room with the reddest face. I found it cute."

I screw my nose up. "I don't think anyone has ever referred to my farts as cute."

Tobias snorts. "Well, you aren't Aria."

I nearly slip on a weak branch, glancing down again as he holds me up by the backs of my thighs. "You relate everything back to her."

He shrugs. "You don't see her the way I see her. Everything reminds me of Aria."

My foot slips, nearly hitting his face, and I giggle out an apology. "Sweet but obsessive. One would assume you were a psychopath, Mr Mitchell."

Tobias is used to our banter, so he just chuckles deeply. "At your service, little one. Can you hurry the fuck up? You're not exactly light."

I fake a gasp. "I haven't trained in a studio for months." Far too long. I miss it. "And you and Aria keep cooking the fattiest foods ever."

"Spare me. Move, or I'll intentionally drop you."

I laugh loudly as I grab a thick branch and pull out of his hold. I sit myself securely, unravelling the camera from my neck and wrapping the strap around the thick trunk. Once it beeps that it's on, facing the river, I give Tobias the thumbs up and head down.

As I descend, Tobias tells me about a time Aria visited with food and a thousand-piece jigsaw of Mount Everest. He flipped it only four times before she decided it was best to do something else. He regrets it and wishes he'd had more patience.

He completely ignores my struggle when a branch snaps beneath me, and I grab on to other branches for dear life. He's leaning on the trunk, ankles crossed, continuing to reminisce while I try not to die.

He huffs when he finally notices me dangling and helps me back down, and I feel ten times safer when my feet touch the forest floor.

He pulls a branch from my hair, flicks it aside and says, "Let's go."

"Where to next?" I ask, trying to keep up with him. I'm out of breath from climbing, and he's soldiering on like I'm a nuisance child who won't hurry up.

He can climb the next goddamn tree.

We walk around the lodge to place more hidden cameras and end up thirty minutes into the forest, his paranoia amping up as we set up another six along the way – all on lower branches or in bushes that require no climbing. Bernadette knows where we are – she sent Kade to shoot me after all – so why isn't she here? It's the biggest question mark above our heads. Her daughter died – it's obvious Kade killed her, since it's his bullet in her skull. Bernadette will know.

She'll know.

It makes me feel uneasy, waiting for her move. Hence all the cameras.

Barry said he'd get someone to do it, but me and Tobias needed a breather, and he wanted to talk to me about Kade's current mental state.

It'll take time until he breaks through, and we're all willing to wait – to help him every step of the way. We all love him, and the struggles he's going through won't break him. We'll make sure of it.

I'll spend the rest of my life by his side, even if he can barely look at me, register that I'm sitting beside him or speak to me. I'll hold his hand when he needs me to. I'll just... be there.

Always.

Kyle took Chris's body and buried him in the middle of the forest before going home.

My brother did give me a cuddle before he left and begged me not to be a stranger. Told me that whenever I need him, he's only a phone call away. He apologised for everything, and promised he'll make sure no trouble comes to us from Chris.

Tobias didn't shake his hand when he held it out to him, but my brother understood. Kyle lived in the same house as me for years and knew his brother was obsessed with me. It wasn't his fault he didn't catch on to *how* obsessed he was. But Tobias sees it differently.

Losing my daughter was the beginning of the end. And it was all because of Chris.

I always wonder what life would've been like for me and Kade if I'd given birth. If we had our daughter, Milo and Hopper, and the house he said he wanted to build for us.

We were so close to having it all.

But then I think of his current state, and my heart shatters piece by piece.

He's been sweating. A lot. And he's got aches everywhere. He won't eat and keeps being sick – is barely drinking water. Aria said that if he makes no improvement today, she'll either get her doctor friends to the lodge or take him to a hospital.

But that also comes with a risk.

When I woke earlier, he freaked out and covered his eyes, repeatedly telling himself to snap out of it. He only calmed when I sat on the opposite side of the room and played music from Tobias's phone.

Chris took mine, and I've no idea where it is. Kade broke his to stop Bernadette from hearing him apologising to me. Barry got us burners, but I haven't used mine much.

I was able to speak to Tylar briefly earlier – she and Dez are still travelling. Her parents had an open day for one of their designs in Rome. She's happy, and she and Dez are having a blast. I have no reason to tell her what's happening at home and ruin the bubble she's in.

However, she did say Dez has been trying to reach out to his friends, but since he's not getting any replies, he assumes they're also living their lives the way he is and can't wait to see them when they arrive back in Scotland in three months.

Kade's asleep right now. He did come out of his room, but Tobias had to tackle him to the ground, because he thought he was being held against his will.

Hallucinations. They're destroying Kade.

Tobias has removed anything dangerous from his room, just in case he tries to kill himself, and we've been taking turns sitting outside his door when he breaks down and wrecks the place.

Once Tobias and I cross one of the wider streams, soaking our shoes, we open the bag and grab another two cameras. "I'm not climbing that," I say, looking up at the tree. "It's your turn to risk your life."

He sighs. "You're very dramatic."

I want to slap him.

Barry calls Tobias and asks if all the cameras are in place yet so he can program them all to his laptop. They bicker then eventually hang up, and Tobias looks at me. "Why are you smiling?"

"You said goodbye without following up with an insult. That's progress for your two's future bromance."

"Fuck off."

I laugh. "Are you going to climb it or are you going to make me?"

He folds his arms. "For your attitude, you can do it."

"Why do I waste my time with you?"

"Because your dad is dead and I'm the replacement?"

Rolling my eyes, I grab a camera and start climbing.

We walk towards the lodge once we're finished. "What time does Luciella get here?"

Tobias smiles, his entire expression changing. "She lands at seven. Barry suggested the driver bring her here instead of me picking her up." He shakes his head. "Asshole."

"He doesn't want you getting caught. I'm surprised you've lasted this long, to be honest. You aren't worried you'll get caught?"

"Nope. I'm good at hiding." He smirks and nudges me with his elbow, nearly knocking me off my feet. "Not even the law can keep me from Aria."

"Are you going to tell me what's going on with you two? When I used to visit, you said you were done because Kade told you to stay away from her. And now you're all over each other like teenagers. I..." I grimace. "I walked in on you two on the couch the other day. Wanted to bleach my eyeballs."

Not that I have any problem with them being that way. I just don't want him to get hurt. She's married to Ewan, and he's a wanted criminal who broke out of his mental institution.

The perfect match made in hell.

Chewing his lip, he sighs. "I haven't been free for a long time. All I know is Aria. Every morning I wake up, I wonder if she'll visit me. I'll reread all her letters. I'll brush my teeth and imagine she's doing hers right beside me. When I sleep, I can smell her shampoo, and if I really try, I can almost hear her giggle in the middle of the night. Now I don't need to imagine it all."

I stare at him, feeling somewhat emotional as he gets annoyed with himself.

He shakes his head. "It's pathetic, I know, but I can't help it. I did a lot to her when we were younger. I fucked up so many times, yet she's still here. Did I tell you I locked her in the bathroom and tried to blow her house up with us both inside?"

My eyes bulge. "You didn't." Some details were kept out of the reports. "That's kind of messed up."

"An hour before, I was fully prepared to hand myself in to the cops for her. But I blacked out, and apparently I did a lot of fucked-up shit. Felt like I didn't wake up for months."

"She forgave you," I say. "She also told you to stop talking about the past, did she not?"

"I know," he replies. "It's weird though, right? How a man at my age is still fucking obsessed with a woman he's been crazy about since he was in his early twenties?"

"Psychotic actually," I say with a smirk.

"Shut up."

My shoulder raises. "And Ewan?"

"He understands. Me and Aria never planned on getting physical together, but Ewan felt his relationship was falling apart and wanted to fix it. He was the one who suggested he watch…" He looks at me, seeing my flattening lips; I'm silently begging him not to go into detail. "Anyway, *look*, they're happier than ever."

I glance down the hill into the lodge to see Aria smiling at her husband as they talk, the other window showing Barry on the phone, probably to his Lisa and Eva, and Jason smoking on the patio. He looks more tired than me. Jason doesn't really speak, unless he's talking to Kade through the door about how nervous his little brother was to take his driving test and when they used to go fishing out in the loch. He keeps going until the banging inside stops, and Kade's breakdown subsides into a deep sleep once more.

"I was never supposed to be here," Tobias continues, helping me down the steep, muddy slope. "I actually asked for the death penalty ten years into my sentence, but Aria fought it until it was thrown out. I was insane and suicidal, they ruled; not capable of making a rational request."

I frown. "You wanted to die?"

"Doing the same thing every single day wasn't a life I wanted to live. I won't return to the institution. I'd rather hide forever, but I couldn't ask that of Aria and my kids. Death has always been my end goal."

I stop walking and grab his arm. "What are you saying?"

Tobias gives me a half-smile – his son's with matching dimples denting. "I think you know what I'm saying."

"You're going to go after Bernadette and Archie once Lu is back and Kade is better, aren't you? It's suicide. They have a goddamn fortress and unlimited security."

"I managed to save you, didn't I?"

"This is *not* the same. You're not rescuing anyone. You're saying you're going to kill the woman who runs Scotland. Her and her husband are vile and corrupt and deep in the underworld. Are you insane?"

"Yes," he replies bluntly.

"Tobias..."

He pinches the bridge of his nose for a second and drops his hand. "Look what they've done to my son. They tried to sell you and my daughter. Of course I'm going to avenge you all." He throws his arm over my shoulders and directs us to the patio. "I would do anything to protect my people, little one."

20

KADE

I blink, needing my eyes to adjust to the lamp shining in my face.

The room is too fucking hot. I sit up slowly, my bones aching as I move. Everything hurts, and I have the worst migraine ever. There's a ticking, like a manual clock is in the room, but my eyes search the place, and I don't see one. I lean down, over the edge of the bed, and look under it.

Nothing.

Is it a clock? What if it's not?

Barry will know what it is. He fixes everything.

I shakily get to my feet, holding the dresser to keep my balance, trying to follow the ticking sound. It's growing louder, mocking me, and I screw my eyes shut and slap the side of my head, but it's still there.

The bathroom light nearly blinds me, so I quickly turn it back off and press my back into the wall.

Tick.

Tick.

Tick.

I try to follow the noise again, freezing when I realise what it is.

There's a bomb in here.

Where?

I overturn everything I can see, but I can't see it.

Where?

I try to open my window, spinning around as the door opens, a faceless man coming straight for me. I try to swing a punch, but I miss, and the person grabs me, holding me down.

"We're… all going to… die." Bomb. Get the bomb.

"It's Jason," the person says. "Please calm down. No one's going to die. Please stop hitting yourself, Kade, please."

His voice is desperate, pleading with me to calm down, until I fist my hand and attempt to push him away – but then there's someone else there, a girl.

She kneels in front of me and places her palm on my cheek. "Kade. Look at me."

"Find it," I spit. "You need… to find it."

Dark hair and a beautiful face lean down to me, and the scent of vanilla and coconut fills my senses. "Kade. Breathe. You're okay." She's stroking my cheek, my forehead, my hair, pushing it out of my face. "You're okay. Me and Jason are here. You're okay."

Tick.

Tick.

Tick.

Tick, tick, tick, tick, tick, tick, tick, tick, tick, tick, tick, tick, tick.

Arms wrap around me, the girl lying on her side beside me. "I'm here," her soft voice says as she presses herself closer. "I'm here. Ground yourself with me. Tell me your three favourite things."

Her hand is soft as it strokes through my hair, gliding down my face, kneading at my shoulder. The feeling is… soothing. The ticking starts to quieten, and all I can do is focus on her voice, on the other person's voice, as they talk about their favourite colours, movies, best memories. Both include me.

I close my eyes and press my forehead forward. "Stacey," I breathe. "Everything."

"I'll grab some water," the other person says. "Keep talking to him."

The bomb is gone, the headache nearly crushing my skull subsiding, and I stay in Stacey's arms while she rocks us back and forth, her voice lulling me to sleep.

21

STACEY

"Luciella and Sebastian are nearly here."

I open my eyes and squint at Tobias, who doesn't give me a second to wake up before he launches the covers off the bed and opens the curtains.

"Wake up."

Screw Tobias and his habit of ruining my naps.

Wincing from temporary blindness, I sit up and rub my eyes with my knuckles. "What?"

"Luciella just arrived. The car's pulling in now."

When Tobias stares at me, waiting impatiently, I pull the covers back over Kade, slide out of bed and raise a brow at him. "Did you say Base is with her?"

"Yes. It seems the Russian dickhead can't leave my daughter alone for a second."

Tobias smiles; it's only a slight curve of the lips, but his eyes are warm. "Are you going to keep being a shitty friend, or are you going to get ready and welcome my daughter home?"

"Sometimes I struggle to find reasons why we're friends."

"We aren't friends. We're family. Now – out of bed."

My heart beats faster when it sinks in that my best friend is here and she's safe. Tobias frowns as I rush to the suitcase Barry brought me and start yanking out articles of clothing, throwing them over my shoulders until I find something decent.

"They landed an hour ago. I think Sebastian intentionally stopped at every traffic light to prolong the journey here."

He glances at Kade, and his smile drops. The big, bad psychopath has a heart, because I see it every time he looks at his kids, at Aria, and I'm sure it grows in size like The Grinch's when she grins at him. When she giggles. When she reaches up and kisses him on the cheek.

When Kade fell asleep, Jason helped me put him to bed. We tidied up his room and sat with him while Jason told me about their childhood. How attached the two were growing up. He's such a broken soul, just like his little brother.

I went to my room for a nap, and Kade had woken up. Jason brought him in here, and he fell back to sleep beside me.

No cuddling. No touching. Just beside each other. Present.

"Is Luciella okay?" I ask as I absently smack him in the face with a pair of leggings and keep rummaging for a pair of fluffy socks. "She's not hurt?"

"Unscathed, Barry said. She just spent the last three days in some secluded house in Russia with Sebastian," he confirms, leaning down and handing me a pair of rolled-up socks.

When I give him a questioning look, he adds, "One of his conditions was to be able to say goodbye. The insufferable bastard thought taking her somewhere like that would be okay."

"A depressing goodbye then," I say as I gather my clothes in my arms, hearing the sound of a car coming up the gravel driveway of the lodge. I walk into the bathroom. "Give me a minute."

I brush my teeth, wash my face and spray deodorant then pull on a hoodie, leggings and my fluffy socks.

"Let him sleep," he says, nodding to Kade when I exit the bathroom. He's sleeping on his front, his face buried in the pillow, the material concealing his face tied behind his neck.

He woke up twice during our nap, yelling at someone to get away, to pull the trigger. To not touch him. To not hurt me.

It breaks my heart to see him this way.

He's exhausted. Three years of constantly being used and abused, drugged and raped, turned into a killer. All for a deranged woman's entertainment.

No one knows her motive for targeting Kade. The sick, perverted woman abused her power and, in turn, a nineteen-year-old Kade lost his free will. He lost everything. His humanity is shattered. The emotions left behind are faded and dark, with only a trickle of the old Kade still shining through.

Regardless of everything he's done for Bernadette, I love him. I'll always love him.

Tobias and I tried to track how many victims fell to his violence, and we stopped when the numbers neared five hundred.

Sometimes, he had contracts to kill buildings' worth of bad people with bombs, and others, he stalked and preyed and took his time while they suffered. He used his hands to strangle, to punch and torture.

He used his gun for slow and fast deaths: firing bullets into areas that weren't fatal, only ending things hours later; or firing into skulls to end them instantly, depending on his mood at the time.

He used his blades to skin and stab and slash.

From footage Barry pulled from Bernadette's system – thanks but no thanks to Chris hacking the database – Kade sometimes talked to his victims. He always used different languages, like he was teasing them while torturing them. In all honesty, I had to stop watching the clips because they made me feel sick.

But he had to do it all. He had to perform and do his job to the best of his ability. Because if he didn't, his family – the people he loved – would become the targets.

I get it, I really do. If I had to choose between becoming like Kade or losing everyone I cared about, I'd choose the former too.

Tobias leaves the room, and before I follow, I walk over to Kade and kneel beside the bed.

"I'll be back soon, okay? I'll bring you water and something to eat."

When he nods lightly, he turns his face to the side, facing me with his eyes closed.

I add, "We'll watch a movie if you want. Or we can just... lie here."

He nods again, and I lean down to kiss his cheek and stop before my lips touch his skin. I don't want to push it and freak him out, so instead, I brush my fingers through his sweaty hair, stroking my thumb against his throbbing temple.

I hold his cheek. "It's all going to be okay. I promise. You're not going to feel like this forever. I'm going to help you. Everyone is going to help, because you aren't alone."

A shaky hand rises to press over my own hand, holding it to his face. I slide my thumb under his eye and smile, even though he can't see me. He pushes his face into my palm harder, clearly starved of this kind of touch.

Tobias doesn't rush me. This is a huge step for Kade to even let me touch his face, to hold my hand to his cheek without flinching and yelling at me to stay away from him. He usually hides his face, but I can see every little part of it.

As handsome as ever.

When his breathing settles and his hand slips from mine, I know he's asleep. I swallow a lump building and stand.

His father closes the door behind us. "I think Aria is right. He needs a doctor," he says as we walk to the end of the corridor and down the stairs. "He looks really sick."

I nod in agreement. "I doubt Bernadette will break into a hospital and take him. But who knows? She's a lunatic."

He hums and slaps Aria's ass as he walks past her. "Our daughter is here, sweetheart."

She blushes and goes to wash the flour from her hands. Jason rushes upstairs to grab his shoes, and Ewan helps Aria untie the apron at her back.

Rain pours from the sky, leaving puddles everywhere. I step in one, ignoring it as I run to the car pulling up.

Even though he's technically the heir to the Russian mafia and marrying into another Russian empire, ultimately making him soon-to-be one of the most powerful leaders in his home country, Base still pales when he sees Kade's father.

"Sebastian Ivanovich Prince," Tobias greets Base as he closes the door to the driver's side. "Why are you alone with no security?"

Base gulps. "They're close."

"Good."

Base gives me a small nod as he walks around the red Aston Martin and opens the passenger-side door. Kade's twin climbs out.

Aria and Tobias snatch her right away, hugging her tight. Aria is crying, smiling, tears trailing down her cheeks as Tobias kisses his daughter's forehead. "You're safe now, baby girl. You're safe."

Luciella sobs into her parents' arms, pulling Ewan and Jason into a group hug. Her head lifts. "Where's Kade?"

"He's sleeping. He's adjusting slowly," her mother says. "Are you okay? Do you need something to eat? Will I run you a bath?"

She wipes her eyes. "I can't believe you're here, Dad."

He hugs her again – she pulls away and kisses his cheek then looks over at me and Base.

She screams when her eyes land on me.

We launch ourselves at each other, and my best friend wraps my arms around her. "Oh my God! I missed you! Are you okay? I couldn't find you. They pulled me out of that room and straight into a car. I was so worried, Stacey. So, so worried."

"I'm fine. I missed you too."

Lu cuddles me back and nods against my shoulder. "I was scared. I didn't know my dad got you until I saw Base. I thought I'd lost you."

I sniff as a tear slides down my cheek and pull her tighter against me. Her dad looks at Base. "Thanks for bringing our daughter back to us."

"It's no bother, big man."

Before Tobias can sneer at him, Barry sprints past us, trailed by numerous guards who begin fanning out around the lodge. "Kade's gone! He ran out the back door five minutes ago!"

My eyes widen as Base drops his bags and runs with Ewan. Aria stares at me in horror as Tobias runs into the woods.

Lu, Aria, Jason and I all join in the search around the woodland, yelling Kade's name, or for someone to go this way or that way, to look for him on the main road and down beside the river.

I trip over something hard and hit the ground, and Lu helps me up, both our eyes landing on a gun… a sniper rifle. The one he used to shoot me? He said he left it here. We both frown, and our heads snap up when someone yells that they've spotted him heading straight for the cliff.

Panic is rising between us with every passing moment, and Aria is in tears, begging out loud for him to stop, to stop running from us.

My lungs are nearly on fire as I run alongside the others, the rain pelting off my face. I slip on patches of moss, my shoes and clothes drenched, and mud splashes up my back. Jason helps me back up just as Base, who's circled back to join us, takes Luciella's hand when she slides.

We reach the cliff, but there's no sign of him. Tobias appears and shoves someone out of the way so he can look down the steep drop. But the rocks beneath are clear – there's no blood from a splattered body.

As I glance around, I have a sudden urge to walk into a small bit of woodland next to the drop. It's dark in there, and it seems like the perfect place to hide.

Ewan, Barry and his men keep searching in the pouring rain. We're so far from the lodge now, there are no cameras in place, and Tobias is fuming that we didn't install more of them further out.

"Does he have a phone?" Base asks, only to be met with an annoyed look from Tobias. Aria shakes her head in response, and they look down the cliff again, just to make sure.

I walk to the small patch of woodland, pulling aside nettles and branches, stopping when I see Kade sitting in the middle. He's hugging his knees with his head down, muttering to himself, far too low for me to hear or understand.

Breathing deeply in relief, I glance over my shoulder. "He's here."

I step closer, and a stick snaps under my shoe. "Kade?"

He doesn't stop muttering – shaking his head and rocking back and forth. There's blood down his arms, probably from falling and running through sharp branches. He's covered in mud, soaked from the rain, and his body trembles with each strangled sob.

There's movement, then Jason comes up behind me, glancing between us both. Tobias and Aria are next, then Lu and Base. We all stay quiet – the only sound we can hear is Kade begging himself to stop, to make it stop, sobbing hard enough to crack his voice.

Jason slips past me, slowly walking towards Kade. He kneels in front of him. "You aren't there anymore," he says quietly, calmly. "You're here, with me. You're safe."

"N-No. I... I..." He shakes his head and starts rocking again. "Make it stop. Make it stop, make it stop, make it stop."

"Look at me, Kade."

He doesn't. "He's not there. He's not there. He hates me. He hates me."

Jason moves closer. "It *is* me. Jason. And I could never hate you. I'm your big brother. I'm the one you call when you get yourself in trouble and need me to bail you out. I'm the one who picks you up when you're drunk and lose your wallet. I snuck you a beer when you were sixteen, remember? And I gave you chewing gum when you didn't want Aria finding out you smoked weed."

Kade stops rocking but doesn't say or do anything.

"I took you to your first boxing class when you were nine, and we got fish and chips on the way home. Do you remember what we did that night?" When there's no reply, he keeps going. "I pretended to Aria you were asleep whenever she came to check on you in my room just so we could play *Grand Theft Auto* until five in the morning."

Aria coughs, but it's more of a sobbed-out laugh.

"When you turned thirteen, I took you skiing in France. You were shit, but I was worse, remember?"

Kade nods once, hugging his knees to himself harder.

"You're with us, Kade. Not there. They can't hurt you anymore. Say it."

"They can't hurt me anymore," Kade repeats quietly. "They can't hurt me anymore."

"No, they can't. Say it again."

Silence, then Kade fists his hands. "They can't hurt me anymore."

"They'll never hurt you again. Look at me."

Lu links our arms as Kade looks up, his cheeks soaked with tears, his eyes swollen and red, the material usually covering his scar lost in the forest somewhere. Everyone can see the damage done to him, but no one speaks as Jason nods.

"See? It's me. You're safe, little bro. You're *safe*. It's going to be hard for a bit, but you'll get through it, because you have all of us."

Kade's face contorts, as if he's in disbelief, and Lu lets go of my arm and walks forward, lowering to her knees beside Jason. "You have all of us, Kade."

Kade looks at her. His eyes brighten, and his voice breaks as he says, "Luciella?"

"Yeah," she replies softly with a warm smile, taking his bloody hand and clasping it between both of hers. "It's me. I'm okay. And so are you."

Base is standing beside me as Aria and Tobias join Lu and Jason. As soon as Tobias sits beside him, Kade erupts in a fit of sobs and apologises over and over, and all four of them sit around him, holding him in an embrace.

Luciella is crying, and I can see how much Base wants to go to her, but this is their moment. His family. They all need this time together. Kade is bawling in his dad's arms while Aria hugs into his side.

"Sorry. I'm so, so sorry." It's like a mantra. A desperate plea for forgiveness as he grabs Jason. "I hit you. I thought you... I'm... sorry. Sorry. I'm so sorry. Please don't hate me. I didn't want to. I didn't... I didn't... I didn't want to hurt them either. They made me, they m-m-made me." His words are rushed out and broken. "Please."

Tobias grabs his face. "You aren't alone anymore, son. If those bastards try to come anywhere near you, I'll make them pay. Do you hear me?"

"I want them to pay," he says, his chin and bottom lip trembling. His body shudders as he tries to breathe. "He hurt me, Dad. He hurt me, and I couldn't do anything to defend myself. Archie. He... He..."

"I know."

His voice cracks. "What if he comes for me?"

Tobias grits his teeth, a tear on his cheek. "He'll never get anywhere near you again, and that's a promise. I'm going to fuck up his life."

"We aren't letting you out of our sights," Aria says. "I'm sorry we didn't do something sooner. We should've known you were in this much trouble."

Base puts his arm over my shoulder. "We should give them their privacy."

I nod and give them all one last look before we leave the small, wooded area. "I have no idea what to do," I admit.

"I don't think anyone knows what to do," he replies, taking a smoke from his packet and offering me one. I take it, and we both light them as we wait. "I need to ask you a favour."

The rain has stopped, but I shake from the cold, my fingers barely getting the cigarette to my lips. I exhale, hating the feeling of it burning my lungs – already sore from running and yelling out Kade's name. "What?"

"Keep an eye on Kade and Ella. I can't come back. I was only allowed to bring her here as one of my conditions for accepting the marriage. Once I leave, I'm gone."

"Are you really marrying someone?"

He sighs. "I have to. It was the only way to get her free. My family is toxic, to say the least. They've wanted me to take over for years, but I always said no. It's not my scene." He shakes his head and blows a cloud of smoke above him. "The girl's being forced into it. Just like me."

"I'm sorry you need to do that, but thank you for getting my best friend back to us. I'll look after them," I say. "Just look after yourself until you figure out how to get back to them."

"Yeah. Do you believe in miracles?"

I shrug. "Do you?"

He just laughs through his nose and takes another draw of his smoke.

22

STACEY

Silence falls between us, and we can hear the faint voices from Ewan and everyone else walking towards us. Tobias or Aria must've called Ewan. But he doesn't go into the trees. Neither does Barry.

We all wait, and nearly two hours later, Aria and Lu walk out of the small patch of woodland, and Base rushes towards them and hugs Luciella. Tobias and Jason have Kade's arms over their shoulders. His head is down. Ewan goes towards them, and Aria tells him that we need to get Kade back to the lodge.

I swallow harshly, and we follow them all the way home. Every now and again, Tobias looks over his shoulder at me, mouthing, *Are you okay*? He winks when I nod.

We get Kade into the lodge, and Jason and Tobias clean him up, get fresh clothes on him and settle him into his own bed. He falls asleep pretty fast, and I want so badly to go to him, but I don't want him to start freaking out again, thinking I'm a figment of his imagination.

It's breaking me standing back, but right now I think he needs some space.

Aria makes us all hot drinks, and I walk to my own room to get changed, catching a glimpse of Base sitting on Lu's chosen bed, her standing between his legs, crying again.

The only thing I catch before I keep walking is him saying, "Come on. Don't be upset, princess. Don't say goodbye like this."

I shower quickly and pull on fresh clothes, heading to the main sitting area where Barry has screens set up on the dinner table, studying them.

"Everything is almost too quiet. Her buildings are empty."

Tobias leans down on the table and stares at one of the screens. "Whose car is that? It's the only one there."

"Greyson's. He's working from the inside. He's not given me updates all day, and I fear he's been caught."

"Shit," Tobias mutters. "When was the last time—" He stops and narrows his eyes at one of the other screens. They both swear at the same time as four black SUVs pull into the small road that leads up to this lodge.

"Fuck!" Barry slaps the table as he shoves away and radios all his men, but people open fire from the cars, and the guards on patrol are downed one by one.

Base and Lu run down the stairs, asking what's happening, and Jason appears in only a pair of shorts, still wet from his shower.

"They're here," is all Tobias says, and everything changes.

Havoc erupts in and around the lodge.

"I want as many bodies as possible guarding my son, right now," he orders, bellowing at people to hurry as they grab their guns, him taking one as well and tucking it behind his back, into his waistband. "Aria, take Luciella and Stacey to one of the rooms and stay there."

But it's too late – the cars are already outside.

Surrounding the lodge.

"Ewan's in the room with Kade," Barry says. "We need to keep them as far away from him as possible."

"And my girls," Tobias says, glancing at Base. "You, go with them."

Base grabs Luciella's hand and leads her upstairs, even as she yells at him to leave her alone, but Aria and I stand our ground.

"Go with them," Tobias barks at us, and we both shake our heads. "Goddammit, go with them now!"

"Now, now, what do we have here?" a voice says as the door opens, and my skin crawls, my blood going cold at the tone of it. I turn around to see Bernadette in a black trench coat and heeled boots, gun in hand as she smiles gleefully at us. "I thought everyone would be excited to see me?"

Aria grits her teeth, Jason grabbing her arm as she goes to pounce at her. "Go to hell, you cruel bitch."

"Hmm," she replies, her eyes snake-like and evil. "So, you're his mother. I should shoot you right now."

"You will not," a deep voice says.

Bernadette's eyes land on the man beside me. It's like the world around her vanishes as she stares right at Tobias. She falters, but something flickers behind her eyes as she looks him up and down.

She visibly blushes and licks her lips. "The famous Tobias Mitchell. I've waited a *very* long time to meet you."

I peek at Tobias, who looks like he's about to punch her in the face. But he's remaining calm. His kids are here, and if he loses it, he dies, and then he can't protect them.

"I'd say it was nice to meet you, but it would be nicer to see you bleed to death. The fuck do you want?"

A wicked grin takes over her face. "I want a lot."

Aria moves to stand closer to him and takes his hand, trembling with rage and fear but unwilling to be intimidated. "Don't you think you've done enough damage, Bernadette? Can't you just leave us all alone?"

"No," she replies, grinning. "Talking of damage, where is my boy? I miss him."

"He isn't yours," I snap, rage injecting into my veins and making my head throb. "He never was. You're an old, decrepit whore who needs her head checked. He was nineteen – *nineteen* – when you preyed on him. What the fuck is wrong with you?"

Bernadette rolls her eyes and huffs. "You must be the most annoying person in the world. Why won't you leave Kade alone? He doesn't want you. You're used trash. Where is Kade?" she asks again, and when Barry reaches for his gun, metal presses to the back of my head; one of her men has sneaked in behind us. "Anyone tries anything, her brains will be on the ground."

They all watch me – Tobias looks like he wants to blow up. Jason raises his hands. "Don't shoot her."

"Don't fuck with me and I won't."

But no one tells her where Kade is, and I try not to breathe with the gun pointed at my head.

She glances at Tobias again. An idea comes to her – I can see it in her expression. When it clicks, her face lifts. "You love your son. You'd do anything for him?"

Tobias doesn't deign to respond, but he does push Aria behind him.

"I'll give your son his freedom, destroy all evidence of his crimes, and he can walk free. But in return, you'll be mine."

Aria steps forward, and we all tense as Bernadette points her gun at her. "Do not test me," she snarls. "You hold no importance. I will shoot you and take him either way."

Tobias yanks her back behind him again, scowling at Bernadette. "Don't you ever point a gun at her again. You hear me? Lower your aim on Stacey too."

She nods to the person behind me, and my lungs fill as I gasp when I feel the metal slipping away from the back of my head.

"I'll fucking go, but you leave the rest of my family alone. Got it?"

My brows furrow. "What?" He's giving in so easily? What happened to taking the empire down and avenging his kids?

"No!" Aria pulls at his arm from behind, but he's like a statue. "You're not going with her! We'll find another way."

Bernadette rolls her eyes again and clicks her tongue. "He was always the real prize. I couldn't get to him, not really. He always wanted you," she says to Aria, the door opening behind her to reveal more suited-up guards – and her husband. "But I guess it worked out well. Your son turned out to be a *really* good boy. Isn't that right, Archie?"

My blood runs cold.

I can feel the horrible vibrations in the atmosphere; the anger between us. Jason's eyes are bulging as he glares at Archie. Tobias seems to be losing his hold on reality as he keeps blinking, reaching behind him to grab his gun.

"You hurt my son," he says to Archie. "I'm going to shred the skin off your revolting body and make you eat it."

Tobias shoots him right in the shoulder, knocking the beast back against the wall with a wail. Guards point their guns at Tobias, but Bernadette huffs. "Lower your aims." She glares at her husband. "I told you to stay outside."

The pig stands back in terror, eyes widening on Tobias, holding his shoulder and hiding behind his wife. "You didn't say he was here," he whisper-hisses. "He's fucking standing right there!"

"He's not a threat. He's trading places with our Kade. Isn't that right, Tobias?"

"Are you insane?" Archie asks at the same time Aria yells, "No!"

Tobias doesn't hesitate to shoot him again, making us jump and him howl in pain and hop on one foot. "You motherfucker! Why are you allowing this?"

Bernadette doesn't care. I don't think she really cares about anything but herself. She tilts her head. "Are you done, Tobias?"

"That's nothing compared to what the fuck I'm going to do to you both," Tobias spits as Archie hops towards the door. "I'll kill your husband in front of you, then I'll make it slow and painful for you."

"Do we have a deal?" Bernadette asks, annoyed now.

Tobias caresses Aria's hand with his thumb and nods once, his eyes blazing, shoulders tense, jaw tight. His gaze is darkening, and I know he's going to close himself off as soon as he leaves with them.

He gestures to the computers. "Delete all evidence you have on my son now, then I'll go. I want him to be able to walk free and have a normal life."

Bernadette sighs. "I knew you all had a foot in my system still. Whatever happened to respecting people's privacy?"

I fist my hand. "We can find another way, Tobias."

"Please," Aria pleads.

Once she removes everything, and Barry checks to confirm, she smiles at Tobias. "When we leave, I want you to fuck me in the back of the car. I wonder if there really is a "like father, like son" thing."

Tobias just stares at her.

Aria's eyes flash with anger. "You're disgusting."

She sucks on her teeth. "Kade didn't think so."

Without giving it a second thought, I lunge for Bernadette, ignoring all the guns surrounding us. But someone grabs me by the throat before I can reach her and shoves me back, so I fall into Tobias.

I try to run at her again, but Tobias and Jason are in front of me now, and we stay frozen in place, guns pointing at us from every angle.

"Lower your fucking aim. I said I'd swap with Kade," Tobias says, reaching back and taking Aria's hand, squeezing it. "You leave my family alone from now on."

"Put your dog on a fucking leash then. I'm sick of her dramatics." She raises her brow at me. "You, missy, need to move on. He doesn't love you. He loves my daughter."

"And you need to die just like your daughter," I retort. "And I hope it's slow and painful."

"As I said," Bernadette says, gesturing to her men to get Tobias, not caring about my comment. "Dramatic."

He shrugs away from them and turns to Aria, who's sobbing and begging him to stay, to find another way, but all he does is smile at her, take her face and kiss her on the lips.

It's more than just a kiss. It's everything he wants. Everything he had. And everything he'll lose. It's a goodbye. A see you later. An eternity of wondering *what if.*

I know what he's going to do.

He's going to raze her empire from the inside, and he's going to take himself out in the process. Because he loves his family, and he'd do anything to save them.

Kade is free, but Tobias never was. He's been a prisoner for over twenty years.

When he pulls back from the kiss, he presses his lips to her forehead. "I love you. Every broken part of me has loved you from the moment I met you."

"I love you too," she sobs. "I need you to come back to me. Please. Please, Tobias."

"It was never going to be an easy road. At least now I can do something good for my family. Live your life the way you were supposed to without me, Doctor."

She breaks down completely. "Please don't. Please."

He steps back from her, nods to Jason and Barry, and looks at me. "You take care of yourself and my kids." He hugs me to him, and I sink into his hold and shake in his arms.

"I'll make it worth it, little one," he whispers against my hair. "Just you watch. Heaven and hell will see the flames of their downfall."

Tobias winks at me as he shoulders into a guard and follows them to the front door. There's no stopping my tears, or the crack in my chest as Aria begs him to come back to her repeatedly. Jason holds her back as she tries to run after him.

Then he's out of sight, a door opening and closing, and Tobias Mitchell now belongs to Bernadette.

A guard radios in that he's in the car. Secured. Locked.

She chuckles as she walks to the entranceway, but she stops and narrows her eyes on me. "One last thing..." She raises the gun, aiming it straight at me. "You've been a pain in my ass from the start."

My eyes screw shut as she pulls the trigger, and there's a harrowing scream, a loud bang that hurts my ears, and warm liquid hitting my face and arms.

I open my eyes to see Kade's brother standing in front of me. He drops to his knees as Aria reaches him, but it's too late.

The bullet is lodged in Jason's skull.

23

STACEY

Everyone dies at some point. It's inevitable. Death is strange and unavoidable. The endpoint to every living thing. There will be a quiet moment in our lives when the world stops moving, our lungs stop working and we close our eyes for the last time.

And that terrifies me.

When my mother died, I was young. I cried. Missed her like crazy. Cried some more. And when we moved away, I tried to forget about it all. Her pale skin and her blue lips, long after the doctors called her time of death.

I tried to forget what her voice sounded like.

How her hugs felt.

The way she always made me feel better on my bad days.

Moving on was impossible for such a long time – it took me

months for a single day to pass that I would feel okay. I never felt complete until I was dared to kiss Kade, then he cornered me in the kitchen and kissed me again and again and again. Everything went uphill from there.

Until I lost my baby girl, then Kade, then my dad. Then everything just fell like tattered dominos into a blazing inferno of fucking oblivion.

I wanted death a few times but never followed through with the dark thoughts that plagued me. There was one moment I let the voices win, and I was fully prepared to jump into the abyss and end my life. But Jason talked me down from the edge of that bridge and proved just how much I wanted to live.

And I didn't want to die anymore, as much as it hurt to keep breathing at the time, so I held on to life with a firm grip. I kept my heart beating even though it was broken, fractured, bleeding from losing everything I had to look forward to.

But that's not always the case, is it? People die every day. Every hour. Every minute. Every second.

One moment, we're here. Next, we're not.

Where does one go when they pass?

Their memories stay with us, their lifeless bodies waiting to be buried or cremated. But what truly happens? Do they become stars? Are they ghosts who stand by our sides when we need them the most? Are psychics legit, and do the dead communicate during readings?

When we get a shiver up our spines and the hairs rise on our arms, is there someone with us?

One blink, we have a life and a future and a purpose. We can breathe fresh air into our lungs and listen to the rain pattering against a window. We meet someone amazing, go on dates and get to know them until the butterflies are unbearable. We buy books that sit on our bookcases and gather dust. We can listen and sing along to our favourite songs until our throats get sore. Watch movies and cuddle on the couch until we fall asleep. We can walk our dogs under the pale moonlight and laugh with our friends while living in the moment.

Make plans for the future and celebrate milestones. Study

and get our dream jobs. Mortgages and car finance to put us into more debt. Fall in love, get married, have kids and watch them have their own lives. Watch them make their own achievements and mistakes. Their own families and careers. Or we can choose a completely different path that's no less fulfilling.

In one stilted moment, we can see the world and all its colours and smell the oceans and flowers. We can eat junk food until our stomachs are full. And dance in a studio, in front of a crowd, or in the kitchen while we cook. Maybe in the shower if the mood strikes.

And in the next, it can all be taken away by a bad decision, an illness, a fatal accident, old age.

In this case, the deadly pull of a trigger.

Jason was getting clean. He was going to therapy, he'd started back at the gym and had a goal to be better. Not just for the woman he loved but for himself.

He was supposed to live. To get his life back. To help Kade get *his* life back and fix his relationship with his brother. He isn't supposed to be gone. He wasn't supposed to jump in front of a bullet for me.

But he did. And now he's dead.

A bullet that was meant for me has penetrated Jason's skull, and he's dead. He's had his final blink. His last moment. His milestones and achievements abruptly halted.

Muffled voices echo around me, and there's a piercing ringing in my ears so powerful my vision blurs. I don't blink. I don't even breathe, though my lungs plead with me for air.

I've seen death. I've killed before and watched Kade murder, but nothing could have prepared me for this. My body is shaking as my eyelids manage a single, hard blink that restarts the chaos all around me.

There's so much blood.

My hands, clothes, face, the floor – all stained with Jason's blood while he lies limp in Aria's arms. I stare at his lifeless body in complete shock, unable to look away.

I don't even realise there's a war going on around us until bodies start to drop, windows smashing from a spray of bullets, pelting us with fragments of shattered glass.

Does Tobias know Bernadette lied? That she killed Jason despite agreeing to leave his family alone? Is he outside fighting like the rest of them?

Someone stands close to me. Black, shiny shoes with suit trousers. His fingers clutch a radio as he pulls another magazine from his stash and reloads his gun.

It's Barry. He cocks the weapon and calls for backup, ordering them to stop the cars from leaving.

"The Russians are here," I hear over the radio, and Barry gives us one last look before taking three quick breaths and running into the war zone outside.

He has a wife and baby waiting for him in his safe house, and he's running outside where bullets fly like birds and take even more lives.

I pray he survives.

A radio nearby beeps, and a voice confirms that they successfully stopped one of the cars, but not the one with Bernadette and Tobias inside. They'd ploughed over one of the new guards and vanished.

Aria sobs in front of me. I sit back on my heels and watch her beg Jason to wake up, her words shattering. She's grabbing his face and yelling his name, screaming for her husband, anyone.

And then the radio beeps again, and a voice says, "We've got Archie Sawyer."

I should be pleased, but I can't do anything but search for ways to comfort Aria.

Barry's voice comes over the radio. "Restrain him and knock him out. Kill the rest."

The radio goes silent, and more shots are fired in the distance. The fight is outside now, and the lodge is filled with whimpers. Our men confirm that they've killed the driver and two are on foot, running through the forest. Heavily armed but thankfully wounded.

But Bernadette is gone. Which means Tobias is gone.

And Jason is... gone.

He sacrificed himself for me. I should be dead. I should be the one lying on the ground. But the angle that he ran in front of me means his head was low enough to take the fatal bullet instead of his body.

I clamp my teeth together and try to breathe through my nose as my eyes burn and my nostrils flare, my ribs tightening with every agonising second that passes.

Aria brushes her fingers through Jason's blood-soaked hair and shouts on Ewan again. He's upstairs with Kade. He'll want to come, but there's no one else left to keep Kade safe.

I lean forward and rest my hand on top of Aria's as she strokes her thumb over the top of Jason's fingers. "I'm sorry," I whisper. "I'm so sorry."

Killing yourself isn't going to make it all go away. If you jump, then it might be done for you, but everyone who cares for you will suffer. Do you know why? Because you are loved, Stacey.

Look at me. Please, Stacey. I lost everything, too.

I lost my fiancée, who's probably already pregnant. I lost my brother. And I've most likely lost the rest of my family. If you jump, then you're leaving me to do this on my own.

My mind skips through every time we've spoken, stopping at one of the last conversations we had, and it echoes everywhere. It makes my chest crack, and my vision blurs with even more tears.

Even if that means taking a bullet for you...

Jason kept his promise.

It's been mere minutes since the shot was taken. Aria's cries grow louder, and her screams for her husband vibrate off the walls, then he's running down the stairs with a confused look, freezing when he sees the scene before him.

His wife with his dead son in her arms.

The boy who was born when he was only eighteen. The kid Aria has raised with him since he was a few months old.

Dead.

"No," he whispers, not taking his eyes off them as he takes slow steps forward. "No. Jason." He falls to his knees by his son's side in slow motion, hands raised, his eyes flickering between refusal to believe and brutal shock. "Jason?"

He grabs his face, and his gaze searches every inch of it, his fingers hovering over the bullet wound. His eyes go wide, his lips moving without any words coming out.

The bullet hole in Jason's head leaks crimson as Ewan shakes his son and begs him to wake up. He shakes him again with a strangled sound in his throat, then lowers his forehead to his as a guttural sob fills my ears.

Ewan becomes erratic. "Wake up, wake up, wake up. You need to, son."

Lu and Base appear in the room next, and she screams and covers her mouth, nearly slipping on blood as she runs to them. "Oh my God! No! Jason!"

I lower my head as my best friend cries for her big brother.

I remember he used to pick her up from dancing when we were fifteen. We'd all blush because of his good looks and giggle when he made jokes to Luciella. I always fancied her twin, but everyone noticed Jason. She'd call him when she was sad. He'd call her when he was drunk and needed someone to hear how badly he played the guitar. Because no matter how terrible it sounded, she'd clap and tell him to keep practising.

He FaceTimed her when he was going to propose to Giana, and she helped him pick a ring.

They were close.

Jason vanishing years ago hurt her more than she'd ever admit. He stopped talking to everyone when he fell into drugs, but recently, she was getting him back.

And I have no idea what to say or do. All I can do is sit here and hold my best friend's hand while she hyperventilates into her dead brother's chest. I'm not sure if it's survivor's guilt or not, but I feel like I'm intruding. Like it's my fault he's dead.

"Wake up! You need to wake up, Jason!" Lu cries, taking his hand and sobbing into his palm while Ewan begs into his shoulder. "Please. Please wake up! Call an ambulance." She looks at her mum. "Call an ambulance! Do something. Why aren't you doing anything?"

A radio beeps then announces that backup is on the way. One of the men in the woods was found, but the other is still on the run.

The TV screens on the table show the massacre outside the lodge. Bodies from both sides have fallen. A white SUV is smashed into a tree, and Archie is lying face down in front of it, his hands cuffed behind his back.

Barry punches him to shut him up.

My attention is pulled back to the family falling apart before my eyes as Lu hugs into Ewan's side. Both are coated in Jason's blood. Both in hysterics, both waiting for Jason to part his lips and take a miraculous breath.

Base crouches behind Lu and kisses the side of her head, and I can see the rage building behind his eyes as they flick to the TV screens. He wants to go fight, but Luciella is his priority.

"You need to open your eyes, Jason. You can't die! I need you. Please. Help him, Base," she cries and falls back into him. "Please help him."

Base looks at Jason then at me and shakes his head lightly. We both know there is no helping him. I think Aria is in shock. I don't think she's even breathing or blinking.

She very shakily presses two of her fingers to the side of his throat, even though it's obvious he's gone, searching for a pulse. A sign of life. A sign that the bullet wasn't fatal. But his unseeing eyes and limp body tells a bigger, darker and harrowing story. When her bottom lip trembles, dimpling her chin, I know she hasn't found any sign of life.

She moves her hand over his eyes, closing them. "I'm sorry, sweetheart," she murmurs to him, a tear dripping from the tip of her nose and falling onto his face. "I'm so, so sorry we didn't protect you. All of you."

"Is he dead?" Lu asks in desperation, her eyes red as she pulls herself out of Base's embrace. When her mother nods once, she cries even harder. So hard I feel splinters sinking into the centre of my heart. "No. There's still a chance! Do CPR! Take him to the hospital!"

Aria slumps on her haunches, at a loss for words, splatters of ruby red all over her. She looks down at her soaked hands, the white dress now red, then shakes her head slowly. Her voice breaks as she says, "He's gone. Jason's gone."

"No!" Ewan yells and pulls his son against his chest tighter. "No, no, no." He rocks back and forth, tears soaking his cheeks as he mouths, *Please, please, please,* constantly. "Wake up, Jason. Wake up. I can't do this without you."

My chest hollows at the sight of him pleading with everyone to bring his child back.

"This isn't how it should be. You can't die, son. You can't fucking leave me. Please. *Please* wake up."

"What happened?" Lu croaks, her eyes swollen with tears. Base is still behind her, holding her, unable to speak as he rubs her shoulders, his jaw clamped shut.

"What happened?" she asks again. "*Who did this?*" Her words are angrier, louder, full of venom. "Who killed my brother?"

Tobias Mitchell's genetics runs deep in her, and with the dark look on her face, the tension in her jaw and the tone in which she snarls each word, I can see that side of him everyone fears.

Luciella is her father's daughter. Through and through.

"She..." Aria gulps, tears sliding down her face as she moves closer to her husband, linking her arm around his shoulder so he cries against her. "Bernadette. She tried to shoot Stacey. He threw himself in front of her. He... he saved her," she says, and I close my eyes as Ewan erupts into a louder cry.

Jason McElroy is a hero. My hero. Everyone's.

The wound in his head is still leaking profusely – blood is puddling beneath us. Our knees are stained crimson, the smell of copper filling our noses, but no one moves.

"I'll get Kade. He's still locked in his room," Base says in a soft voice. "What do you want me to do?"

"Kill them all," Ewan snaps, his eyes blazing as they lift to the Russian Scot. "You have power. You have two armies behind you. You want to help? You kill them all. I want that family to burn alive and be wiped from existence."

"It was my team who stopped one of the cars," he reports. This is a side of him I've never witnessed. Serious. Unsure. "I'll see what else I can do, but I hold very little power until I'm fully sworn into the empire." Base stands still, not blinking, his throat working on a swallow. "I'll speak to my grandfather."

He looks at Luciella for a second; nods to her as if to ask, *Okay?* And when she gives him a sad half-smile, he kisses the side of her head, snatches his phone from his pocket and walks back upstairs.

The shooting outside has stopped.

But Barry and his team are still hunting the forest for the final guard who managed to run when they stopped one of the cars. Ewan continues to cry for his son. I look at Aria, wiping under my eyes with my hands.

"What do we do about Kade?" I don't even recognise my voice. "I don't think he'll survive this."

He should know what's going on. But I'm not sure if he'll be able to handle any of it. This could be the very thing that knocks him off course, losing himself forever.

No one answers.

"I'm taking him to the hospital." Ewan stands and lifts Jason's body into him, barely struggling under the weight. His cheeks are drenched in tears. "I can't just sit here." Ewan settles Jason on the sofa, crouches beside him and rests his hand on his chest. "I need a car."

When Base comes back in, he's pale, and I know the call didn't go well. "I can have you transported to the hospital," he tells Ewan. He says nothing about the phone call, but he gives Luciella a look that says he's failed.

"We need to tell Kade," Aria decides, sniffing, wiping the back of her hand across her mouth, smearing more blood. "He should know what's happening."

I get to my feet, but I'm unbalanced, and I grab the sideboard. "I'll get him."

"I can go to him, if you want?" Base offers.

I shake my head. "I'll do it."

24

STACEY

The walk to the room he's in feels like miles. Every step I take has my heart beating harder, leaving bloody hands on the banister as I ascend the steps. The lodge is huge – but surely he heard the gunshots?

Unless he assumed they were hallucinations.

The corridor is long and narrow, and when I make it to the door, I freeze.

This is by far the last conversation I want to have with a barely lucid Kade. But as I unlock the door and push it open, my head turns in the direction of the bathroom. The shower is running, and the steam creeping under the door is causing condensation on the window.

I close the door behind me with a click, leaning against it. "Kade?"

The shower cuts off, and a few seconds later, the door swings open, a gust of hot air hitting me as Kade walks out and wraps a towel around his waist. The cloud of steam dissipates around him. His hair is wet, and drops of water slide down his chest.

It's the wrong time to be looking at him this way, but I haven't seen Kade like this in so long, I'd forgotten just how handsome and perfect he is. My eyes fall on the scar he hasn't covered, my gaze following the purple line from the corner of his mouth, all the way down his throat to where it stops, above his heart.

He follows my gaze, and when he looks back up at me, he doesn't try to hide it.

"She did that?" I ask.

Half a beat passes before he slowly shakes his head. "She made me do it to myself."

His voice isn't shaky. It's clear and deep and makes the butterflies I've had since I was fifteen go wild. Even though he just told me that bitch made him cut himself.

"You don't need to keep hiding it from me," I say, taking a careful step forward. Blood rushes in my ears, knowing that this more controlled version of him is about to shatter. "But we're going to make her pay for everything she's done."

I go to tell him that she has his dad, but I can't. The words get trapped in my throat, and I have to grit my teeth together to stop myself from letting out a broken cry.

I should have yanked Tobias's gun from his waistband and shot her and damned the consequences. She hurt him, and I didn't do anything about it. But I know she has a failsafe in place – Barry mentioned it before – so even if we'd been able to survive the onslaught of her men once she fell, there still would've been consequences.

Taking her out in a fit of rage would have resulted in everyone's death.

Kade's eyes drop down my body, taking in the blood soaking my clothes and staining my skin. "Are you hurt?"

I shake my head, unable to speak as my eyes burn.

"You're covered in blood." He says it with such… normality, as if me being covered in blood isn't a big deal, as long as I'm not hurt.

"It's not mine," is my reply, my eyes watering as I attempt to find the words to tell him exactly whose blood is on me.

"Do you want to use the…?" He gestures behind him, truly confused. "I won't watch you."

My cheeks heat. "No. I'm fine." I fidget my hands in front of me. *Tell him, dammit.* "Kade, something—"

"I owe you an apology," he cuts in, walking over to a pile of clothes neatly folded at the bottom of the bed. In amongst them is another face covering to replace the one he lost in the woods. Although I said he didn't need to hide his scar, he wraps the black material around his face, covering his neck, so it sits just above his top lip. Then his voice is muffled as he says, "I've been a bit of a dick."

I tilt my head at his actions. He seems more lucid than earlier, as if he's finally snapped out of his breakdown. But his eyes are still bloodshot, both hands still shaking as he attempts to tie the material behind his neck like a bandana, and he drops his top twice when he tries to pull it on.

When he struggles to get his feet into his boxers while holding his towel in place, I move towards him. "Let me help."

He huffs and runs his hands through his hair, not looking at me while I kneel at his feet and pull his boxers up his legs, stopping at the hem of the towel so he can do the rest himself. I don't want to cross any boundaries and make him uncomfortable.

Tell him, Stacey. Maybe I can say Jason got hurt and Ewan has taken him to hospital? But then again, that would be me withholding information, sugar-coating a lie.

No more lies.

If he goes downstairs and sees the blood, the destruction, the bodies of some of the men he hired when he formed his own team, he might fall back into that hole in his mind.

I have no idea what I'm doing. I have no idea how to tell him his brother is dead. That his father is gone. I shouldn't have volunteered to come up here. But it's Kade.

"My body hurts," he admits, his jaw tense, and I can tell he's fed up and pissed off at himself. "It feels like I've pulled all my muscles. I can't pick anything up without fucking dropping it." He flexes his hands then fists them, the veins bulging. "I felt this way before when Bernadette locked me up for two weeks." He laughs darkly and shakes his head in disgust, his pinkie spasming as he pinches the bridge of his nose. "So I know what's up. I'm a junkie with the shakes and seeing shit, needing my next hit."

"That's not true," I say, pushing up to my knees and taking one of his hands. When he doesn't flinch from my abrupt touch or yank his hand away, I hold it. "You went through a lot, Kade. For years. It'll take time for you to get used to not being on alert."

He grimaces and looks down. A few seconds pass, and his voice is low, a rumble in his chest, when it comes. "Why are you here?"

To tell you your brother is dead and your dad is gone, is what I should say. But I don't; I lick my lips and tighten my hands around his. "Because I care about you."

He sighs and uses his free hand to pull his boxers up the rest of the way. His eyes flicker to the side, his cheeks going flush. "I need you to help me with..." He glances at his shorts. "I won't be able to... My hands hurt."

I get to my feet. "Of course," I say, folding the towel aside and helping him into his shorts. "You need help with anything, I'm here."

He stays silent, staring at the ground and rubbing his hand down his face and sighing.

His blue eyes flick up at me. "How do I know any of this is real?" It's a serious question – I can tell from the look on his face.

I slant my head. "Do you think it is?"

"I don't know, and it's fucking annoying me. There were gunshots and yelling, but it all stopped. You're covered in blood. It makes no sense. But you're here... helping me. And my dad and brother are here – they were in the forest. It all seems too good to be true."

I gulp down a solid rock lodged in my throat. "Kade, I need you to listen carefully, okay?"

"Can you ask Jason to come up here? I need to talk to him." He blows out a breath, shaking his head. "I fucked up bad, Stacey. I beat the shit out of him for that video."

"He understands."

"Regardless, he deserves an apology from me." He stands, rolls his jaw and blinks a few times. "We were close, you know? I always went to him for shit. I want my big brother back."

I release a crackly sob and try to hold back tears. "Kade..."

"What?"

Before I can speak, he frowns in confusion and looks around the room when two people start yelling outside, just below his window. One is Russian and angry, and the other is Barry.

"Wait." He steps back. "You *aren't* real, are you? This is all in my fucking head again."

"No," I reply, taking his hand and placing it against my cheek. "It's me. I'm real."

He gives me a wary look, searching my face. "I don't know. You're always there, but you're not."

"I am," I urge, moving closer. "I'm here, Kade. I'm never going to be anywhere else. I promise."

His thumb swipes against my skin, against the wetness from the tears on my cheek. "But why are you crying? Why are you covered in blood?" He pulls his hand away, the pad of his thumb coated with his brother's blood. "What the fuck is happening?"

A car door slams outside. I hear Base yelling in Russian.

I bite my lip and close my eyes, burying my face into his palm. My chest shudders in a sob, and I try to take a breath that doesn't rattle my body and fail. Saliva builds in my mouth as I screw my eyes shut, feeling the world around me shrinking.

"Hey," he says softly. "Talk to me, Freckles. Why are you so sad? Did Chris hurt you again?"

I shake my head, my chest tightening. "No. Chris is dead," I reply with a wobbly bottom lip, opening my eyes to look at him. "We killed him. Me and you. He can never hurt us again."

"Never again," he repeats with a frown, and I nod. "But that's not why you're crying. Was it me?"

I heave in breaths. "Was what you?"

"Did I hurt you again? I can't remember much from the last few days, and I think I hurt you."

"No." I strangle out the word. "You've never hurt me, Kade."

"I don't know." His unfocused gaze drops to the floor between us. "Can you get Jason for me?"

I freeze, my breathing stuttering in my chest and rendering me speechless. I've dragged this out for too long, and now we're standing mere centimetres apart, and I want to hug him. I want him to let me hug him, but I don't know his limits.

I miss him so much, yet he's right here.

"Earlier, I wasn't myself. I remember his voice. I need to see him. Fuck, I'm such a fucking asshole." The last word is gritted out, and he shakes his head again. "I pushed him away when he needed me the most. I pushed you both away."

"Jason..." I stop and chew the inside of my cheek. Aria said he should know, but I have no idea if he's in a state to survive it. "He..."

He tilts his head, looking more tired every second as his hand spasms against my cheek. "What?"

I sniffle and drop my head to his chest, at a loss for words. Do I tell him to come downstairs and see the havoc? Do I tell him Jason was hurt but Kade needs to stay in the room? He should know, but I have no idea how to tell him.

Then I need to tell him that the woman who made his life hell now has his father.

The only positives are that Kade's files are clean and we have Archie. Although I'm sceptical of the former, despite Barry's checks.

Come on, Stacey. "I'm so, so, so sorry, Kade, but..."

There's a harrowing sound downstairs as someone weeps louder, and I know it's Aria. Lu is screaming at someone as wheels crunch over the gravel outside – she's begging them to stay.

Base. He's leaving?

He frowns and looks at the door over my shoulder. "What's going on? Why's my mum crying? Can you hear crying?"

He doesn't wait for me to reply as he pushes away and side-steps me.

"Kade, no, wait!" I call after him as he heads to the door.

But when he swings it open, the sobs and wails become more prominent. He freezes for a beat, glances over his shoulder at me then rushes down the corridor.

I barely catch up to him before he's heading down the stairs, bumping into walls and nearly falling over his feet.

"Kade!"

I almost slam into his back as he stops at the entrance of the sitting room. His brother's body lies limp in his stepfather's arms as he struggles to lift him towards the front door with Aria trailing behind, distraught.

All eyes turn to Kade.

"Kade." I walk around him to see his face, his eyes searching the room. "I'm so, so sorry. I didn't know how to tell you. I..." I trail off, stumped. "Kade."

He doesn't go to Jason's body. He doesn't move, blink or speak a word. He's deadly quiet, his eyes darkening with every passing second.

Aria looks over her shoulder, and her face contorts when she sees him. She reaches her hand out to him. "Oh, sweetheart."

But instead of walking to her, Kade takes a step back. Then another and another. He's silent. Emotionless. Like a veil has fallen over his eyes and he can't see the blood all over the ground or the dead bodies his mother steps over to reach for him.

He flinches away from her.

"Sir," Barry says as he walks in, a bullet wound in his shoulder. "We need to leave this place. Tobias is gone. We need to leave. Right now. We're getting the vehicles ready."

Kade doesn't acknowledge anyone.

Barry limps towards him. "We have Archie Sawyer. She'll send her team to collect him. What are your orders?"

Barry is handing Kade back his power, the reins to what he built behind Bernadette's back. He's telling him to lead them on their next step. He's giving him focus. A target. And when Kade eventually looks at him, I see it settling into his blood.

A devastating hunger for revenge.

"What happened to my dad and brother?" His voice is eerily calm.

Bless his soul, Barry doesn't falter once as he tells him, "Your father made a deal to swap your freedom for his. Your files are wiped. But when they were leaving, Bernadette tried to shoot Stacey. Jason shielded her and took a bullet to the head."

Kade glances at me and drags his gaze down my bloodied clothes then up again. When his eyes clash with mine, I see nothing but darkness behind them. No emotion except anger.

Any closeness we just had in the room is pushed aside as I watch him think.

His hands fist at his sides, his once sleepy eyes filled with something dark and sinister. I think of the videos I've seen of him torturing people. I think of the way he had no expression as someone begged for their life and said they had children. Or when he stalked people and drove them into a mental hole.

Regardless of that side of Kade, I still love him anyway.

He looks at Barry again. "Put Archie in the walk-in freezer in the manor and turn it off. I'll deal with him. I want the place fully guarded. Call in everyone we have," Kade orders in a deep voice, blinking as he rolls his neck and shoulders. "The fact she walked out of here, with my father no less, pisses me off, but I understand the situation."

Barry nods. "I'll make the calls now."

"Good," Kade replies, looking down at the puddle of blood on the floor where his brother was lying.

He's so blank, I'm terrified. There aren't any tears – just anger.

"They want a war?" he says. "Well let's give them one."

25

KADE

Archie rattles the chains as he struggles, his restraints cutting into his skin. Cuffed at his wrists and ankles, he stands spreadeagled in the centre of the walk-in freezer with nothing but his underwear on.

I cut his clothes off while he was passed out. I wanted him fucking exposed while I carved my name into his back.

My mum refuses to come down to the basement. It's dark and cold, and the walk-in freezer is covered in melted ice cream and defrosted meat. And blood.

It stinks.

Barry leans his uninjured shoulder against the entrance to the freezer while I pace around Archie. "It's funny to see you like this. Helpless and scared. Waiting for your wife to save you?"

Archie spits at my feet, his face half scalded, one ear missing.

Infection has set in from my dad shooting him, and the wounds are starting to smell.

He's pissed himself for seven days straight. I've only fed him kibble and the odd glass of water to keep him alive and extend his torture. I want enough video evidence to rile up Bernadette to come out of hiding.

One of the guards was on watch earlier – recorded himself as he used a water gun to spray all of Archie's wounds with vinegar. It was the most pathetic thing I'd ever seen, watching a grown man scream because of a fucking water gun.

He glares at me, trying to follow my steps as I keep circling him. "Your father will be dead soon, just like your brother," he says, letting out a laugh.

I smirk. "How does it feel? You've been married since you were eighteen, yet your wife sought out a teenager to get pleasure. She was so damn bored of your pathetic ass that she used drugs and manipulation to get others into bed."

He laughs again. Several of his teeth are missing. "You think this is revenge? When I get out of here, because I will, I'm going to make you cry again. I'll make you bleed and hate your own body more than you already do. Do your men know you begged me to stop? I'll make it ten times worse when I'm out of here, boy."

I sigh, unaffected by his threat. "I'd love to see you try." I turn to Barry. "Get me the nail gun."

Archie's eyes go wide as I walk towards him with it. He thrashes as I press it directly to his crotch and screams as I shoot a long nail right through his limp dick, pinning it to his inner thigh.

I lower my voice, whispering into his ear. "You'll never touch me again. I highly suggest you keep your threats to yourself, or I might just order my largest guard to split you in two."

I toss the nail gun on the ground as he wails in agony and head out the door. Barry follows, locking the door behind us.

Stopping in the corridor, I lean against the wall, bending forward to hold my head in my hands. "Fuck," I murmur to myself. "Fuck."

"You good, boss?" Barry asks, patting my back.

I shake my head. "Nah."

"Let's get some fresh air."

When we get outside and I fill my lungs, I close my eyes. It's fresh, cold and quiet. The moon is high, and there's a cool breeze against my heated face.

"Where's Stacey?"

"With the dogs in the sitting room. She's watching a movie with your mother and sister."

I nod. "Any updates?"

He shakes his head. "She's probably created a new system database. The one Christopher Fields was in is now dead. Like it never existed. But we'll find her."

"Your father will be okay," he reassures me. "I'm fully expecting him to walk through the manor gates with Bernadette's head under his arm."

I roll my stiff shoulder. Everywhere is stiff from tensing my body. The shakes are worse, and my muscles still ache like I've crashed my car again.

"Before you sign off for the night, could you bring a nurse in?"

Barry tilts his head. "What for?"

I feel comfortable talking about this with him. He's very aware of what I've been put through and the rules I had to stick to. He tried to get me out a few times and failed. I didn't want him getting caught and risking everything, so he kind of just aided me, my crutch when I was in a really dark place.

When I left for Russia a year ago, I blacked out so many times, I have no idea if I wore a condom when I was forced into sexual contact. Bernie definitely didn't let me use one with her.

My teeth crush together. I should have told her to fuck off and to shove her rules up her ass. I did everything she asked. Everything. And degraded myself in the process. Following the shitty rules hasn't kept my family safe, has it?

I'm done being her chained pet. The defective Kade Mitchell with no free will who was drugged and fucked by her family to save his own. Raped by men *and* women.

Pathetic.

Dirty.

Useless.

I crack my neck to each side. "I want to make sure I'm clean."

"Ah, yes," he says with no judgement. "I'll get one first thing in the morning." Then there's a long pause. "Do you want to talk about it?"

He could mean any number of things. I just shake my head, because if I even attempt to speak about what's going on in my head right now, I might slip off the deep end.

I pull the joint from behind my ear and roll it between my fingers, fidgeting to control the tremors. "How old is Eva now?"

His entire demeanour shifts to pure happiness. Proud. Fatherly. Something I can't relate to. "She just turned one."

The spark in his eyes makes the corner of my lips curl in a soft smile. I truly consider him a friend and my right-hand man. He's spent so much time keeping together everything I've built over the years. The glue of my company and sanity. He stayed by Stacey's side while she was in America and was even helping my dad.

Fuck, he even pointed a gun at me when I met up with Stacey after shooting her. He cares for her. He puts her safety before mine.

And that's what I need – Stacey safe at all costs.

He's already secured the manor, set up contacts with the outside to help bring down Bernadette and is liaising with the cops to make them listen. Information for protection. Information for the promise that Bernadette and her fucking cult are taken down without any risk to those I love.

Barry's done all this, all while being a first-time father. The travelling he does back and forth between here and the safe house up in Aberdeen is a mission in itself. He needs to be careful – but he's committed.

I inhale the cold air through my nose, letting it out through my mouth before putting the joint between my lips. "Go to your family. Nothing's happening right now anyway. You should be with your wife and daughter."

He frowns, his hands shoved into his pockets as we start walking along the edge of the loch. "Are you sure?"

"Yeah. You've done a lot for me while I've been away." I place my hand on his good shoulder, squeezing it. "You kept the ship from sinking, and I appreciate you for it. But you need to go and spend time with your family. I've taken you away from them enough. Go and join them at the safe house."

"What if there's a development? And what about Archie?"

"I'll deal with Archie." I raise a brow. "And if there are any developments, you better answer me when I call."

Barry lowers his head. "Thank you, sir." His eyes flicker to the side. "And I'm sorry for your loss. I know I haven't said it yet, but I truly am sorry. Don't beat yourself up about it, alright? Eat something. Drink water. *Sleep.* Jason knew the position you were in when things went down with Stacey. He forgave you. He loved you."

I stiffen at his use of the past tense, letting go of his shoulder and stepping back. "Make sure you have eyes on you and your family wherever you go. I'll let you know if there are any changes." I nod to the house. "Go rest, then take one of the cars."

Barry gives me a quick nod and pulls his earpiece out, yanking the black box from his waistband and disconnecting the wire as he walks back to the manor.

He looks over his shoulder and raises a hand in farewell, and I do the same before he vanishes inside. It's three in the morning, but every light is on. Mum is sitting on the porch steps with a glass of wine, looking more drained with every minute that passes.

Ewan reported Bernadette, and, shock, there was no evidence to prove anything. Barry checked Police Scotland's records, and all he found was a closed file that noted Jason McElroy had been found deceased. His death is marked as unexplained but not to be investigated.

That's fine. Keeps the heat off my back.

Mum's eyes land on me as she takes a large gulp of wine. She's been drinking. She's never drunk, but she's not exactly sober either.

"The doctor said you've to rest as much as possible," she says, her eyes sunken from nights spent staying awake and crying. "You should sleep."

I fidget with the joint between my fingers. She's not yelling at me to throw it away – she's definitely not doing good. "So should you."

She smiles and takes another drink as I sit down beside her, resting her chin on her palm and staring off into the silent and steady waters of the loch. Dazed. Tired. Heartbroken.

"I take it the movie's finished?" I ask, gaining her attention again.

"Yeah," she says blankly.

"You know he'll be okay, don't you? Dad can handle himself."

Her smile is fake. "I hope so."

For a minute, I sit with her in comfortable silence before I walk over to the pool house. It's the only place I can get some peace given the number of guards Barry's brought in.

We have patrols all over the manor. All armed. All standing around inside and outside. Watching. Waiting. It'll not be long before Bernadette strikes again, but we'll be ready. I'll be ready. Not shacked up in my bedroom while she singlehandedly ruins my family in one breath.

I abruptly and harshly blink multiple times, then screw my eyes shut to stop myself. I sit down on the edge of the drained pool, my legs dangling over the side as I pull my lighter back out to try relighting my joint.

It takes me five tries with my unsteady hands to spark a flame, and I inhale deeply, until my lungs burn more than the thoughts running rampant in my mind.

Dirty.

Pathetic.

Useless.

You were raped by men and women.

Your dad is going through it all now.

And your brother is dead because of you.

26

KADE

I drop my head and keep my eyes closed, focusing on the one thing keeping me stable, keeping me on this side of the fucking world of sanity.

Revenge.

My dad thinks he's a hero for swapping with me, but he's wrong. Bernadette is evil and vile, though her connections are worse. His emotions have been carefully learned over years of studying and therapy, so he can just shut them off. He won't follow her rules or allow her to abuse him like she did me.

He won't hesitate to snap her neck if she tries to force him into anything. Maybe he already has and that's why she's been a ghost?

He'll survive through violence, not the pressure of keeping his family safe, because he isn't wired that way. He's impulsive and dangerous. Un-fucking-hinged.

In the end, I survived because I kept holding on for *her*, even when I didn't realise it – promising myself I'd get back to Stacey as the same eighteen-year-old kid who fell in love with her.

But I didn't survive. I might be free, but I'm still there. At least mentally. I hear the voices. The laughter. Feel the pain, the unwanted touches, the warmth of my own blood leaking out of my body.

Even now I can barely open my eyes without feeling the walls closing in, hearing so many different voices from past clients, and feeling their hands all over me.

I tried to burn my palms on a hotplate to get rid of the feeling, the dirtiness, the invisible blood, but Mum stopped me. Hence the doctor she called in and how many meds are in my system right now.

I was in a dark-as-fuck place when we were in the lodge, and although I feel like I'm slowly climbing out of the void, something is trying to drag me back down. Its claws are deep in my soul, and I'm barely holding on.

I know Stacey was there with me most of the time. I could hear her talking, even when I was disconnecting, battling with reality. Her fingers were brushing through my hair while she talked about everything we used to do when we were normal. Just two eighteen-year-old kids getting to know each other.

She doesn't know me now, and I'm not sure I want her to.

The joint burns between my fingers with each harsh inhalation, and the smoke dissipates above me in a cloud as I blow out. I nearly drop it given how ridiculous my hand-to-mouth coordination is.

I hear a radio beeping faintly to my right as a guard walks by during his patrol. I sigh and rest my elbows on my knees. When my eyes lift to the kitchen, which has a large window that looks onto the back of the grounds, I see Stacey filling a glass with juice. The view is blocked mostly by the trees that circle the pool house, but there's just enough of a gap that I can watch her gulp down the liquid and wipe the back of her hand across her mouth.

My chest aches with how beautiful she is. How, after everything I've put her through, she's still here. Still fighting for me. Fighting for us. Not to be in a relationship, because we're both too fucked for that, but to find level ground.

She should kick me to the kerb and tell me never to speak to her again after I pushed her out of my life for two years. After I shot her. The wound is almost healed, but will definitely scar, and I stare at it every time I see her.

I want to go to her, to kiss her and touch her and ask her to love me, but I can't.

I was in a bad place those first few days after I got away from Bernadette. I couldn't even take a piss without freaking out. But what happened in that lodge kicked me back into reality. Well, a little. There are parts of me that are still struggling, but I'm zeroed in on Bernadette, her husband wasting away in my basement and how much I'm going to make them regret even looking in my direction.

Stacey leans her palms on the kitchen unit and closes her eyes. When she drops her forehead to the counter, I wonder what she's thinking about. What's making her so upset?

Could be several things.

Her dead brother. My dead brother. My soon-to-be-dead father. Or me. Her vile ex who can't even look at her without feeling his hands tremble and hiding his face like she'd judge him. I've kept my distance, and I intend to keep doing so.

Maybe she's just tired. Tired of all this bullshit. I know I am.

I miss her. I miss her infectious giggle. The dimple that dents when she smiles at me after I kiss her. Her snarky texts. The way she always wants to laze around and watch TV with the dogs. I miss watching her dance, deep in a routine, or watching her unravel with my tongue inside her…

I get a flash of what I did to her in front of her stepbrother and feel myself recoil, a painful twist in my chest. Something we haven't spoken about. Something we shouldn't have done. Something I can barely remember.

Being like this sucks. I keep either dissociating or going completely blank. Sometimes I seize; sometimes I just stare at nothingness, trapped in my own mind, yelling for someone to help me. Most of the time I don't realise it's happening.

I never truly knew what it was like inside my dad's head, but

I think I do now. It's fucking scary and lonely, and I get so damn angry all the time.

Stacey disappears from my view, and I lower my head again, running my middle finger across my lips to feel how dry they are, flinching when I feel rough skin at the corner.

I wear the face covering less, but when I'm around her, I make sure it stays in place. She looks at it when it's accidentally in view, like everyone else, and her expression turns to pity.

I don't want pity.

I want everyone to leave me the fuck alone and let me focus on getting Bernadette six feet under after months of torturing the sadistic bitch. I want her to see how much I can ruin her husband.

There's an abandoned dog shelter I now own that I can take her to. I'll stuff her into a crate and watch her suffer. My dad did the same thing before he was arrested twenty-three years ago, and it only seems fitting that I follow in his footsteps.

Barry located the eroding building with the plaque outside for my aunt Gabriella – a remembrance. She was killed there by Dad's lunatic friend, but that's an entirely different story.

There's a team up there now securing the place. There are cameras, computers and a room they've reconstructed into a shiny new cell for one. I'll make her watch me ripping her husband to shreds, then I'll strangle her with his intestines.

With over two hundred client names on file, and hundreds more she has connections with, I have enough evidence to take down most of them. But that family deserves more than fame as criminals. They deserve death, over and over again.

If I can save my dad in the process, then it's another win, but I won't hold my breath.

As soon as Dad is introduced to that world, he'll be gone. He was suicidal his entire life until he met my mother, and it got even worse when he was locked up with only small pockets of time with her. Now, he doesn't have his meds, so he won't last long in the underworld.

Or he'll fit right in and revel in how twisted it is, who the fuck knows? Either way, I'll have lost him.

Once my joint is done, I flick it aside and pull out a cigarette and light it. I've smoked so much green over the years I barely feel the calm. It's frustrating.

Movement to my left catches my attention, and my heart stops when I see Stacey walking towards me. I take a drag of the smoke and watch her as she comes straight to me, sitting down beside me on the edge of the pool.

My throat bobs as she takes the cigarette from between my lips and puts it between hers. "My name is Stacey," she says, smiling and making my lungs stutter. "I joined Luciella's dance class a few months ago."

My eyes stay on her as she takes a long inhale and blows smoke out above us. I think I might be having a heart attack. My heart hurts, it's beating so hard.

Her green eyes twinkle beneath the moonlight, her freckles dusting her cheeks and nose, and her jawline is as impeccable as ever. I want to touch her, but I can't. I'd hurt her. I don't know how to be gentle.

I was the luckiest guy in the world once upon a time. She was mine, and I lost her.

In the same place we met properly when we were fifteen, I shake my head at the déjà vu.

"You should've taken my heads-up and stayed away from me." I gulp, gripping the edge of the pool with both hands until my knuckles turn white. "You'd be in a much better position now if you had."

She tilts her head, leaning back on her hand. "Falling in love with you didn't ruin my life, Kade. Chris did. Without you, he would've locked me away and called me his pet forever."

Can I resurrect a dead man and kill him all over again? Another death I barely remember. That pisses me off.

I look away. "You wouldn't have known the world Bernadette dragged me into."

"No, I wouldn't have. But I still don't regret anything."

I pick at the paint on the pool's edge. "You should."

"Shut up," she says with a tut, still puffing away on my cigarette. "Milo and Hopper are looking for you. They keep pacing around the sitting room and jumping up on the window ledges."

"I'll go and see them. It might be best if I put them in protection. A safe house." I sigh. "Bernadette knows what they mean to me, and I can't have her doing something to them." I chew my lip and glance at her. "I doubt you'd go to a safe house if I asked you to."

"No."

"Yeah. Thought not."

"How are the meds?" she asks, shifting to cross her legs and face me. "You haven't spoken a word to me. I want to know you're okay."

"I'm fine," I lie.

She huffs, knowing I'm talking shit.

I change the subject before it gets awkward. "Barry's going home. If he hasn't spoken to you already."

Everything goes warm, butterflies deep within as she smiles. "He deserves it. Wait until you meet Eva. I miss her so much. She's so full of energy and life and has the most adorable smile."

I won't ever meet Eva. What good would that do? *Oh, hey, kid. This guy here is a fuck-up and is basically dead inside. He has no idea where his soul is, and his heart is practically upside down and inside out. You see his face? Hideous. He's killed hundreds and regrets only half of those deaths. He's the monster that hides under your bed.*

"Hey."

Stacey pulls me out of my head, but I start blinking rapidly again. I screw my eyes shut when I struggle to stop.

"I'm here with you."

"Y-You should get some sleep."

"Let me help you, Kade. We don't need to talk – just let me be here with you."

She moves closer, and I stiffen. "I love you, Stacey, but I'm not ready for any of this," I say, getting to my feet, her eyes lifting to follow my movements. "I'm sorry."

Her gaze drops. "I just want to help you."

"I know you do."

She takes my hand when I offer it to her, helping her to stand. The touch is electrifying, and it takes me everything not to yank her into my chest and kiss her.

I'm not sure how to feel about it. I'm in no position to offer her anything.

Why is this shit so confusing?

While I follow her inside, my gaze lowers to the sway of her hips in front of me, her wavy hair flipping side to side. The need to grab her gets worse, but I fist my hands.

At least I know my dick still exists. I feel the twitch and hate myself.

I walk her to the room my mother has given her, right next to Luciella's. She stops outside the door and nibbles on her lip as she turns to me.

Is she nervous? I'm nervous.

Do I fuck my own inner turmoil and kiss her anyway?

No. She'll feel my scar and I'll probably pass out. I already feel faint thinking about potentially hurting her.

"I know you need your space to normalise with everything again, and I'm going to give you as much as you need. But I want you to know that I'm here."

I stare at her for a beat then drop my gaze. "You can do better than me, Stacey. I'm not the same person I was before. That version of me doesn't exist anymore."

I don't think this version does either.

"I changed too." She hugs herself, and I hate that I've made her feel anxious around me. "I want to help you. I want to *be* with you. However long it takes for you to get better." Her voice cracks, and I think something in my chest does too. "You said you still loved me."

"I do," I reply without hesitation. "I would die to get that time back with you. But I've no idea how to be in a relationship. Not anymore."

"I understand. I don't want that either. It's not something either of us is ready for." She chews her bottom lip, nods once and looks to the side. "I just… I don't know what to do or how to act."

I lower my voice. "I know."

She tucks a strand of dark hair behind her ear. I wish I could feel how soft it is between my fingers. I used to always play with her hair.

She was my anchor. I think she still is.

I run my thumb against the rough skin at the corner of my lips, and weirdly, I don't feel the need to hide it from her. It's been out in full show all night and she hasn't once looked at it or let it grab her attention.

Or maybe I haven't noticed because it hurts to look at her.

"Can I get your new number?" I ask before I can stop myself. "Us texting is fine, right?"

A warm feeling fills my chest when she smiles. It reaches her sad eyes. "Yeah. Type yours in and I'll text you," she replies, pulling her phone from her pyjama pocket and giving it to me.

As soon as I unlock the screen, I see her search bar is open. She's been hunting on Google for any news on my dad.

She tilts her head at my pause.

"You were close with my dad."

"Yeah. I visited him every day when I was in America."

I hum, typing my number. "I'm glad you had someone. Barry said you were close with Lisa too. And sometimes gave him a heart attack when you'd slip security."

She giggles, and my fingers freeze over the screen for a second.

"Aria said Archie is still alive. What are you going to do with him? Are you going to go after Bernadette?"

I ignore her, because I can only focus on one thing at a time, and my thumbs are shaking while I try to type my number into her phone. I've input it wrong twice already.

"Are you going to go after her?" she asks again, and I glance up to see the worry in her eyes.

Nodding, I hand her back the phone. "Yeah. I'm going after them all."

The idea of getting on with my life without watching them burn makes me rage, and when she notices the shift in my mood, she stops asking questions.

I step back from Stacey when our fingers touch and her breath hitches. I move away enough that I can't smell her shampoo. "Go to sleep," I say. "Text me, but don't feel like you need to."

She wraps her arms around herself. "Goodnight, Kade."

I don't say anything back as I watch her slip into the room and close the door. The urge to open it and beg her for forgiveness smacks into me, but I can't let myself drop the control I've cultivated.

I need to stay focused.

My phone vibrates in my pocket while I find the dogs and head to my room.

Unknown Number*: Is it weird I'm all giddy as if I've just been on a first date?*

Me*: Were you nervous?*

Stacey*: Very...*

Me*: I'm sorry.*

She types, deletes, types then deletes again. Then there's nothing. Should I have pushed the conversation? Flirted with her? Admit that spending those ten minutes with her quietened the voices in my head?

I pull off my top and shorts then toss them at the basket and climb into the shower. The water scalds my skin as I press my forehead to the tiles.

The walls close in around me, and I struggle to breathe.

I want you to call me Stacey. Would that get you hard? Close your eyes and imagine I'm her. If you don't get hard, Kade, I'll go get Archie.

That's it, such a good boy. Fuck her harder in front of all of us.

Now put a bullet in her head.

Good boy.

Good boy.

Good boy.

The tile cracks as I drive my fist into it.

27

KADE

The next night, while in a briefing with some of my team – with Barry on a video call – to discuss where Bernadette is and her next steps, I realise a lot of my shit is still at my apartment in Stirling.

Mainly, my laptop and paperwork.

Some of the guys were going to go up, but I refuse. I want to go.

Barry arranges for me to get escorted up, but I tell him I'll drive up on my motorbike and whoever is shadowing me can follow behind. I doubt Bernadette will try anything. She knows if she targets me, I'll make it worse for Archie.

She'll be on alert, yet still smug that she has my dad.

Once everything's arranged, I stand out on my balcony with a joint. It's dark out, cold. Winter is fast approaching, and it makes me think about Christmas, though it's still a few months away.

Will I still be alive then, and if I am, will it be weird to buy Stacey a gift?

My eyes catch a drone flying by. Barry's great idea – half the team don't have a clue how to control them. I lean my elbows on the stone wall and glance over, seeing Stacey over at the pool house, talking to someone on the phone.

Her hand is waving around like she's mad and trying to explain something. Maybe it's her brother? Or Barry's called her for something. She's close with him now too.

She hangs up, and I pull back just as she glances in my direction.

I haven't spoken to her at all today. She and Luciella stayed in the studio downstairs and tested out all the new aerial equipment. I stood outside the room for a little; I heard my sister crying then Stacey telling her to dance until the tears stopped.

The music played for hours.

I might have stared at a screen for hours watching Stacey stretch and work her way around a pole, twist herself in fabric dangling from the ceiling then do some bendy routine on an aerial hoop after my sister left.

Spending time together yesterday, even if it was only a little while, made me get my first night's sleep without waking up soaked in sweat or on the bathroom floor, dazed and unsure about what the fuck's going on.

I open Stacey's contact and type fifteen messages before settling on one. It's stupid, considering I just told her I wasn't fit for a relationship or anything else, but she makes me feel calm, and being around her makes me forget all the shit in my head.

And I really do fucking love her.

I don't want to confuse her, but I also don't want to push her away. I'm at a crossroads, in all honesty. I want Stacey. I need her. But I'll hurt her, both physically and mentally. What if I lose myself during sex and hallucinate? What if I shoot her in my sleep?

Maybe I can ask her to be my friend?

***Me:** Why aren't you asleep?*

The reply is rapid.

***Freckles:** Stalker.*

***Freckles:** Kyle called me. Why are you awake?*

I put the joint between my lips and use my two thumbs to reply.

***Me:** I need to head up to my apartment in Stirling. You game?*

Fuck, I'm an idiot. An impulsive, idiotic idiot. What am I doing? She deserves way fucking better, and I'm dragging her along with my bullshit. Why would I ask her to come with me? Why? Fucking why?

***Freckles:** Are you sure? I don't want you to force this.*

***Me:** We can hang out, Stacey.*

***Freckles:** When are you leaving?*

***Me:** Now. Meet me in the garage. We're taking the bike up.*

***Freckles:** I'm having flashbacks, and I think I'd rather stub my pinkie toe than have a repeat, but thanks for the horrendous offer.*

***Me:** Shitebag.*

***Freckles:** I hate you. I'll be there in ten minutes.*

Once I pull on a thick hoodie and sweats, not bothering putting on my leathers, I stare at the material sitting on my dresser for far too long before giving in and fastening it around my mouth.

She's waiting by my bike when I get to the garage – wearing comfort clothing like I am. She's even wearing a woolly hat.

I grab the bobble at the top and pull it off, messing her hair. She frowns at me, and I gesture to the helmet. "You're wearing that."

It's big on her, but it's better than nothing. I keep the visor open as I fasten the clips under her chin, feeling a bout of butterflies hitting me with the way she's watching my every move.

Being loved by Stacey Rhodes is a dream. Why does my dream need to be a nightmare?

"Can I drive it?"

I laugh and pull my own helmet on, and when she crosses her arms and pops out her hip, I stop laughing. "You're joking?"

"No. We can go somewhere and you can teach me, like when you taught me how to drive a car."

"You crashed four times."

She tuts. "How many cars have you written off?"

I stay silent, narrowing my eyes at her.

There's a smile on her mouth. I can't see it, but I can see it in her eyes.

"You can drive it down to the front gate," I say, moving over to the bike and patting the seat. "Sit in front of me and I'll hold your hands over the handles and shift our balance to move."

She climbs on, wobbling a little before I jump on behind her, unsure where to put my hands at first as I point out each part of the bike. She listens, nodding, and when she adjusts herself, she pushes her ass against me.

My hands fist, my teeth gritting at the feel of her entire body pressing against my front, and it only gets worse as I cradle her, placing my hands over her on the handlebars.

"Ready?" I ask.

"Ready," she confirms, and the bike stalls.

"You let go of the clutch too fast. Slowly, the same way you do in a car."

This time, we move forward, and I already regret my decision as we pull out the garage and, very messily, zigzag all the way down the driveway.

My guards watch us, and I know they're probably wondering what the fuck is going on. The SUV follows behind us, and I slip my fingers between hers to gain more control and drive us to the gate.

"Can I keep going?" she asks through the Bluetooth. "Just to the end of the road."

"Don't kill us."

She giggles, and when the gate opens, her wrist curls, and we jolt forward so hard, my helmet smacks into hers. "Shit," she blurts. "Sorry, but you are the worst teacher."

"You're the worst order-taker. Go fucking slow, or I'll take over."

"Yes, sir," she says sarcastically, and I knock my helmet into hers lightly.

We make it to the end of the road, but only because I take over, with my fingers between hers, my front pressing to her back, leaning left and right as we move. As soon as we hit the main road, I pull in.

"Can we stay like this?" she asks.

I keep the bike up with my feet flat on the ground while she dangles from the seat, pulling back and letting go of the handlebars. She twists her body to look at me, flipping up her visor, and I see the excitement in her eyes.

"It's a two-hour journey," I say, pulling my phone out to connect it to our helmets just as the SUV stops behind us. "But we can go for a bit and stop for some food."

She nods excitedly. "I'd like that."

I sigh, waiting for my playlist to start. "Hearing Damage" by Thom Yorke plays, and Stacey groans. "I love this song."

I know. I know everything about you, Freckles.

We take off again, and at some points in the drive, she tries to take control, but I value her being alive, so I make sure I dominate her movements, but only enough so she still thinks she can drive a motorbike.

I like this. It's calming, hearing her little gasps when we speed up, seeing her hair flying around, feeling the cold air on our skins. The SUV keeps up, even as we swerve between cars on the motorway.

We stop for food, eat it in comfortable silence then we're off again.

The entire way to Stirling, Stacey sits in front of me, and I feel her against me, and I like it. I wish I could stay here.

We pull up on my driveway, and the garage opens as I direct us into it. She lets out a long breath. "That was amazing," she says, taking the helmet off. "My heart is going so fast. Feel it." She takes my hand and presses it to her chest, and although I freeze everywhere, I can feel the beating heart that belongs to me.

She uses her free hand to pull up my visor when I stay silent.

"It's the adrenaline," I say, holding her eye contact. "Sometimes it can get really overwhelming."

"My heart's been pounding in my chest since you asked me to come here with you."

The corner of my lip curls. "You're getting soft in your old age, Stacey."

She smacks my hand away and swings off the bike. I follow, hearing the SUV pulling into the driveway.

"Stay here. I'll only be a minute."

She nods, and I leave her in the garage, knowing my guards are right outside, while I hunt for my bag and laptop, finding them both in the office I rarely use. I check for the charger and stuff the laptop in the bag, then riffle through the drawers of my desk for paperwork.

I glance up when I hear movement – Stacey is standing in the doorway with a piece of paper in her hand. "What's this?"

My eyes don't stray. "Nothing."

"You're addressing everyone in it and apologising for everything as if you're going to die." She scans the words, turning the paper over and pausing. "*And lastly, the most important person in my life, my girl Stacey Rhodes. My Freckles. My forever. What can I say to make any of this better? I hope my death means you're free, and that—*" She glances up. "Why did the note stop?"

I look down. "It's nothing."

"It looks like a suicide note. I..." She pauses again, glancing over her shoulder and gasping. "What happened in there?"

Shit. Fucking shit.

I drop my bag as she walks into my destroyed bedroom, stopping when she covers her mouth on a gasp. Speechlessly, she lowers herself to her knees and picks up the ultrasound picture of our daughter. Her grip on it shakes, my suicide note in the other hand.

"Stacey..."

Her bottom lip trembles as she crawls forward over the broken glass from me punching my mirror, snatching up the princess dress. "Oh God," she sobs, cuddling it to her chest as she screws her eyes shut. "You had everything. I-I-I-I only had the ultrasound picture. Chris burned it, and after we broke up, I had nothing from when I was pregnant with her."

I step in slowly, glass crunching beneath my shoes, and lower onto the bed, sitting in silence as Stacey rocks back and forth with tears streaming down her face.

She looks to the left, seeing the drawing of her I did all ripped up then lifting the piece of paper that has my five rules on it. She shakes her head, another sob dropping before she lets it slide from her fingers.

"Why is life so cruel?"

"I wish I knew," I reply. "I lost control the last time I was here and wrecked the place. I never intended for anyone to see this. I forgot when I asked you. I'm sorry."

Stacey sniffs, the dress still in her lap as she picks up a picture of us two. She rubs her thumb over our smiling faces. The only worry in the world we had back then was how my sister would react to our relationship.

"We're never going to be them again, are we?"

I shake my head. "No."

"I miss how happy we were," she says, sniffing some more as she rests her head on my knee, cuddling the dress and holding the picture. "I'm sorry Jason jumped in front of me."

I frown. "You have nothing to apologise for."

"I do though. If I'd gone upstairs when your dad told me to, then I wouldn't have been there. Jason would still be alive."

My hand shakes, but I manage to lift it and place it on her head, brushing my fingers through her soft hair. I inwardly sigh, our closeness something I need but can't have. "Jason's gone," I say, the words getting twisted in my throat. "There's no point dwelling."

We just need to get the funeral out the way. I'll figure out the next steps once I bury my brother.

The thought alone makes me feel nauseous.

Stacey lifts her head up and moves so she's sitting beside me on the bed. Then she drops back, holding the picture and dress, staring at the ceiling. I slowly lie back too and fight the urge to talk. To tell her how dark my head is. To ask her to stay by my side. To beg her to make the pain go away.

The crippling grief I'm trying to ignore.

The paranoia about my father's whereabouts.

The rage I feel towards Archie, still trapped in my basement, starving and in pain from my constant beatings.

Stacey turns her head, looking at me. She lifts her hand, and I take it without hesitation. The contact has butterflies going through me again, and I close my eyes, loving the touch, ignoring the demolished room around us.

If only we could stay like this forever, here, in this position. Together.

Hours later, I wake up to Stacey's head on my chest, her leg trapped between mine, the dress between us. I inhale, smelling her shampoo. I trace my finger over the mark on her cheek – I did that to her. I didn't mean to.

When my eyes lift to the guard standing by the doorway, his back turned, I sigh and wake her up.

We pack the box again, even the ripped-up sketches of her I drew, and she makes me take my pencils and sketch pad too before we head back to the manor.

28

KADE

Mum and Ewan are watching a movie in the sitting room, and my sister has had Stacey in the studio for hours, so I've spent the last three hours torturing Archie.

He's weak. His skin is a little yellow. Well, the parts I haven't already cut into. He's slobbering everywhere, and I think he might have an infection in his dick from the nail gun.

He wails in pain as I stub my cigarette out on his cheek.

"Are you going to give me any information on those bastards in the underworld, or am I going to start pulling your fingernails?"

"Go f-f-fuck yourself."

I shrug and grab a pair of pliers, and blood squirts all over my face as I yank his pinkie nail out. I chuck aside the tool and cross my arms. "I'll be back in a few hours. Pour bleach on his wounds,"

I order one of my men.

"Yes, sir."

I unravel my shirt sleeves, refasten the cuffs and head out into the corridor, stopping when I hear music – "Dead Man" by David Kushner. I push the door to the studio open to see Stacey mounting the aerial hoop.

Throughout the song, I watch as she dances in a routine. She forms shapes that would break my bones and kill me, and she spins so slowly and sensually, I know she's feeling the music, zoning out and letting go.

I gulp and lean my forehead on the doorframe, hidden enough that she won't see me watching the way she bends and moves, the light sweat working on her skin.

We've been texting back and forth today. Nothing flirty or about the other night. She's given me soft smiles and even nudges me playfully when we're eating at the dinner table.

We've walked the dogs together too. She still can't handle holding both leashes without letting go when they pull.

Her routine ends, and she drops from the hoop like a cadaver and lies on the thin mat, her chest rising and falling. She wipes her face, then she starts stretching.

A throat clears behind me, and I turn to see Ewan holding a bottle of bleach. "I was told to bring this down."

Luciella and I haven't really talked. Me and my sister aren't the type of twins to connect with our emotions – we aren't synchronised.

She cries a lot. She's very open about her emotions. She gets mad and yells; she cries and screams. And she begs my best friend every hour to come home to her. But he can't.

Base hasn't spoken much either. He's busy with the Russian drama. I get it – he had a life outside of my bullshit, and I respect the hell out of him for saving my sister. And Dez is on his way home too. He and Tylar will be back in time for Jason's funeral.

My phone buzzes on my dresser, and I try to sit up, but the dogs are on top of me. I slide them off me – somehow they stay asleep – and reach for my phone.

***Freckles**: Why are you awake?*

***Me**: Who's the stalker now? I'm watching TV. You want to come up?*

***Freckles:** I might accidentally fall asleep in your bed though.*

***Me**: Then I'll let you sleep in my bed.*

***Freckles**: Only if you want me to.*

***Me**: I do.*

***Freckles**: Please don't start vacuuming your curtains and freaking out again. I'm coming up now.*

I frown at the screen in confusion, then it clicks that my mum must've told her she walked in on me doing just that when Stacey was coming up when we were teens.

The fucking traitor.

Then there's a pressure on my chest, because Stacey is coming up here, and I have no idea what the fuck we are or what we're doing.

I drop my phone and stand, pacing the room with my hands in my hair until I get dizzy and have to sit down. When the knock on the door comes, I grab the face covering and secure it in place.

After I glance over my room to make sure it's tidy, the balcony doors wide open to eliminate the smell of weed, I close my eyes and take a deep breath. My lungs give up as I swing the door open to the girl I've been obsessed with since I was fifteen.

She wears silk pyjama shorts and a top, and fluffy slippers with dog faces on them. She smiles sleepily and walks in as I step aside. The dogs run over to her – she crouches to see them before flopping down on the bed.

"I would say I missed your room, but I slept in here for weeks."

"Why?" My brow arches as I close the door and lock it. *Wait, is it normal to lock the door if it's only a friend?*

She shrugs, star-fishing. "Like I said, I missed you. I felt close to you, even though you weren't here."

"Sounds a little psychotic and obsessive. I think you spent too much time with my dad."

My dad. Who's with—

I blink away the thought and cross my arms. Her smile stays on her mouth, but it leaves her eyes. "Maybe. Or maybe I just wanted to hang around with the dogs." She pets them and shifts so Hopper can rest his head on her arm.

I snort. "They still like me more."

"Debatable."

"Get properly into bed and I'll put something on," I order as I grab the TV remote and turn it on.

"Are we actually watching something? Can't we just go to sleep? It's four in the morning."

I smirk and pull the duvet back. "I knew you just wanted in my bed."

She laughs softly, and fuck, I missed that.

Wait. Are we flirting?

We are.

I think.

She rolls her eyes. "I'm never going to sleep if you have a movie on."

Regardless, I need something on. Background sounds drown out the voices in my head. It's stupid, but I've tried everything else to stop them – trying to sleep is torture. Sometimes they're so loud, I believe they're real. I believe I'm in her bed and waiting for her to cut me or drug me, or for her to bring in our next victim.

"I'm not expecting anything from you," she says in a serious tone. "I just want to be here for you, okay? If you need my company, have it. If you need me to keep your mind off everything, then I'm here."

I furrow my brows as I get into bed. "I don't understand you at all." She tilts her head, confused. "I tried to shoot you. I chased you down in your car and held a gun to your head. You—" I gulp. "You were raped after losing our daughter, and I left you."

She's unfazed as she raises a shoulder. "All relationships have their obstacles, Kade. You weren't in control of any of yours. What's done is done. All we can do is go forward, right?"

My voice lowers as I reply, "But I don't know how to move forward."

She rests her head on the pillow, and I turn to face her on mine. She reaches forward and tugs the material on my face. "Take this off. You don't need it."

I shake my head.

"You don't need to hide from me."

I do though. And *she* should be hiding from *me*.

"Bernadette made me take a blade to my own face. It was either that or she'd hurt my sister."

I think I've already told her this, but her eyes water anyway as her nostrils flare. "She's a monster," she sneers. "I've never hated someone so much in my life. Her and her stupid, vile husband."

I look at her, wondering if she knows just how much they both violated me. Would she see me differently if she knew I was raped by them both? That I was raped by both men and women, sometimes at the same time?

A part of me thinks she does know. Yet she's still here, in my bed, spending time with me. She doesn't think I'm disgusting or used.

"Do you want to talk about any of it?"

"*No,*" I retort, hating myself for the shitty reply and the way she flinches. "Shit. Sorry. No. You'd run for the hills if you knew half the stuff she made me do." I shake my head. "You saw what I did to your stepbrother. That pales in comparison to everything else. One time, I made a guy eat his own intestines."

Her eyes widen in surprise. "Oh."

"I wanted to make Chris do the same, but I think I got sidetracked.

I don't remember much." I chew my lip. "I'm sorry about what I did to you in front of him."

Her expression stays the same. "I wish you'd fucked me in front of him. It would have hurt him a lot more."

I study her face – how beautiful she is. "I would've hated myself more if I'd fucked you."

"Why?"

I let out a mocking laugh. "Why would you want me anywhere near you?"

"Because I love you. Because I've always loved you. Regardless of what you've gone through and the changes we've both had to make to our lives, my feelings remain the same, Kade. I won't stop loving you."

"I wish I could be the old me again," I admit quietly. "I hate who I am now. Because all I can think about is killing people."

She shifts but not out of discomfort. "Who do you want to kill?"

"Everyone who's ever wronged you, hurt you, touched you without your consent. I want to rip them all apart. I'd ruin myself to keep you safe."

"You have a beautiful soul," she says. "You're worth more than death."

I want to lean forward and kiss her, but I banish the urge. "Go to sleep."

"You go to sleep," she fires back.

I roll my eyes then close them. "I forgot how insufferable you are."

"I forgot how much room you take up in bed. Stay in your half!"

I chuckle when she kicks my shin in a lame attempt to show dominance of her side. I grab the back of her thigh and pull her towards me to close some of the distance she's put between us.

It's an absent-minded move, and we both open our eyes, our gazes clashing at the feel of my hand on her bare skin. It lights a fire within me that I'm desperate to put out. I get flashes of the times I've been on and in her, and heat coils up my spine.

She's the only person I've ever willingly wanted. The only person to turn me on. The only person I've pictured spending the rest of my life with.

Her leg hikes up to my hip, and I try to drag my middle finger up from her ankle to the back of her knee, but she grabs my wrist. “I need to shave.”

I let out a breathy laugh. “Felt like I was touching a cactus.”

She moves back and takes her leg with her. “Rude.”

I smirk and close my eyes again, my skin burning for another touch. “It’s nearly five in the morning now.”

“Great observation skills, Mr Mitchell.”

I open my eyes to see her pull the duvet to her chin. “Stand beside me at the funeral on Saturday.”

She nods. “I will. It’ll be okay. I’m glad they finally released his body.”

I hum as I pull off the face covering. “Yeah.”

I turn off the lamp, leaving only the glow from the TV playing, the sound of whatever show I clicked on a gentle murmur in the background. I haven’t been this nervous since our first kiss, but I need to give her something. For me and for her. I need to try.

Leaning over and pressing my hand to the pillow beside her head, I look down at her. “Don’t move.”

She gives a little nod, watching me lower myself to her, my hair falling over my eyes.

I kiss her cheek, hovering for a second when she makes a cute hum in her throat. I press my lips down a bit, closer to her mouth while she stays still but breathless.

I shut my eyes and focus away from the voices, screams and gunshots that echo in my mind. They almost prevent me from kissing her again, but she grabs my chin. “You’re in control.”

I’m really fucking not.

“You can go as far as you want. You’re in control of this, Kade. I’m yours,” she says, and her eyes drop to my mouth. “And you’re mine.”

“Yeah?”

“Yeah.”

When I lean down again, my nose nudges hers and slides against her cheek – our lips are millimetres apart, and my breaths come out in a rush as I try to be in control.

“Kiss me,” she whispers against my mouth, knowing how

desperately I want to do just that. "It's just me and you. It's always been me and you. Against the world."

My heart stops and restarts when my lips press to hers softly.

I kiss her slowly at first, like the first time we ever kissed, and my nerves are on fucking fire. She keeps her hands to herself, while mine rest on each side of the pillow.

My teeth graze her bottom lip gently, and she parts her lips and sucks on my top one. She drags slow, chaise kisses to the corner of my mouth, and I hold my breath as she presses her mouth to my scar, trailing down to my jaw then back to my lips.

She carefully takes my face between her hands, her pupils dilating more with every second. "I love you. I've loved you since we were eighteen. And I'll love you until we're old and grey and we've lived our whole lives together."

My entire world feels close to collapsing at her words, and I want to smother her with everything I have and protect her. I want to take her away from all of this and start a new life.

She might die next.

I slip my tongue between her lips, and my hand cups her cheek, sliding down to her throat and stilling when I get a flash of how many people died from me strangling them or snapping their necks.

I snatch my hand away at the visceral need to strangle her and fist it at my side as I pull away from her.

Did all the oxygen vanish in the room? Why can't I breathe?

She sits up, her dark hair falling over her shoulders, and studies me as my lungs burn – my brain is fucking failing to work as my vision blurs. "Are you okay? You've gone pale."

I try to sit up and attempt to breathe, but it's like my mind isn't connecting with my body. There's a ringing in my left ear, and I hear a gunshot go off.

Good boy.

Good boy.

Good boy.

Another gunshot goes off.

It makes me flinch, but I know it's not real.

It's never real now.

There's a tingling sensation all over my body, and I feel like I'm falling. A big drop. I flinch again.

And again and again and again.

I can't talk. I try to tell Stacey that everything's going numb, but the words come out slurred. My vision blurs, and the last thing I hear is Stacey gasping as my body violently jerks before everything goes black.

29

STACEY

The deadly silence fills the cemetery as we walk slowly behind the black coffin, a spray of white roses on top. Luciella is beside me, holding my hand while she grabs her mother's. They're sobbing, wiping their tears away with a handkerchief.

I keep my eyes forward, the large umbrella above our heads keeping us dry from the downpour of torrential rain.

The group of people follows behind us, all in black, all silent except the whimpers full of sorrow. Dez and Tylar are right behind me. They arrived at the manor this morning, just in time for the service.

Other than whimpers, it's so quiet, I can hear every drop of rain, every crack of thunder in the distance and Lu's hyperventilated hitches of air.

Kade and Ewan are carrying the coffin, along with four of Jason's friends, and the funeral director is leading the way to a deep plot. It was reserved years ago for Ewan and Aria; no one knew Jason would be the first to fill it.

When we reach the plot, I glance behind me, the air nearly knocked from my lungs with how beautiful the view is, despite the rain. We can see the entire loch from here, the Munros crowding the sky – in the near distance is the manor surrounded by trees. During summer it will be a wonderful sight.

We gather around the hole in the ground, and my eyes stay on Kade, who is completely emotionless as he helps them lower Jason's coffin onto the wooden slats covering the plot before dropping the ropes they'll use to lower the casket.

Ewan is a mess. His eyes are red, and tears are soaking his cheeks as he audibly weeps for his son. He's covering his mouth with one hand, the other on the casket.

His teeth chatter as he looks around everyone, his gaze finally landing on his wife. Aria reaches out and takes his hand, pulling him close, and he barely holds himself together, his body shaking in her hold.

Kade stands beside me, his stare blank as he looks at the grass way past the coffin. I notice the tension in his expression; he's trying so hard to stay calm. He's either going to break down in tears, or he's going to break something or someone.

I try to take his hand, but he pulls away, and my heart sinks.

An older man in a long suit speaks of life and death, about Jason and how adored he was. He speaks of peace and love, until the words blur together like my vision, and I lower my head.

When he stops talking, he asks for the carriers to come forward again, and Jason's favourite song – "The Woods" by Hollow Coves – plays as they slowly lower the casket into the grave.

Kade is still a statue – his movements almost robotic. His gaze is cold, unyielding, and he's barely giving anyone attention. He isn't even looking at the coffin – he's looking past it.

He's just a shell of breaking emotions, and I have no idea what this means. Is he a ticking time bomb? Is he going to lose himself? Will he explode at the wrong time? Will he get through this?

Kade's hair is soaked, falling over his forehead as he licks a droplet from his lips, his nostrils flaring.

Rage. It's growing inside him like a blazing inferno.

We all stand in silence as the song fills the quietness, the lyrics very fitting considering we're at the top of a hill and the view of the trees below is beautiful.

He'll be here, standing with us, probably bobbing his head to the song while we all muffle our cries and blow our noses. He won't want us to be sad and miserable – he'll want us to live our lives and be happy.

I glance over my shoulder, and my teary gaze lands on a heartbroken Giana. Her bottom lip quivers, and she doesn't appear to have slept a wink in days given the black rings under her eyes. She's shakily holding a rose in her hand, the thorn cutting into her skin as she fights to fill her lungs.

She hasn't reached out to anyone – no one has reached out to her either. They were hoping to work on things. He was getting better for her, and now he's gone.

As the song ends, Kade comes back over to stand beside me while Ewan struggles to speak. He tries to thank everyone for coming, to say that every single one of us meant a lot to Jason and he'll stay alive in our hearts, but his voice keeps breaking, and he eventually needs his wife to comfort him and lead him back to the crowd.

Luciella moves to stand beside the coffin, and I hold my breath. My best friend hasn't been the same since leaving the lodge. She cries all the time, and she eats even less than Kade.

I've tried to keep her in the studio room with me – we exercise, dance, stretch, lie on the crash mats and I listen to all of her stories about Jason growing up.

She clears her throat and unfolds a piece of paper, then takes a deep breath.

"On your twelfth birthday, I..." She pauses. "I took my first steps and walked straight into your arms. When I turned four, I started my first day of school and you were the only one wh-who managed to calm me down when I cried. M-m-my first school disco—"

She nearly drops the piece of paper. Kade is stiff as a board beside me, emotionless, but I can see in his eyes that he's battling how he feels. He's witnessing his twin sister falling apart in front of everyone.

Base isn't even here to comfort her. He's in Russia, battling with his family to cancel the arranged marriage he agreed to and get back to the girl he loves.

I offer Kade my hand again, and I hold my breath until he grips it like a vice, his throat bobbing.

Lu wipes her eyes. "Sorry." She blows out a breath. "No one would be my date at the school dance, so you danced with me in the playground." Her throat cracks. "You danced with me until the music from the hall stopped. For prom, I didn't like my shoes but didn't want to tell Mum, so you used your first wage to buy me a new pair. I was afraid of the dark, so you and Kade slept on my room floor whenever I had nightmares."

Kade's fingers tighten around mine, and I glance up to see a lone tear sliding down his cheek, the muscle in his jaw ticking with each blink. I stroke my thumb against his hand and rest my head on his shoulder.

Luciella's shakes worsen, but she keeps going. "You moved out, and I felt like a piece of my soul was missing. You were going to walk me down the aisle. Hold my first child. Watch me grow up."

She stops and presses her hand to her mouth, and Aria nods her head, smiling warmly. "You're doing well, sweetheart."

"You... you were – *are* – the perfect big brother for me and Kade. The best. Caring, supportive, funny and exactly the kind of sibling everyone deserves. I love you, Jason. I-I miss you."

Kade lets go of my hand. "Fuck this," he spits through gritted teeth and shoulders his way through the crowd.

I don't hesitate to go after him. Neither do five of his guards. But before we catch up with him, he staggers to the side, drops to the grass and starts seizing again.

"Psychogenic non-epileptic seizures," the doctor says, reading from his clipboard. "From your EEG during your third episode, there weren't any spikes in electrical activity to indicate epilepsy, so we can likely rule that out, though not completely. PNESs are not uncommon for someone who sustained as much trauma as yourself, Mr Mitchell. Your father suffered from pseudo-seizures too."

Aria sits down beside Kade. "They only stopped about ten years ago," she says. "He had triggers that brought them on. Anything from a word to a feeling to a smell set him off. That's why he wasn't allowed to drive when he was younger. He crashed while blacked out and nearly killed someone."

Kade's jaw ticks as he stares at his bouncing knee, legs parted wide as he slouches on the sofa beside me. I don't think he's even listening.

As soon as Aria got him to her colleague's office, he was sent for testing, and they happened to have caught a third seizure that got him a solid diagnosis. The doctor had said he was lucky, because it can take years for someone to catch this type of seizure on an EEG.

"Pseudo?" I ask, tilting my head.

"Pseudo-seizures," the doctor clarifies. "They mimic epileptic seizures, but they're brought on by stress, anxiety and other mental factors."

"How did Tobias stop them?" I ask, badly wanting to take Kade's hand but not knowing how he'll react. I already feel like I'm overstepping by just being here, but he forced me to sit with him.

The doctor looks at Aria, and she gives me a warm smile. "Time. And a lot of help from the institution. He said he could always feel them coming on, and he had no idea how to stop them. Not that they can be stopped. Just… with time, they started to come on less frequently until they were weeks apart, months apart, and then years."

Kade closes his eyes with a deep sigh and pinches the bridge of his nose. "I don't have time for this bullshit."

The doctor clears his throat as he packs up his things. "I recommend plenty of rest. Relax for a few days. Don't take part in any strenuous exercise." He gives me a pointed look and goes back to Kade.

"I'm too busy to rest."

Correction: he needs to continue torturing Archie in the freezer.

Aria sighs. "He'll rest. Thank you, Doctor Shique."

The man lowers his head in acknowledgement, and Aria walks him out of the manor as Kade scowls at the back of his head.

I turn to him, and his eyes soften a touch. "How do you feel?"

"Fine. I just need this fucking day over with."

I chew my lip and sit back as Aria walks back into her office, rubbing her arm. "Why don't you grab a shower and have an early night?"

Kade doesn't respond – he just gets to his feet and storms out, but before he can vanish, I spot him blinking excessively again.

"We need to keep a close eye on him," Aria says to me. "I think Kade is very unpredictable at the moment, and you might be the only person holding him together. Today must've been too much for him to handle."

I don't feel an ounce of embarrassment as I tell her, "He kissed me. The other day, seconds before he had a seizure, he kissed me. I think that triggered him. It was the first time in a year we'd been… like that."

I don't mention him fingering me in front of Chris. That was different.

"We don't know if that was a trigger."

I nod as I stand and smooth down my dress. "How are you? I know today has been hard."

She raises her shoulders shyly. "I don't really know how to answer that."

"Yeah." I give her a tight smile, and it drops as I step forward nervously. "I'm truly sorry about Jason. I know if I wasn't there, he might not—"

Aria raises a hand to stop me. "No. Don't do this again, Stacey. You're not to blame. None of this is your fault. It's that vile, horrible woman."

I nod again. "Luciella's asleep. Tylar went home to pack some clothes to stay here for a while."

"She'll love having all three of you together again. My best friend and I lived together. It was like having a sister."

"Yeah," I reply. "Gabriella."

Her eyes brighten. "We buried her a few plots over from where Jason is now. I go every Friday and lay fresh flowers. I talk to her, you know? I tell her about my life and my kids, about what we'd be doing if she was still here. I asked her to look after Jason for us."

Her best friend was murdered by Tobias's best friend. He bludgeoned her skull with a hammer. Aria stabbed the killer to death then accidentally drove the blade into Ewan's side.

Horrid.

I gulp. "I'm worried about Kade."

"He's been through a lot. We're lucky we got him to a semi-sane state so quickly. Doctor Shique thinks he's in denial too, but I think he's just focused on getting his father back and taking his anger out on the man in my freezer." She grimaces. "It smells terrible down there."

Against my wishes, a smile breaks through. "He deserves everything that's coming to him. At least we can't hear his screams while we try to sleep."

"I agree, which is why he's still there. But I can assure you, Kade Mitchell will be on his hands and knees bleaching that entire freezer before I restock it."

I grin at her, but it slips again. "If it helps at all with the seizures, I'll stay away from Kade… romantically. I know there's a chance I did trigger one, and I don't want that to happen again. I'll be there for him and be his friend." The word friend sticks in my throat. "I can't walk away from him."

"Of course," she replies, resting her hand on my shoulder. "You've both been through a lot. Let's not forget what you had to endure. Go at a pace that suits you both if you can. He lost control of his body once, and he'll feel like it's happening again with these seizures. He loves you very much. I see it every time he looks at you."

"I love him too."

Kade clears his throat; he's standing on the threshold of the room, glaring between the two of us. "Ewan is looking for you," he says to his mother.

30

STACEY

Aria walks past Kade and pats his chest, then she's out of sight.

His eyes land on me. "I won't be bleaching the freezer."

I cross my arms and jut out my hip. "You really shouldn't eavesdrop. It's rude."

He breathes deeply through his nose and walks in, closing the door behind him. He shoves his hands in his trouser pockets and steps forward. "Do you believe me now that I don't know how to be in a relationship?"

I lower my head. "It doesn't mean that at all."

"You said so yourself. It triggered me. And it pisses me off, Stacey."

I nibble my lip. "I know."

He pulls a hand from his pocket and aggressively taps the side of his head with bared teeth. "It's Bernadette. She's in my head all the fucking time. Every single thing I do, I hear her voice, smell her fucking perfume and feel her nails clawing into my skin. I'm trying so damn hard to push it all aside and be good enough for you." He eats up the distance between us, making my pulse race. "I. Don't. Know. How."

I fight tears, seeing into his abused soul through the deadliness of his eyes.

"But, despite every reason not to, I want to be with you. I need you."

My head tilts as a tear slides down my cheek. "You do?"

"Of course I do," he says with a frown, closing the remaining distance between us and wiping the tear away with his thumb, stroking beneath my eye as he cups my face. "But I've fucked up too much, and I don't know how to fix any of this."

"I forgave you," I reply, my voice shaking.

"I don't know how to forgive myself for everything I've done, so how can I expect you to do the same?"

When he lowers his forehead to mine, I part my lips on a rushed breath, feeling warmth crawl up my spine all the way from my toes. "Then you need to learn how to forgive yourself, because I'm not leaving. I'm always going to be by your side."

My nerve endings tremble, ready to combust as he curls his fingers around my nape, stroking his thumb behind my ear. I grow warmer from his touch. His white shirt is pulled taut over his muscles, his cuffs rolled to his elbows, showing off his expensive watch.

"I need you too," I add.

"Even if I'm a bag full of trauma?"

I smile. "I have my own bag. We can swap when they get too heavy and we need a balance."

Kade huffs out a laugh, nudging his nose against mine. "I want to try and kiss you again. Can I?"

"Promise me something first."

He arches a brow. "What?"

"Don't push me away."

He brings his mouth close to mine, fire igniting within me as he whispers against my lips, "What if it's for your own good?"

He tries to kiss me, but I press my fingers to his lips. "I don't want you to think you need to force this and you end up seizing again. We can wait. We can go slow."

"Slow," he repeats with a slight grimace, as if the word sickens him. "I never want to hear that word from you again when it comes to me and you. We do whatever the fuck we want."

His lips are so soft beneath my skin, and the tip of his tongue pokes out, swiping at my fingertips. I snatch my hand away at the electricity flowing through it.

He's not wearing his face covering. I'm glad; I don't want him to hide from me. When I kissed his scar before, I was showing Kade that it's a part of him, and I love all parts of him. Even the darker ones. I'll always love those parts of him.

It's not ugly or something that should be hidden. It shows his courage, how he stopped his sister from being tortured by cutting himself and surviving the punishment.

Nothing about Kade scares me. Even if he did chase me down a highway on a motorbike and point a gun in my face, shoot at me, finger me while covered in blood, along with all the other messed-up things he's done. He doesn't scare me. That side – the scary, vicious and extremely dangerous side – is the one everyone sees, but I get to see a different Kade.

The real Kade.

The one who went on holiday with me. Got drunk and sang karaoke, swam in the sea and kissed me under the sunset. He's the one who sent me good morning and goodnight texts every day without fail, and we shared all of our firsts.

Everything he's done in his life – kill, fuck, torture – he did to protect those he loved. Including me.

I almost smile, elated deep within as butterflies bloom, as I look into the eyes of the only person I want to be with. He's the only person I've ever wanted to be with.

Kade Mitchell loves me.

I'm his. And he's mine.

My lungs stop working as his other hand comes to rest on my hip, walking me back until I bump into the desk. I pull myself on top of it without thinking, my dress riding up my thighs as I open them wide enough for him to slot himself between them.

I pull him by the shirt, bringing him closer to me, until I feel every bit of his warmth.

"Your little speech to my mother isn't happening. I don't deserve you. I don't deserve your forgiveness," he says, making my body sing as he brings his mouth to my ear and lowers his voice. "I don't deserve to even be in your fucking company."

Shivers overwhelm me as he presses a kiss against my heated skin.

"But I want you. I want everything you'll give to me. I want you around me, beneath me, on top of me."

My chest rises and falls as he sucks on the skin behind my ear then bites at my lobe, bringing it lightly between his teeth.

"I tried so hard to keep my distance, Stacey, but I can't do it anymore."

"Wait." My back arches, and I let go of his shirt to lean back on the desk. "You might push it too far and seize again."

He scoffs and lowers his forehead to my shoulder, shaking his head. "I'm not going to let some neurological bullshit passed down from my father stop me from getting what I want."

I'm not quite sure if that's accurate, but I don't want to correct him.

I raise a brow as he looks up. "And what is it you want?"

"You. I want to be the person you think of when you wake up, when you go to sleep, when you slide your hand between your legs and find pleasure."

His hands have a bruising grip on my trembling thighs as he drags his hungry, hooded gaze down the length of my body. He's trying to control himself.

"What else?"

He sucks his bottom lip into his mouth then holds it between his teeth as my dress slides further up my thighs, exposing my definitely soaked underwear.

"Your body. I want to be the only person to touch, kiss and fuck you. I want to claim all your emotions. Fear. Anger. Misery. Happiness. Love." He presses his thumb against my clit through my underwear, and I let out a soft moan from the abrupt sensation. "I want your heart, every single fucking fragment that I've broken over the years. I have your past and your present, and I want to be a selfish asshole and have your future."

"You already have it," I breathe, letting out a quiet whimper as he pinches my clit. I lean further back, my palms pressing into the desk as he circles, and feel him harden against my inner thigh. "You have all of it."

"The monster in me wants you to be terrified. I want you to run to the other side of the world again and stay there." He pulls his thumb away, leaving me panting with need. "I want you to be scared of me."

I tip my chin as I sit up, my arms wrapping around his shoulders slowly, taking in the stiff muscles beneath my touch. "I'll never be scared of you," I say quietly, my voice soft and honest. "Never."

My hands slide down to his sides and snake around his waist, and my eyes widen when I feel a gun at the back of his waistband.

He snatches my wrists and presses my hands back to the desk. "You should be scared of me. I might worship the ground you walk on, but you don't have the faintest idea what I'm capable of. I could snap your neck without blinking, mistaking you for a client. I could fuck you so hard you pass out. I could really hurt you, Stacey."

I hook my ankles behind his thighs when he tries to step back. "You once told me not to be afraid of you. That sometimes people need to change to survive."

He sighs and slides his palms up to my thighs again, pushing them further apart. "I did say that, yeah. What's your point?"

"You survived."

The deep groan vibrates through my bones as he yanks me to the edge of the desk, pressing his hard cock right against my drenched panties. "Did I? Because it doesn't feel like it."

"You're here," I say, lowering my hand between us and palming his thick length through his trousers, making his fingers dig into my skin. "You're alive. You're fighting back. That's survival, Kade." I smirk as his pupils dilate. "Now you're mine and only mine."

It's been so long since I felt him. All of him. I forgot how large he is. He's thick, long and veiny. I might actually die if he pushes inside me.

He thrusts against my palm, and I twist my free hand into the material of his shirt, bringing his face closer to mine. "What will you do with your freedom?"

Kade stares at me for a long moment, breathing the same air while I touch him through his clothes. "Win my girl back."

My heart sings at his response, and I grin. "Yeah?"

"Yeah."

He lowers his head and drags my bottom lip between his teeth until it snaps into place. When he pulls back, I chase his lips and grab the back of his head, forcing him to stay as I devour his mouth with desperation.

The groan he lets out makes my pussy throb, and I can feel him growing harder.

I kiss every inch of his lips, his scar, nibbling along his jaw as I curl my fingers around his cock through the fabric, trying to unfasten the buttons of his shirt with one hand so I can kiss the scar trailing down his throat.

He stiffens slightly, so I go back to his mouth.

Kade slips his tongue against my own; he tastes of smoke and mint and something that's wholly mine. The grip on my thighs turns painful, but I revel in it. It makes me breathless as he kisses me like he'll die if he can't taste my tongue with his.

"Fuck," he mutters into my lips.

"Keep going."

We're biting and sucking tongues and moving our heads to deepen the kiss, and he whispers my name against my lips as he thickens even more in my hand. But when I reach for his belt, Kade grabs my wrist.

He doesn't release it, instead pressing it to my chest and pushing until I lie flat on the desk, my legs dangling over the edge.

He takes the gun from his waistband and places it beside my head, the deadly weapon so close I can smell the acrid scent of metal and gunpowder.

"If you keep touching my dick, I'll screw your plan of going *slow* and fuck you on this desk until we crack the wood." He lets go of my wrist and steps back enough to hook his fingers under my panties and slide them down my legs.

He lets them fall at his feet, staring at them, then lifts his gaze to the sensitive area between my legs that's buzzing for touch.

"I dream of you," he says in a deep voice, his eyes darkening as he pulls his belt from the loops of his black trousers. "Every night, I dream of you."

"Seems very psychotic and obsessive of you," I say, using his own words against him, flinching as he moves forward and massages my legs, close to the apex of my thighs, each caress parting my pussy for him. "What happens in these dreams?"

Everywhere tingles as he bends forward, breathing against my pulsing centre. "Everything."

My head falls back on a loud moan as he sinks two fingers inside me, his thumb pressing to my clit.

He thrusts his fingers all the way in and out while circling my clit. "Whoever touched you while you were in America, I'll kill them." He speeds up, fucking me harder, and I have to cover my mouth to stop the entire manor from hearing me moaning on his mother's desk. "I'll track them all down and make them wish they'd never laid eyes on you."

"I wasn't with anyone," I breathe. "But continue with your threats."

He pulls his fingers out and shoves both my legs up so my knees are bent, and I cry out as his teeth clamp down on my clit, sucking away the pain.

I grip the edge of the desk with one hand, knocking paperwork and a pencil holder over as I try to grab on to anything with the other, settling on burying my fingers into his hair as he eats my pussy.

Kade traces around my clit and entrance with the tip of his tongue, before sucking on the bundle of nerves again and making my spine twist, my back arching from the desk.

When he shoves his tongue through my entrance and devours me, I tug at his hair, pulling him firmer against me, grinding against his mouth as he switches between sucking, licking and biting, driving me to the edge.

His lips wrap around my clit again, and he sinks two fingers back in, adding a third then curling them, pumping in and out until my body spasms, a coiling sensation wrapping around each vertebra.

He mutters something in a different language against my pussy, and it almost sounds like praise from the tone he uses. Then his gaze clashes with mine, and I watch him lapping every inch of me as my lungs give up.

The orgasm smacks into me like a car crash, overtaking every single one of my senses as my vision blurs, my throat cracking on a loud moan of his name, his hair soft beneath my fingers as I tug hard and grind through my release.

He keeps going as it flows through me in waves, groaning against my pussy, and my inner walls crush his fingers with each pulse until I'm completely spent on the desk.

Someone knocks on the door, and Kade moves his face away, keeping his fingers inside me and making my eyes roll.

"What?" he calls out abruptly when the knocking sounds again.

"We have some information, sir."

He licks his glistening lips, and, instead of stopping, he keeps finger-fucking me then pulls out, yanks me off the desk and bends me over it. "Give me an hour."

He reaches in front of me and rubs my clit, the head of his cock pressing between my legs. "You see that gun there?" he says quietly so the guard doesn't hear, and I nod, frowning as he grabs it and shoves it into my hand. "If I hurt you, shoot me."

I don't have the chance to reply before he fills me in one punishing thrust. I struggle not to cry out from the fullness, my nails sinking into the wood of the desk while I grasp the gun.

Buried deep, not moving, he pants and takes my throat with his free hand, pulling me up so my back is against his chest and squeezing hard enough to put pressure behind my eyes.

"Don't make a fucking sound," he warns, speaking in my ear as he throbs inside me. He eases out slowly and fucks into me with one more thrust, and my body trembles, vibrating against him.

Skin slaps skin as he thrusts in and out, and I silently cry, the intensity overwhelming me yet bringing me close to another orgasm.

I almost lose my vision, but he releases my throat and bends me over the desk once more, holding me down by my nape just as the door is knocked again. I look over my shoulder to see his eyes darken to deep voids as he swears under his breath and pulls out of me.

He stuffs his cock into his trousers, takes the gun from me and storms to the door while I rush to get my dress back down. I yelp as he swings it open to point the weapon at the guard's head. His eyes widen, and he raises both hands.

"The fuck do you want?" Kade snaps as he cocks the gun.

"Bernadette Sawyer was taken to hospital and is in a critical condition."

Kade blinks twice and frowns. "What happened?"

He lowers his head. "Follow me."

I go with them to the main dining room, where Kade and his team have regular briefings to discuss the next steps of their search for Bernadette. All the screens are on, dotted around the room. One shows Archie, slumped on the floor of the freezer, covered in his own shit.

Aria gives me a welcoming smile as I walk behind Kade, hugging myself while he sets the gun on the table and leans in to see the footage.

"We managed to locate this file," Barry says through the speaker of a laptop. "It took place six hours ago."

In the recording, we see a bedroom, and Tobias is walked in with guards crowding him. He's only in a pair of boxers, and when he elbows one of them in the face, they all attack him with batons and the butts of their guns.

He laughs maniacally as his face fills with blood, then he grabs a guard and sinks his teeth into his cheek before kicking another in the face and knocking them clean out. One of them injects something into his neck, but he doesn't flinch until a second dose is administered.

He grows weak, and they sit him down on the edge of the bed, all of them backing away in terror.

When they leave, Bernadette walks in wearing a silk robe. She's speaking, but there's no sound in the clip. She strokes his cheek and licks the blood from his face, which makes my stomach roil, then slowly drops her robe.

She's naked as she climbs into his lap, and Aria turns away.

Kade crosses his arms. "I'm not watching my dad fuck her."

"Keep watching," Barry demands.

She tries to kiss Tobias, grinding in his lap, but he stands abruptly and knocks her on her ass. He's heavily drugged, but he still has control. I shouldn't be surprised, considering he's Tobias, but I am. He should be knocked out by now.

Bernadette crawls back, but she stops when he grabs her jaw. He says something that makes her smile, and she's licking her teeth and lips.

She gets into a position that would indicate she's going to suck him off but starts thrashing in his hold as his grip on her tightens. I can almost hear the crack of her jaw as she releases inaudible screams with terrified eyes.

No one enters in time to stop Tobias from lifting her from her knees by her shattered jaw and slamming her back into the wall with brutal force. Once, twice, three times. Blood marks the wall where her head's smacked into it.

She's out cold as Tobias punches her right across the face and throws her on the floor.

"Shit," Kade blurts out, looking at one of his team. "Where is my dad now? Is he still alive?"

The older man looks at me then opens another file and stands back.

The clip plays an unaired, pre-recorded news report. The reporter is standing in front of a cliffside, wind whipping at her hair as she addresses her audience.

"Officials have recovered a body from the car. The individual has been identified as convicted killer Tobias Mitchell. He escaped his institution in the US not long ago and has been on the run ever since. It seems the hunt for the psychopath has now come to an end. There will be more information in the coming days."

31

STACEY

No one speaks as Aria rushes for her phone, dialling a number with flying fingers and pressing it to her ear while covering her mouth with a palm. She's muffling a sob, her body shaking.

It's a silent cry. A scream is trapped in her throat as the line rings. And rings. And rings.

It's all we can hear in the silence of the room.

I glance over my shoulder to see Kade staring at the monitor, the screen paused on the reporter's face, the banner text at the bottom mocking us about Tobias's possible death.

It knocks the breath out of me, thinking it might be true. There's a hole in my chest, and if I feel like this even though he wasn't my father, then what the hell do his family feel?

Kade's tapping his middle finger on the table with haunting

slowness, his jaw clenching, his breaths steady but harshly exhaled through his nose.

Tap. Tap. Tap. Tap. Over and over again. *Tap. Tap. Tap. Tap.*

He's thinking. The mind of a killer in overdrive. Dangerous. Deadly.

The footage Tobias and I saw of Kade draws my mind away from the present, and I feel like throwing up. I see him stalking his victims in alleyways and dragging them into darkness, stabbing them, leaving no trace behind so he'll never be caught.

Driving over someone's skull repeatedly because he stepped on his foot.

Tying rapists to chairs and carving the names of their victims into their skin.

Putting bullets into a man to finish a contract before fucking me beside the dead body.

Shooting a gang leader for touching my ass.

Pulling the trigger and nearly killing me.

Strangling.

Smashing his lethal fists into a face until its owner is unrecognisable.

Driving a knife into the skull of a woman for giving him a dirty look then leaving her body in a Russian river.

He's unhinged and completely off the rails when mad.

And he's thinking.

With his state of mind and everything going on, I know that's a really bad thing. Destruction ready to happen. He's the son of Tobias Mitchell; it's in his blood to rain havoc down on everyone.

If it wasn't for his love for me and how much he cares about his family, I'd say all of the trauma and abuse had made him sociopathic.

I know his new therapist has spoken to Aria about dissociation, and the possibility of Kade compartmentalising certain emotions, keeping them on a shelf in his mind and making sure they stay there. He told his therapist that when the abuse took place, he would go elsewhere mentally, which is what may have caused the disorder.

Aria pulled me aside and told me that Kade was in a dangerous mindset, and that he had no idea how to pull away from it. The only thing that could help is if he gets revenge.

And he will. He'll kill everyone to protect us. I've watched hundreds of videos of Kade brutally taking lives with his bare hands and with weapons. He'll use those same hands to kill Bernadette and Archie. They killed his brother, and now possibly his father. He'll not think of the consequences of his actions.

His gaze flickers to me, and my heart skips a beat at the look in his eyes. He's dropping into the abyss, and he doesn't want to stop himself.

"Stay with me," I whisper to him, but he looks away.

A soft voice gets our attention. "Aria Miller. I'm Tobias Mitchell's next of kin."

I lower into one of the chairs and sit on my hands, in complete denial as Aria's facial expression contorts into pure rage. I jump as she slams her palm down on the table. "Then put me through to someone who can fucking help me!"

It takes a lot for her to get angry. She did years and years of therapy after what happened with her and Tobias.

Now I see another side as the mask drops, and flickers of Kade shine through. She grits her teeth as someone speaks, and angry tears slide down her cheeks.

She repeats, "Then put me through to someone who can help me." Her tone is calm, yet she's anything but.

Kade pushes from the desk and huffs as he jams in an earpiece and has a whispered conversation with someone on the other end. I hear him mention Archie, files and exposing something. He also asks them to get information about Bernadette's current state and what hospital she's in.

I furrow my brows at him as his eyes lift to me; it's been just a few minutes since he had me bent over a desk and was inside me.

I can still feel him.

My neck hurts. He gripped me too hard, and I know I have marks on my skin. He's staring at them, and as I press my palm to my throat, hiding them, he fists his hands and turns away from me.

There's silence, and Aria starts pacing , her hand over her mouth again. Then her footsteps falter. "You're putting me through to who? Why are you...?" Her eyes widen, and they land on Kade, who doesn't pay her any attention as he starts muttering into his earpiece again. "Is Tobias really dead?"

Whatever they say as a response knocks Aria off her feet, and guards rush to grab her from the floor as she lets out a harrowing scream that shakes my bones, just like she did when Jason was shot in the head.

The sound cracks my chest open and painfully squeezes my heart, knowing that I'll never see Tobias again or hear him call me *little one.*

No. Tobias Mitchell cannot be dead.

I refuse to believe it. He took two doses of something that should've knocked him out cold, yet he still managed to push through and attack Bernadette. There's not a chance in hell his end comes from crashing a damn car.

"Contact the Russians and tell them the deal is off. Demand their presence immediately," Kade says, completely monotone, and an older man from his team leaves the room with his phone to his ear. "Barry, I need you to set up a live feed and get every single one of our team on foot. I want *everyone* called in over the next week."

A lady in a suit nods and goes to a computer, typing rapidly into a coding system that sends out a signal to every member of Kade's company.

Is it a company? A gang? An organisation? His own empire? I have no idea. All I know is that he has hundreds of bodies beneath him – they get paid a hefty amount for their work, and he's the boss of them all.

If the Russians do get involved, I think this will be quite the battle, possibly a war. I know Base will do everything he possibly can to get them over here, or at least get Luciella to him.

Aria is still crying, and my nerves are shattered, because I'm either too numb to let tears fall, or I'm terrified about what Kade is going to do.

I want to grab his face and force him to look at me, to breathe through it, to focus on my voice and not the ones in his head. But when I stand up, he punches the desk with so much force, the wood cracks and a monitor falls on the ground.

Kade pushes from the broken desk, grabs his gun and marches

out of the room. I try to follow, but he points at me and speaks to his tallest guard, who's wearing a black suit. "Keep her in here."

"What?" I ask, frowning as the man stands in front of me. "Kade..."

He doesn't look at me. "Stay in the fucking room, Stacey."

I bite my lip, wanting to refuse, but I know this is a side of him that thrives on power and control. Uncontrollable rage. His blinking is worse than ever, and his body is rattling with anger as he slams the door.

Aria is back on the phone, demanding she be allowed to view the body, to identify him. But when she's told to call back later, she screams at them until they hang up. Her phone smashes off the wall as she slides down it. The guard who was to keep an eye on me rushes to her.

Against Kade's wishes, because I'm an asshole who doesn't want him doing anything alone, I check no one else is looking as I dodge another guard and run out of the room. He shouts for me to come back, and even tries to chase me along the landing, but I duck from his hands and make him tumble. Although I'm in a dress, it isn't tight or restricting my movements, and I've been back in the studio often enough now that my stamina is getting back to what it used to be, so I easily outrun him and make it to Kade's side of the manor.

Stopping at the top of the black, metal spiral staircase – the one he once made me crawl up while he touched me – I raise my fist to knock on the door but drop my hand on a breath. I falter and decide to turn the handle, and it opens.

I see him pulling a black hoodie on, his face covering in place to hide the scar. It matches his gloves, boots, combat trousers and hair.

Kade Mitchell is the haunting definition of darkness.

"I told you to stay in the room," he says without looking at me, pulling his hood up over his head to hide his hair, barely concealing his wavy fringe. Blue eyes burn into me as he turns. "Go back."

I gulp. "Your mum needs you right now. We need to tell Luciella about your dad. I don't want you to act on impulse."

"Then go tell Luciella," he snarls, his voice laced with venom.

He snatches an army pocketknife from a bag and tucks it into his boot.

I try to grab his arm, but he flinches away from me.

"Seriously, go back to the fucking room, Stacey."

"What's your plan?"

He glares at me for a second then averts his gaze. "I won't repeat myself."

He grabs a blade from his bedside unit and slots it into a leather strap on his thigh, then fits a gun into his holster under his hoodie before pulling a second weapon from his dresser and settling it into another holster on his thigh.

Kade fills a bag with more weapons as he sternly speaks to someone in his earpiece about a tripod and live-streaming networks. Then he grabs a duffle bag and packs it too. Handguns, blades, and…

"Why do you have grenades? What are you going to do?"

He grazes my arm as he reaches for something behind me, and when his hand rests on my hip for a moment, the world stops moving. I stare at him as he caresses his thumb over my hip.

"Let me do this, Stacey."

His eyes are on my neck again, then he frowns, lets go of me and turns around.

"Anything from Barry? Good. Tell him not to come here, just to stay where he is. Contact Sebastian Prince and tell him to fuck off his wedding and get his ass here. Whereabouts in the manor is my sister? Right, make sure she's watched. Ensure my mother is escorted to her room. Turn Dez and Tylar away at the gates. And take Archie Sawyer to the main office."

Whatever they say in his ear, it pisses him off. He closes his eyes and grits his teeth. "That was a fucking order."

"Where are you going?"

He ignores me, continuing to pack even more weapons and ammunition.

His shoulder touches mine as he passes. I release a shaky breath, and my voice breaks. "Talk to me, Kade."

He stops and shakes his head, then turns and walks to me. He grabs the hair at the back of my head and pulls our foreheads together as my fingers instantly wrap around the strings of his hoodie.

"They took everything from me. Everything. We had a chance, but they took that as well." He presses a firm kiss to my lips then shoves himself away, backing to the door while putting a fresh magazine in his gun and loading it. "Watch me destroy every last one of them, Freckles."

I follow him in a rush back to the office, taking two steps for each of his, where Aria is sobbing in the arms of one of her closest workers – a lady named Vera with long grey hair who's here to cook and clean but gets annoyed when Aria helps her around the manor. Vera strokes Aria's head and tries to shush her comfortingly while tears soak her face. Aria is muttering about how she was supposed to keep him safe – him, Jason, her children, all of them. She failed, and she doesn't know how to fix it.

Kade ignores her, settling two of his bags in the middle of the table. Two minutes later, as he sits on the desk chair and taps his finger, a guard drags in a thrashing Archie, completely covered in dry blood, smelling like shit, in only a pair of briefs that are stained with blood, piss and his own mess.

Is there a nail in his…? Oh God.

Instead of being scared and begging for his life, Archie scowls at me and tries to lunge in my direction, but a blade is through his hand, pinning it to the wall before any of us can blink.

He lets out a strangled scream as Kade sinks the blade further. The void of his eyes is the only thing we can see with his hood up and his mouth covered. "I wouldn't try that again if I were you."

Then he pulls the blade free and wipes it on Archie's chest, slicing the skin there.

"What do you want?" he sneers, wobbling. He can barely keep his balance.

He's very thin, his bones nearly protruding from his skin, and his eyes are sunken into his skull. I sometimes forget that he's locked in the basement – just along the corridor from the home studio where I spend so much time dancing.

Kade nods to the computer. "There's a file I want you to open."

Archie snorts. "Can't use your fancy gadgets now, can you, boy?"

Kade grabs his chin and squeezes. "Don't fuck with me. Open the damn file."

His rotten teeth bare. "Or what?"

"I'll put another nail in your dick."

Archie's eyes go wide at the threat, and the fight in his eyes vanishes as he tries to get free of Kade's hold. "What file?"

Kade shoves him towards the desk, and I need to cover my mouth and nose with the smell coming from him.

He snatches the back of his head and digs his fingers into his skull. "Open it."

"This file? No. Absolutely not! Are you insane?"

"Yes," Kade says blankly. "Open it."

He types slowly, because he's trembling so much that he can't coordinate his fingers properly. He fails the passcode six times before it cracks, and Kade launches him off the chair, causing him to land on the floor on his back. "We're both dead if you release those!" Archie yells, spit hanging from his mouth.

Kade points a gun at his head, not looking at him as he scrolls on the computer. "There are over five thousand files here."

Aria rises and slowly walks to stand beside him, and I follow her. I freeze behind Kade, looking sideways at Archie as he studies the new wound in his hand, rolling his jaw before he picks something from his unbrushed teeth.

A gasp draws my attention back to the computer, and I see Kade scrolling through hundreds upon thousands of folders. Each one has a name, and when he clicks on the contents of one, both Aria and I turn away and gag.

"You recorded everything," he says, scrolling through more folders and clicking random files. I want to slap Archie when I see an image pop up of himself with a girl who looks not a day over sixteen. In the same folder, there's a clip where Bernadette joins in.

I feel sick. These people are twisted.

There are so many files. Evidence of their crimes. Like they've created their own diary of the times they've had. Some have long captions describing their victim's bodies, and the way they screamed for help.

Kade stops scrolling and opens Cassie's file. "Why do you have a folder on your—" He pauses, narrowing his eyes at the screen, then glares at Archie in disgust. "You fucked your own daughter?"

Archie spits at him, uncaring. "She was a good girl."

Kade huffs at the ridiculous comment then nonchalantly says, "I was the one who killed her."

Archie's smile falls. "I'm aware."

Kade cocks the gun and presses it to his forehead. "She was an annoyance. I didn't even need to think before pulling the trigger. She was just like her mother and irritated me like you do."

Rage fills Archie's face. "You're lucky your baby girl is dead, or I would've made a file for her."

I punch him across the face without thinking at the same time Kade does, and although my knuckles sting, I put as much force into it as possible as I throw my fist at his face a second time, knocking him on his side. Kade boots him in the ribs as my nails score down Archie's cheek.

Kade pulls me away from him as I scream bloody murder. "You piece of shit!"

"Stop. I'll make it hurt," Kade whispers into my ear. "I promise."

Stepping back on heavy breaths, I shake the pain in my fist out and enjoy the burn searing across my knuckles as he wipes blood from his lip.

"I understand now why my wife was so interested in you. Feisty girl. I like it."

"Stop talking," Kade snaps, hitting the butt of his gun into Archie's head and knocking him into a semi-conscious state. "Fucker never knows when to keep his mouth shut."

"There's a folder named Sebastian Prince," Aria says. "And one for you." She wipes tears from under her eyes and moves closer to the screen. When she clicks on Kade's folder, she gasps and pulls away, covering her mouth on a loud sob. "Oh God. What did they do to you?"

I catch a glimpse of a naked Kade, unconscious and coated in blood, surrounded by dead bodies, before he shuts it off. "I think it's time for you both to leave." He nods to a guard. "Take them to their rooms and make sure they stay there."

"What the fuck is wrong with them?" Aria yells as her chest

shakes. "They are sick and insane!" Then she grabs the gun Kade had set on the desk and points it at Archie's head. "You monster!"

"You like what we did with him?" He laughs groggily, semi-awake. "Your daughter is next."

Since she has no idea how to shoot, she throws the gun at Archie and hits him in the face. His nose bleeds all over her polished floor, but she ignores it and turns to her son. "This is what you've been going through? I knew they were abusive, but those images?"

Kade snorts. "If you think that one glimpse was bad, then you have no idea."

He gestures to one of his team. "I want you to send this file to every organisation in our system, and send it to all the police stations, news stations, TV stations, CIA, MI5, even the fucking army. You name it, everyone. And make sure it's known who they came from. There's no pushing this shit aside. The Sawyers' standing in the underworld is about to be blown sky-high."

Archie's eyes widen. He's speechless.

I watch the man type on a laptop, giving Kade one more look. "Are you sure, sir? Your file alone will criminalise you."

"No," I say, moving forward. "Kade. Don't send yours."

"I'm in hundreds of those folders, Stacey. Who do you think killed them all?"

He blanks me when I try to take his hand, and he glares at the man with the laptop. "When I give an order, don't question it. Send. The fucking. File."

He types on the computer, and within a few minutes, it's done. The incriminating files have been sent, and nothing will ever be the same.

I worry my lip. "Kade."

"Don't cry." He takes my face and wipes a lone tear from my cheek. "Stay here. I can't focus when you're around, and I *need* to focus. Do you understand?"

I nod, and he presses a soft kiss to my forehead. "I'm going to make the world a safer place for you. Let me do this."

Everything cracks inside me, and I release a sob. "Okay," I croak as he pulls away from me.

When he opens the door, yanking Archie alongside him by the

only ear he has left, Lu is standing at the threshold, completely confused. "Um... What's going on?"

"Dad's dead," he says bluntly, and her eyes go wide. "Comfort your best friend, Stacey. Don't follow me."

He did that on purpose.

Luciella stares at her mother, then at me with furrowed brows. "What is he talking about?"

"Lock the fucking door."

Lu scoffs and folds her arms. "What? No. You can't keep us here."

Kade glares over his shoulder before the door closes, and a guard locks it.

"Kade!"

The images in his file keep flashing behind my eyes. He's been so abused, so brutalised by these people, I kind of want him to let loose his demons and destroy everyone.

But I also don't want him to get hurt. Really hurt. Whatever comes from these files, Kade will be a wanted man for hundreds of murders.

It was forced though. He was drugged and attacked and made to do all those bad things. Will the law think the same? Will the world of social media know he's innocent now everything is leaked?

I cross my arms to keep them from trembling, my heart thudding in my chest as I listen to Aria explain to Luciella that Tobias was found dead. Her daughter is in disbelief, but Aria plays the clip of the reporter for her.

Luciella frowns at the screen then wipes her eyes and shakes her head. "I refuse to believe he's dead until we see his body."

Aria lowers her head. "I think we should prepare for the worst, sweetheart."

"Dad isn't dead," she says firmly.

I move over to the window and see Kade, holding his gun in one hand, dragging Archie by the ankle across the grass and dropping him there. He scratches the side of his head with the barrel of the weapon then kicks Archie in the face, knocking the man on his back. Then he points to where there's a tree swing next to the water on the manor's grounds. It's at the start of the forest that stretches for miles. He tells the guard beside him something, and the person runs back inside.

Kade walks around Archie, circling him like a lion stalking its prey, and if he didn't have on the material covering his mouth, I know I'd see his lips moving. He's probably teasing the disgusting man about how pathetic he looks.

He kicks him between the legs, and Archie throws his head back on a yell and tries to kick him away.

Kade shoots him in his good foot. There's no way he'll be able to run.

The person comes running back out with a torch and a tripod, and Kade grabs Archie's foot again and drags him towards the woods. He drops him at the tree swing then lets his bag down beside Archie, opening it while the guy with the torch sets up the tripod.

Then he fixes what I assume is a phone to it, positions the torch so it's on Archie and Kade, then gives the thumbs up as he runs back into the manor, leaving his boss to stalk around his new target.

The screen comes to life on the main computer, and I gasp when every single one of the screens lining one wall turns on, showing Kade and Archie.

He's live-streaming this to the world.

32

STACEY

Kade isn't recognisable. He's concealed his identity, which is a relief.

Luciella pulls her phone out and shows us the same live feed playing on her screen. "What is he doing?"

Even his guards are frowning at the screens.

He looks evil, his eyes filled with death. A killer. Dark and dangerous as he swings a hammer at Archie's face and knocks him to the side. He chuckles deeply, and it's a haunting echo in the room as Aria and Luciella stand beside me.

On the screens, Kade tosses aside the hammer and pulls the blade from the holster on his thigh, grabbing Archie by the hair and bringing his bleeding face to the recording. His terror takes over the screens.

"Tell them who you are," Kade demands, not even trying to hide his voice. "Tell them who your wife is."

"Fuck you," he seethes, and Kade drags the blade down the side of his face, making him scream in pain and try to get out of his hold. He fails miserably.

"Everyone will see," Kade continues, yanking his head back and pressing the blade to his throat. "They'll know you fucked your own daughter, abused children and even your own wife. Did she know you were drugging her as well as your little test subjects?"

"Fuck you," Archie says again with less fight.

"By the end of this, you'll be a wanted man. Tell the world who the fuck you are." The blade is pressed to his throat hard enough to make beads of blood well up, and Archie whimpers as he pisses himself.

"Ar-Archie Sawyer," he stutters. "My name is... is... is Archie Sawyer."

"And your wife?"

"Bernadette Sawyer. Head of Police Scotland and... and..." He chokes and attempts to get free from Kade's hold. "It was all her idea. I fucking swear it."

"What was?"

"She wanted your father," he says, choking on his own slobber. "We watched him for years, and then we watched you. You were twelve."

Jesus.

"I already know I was fucking twelve. I saw all the surveillance photos."

"That's when we first got the idea," he says, gasping for air as more crimson spills from the blade.

"Idea for what?" Kade asks, tightening his grip on Archie's hair and making him wince.

"To use you. You looked like your father, and he was untouchable for us."

Aria covers her mouth, and Luciella scowls at the screen. "What the fuck?" she snaps.

"When she finally got you to our place, pretending she'd help with your father's case, she slipped you something to make you pass out. I had no idea she wanted you for sexual reasons." He licks his teeth like the vile man he is. "I can't say it wasn't enjoyable though."

Kade has had enough. He pulls a grenade from his bag, and his eyes stare into the camera. "Watch your husband die, Bernadette."

My eyes widen as he grabs Archie's jaw and pries it open, his gloved fingers curling around his top and bottom teeth and separating them with force. His gums split first, and blood pisses from his mouth, then the bones crack at his jaw, so it's wide enough for Kade to jam the grenade into his mouth.

Luciella turns away, grimacing. "I can't watch this."

The fact that I can watch it and feel no remorse or even a touch of sadness for the monster speaks volumes as to who I am now. Before, I'd have been mortified and felt ill. I'd have been gagging into a bag and calling Kade vile.

But they're the vile ones.

Archie's eyes are filled with panic and agonising pain, but for once, I want Kade to keep going. I think Aria does too, but at the same time, she doesn't want to watch her son do this.

It's live for the entire world to see.

Aria turns to a guard. "Unlock that damn door."

"No can do, ma'am."

"I own this house," she replies, her patience non-existent. "My stepson just died, the man I love might be dead, my husband is living in a hotel room and my son is in the middle of slaughtering someone on my lawn. I will not stand here and do *nothing*. Open the door before I fire you."

He stands taller. "No."

Everyone turns when a shot is fired, and on the screen, Archie clenches his teeth over the deadly metal of the grenade as Kade shoots him in the kneecaps. His sadistic laugh echoes around the room as Archie falls to the grass. It should cause shivers to go up my spine and make me as horrified as his family, but I'm proud of him.

Archie has abused him since he was a teenager, causing unimaginable pain that'll stay with him forever. He has nightmares about everything that happened while he was with that horrible family, but I think what that man did to him has impacted his psyche the most.

Archie silently begs for mercy, the grenade still lodged in his mouth.

"This man and his wife are responsible for years upon years of corruption and death..."

Kade speaks to the camera, and my heart stutters at the silvery-blue eyes blazing right at me. He starts reeling off names. The dead and the taken. Children and their ages. Who pays who and the connections Bernadette has that keep her on her pedestal.

"In the file I've sent out, you'll see twenty-eight locations all over the world. Those organisations hold over two thousand missing children and adults. Act fast. Dispatch every unit you can to rescue them."

He mentions four prime ministers, two presidents and various other world leaders who have their hands in the underworld. He talks about the files that have been released worldwide to every news station, law-enforcement organisation and social-media platform, explaining how everyone else can access them too, if they dare to look.

He knees Archie under his chin, knocking him on his back, the grenade somehow still in place.

"I was nineteen when they first abused me. I was threatened to do things or my family would be targeted. I was trained to kill mercilessly and fuck like a monster, and they ruined my life in the process. My name is Kade Mitchell, son of Tobias Mitchell, and I will not be fucking silent anymore."

My mouth opens with a gasp. Aria releases a rushed breath, and Luciella closes her eyes and turns away.

He just told the world who he is. In the middle of committing a murder.

"Jason McElroy was my brother, and he died protecting my girlfriend at the hands of Bernadette Sawyer."

I can't control myself – I fall against the wall and slide down it, hugging my knees as I keep watching.

"If you look at my file, you'll see what they turned me into. I was *twelve* when she first started watching me. She waited for just the right moment to approach me, and I was dumb enough to buy into her bullshit."

He pulls off his face covering, showing the thick scar from his mouth all the way down to his chest. He grits his teeth, letting out a dirty laugh.

He looks demonic, satanic, like he has no humanity left.

"My file tells the rest of my story."

A tear slips down my cheek, but I don't wipe it away. I look up at the guard. "Please unlock the door. I need to stop him before he criminalises himself even more."

"Please," Aria begs the man, helping me to my feet. "Please."

Luciella stands beside us. "We want to help him."

He hesitates then looks at his colleague, who nods once, his eyes sliding shut.

But before he can unlock it, Kade says, "Let's see you get yourself out of this, Bernadette. And if I find out my dad is really dead, you better hide, because nothing will stop me from breaking every bone in your body."

People wince around us as Kade pulls a blade longer than his forearm out of one of the bags and, with a completely blank expression, cuts off Archie's hand.

The sawing motion he uses means it doesn't detach right away, and we can hear the monstrous man screeching both through the screen and from outside like an animal being slaughtered. Blood gushes everywhere, even hitting the phone recording it all.

The door is unlocked, but I freeze at the threshold when Aria yells, "No!"

My eyes find the screen again, just as Kade pulls the ring on the grenade and kicks Archie in the chest. He starts walking backwards as he spins it on his middle finger. "Die, you little bitch," Kade taunts as he hides behind a large tree trunk. "I'll make sure your beast of a wife sees you in hell pretty soon."

Archie's eyes go wide, and the recording ends just as the explosion flashes, a roar of something like thunder following right after.

The eruption shakes the windows, the lights flickering, and then it's done. Over.

We all get to the window, relieved to see Kade returning, unscathed from the grenade exploding in Archie's mouth. He walks towards the manor, but his steps are slow, his head bowing further and further with every footfall. He drops to an unstable knee then struggles to get back up, and when he does, he only takes a few more steps before going down again.

I'm out of the manor and sprinting across the grounds before Aria can yell his name.

I fall to my knees in front of him and take his face in both of my hands. There are pieces of flesh all over his clothes and face from either shooting or cutting or blowing up Archie. His eyes are on me as I stare at him, but he's looking right through me.

"It's me," I say softly. "It's me."

He seems to breathe for the first time in hours.

"They're loud," he says, fighting the excessive blinks, his right eye twitching. "So damn loud, Freckles."

I nod, knowing that the version of him that thirsted for revenge and pain and blood has gone to sleep in his mind, and the voices are taking over. The ones that mock him and make him freak out. I've no idea what they're saying right now, but Kade screws his eyes shut and drops his head to my shoulder, wrapping his strong arms around me.

After Archie's murder was just live-streamed to who knows how many TV screens, the police are most likely on their way here.

I bite my lip to hold in a whimper as Kade digs his fingers into my skin. "I'm tired, Stacey."

"I know," I reply, rubbing my hand up and down his back. "Do you want to go to your room?"

His team is starting to circle us, everyone silent as Kade cuddles into me on the grass, both of us on our knees. Aria and Luciella hold each other, and when Kade lifts his head from my shoulder, his eyes go from left to right, taking them all in.

"I fucked up," he slurs at them. "You're free to go home. No one needs to stay."

Most of them had no idea what Kade had been through. They must've thought he was just a rebellious kid who wanted revenge on someone who'd wronged him. They were paid to guard, to debunk, to hack and to fight, and now they know.

I can see the respect they have for him.

None of them move to leave; they just lower their heads, showing their unmoving loyalty.

Kade looks exhausted as he glances at them all then at me. "I'm sorry."

"Don't be." I kiss his forehead despite the blood, and it makes him slowly close his eyes for a moment. "Do you want to go to your room?"

He nods. "Yeah."

I reach for his gloved hand, and he lets me take it, lacing our fingers. I help him up with the aid of two of his guys, and we lead him into the manor.

He stops beside his mum. "We don't believe Dad is dead until we see proof."

Lu hugs him. "I said the same thing. You need to sleep."

Aria also agrees. "Yes, sweetheart." She brushes her fingers through his hair as Lu pulls away, pushing his hood down. "Go shower and sleep. I'll have breakfast ready in the morning."

Aria tells Luciella to go to sleep too. "Go. I'll have the mess cleared."

The glaze in her eyes tells a thousand stories, all of them ending in heartbreak.

We all know there won't be any breakfast in the morning.

Kade doesn't speak on the way to his room, but he does stagger a few times, and I'm certain he's going to seize again as he drops to his knees and vomits on his staircase.

As soon as we get to his room, he falls against the closed door. "I fucked up."

"It's okay. Where are your meds?"

He points to the drawer next to his bed. "I fucked up," he says again. "They're coming for me. Please run."

I make sure he gets the right dosage, then he swallows a benzodiazepine, something new that was prescribed to help calm him during what they assume to be schizophrenic episodes.

I turn the TV on to a music channel, hoping the songs will

drown out the voices for him. "medicine" by onte plays.

A few minutes pass of him breathing and watching me get clean clothes ready. "You should leave," he says. "If you're caught with me, they'll arrest you too."

"I'm not leaving you," I say, slipping into the bathroom to turn on the shower. "Come on."

The tears don't start until I'm stripping him of his clothing, and he keeps apologising to me for everything. He thinks he keeps blacking out. He can't control anything. He doesn't know what to do. He doesn't want to die.

He wants us to be together but has no idea how, especially now.

I help him into the shower, and he pulls me in. Warm water cascades over us from two different shower heads, and my dress is quickly soaked. I move wet hair from my face and grab a sponge, cleaning off the evidence from Kade's body.

His muscles pull taut at the touch of the sponge, and he flinches a little. He's still tanned from being all over the world, with far more scars than he had a year ago, and his hands are trembling as he tries to take the sponge from me.

I let him take it, and after he pulls the straps of my dress down, one at a time, it pools at my feet. He uses the sponge on my body, and my eyes burn. I know this could be one of the last times we ever spend together.

I'm not wearing a bra, and he doesn't try to remove my panties, because this isn't a time to have sex.

"I love you," I tell him, my voice cracking. "No matter what happens next, please know that."

The sponge stops at my neck, then it drops at our feet beside my dress as his finger traces my pulse. "I bruised you. Where I grabbed your neck earlier, you have a bruise. I hurt you. I knew I was doing it, but I couldn't stop, even though my mind was yelling at me to let go of you. I never wanted to hurt you."

"I think you dissociated," I say.

He stares at me, then it's like his gaze goes right through me as he continues to move his hands around my body against the water. It's not sexual but as if he's memorising my every inch. "My meds are supposed to help. They're not."

"You've not been taking them that long. They're not going to work right away. But the fact that you're taking them is a good thing. It takes a lot for someone to ask for help. I'm proud of you."

"After what I just did? Have I not made you afraid of me?"

I shake my head. "No. Archie deserved it."

He chuckles deeply and shakes his head, his eyes so, so tired. "My little sadist."

"Maybe," I say, smiling as I slide my arms around his neck and bring our bodies together. "I'm glad you overheard me telling your mother we should stay friends when we were in the office."

"Yeah?"

I nod and fight more tears. "I missed your touch."

"I was terrified I'd hurt you, so I held back, especially when I kissed you in bed," Kade replies, resting his forehead on mine. "But when I heard you saying you'd just be my friend, I couldn't think of a worse sentence to hear." He nudges my nose with his. "I had to reclaim what was always mine, even if I blacked out for most of it."

I laugh and rest my head against his chest. "I was always yours."

He strokes my hair. The water's starting to get a little cooler. "I didn't finish inside you, did I?"

"No. You were inside all of three minutes."

"Shameful."

I roll my eyes.

"But I didn't wear a condom."

"No, you didn't."

"I'm clean. I got tested when we arrived back here." Then his hand freezes. "I assume you're not on birth control?"

I shake my head.

"Tell my mum to get a nurse in. They'll give you a Plan B, just in case. You don't want to have a kid with someone who'll be an absent father."

I narrow my eyes at him. "You wouldn't be."

He rests his back against the cold tiles, one of which is cracked, still shaky on his feet. "You know I will be, Stacey. I just killed a man live, outed over half of the underworld and exposed Bernadette's empire. If I'm not arrested, I can assure you there'll be a number of pissed-off people hunting for me."

His speech is less slurred, and I guess the benzo is working, since some light is returning to his eyes.

"We could go to the safe house you were thinking of sending the dogs to. We'll leave now."

He stares down at me. "I wouldn't let you ruin your life by being on the run with me forever. Whoever gets me first, I'll surrender."

I step back, putting minimal distance between us. "You can't just give up. There's a chance your dad is still out there, and Bernadette is still alive."

He shrugs. "I have no plan, Stacey. This, right now, was my last resort to stop her. I wasn't supposed to kill Archie. I had nothing set up for after."

"What about me?"

He smirks weakly. "Go dance and live your life. Think of me when you do, and picture me sitting in the crowd, right at the very front."

"You say that like you'll be dead."

"I might be," he replies, not a trace of sarcasm in his voice. "I'd be better off dead."

I shake my head. "You're not giving up, Kade."

He tilts his head. "I have no hope, can't you see? I need medication to stop people talking in my head and seeing shit that isn't real. I black out, dissociate, and I hurt you. Everything is tainted. Even sex to me is violent. I just fucking killed a man while live-streaming because I'm too impulsive. I wasn't supposed to kill him; I just wanted the piece of shit to expose himself and his wife's empire. And then I declared war on *thousands* of people. Any idea how to get me out of that? I'm all ears."

"People live every day with blackouts, dissociation and seizures. Your condition *is* manageable."

"According to people who've never experienced it. Do you have any idea what it's like to have no control? To have your free will and consent taken away from you?"

I lower my eyes. "Yes."

Silence – so much silence fills the bathroom as I remember Chris and everything he did to me.

Kade swears to himself. "I'm sorry. I wasn't thinking. I'm sorry."

I turn away to hide my tears, the tremble in my chin, the way my chest is rising and falling. Kade pulls my back to his chest and presses a kiss to my pulse.

"You're stronger than I am. To go through what you did and still put others before you... I envy your strength. I want a normal life with you, but that's not on the cards for me. If I could run and guarantee your safety, I'd run."

"I want you to run with me," I say, sniffling. "Please."

He kisses my shoulder gently. "I love you, Freckles."

My teeth chatter. "I love you too."

Silence follows, and we stay under the water until it turns cold – then we brush our teeth and don clean clothes. I'm wearing a black top of his that nearly reaches my knees, and he's in a pair of sweats.

We sit on the balcony while he smokes. I stay in his lap, my back to his chest, as we stare at the stars. All the while, Aria is running around with Kade's team, cleaning up the mess he left behind.

After he sighs and flicks his cigarette over the balcony, he wraps his arms around me and lifts me up. "Let's go," he says, kissing my cheek as he carries me to bed. "I want to sleep with my girl in my arms one last time."

33

KADE

A fist drives into my gut, and I'm knocked to the floor, a cough spluttering from my throat.

I clench my teeth and try to push up, but someone kicks my head with steel toe cap boots, and I'm down again.

"When I tell you to do something, I expect you to do it. No questions, no refusals, no fucking cheek."

On my hands and knees, I spit blood on the ground, my entire body shaking from the beating from her four guards. I try to stand, but a heavy boot lands on my back and shoves me back to the concrete floor of the basement. "Stay down, boy."

Bernadette's shoes click as she walks around me, the sound vibrating in my ears. Her husband smacks her ass as she scrapes her nails across his chest. "How do we make him compliant?"

"He's a troublesome teenager," Archie says, pressing his boot harder

into my back. As much as I want to stand up and punch the fucking smirk off his face, they injected me with something that's making me weak. "We could add more of an incentive. Maybe a family member?"

She clicks her tongue, and the boot vanishes from my back. I push up, falling and stumbling, until I grab hold of a pipe attached to the wall and stand tall. But with the damage to my leg, I struggle. The red-haired she-devil grins at me. "You have an order, Kade." She points a manicured finger at the man strapped to a chair in front of me. "Kill him."

I shake my head. I'm not going to kill someone. The fuck is wrong with these people?

One minute, I was looking at a file she'd retrieved from her office about my dad's case, another appeal that's due to fall through, then something sharp stabbed at my neck, and when I tried to grab Bernadette and push her off me, Archie shoved a knife in my leg. Some time after that, I woke up beside Bernadette with a condom still attached to my dick, and I've been trapped here ever since, hating my own skin.

They're evil rapists.

She stresses each word as she walks towards me. "Kill. Him. Now."

"Fuck you," I manage, gripping the pipe to stay standing as my leg spasms. I notice the stab wound has started bleeding again.

Bernadette narrows her eyes then looks at her husband. "Archie, bring up the live footage we have of little Luciella Mitchell."

All the blood drains from my face when he shoves an iPad at me, the screen showing my sister walking with Stacey and Tylar in the mall. They're laughing together, but my gaze is on the face I see every time I close my eyes.

It's been two months since I left her and beat up my brother. I haven't spoken to either of them.

How can I be so mad at her yet hang on to every memory of us like they'd keep me alive?

"Kill him, or I'll make sure your sister and her friends don't make it home."

I gulp, picturing Stacey fighting for her life while my sister and Tylar lie dead beside her. Even the thought of them being harmed has me seeing red flashes behind my vision.

She obviously doesn't know Stacey is my ex, or she'd threaten me with her instead.

"Leave my sister alone," I grit out.

"Then kill him." She places a gun in my hand, and the metal is so heavy, so fucking deadly, that I drop it as if it's burned my skin.

She chuckles and looks at her husband. "It seems our pet doesn't know how to fire a gun."

"Such a pathetic little boy."

I want to rip this motherfucker apart, but my mind is blanking, and I can barely stand with how much the room is spinning. I don't know why they're doing this. Or why me.

My attempt to escape this morning was pointless. Archie stuck another needle in me and pulled my trousers down while I clawed at the carpet until I passed out.

For the first time in a long time, I want my dad. I want Ewan and Jason to find me. Even my mum. If they knew where I was, they'd fight tooth and nail until they saved me. But with security everywhere, and how brutal they are, I doubt I'll be rescued anytime soon.

Will they be looking for me? What if Stacey needs me? Who will walk and train my dogs?

I stand back, glancing at the terrified man with black tape over his mouth and eyes. He's shaking in the chair, his hands bound behind him. "How?"

"You can choose," she says, crossing her arms and popping her hip out as her shoe taps the ground. "But hurry up. We have a party tonight, and I need your wound tended to before you meet your first client."

I frown. "First... client?"

She smiles, the lines around her eyes crinkling. "You're going to make me a lot of money, Kade. And if you're a good boy and do as you're told, your family will be safe." She shrugs. "I'll even give you a percentage, so you'll have some benefits."

Archie shows me the screen again, and my heart stops when I see two guys in suits following my sister and her friends through the mall. "The next shop they go into, they won't come back out."

"What the fuck is wrong with you?"

Bernadette's eyes darken, her fake smile slipping. I sigh and close my eyes, then look at the thrashing man in the chair again.

Each limping step I take towards him has bile rising in my throat, and I want to apologise, to say I don't want to do this, but I need to keep those

I love safe. When I wrap my hands around his throat, making him still in shock, I shut my eyes for a second.

I apply pressure but nowhere near enough to kill him. I'm shaking.

Archie chuckles like I'm pathetic. "Tighter."

"Press your thumb into his carotid artery," Bernadette says beside me. "And tighten your grip. Make sure he can't breathe."

I do as she says, and the man struggles for breath, doing everything he can to fight against me. But he's tied up and useless. He can't see me – can't see the look in my eyes as I strangle him.

"That's it. The blood flowing to his head is reducing," Bernadette says, moving closer. "The brain is being starved of oxygen and nutrients." She walks around the man, ruffling his hair as I keep my eyes on my hands. "Watch his skin change colour, Kade. Watch how you rob him of breath, of life. Take him away from his daughter, his wife and the future they should be having."

A tear slips down my cheek, but as I loosen my hold to let him breathe, I think about Stacey and what could happen to her and my sister if I don't do this.

I push forward hard enough to make the chair tip back, and Bernadette moves out of the way before the man crashes to the ground, likely dislocating both his shoulders. I lock my elbows and put all my weight into my hands as I climb over him and press as hard as I can against his neck.

"I'm sorry," I say, spit falling from my mouth as I keep repeating those two words. "I'm sorry. I'm sorry. I'm sorry."

He's not conscious anymore. He never will be again.

"Good boy – that's it. Hold him there until he's dead. He'll be the first of many." Bernadette crouches beside me and grabs my chin, making me look at her as I keep all my weight on his neck. "You are mine. You'll always be mine. You will follow every order, and you'll come to my bed whenever I say."

"No," I croak.

"You have no choice."

She licks a tear from my cheek then takes my earlobe between her teeth. I want to vomit everywhere when she slips the strap of her dress down, her other hand sliding up my thigh as I take this man's life.

"You can stop now. He's dead." Bernadette's voice changes to something

softer, and there's a slight panic in her tone as she presses against my chest. "Kade. Stop."

My hands grip tighter around the man's slim throat.

"Kade!"

I blink, and Stacey is beneath me.

"Fuck." I throw myself back, releasing her throat, and climb off the bed, putting as much distance between us as possible until I knock into the wall. I screw my eyes shut and slide down it. "Fuck. I'm sorry. I thought you were... Fuck. He was..."

There's no knife wound in my leg. I'm not in the basement. Bernadette isn't here.

Stacey coughs and holds her throat, which I had my murderous, dirty fucking hands around. "It's okay. You were having a nightmare. It's okay, Kade."

My eyes fly open. "It's not fucking okay! I just strangled you. What if I didn't wake up?"

"You were sleeping." She gets to her knees on the mattress and reaches a hand out to me. "Please. Come back to bed. I'm fine, I promise."

I drop my head between my parted knees and try to calm my breathing, my heartbeat, to banish the fucking image of her struggling beneath me. If I hadn't woken up, if I hadn't snapped out of it, I could have really hurt her – killed her.

"Hey," she says, lowering herself in front of me. She's still wearing my top, and it's so large on her small frame that it slides off her shoulder. "Look, I don't have any new marks. You didn't do it hard enough for that."

I open my eyes. She's pulling her hair over her shoulder to show me her throat. "I promise you didn't hurt me. Come back to bed. Please."

She's right, there aren't any new marks – but the ones from earlier are there. I was gripping her so tightly...

"You're the last person in the world I'd ever want to hurt," I tell her, taking her hand and pulling her towards me. "But I'm scared I do. Why won't you run from me?"

"The only way you could hurt me is if you pull away from me again." She straddles my lap as I straighten my legs out, her arms wrapping around my shoulders. "I don't know why we're still here or why the police haven't blown into the manor, but we should make the most of every minute we have." Her forehead settles against mine. "Come back to bed."

"There's no doubt I'll be arrested," I say, glancing outside through the balcony door, which is slightly ajar. "It's been a few hours. I probably won't have long until they come for me."

I snake my arms around her, and I wish I could stay here forever. With my girl in my arms. "I'll go willingly. What will you do? I can get Barry to take you and the dogs out of the country."

She shakes her head. "I'm staying here. We'll wait for you."

"I'll be in for life, Stacey."

"Then so am I," she replies, chewing her lip, and I want to take it between my teeth as I palm her ass and pull her closer to me. "If you try to push me away or force me to leave you, I'll hate you."

"So you'd still be my girlfriend even if I'm in prison forever? That's not a life you deserve."

She grins, her cheeks going a lovely shade of red. "I don't believe we've crossed that bridge."

I pull a brown strand from between her lips. "What bridge?"

"The one where you ask me to be your girlfriend again."

Something swells in my chest, and the tip of my nose touches hers. "Will you?"

In all honesty, the title "girlfriend" seems minuscule and immature considering what we have. I'm madly in love with her, and she's made it clear she feels the exact same way. If we were in a different position, and I wasn't about to be arrested and taken away from this life, then I'd marry her and put an army of kids in her.

I'd burn the universe just to see her smile at me the way she is now.

She's my entire fucking world.

"Your girlfriend?" Her nose scrunches as she fake grimaces. "Ew. No."

She squeals as I shove her so she's on her back and I'm on top of her. I cup her cheek in a palm as her legs wrap around my waist then swipe my thumb over her plump lips.

"So much patience for someone who left you at your lowest point. I'm a scumbag who doesn't deserve you."

She rolls her eyes and bites my thumb, sucking it into her mouth and making my dick twitch. Against my thumb, she says, "You can make it all up to me by coming back to bed and watching *The Greatest Showman* with me."

My lips curl as she releases my thumb, and I slide it down her chin. "As long as you promise to sing, Freckles."

She giggles and presses a gentle kiss to my lips, smiling as she replies, "Every single lyric."

As soon as her mouth is on mine, I let it all out in the way my lips smooth over hers, the way I kiss her like I haven't in a long, long time – I take her bottom lip between my teeth and suck and bite, and let my hand travel from her hip to her knee, squeezing.

There are no voices, so I listen to her breaths and focus on how soft her body feels beneath me.

She gasps into my mouth, and I take that opportunity to taste her tongue with my own, tilting my head to slant our mouths.

Her legs tighten around me, and I grow harder against her.

"Is this okay?" she whispers against my mouth as she rocks her hips, rubbing herself up and down the underside of my cock.

I nod and thrust my tongue into her mouth again, tasting her as my hands dive into her hair, tugging her head to the side so I can suck on her pulse. I feel it fluttering on my tongue as I rock my hips into her.

Through my sweats and her underwear, I can feel how warm she is, and I know if I drop my hand between us, her panties will be soaked.

I pull back and stare down at her, taking in the way her dark hair covers the floor, her dilated pupils, how her chest rises and falls. My hands splay on her torso, under my top, and her back arches as I grab her tits and caress them while rubbing my dick against her covered pussy.

"I don't understand."

She tilts her head, breathless and spasming as I pinch her

nipples. "Understand what?"

"With all the shit I've done, how I'm lucky enough to have you."

She blushes, gasping as I drop one hand between her legs, feeling her drenched panties as I shove aside the material and sink two fingers into her pussy. She crushes my fingers, tight and fucking mine.

I bite my lip and wonder if I should just fuck her, no condom, no birth control, with such a slim chance of being here if she falls pregnant. Is it bad that I'd happily tell her not to bother with the morning-after pill today? I was inside her already – it's not impossible for her to fall pregnant from that alone.

Her back arches as I fuck her faster, and she moves her hips in time with my fingers, grabbing at the hand that's groping her breast.

I already know what she looks like with a small bump. I know the way her tits feel when they're heavy, how much she glows and the way she smiles talking about becoming parents. I could fill her with my cum, impregnate her and she'd be tethered to me forever.

Fuck, I shouldn't be thinking about any of this. Not in our position.

"Why are you staring at me?"

I blink, three times, and I calm my breathing when my fingers twitch on her breast. My fingers have stopped inside her, and I must've zoned out. I kiss her and curl my fingers, swallowing her moan as her cunt flutters around me.

"Tell me you're mine," I demand against her mouth, sinking my teeth into her bottom lip. "Tell me you'll always be mine, Freckles."

"I'm yours," she moans. "Always."

I look at her, keeping myself steady as I blink unevenly again. "I won't hurt you."

"I trust you," she says, and it's more than enough to slow my rampant thoughts.

I don't want my body to fail me when we're having such a close-connected moment. My arms tremble. If I seize right now, I'll be so pissed.

I flinch as she moves her hand to my sweats but nod when she silently asks for permission to touch me. She reaches inside them, and as soon as her hand wraps around me, my eyes fall shut. I add a third finger as my thumb rubs her clit, eliciting another moan against my mouth.

"You aren't on birth control, and I don't have any condoms." I hate myself as I thrust into her hand anyway. "But I want to feel your cunt wrapped around my cock."

Her throat works on a gulp. "I'm going to take the morning-after pill. Just... fuck me."

"That's probably the most irresponsible thing you've ever said."

She shrugs. "Do you disagree?"

"No."

I groan and grit my teeth as she swipes precum from the tip with her thumb. "But I don't know if I can."

Annoyingly, she lets go of my dick and grabs my wrist, stopping me from fingering her. She's not mad at all; her voice is soft. "We said we'd go slow, so just go slow until you're comfortable. Even if that means waiting until we're in a private room after your sentencing."

"That sounds like a terrible idea. Go back to being irresponsible and let me fuck you."

Stacey slaps my chest. "You're insatiable, do you know that?"

"Only for you." I force out the words and focus on her. "I've been attracted to you since we were fifteen. But why is it that even after all the times we've been together, I want more? It makes me crazy. *You* make me crazy."

She smiles, and it touches her pale green eyes. "Does it also make you want to take me to the bed? The floor is hurting my back."

I laugh a real laugh and get up to my knees, tucking my dick away and taking her hand before throwing her on the bed. "Put the damn movie on and stop distracting me." She reaches for her phone, and I shake my head. "Not yet. Reality can wait."

Her voice is quiet as she looks down. "Reality scares me."

"Then ignore it with me. Hide with me until reality slams through that door and takes me away from you."

She fights against her tears as she nods. "Okay."

I press my forefingers to the corners of her lips and drag them upwards to make her look like she's smiling. "Stop being miserable."

She slaps my hands away and kisses me, then my cheek then lies down. "I'll try."

The movie starts, and Stacey rests her head on my chest, probably hearing how hard my heart is beating, getting faster when she hums to the lyrics.

"I thought about these moments," I tell her. "When I was forced to do things, my mind always brought me back to the times we've spent together."

"What times?"

"I mean, my favourite was when you did your fancy little dance then sucked me off."

Snorting, she covers her mouth. "You mean the time you nearly passed out?"

"Yes," I reply, narrowing my eyes at her head. "It was my first blowjob – give me a break."

I had to take a breather and fell against the wall to stop myself from passing out. To say I was an embarrassment when I was younger is an understatement.

"My favourite was when I realised I was falling in love with you," she says, taking a deep breath. "We were driving to London, and I kept staring at you and thinking how lucky I was. I knew then that you had my heart. When we split, I missed you. I always came to your room when you were away and cried in your bed."

My chest tightens, both with rage at myself for leaving and the idea I affected her so much after the split. I thought she didn't care – that she was living her life like we didn't happen.

"Can we look in the box?"

She tilts her head. "Yeah."

I move to the edge of the bed and lean over, pulling the small box out. I unlock it and give it to her. "I know you saw everything sprawled over my floor, but let's look properly. I kept everything."

She cries as he picks up the dress. "She would've looked like a princess in this."

I suck in a breath and hold it as I nod. "Like her mother."

"I hate this," she says, picking up the five rules I made. "Did you ever break the fifth?"

"I did."

She smiles weakly. "I'm sorry."

"Don't. The rules are void and mean nothing. They shouldn't exist. Keep looking."

"The little booties too." She wipes tears from her cheeks and looks at me when she sees the paper rose I made from a napkin. She wore it behind her ear the entire way home from a dinner we had in Edinburgh. "You really never stopped loving me?"

I shake my head. "Not once. I watched you all the time."

She keeps going through the box, sobbing when she sees a hospital letter about entering the second trimester. The pictures I drew. Pictures she took. The top she left here that I never returned.

She glances at me as she shuts the box. "You watched me?"

"Probably more than I should have. I, um, beat the shit out of every guy who went near you."

She sits up straighter, mouth open. "You did?"

I shrug and put the box under the bed again. "You were mine."

"I thought you hated me, and I was single."

I drag her to my side, squeezing her ass and hiking her leg over me. "I never want to hear that come out of your mouth again. Regardless of where we were in our relationship, I would have slaughtered an entire room filled with people just to get one minute of this with you."

"Cute – but a little scary. No more killing."

I chuckle. "I have one more person to kill, then I promise never to lift a gun or use my hands for anything but pleasuring you for the rest of my life."

"How do you plan on killing Bernadette if you're arrested?"

She looks up at me, and I wink. "I always find a way."

I play with her hair as she settles her head back on my chest, and it's probably the first time we've watched the entire movie without her belting out the words.

She tells me she loves me, and I say it back. She tells me that we're going to have loads of babies, and I tell her we'll start right away, but she thinks I'm joking. She tells me that she'll find a way for me to see the dogs while in prison, and I tell her they'll keep her warm in bed since I won't be able to.

Stacey falls asleep on me, and I close my eyes, not sleeping, just enjoying the time I have with her.

I shouldn't have said my name and showed my face in that video of Archie, but in my reality, I don't get a happy ending. All I can hope for is that I take the fall for everything and my team, Stacey, and my family walk away.

They could all be arrested too.

I swallow the lump threatening to strangle me, staring outside at the sun rising behind the hills and treetops. I hear voices, probably my team still cleaning up my mess.

Then a knock sounds at the door, followed by one of the manor's workers announcing that breakfast is ready.

34

KADE

Stacey takes my hand in hers as we descend the staircase, and she squeals as I lift her at the bottom and press her to the wall to steal a quick kiss.

She's wearing my cotton shorts and another black top that's far too big for her, her hair pulled into a ponytail, fresh-faced from our shower. She smells like me after using my shower gel. She smells like mine. She *is* mine.

The quick kiss turns heavy as her hands tug at my hair and my tongue moves with hers, and then she's grinding against me, making me hard again as a moan slips from her lips.

Fuck, I'll never get enough of her.

"Stop," she says, laughing. "Someone will see."

I shake my head. "No one comes to my side of the manor."

"Cameras, Kade. Cameras."

I huff and let her down. "After breakfast, we're finishing what we started."

She raises a brow as I take her hand in mine, revelling in the energy zipping between our palms. "Really?"

I hum a *yes* and drag her down the lobby before wrapping my arms around her from behind and walking forward a few steps. I whisper against her ear, "Unprotected. Hard. Fast. Slow. Long. Gentle." I bite her neck and make her shriek. "*Loud.* Take your pick, Freckles."

She elbows me and settles her head against my arm as we walk to the main dining area. I stop when I hear multiple voices, and Stacey halts her steps too. We frown at each other before walking into the kitchen.

Mum has made a huge breakfast spread. The dining table is filled with different foods: cereal, fry-up food, tea and coffee jugs, and loads of different kinds of omelette.

Dez and Tylar are here, sitting beside Luciella, Mum and Ewan. He must've saw the footage and decided to leave the hotel he was staying at. He needed space, to breathe and think.

Ewan's arm is resting on the back of Mum's chair as they talk about one of the times we all went to America. My mother offers food to the workers. Two guys from my team are sitting at the table too, devouring fruit.

Mum looks up at me and rises from her chair. "Oh, you're both awake. Come. Eat."

Tylar jumps up and pulls Stacey into her arms, hugging her and asking if she's okay, and Dez nods at me, patting my shoulder. "It seems we have a lot to catch up on."

"A lot is an understatement."

"Fuck, man."

"Language," Mum scolds Dez. "Don't let your toast get cold, Desmond."

We settle into seats, my hand on Stacey's thigh as we dig in, filling our starved bodies until we're both full, thankful I'm able to hold food down now. I pour her a tea, and she passes me a bowl of grapes while Dez and Tylar tell us about their travels.

I welcome the subject, since no one wants to talk about the

elephant in the room, or the fact that I ripped Archie's body to shreds last night and his remains are in buckets in the walk-in freezer. I'll use them to taunt Bernadette.

Stacey rests her head on my shoulder and smiles at Luciella as she returns the smile despite the circumstances, glancing between the two of us. I guess she isn't pissed at us. Not that I give a fuck.

Ewan whispers into Mum's ear, and she lowers her head. "Kade, have you seen the news or... looked outside the main gates?"

I shake my head, my brows knitting together. "No. We've kept our phones off, and I haven't checked my laptop. I kind of expected a raid hours ago."

"There will be no raid, I don't think."

I tilt my head in confusion, and Ewan grabs the remote, turning on the TV that's on the wall opposite the table. I rise from my chair when I see the crowds at our main gate – members of the public all standing with linked arms, placards held aloft, chanting.

"What the fuck?"

Stacey leans her elbows on the table, watching it with me.

Luciella speaks next. "There's been a huge social-media outpouring – reports of corruption in both the police and armed forces from the file you released. Victims have come forward and given evidence. Everyone is backing you, Kade. And I mean *everyone.*"

She pulls up something on her phone and shows me.

"Four petitions to have whatever charges they hand you dropped and Bernadette removed from her position. Over ten million on one petition alone in just six hours."

I gulp, looking around the room, then at my mother. "But I'm not the good guy."

She smiles weakly. "Yes you are, sweetheart."

I should have been arrested hours ago, but by the looks of the screen, an army is preventing the police from entering.

I walk over to the patio door and open it, and low and behold, two helicopters are hovering over the manor. One is Barry's, and the other belongs to the police. But I also notice the chain of people, loads of them, stretching around the manor grounds, only stopping at the loch.

Stacey stays beside me as we follow my mum out into the front entranceway of the manor, into the grounds, and down the cobbled path to the locked gates.

The sight has me frowning.

Justice for Jason!

Justice for Tobias!

End corrupt cops!

Arrest the real murderers!

Keep Kade free!

We stand with the Mitchells!

The signs and banners are dotted around the crowds outside the gates, hundreds of them – when they spot me, they all cheer and clap, and I forget how to breathe. Stacey covers her mouth on a happy sob, but I'm blank, staring at them all. All these strangers are here for me.

"Is that her?" one asks the other, staring at Stacey. "Wow, she's so beautiful in real life."

Am I in an alternate reality, or am I fucking dreaming?

There are people of almost every age in the crowd too – from teenagers all the way up to seventy plus – all rallying around the manor to protect me.

A hand slides into mine, and I curl my fingers. "I think we should turn our phones on."

"Yeah. That's probably a good idea."

A police car is sitting in the distance – a news reporter too, filming the scene.

Some of the people have their phones out, recording me and Stacey and calling out to my mother. I pull Stacey to me when I feel an overwhelming crack in my gut – I need her to be here with me. Her back to my chest, I wrap my arms around her and rest my chin on her shoulder.

We watch everyone fight for us.

Luciella comes up beside me. "I'm proud of you, Kade."

"Why?"

She glances up at me, her eyes watering. "You survived."

She cuddles into our mum, and Stacey kisses my cheek. "I told you, didn't I? You aren't alone. Not now, not ever."

I kiss her back then wave to the ones grabbing the walls for dear life while the guards warn them to stay on their side of the fence. The bodyguards are wearing bulletproof vests and helmets, guns strapped to them, all lining the perimeter to make sure no one gets in.

As happy and supportive as they all seem to be, someone in among them could be a spy or against us. Maybe even part of one of the empires I threw under the bus.

If I'm marked for assassination, they could all be in danger.

"Come on," I say to my mum and Stacey, Luciella trailing behind. I lower my head and turn around. My heart is racing, and my blinking is getting a little out of control. I think it's the overwhelming feeling of having so much support. "I need to get back inside before they see me freak out."

Stacey is watching me as I walk back in. She looks tired, so I take her hand and direct us back to my side of the manor while thanking my mum for breakfast.

One of my men stops me before we enter my wing.

"Sir, Barry has passed on word that Bernadette Sawyer is being transferred to a hospital in Edinburgh. She's due to be discharged in the next few days. He's also keeping an eye on police reports, and so far, they only want you taken in for questioning. No listed charges."

Fuck, what does this mean?

"Right. Anything else?"

"Sebastian Prince will be arriving in two days. He couldn't cancel his wedding to come sooner."

I was hoping he'd be here as soon as possible.

He straightens and smooths down his tie. "He'll also bring a squad of soldiers to keep the manor protected. You have... quite the bounty on your head, sir."

I expected as much. "Thanks. Tell Barry to stay where he is. Why are you and everyone else still here? I told you all that you could leave."

"As much as we appreciate the offer, our loyalty remains with you, Mr Mitchell. No one's left; nor do they plan to. We will protect you and your family and" – he glances at Stacey – "your partner with our lives."

I pat his shoulder. "Thank you. Really."

He lowers his head to Stacey then strides towards the dining room. I blow out a breath and take Stacey's hand again.

"No charges?"

"No idea. It might take a while to show on the system, or it's all being conducted under the table like the corrupted pricks they are."

"Where are we going?" she asks.

"I'm taking you to bed."

"Oh."

I glance at her – she's blushing. "To nap," I clarify.

"Can we do that?" she questions, trying to keep up with me. "Shouldn't we figure out what happens next?"

"I think the crowds outside have bought us a few more hours. Hopefully the Russians arrive before trouble does, and Barry will keep track of Bernadette and the police movement. We're going to bed, and we're going to cuddle and sleep and talk then cuddle some more."

"We can watch *The Greatest Showman* again and eat junk food all day?"

I laugh and let go of her hand, grabbing the backs of her thighs and lifting her as we reach my spiral staircase. She wraps her legs around my waist, slides her arms around my neck and grins down at me. We make it four more steps before I'm pressing her against the railing and kissing her until our mouths hurt.

"If that's what you want," I whisper against her lips.

35

KADE

I wake to Stacey's cunt strangling my cock.

She's facing me, both of us on our sides, her moaning against my ear as we rock into each other, her breathing unsteady, mine non-existent.

I open my eyes one at a time, blinded by the sun beaming through the window. Stacey's writhing beside me. My top is pushed up over her breasts, one of which has teeth marks imprinted on it. I must've done that in my sleep.

Hard, pink nipples. Flush skin. Parted lips letting noises I haven't heard in so long slip out as she grinds against my dick and whimpers.

Looking down between us, I watch her take more of me, barely accommodating my size as her walls crush around me, her soaked pussy stretching with each short thrust as she takes another inch.

My balls tighten as I push into her more, and her moan makes me even harder. I grab her ass, dig my fingers into her skin and fuck into her in a way that drags a deep, breathy groan from me.

It takes me a second to figure out if this is another dream, me blacking out and picturing Stacey, or if this is actually happening.

"Kade," she whisper-moans, and I close my eyes and sigh in relief. "Deeper."

This is real. She never speaks in my dreams. My girl really is in my bed, her hair wild on my pillow; I can feel her soft skin beneath my palm as it explores her body.

Her hip. Waist. The way her thigh hikes over me as she fucks me.

She whimpers as I dig my fingers into her flesh and pull her closer to me, making me go deeper, hitting a spot within her that has her moaning into my ear.

This is Stacey. My girl. It's really Stacey I'm fucking while half-asleep with my shorts and boxers tangled at my ankles.

I should stop this. She's not on birth control. I could get her pregnant. Why am I still thrusting into her?

Her leg hooks at my side, and she absently rolls her hips to take more of me. I can hear and feel how wet she is; it's dripping onto the mattress between us.

The tip of my nose slides against her cheek, bringing my mouth to hers but we only breathe against each other. Stacey's eyes flutter beneath her lids, and it hits me that she's still asleep.

I groan, and against everything in me desperate to wake her, drag her on top and demand she rides me, I hold Stacey's hip to stop her moving against my dick while she's not fully conscious. I stop thrusting too, as much as I want to push her onto her back and fuck every last breath out of her. Sweat coating my skin, I move strands of brown hair from her face. Her dancing green eyes open gradually, and she smiles at me sleepily then looks down between us.

She licks her lips, the blush on her cheeks a deeper shade of red that spreads to her throat. "Oh."

I don't miss the way her pussy tightens around me; her inner walls are crushing me like a wet fist. She looks up at me, pupils dilated, then flinches as I run the tip of my thumb over her nipple. My chest rises and falls. "We sleep-fucked," I say.

"Should we..." She chews her bottom lip as I keep circling her nipple, needing to put it in my mouth. "Is this okay for you?"

I pulse inside her as she rolls her hips back ever so slightly, my swollen tip still inside, making me want to grab her and shove myself deep to the hilt and hear her scream. But it's not the tightness of her around me or the weird feeling in my chest that I've woken up with her making my heart race.

I don't want to hurt her.

"Can we keep going?" I ask her. "I want your cum all over my cock."

She nods enthusiastically and pulls her top completely off. "Make me come, Kade."

Fuck. "I need you to be patient with me," I say as I roll her back, my cock still inside her as I settle between her legs. "I don't want to hurt you."

"Keep your eyes open," she says, gasps falling between us as she lifts her hips, taking nearly all of me. "If it helps, don't close your eyes. Watch what you do to me, under your terms."

Doing as she says, I keep my eyes on her as I tense my jaw and pull back so just the head stays in. And when I thrust forward, fully sheathing myself in her warm cunt, a deep growl leaves my throat.

It hasn't felt like this in so long.

Yeah, I was inside her when I had her bent over the desk, but I was zoned out and barely holding on to reality. This, here, with her, is real. It's as real as it's going to get for us.

Each movement draws sounds from her I'll never forget, and my spine tingles, a warmth already building at the base, my balls tight, my head throbbing as she chokes my dick.

Stacey kisses me, grabbing my face and slamming her mouth on mine, and it's the only time I allow my eyes to shut, tasting her, feeling her, fucking the girl I'm in love with as she pants and whimpers into my mouth.

I swallow each moan I pull from her, hammering harder, knocking her up the bed until her head hits the headboard. I hold her hip with one hand and grab the metal frame with the other, using it to go harder, deeper, her pupils fully dilated as her mouth drops open, and her eyes glaze over.

I press my hand to the pillow beside her head, leaning up to watch her. "I love you," I pant. "I'm going to prove to you every day for the rest of my life just how much I love you."

She shoves my chest, and I roll onto my back so she's on top. "I love you too – so, so much." She goes onto her knees, my swollen head still between her slit. "Take control, Kade. Fuck me. Show me I'm yours."

I grab her hips and drive my own up, making her head tip back on a loud moan. Then I palm her tits, bring her nipples to my mouth and suck harshly as I fuck up into her wet pussy.

Her fingers tug at the hair at my nape, and my head rises so she can kiss me. Grabbing her waist, I move her on me, controlling how hard and fast she grinds her sweet cunt on my cock.

"I'm..." She shakes in my hold. "Oh God. Kade!"

I circle her clit, and Stacey moans into my mouth as her orgasm smacks into her. I ride her through it, feeling her pleasure; how soaked she becomes as she pulses and throbs. I pinch and circle, dragging my lips to her throat and sucking on the flesh there.

She comes down from her high, panting, but I'm not done. I'm going to make her explode again, then I'm going to fill her with every fucking drop of me.

I slam her down on my dick, and she screams.

"Fuck. I missed this."

"This?" she barely says as she grabs at my shoulders with each powerful thrust.

Her back hits the mattress then, and I turn her around so her chest is against the bed and sink into her pussy from behind. "Being in control. You. Us. All of it."

Her whimper mixes with a pleasurable scream as I keep going, and the tightness in my chest comes back at watching my girl fall apart once more, gripping the sheets. It only takes me a few more pumps before I sink in once more and fill her with my cum.

I drop onto the mattress once my dick stops throbbing inside her, and she rolls onto her back beside me. She pants, both of us looking at the ceiling. "Even when we're asleep, we want each other."

"Yeah," I reply, turning my head to watch her – the way her tits move with each breath, her freckled skin, the smoothness of every inch of her. "You still take it like a good girl."

She rolls her eyes, but her smile stays there. "Shut up."

I want to memorise everything about her, from the softness of her skin to the dimples as she smiles to the sound of her laugh when we banter with each other. I want to hear her voice telling me forever that she loves me, and that it will never change.

It's a miracle the police haven't barged into my room and cuffed me yet. I'm still in bed, with my girl, and I'm going to make every second of it count.

Starting by getting everything out in the open.

I turn onto my side. She shivers as I circle her nipple.

"I know I apologised already, but I was fucked up at the time. I should have heard your side with that video, but I also should've realised you were being abused at home. I would have killed him, you know? The first sign of him hurting you, I would have killed him."

She rests her hand on my cheek, and it feels like I've not been touched this way for years. "I lied and kept Chris hidden, so you wouldn't have been able to know what was happening at home."

"I should have noticed," I say, and I feel my eyes burning. I shut them and sink my face against her palm. "Things could've been so different if I'd just noticed."

"Stop blaming yourself," she replies and moves so she's straddling me. Naked still, may I add. "From this moment on, no more apologies. We heal. Together."

"What about yesterday?"

She tilts her head in confusion, and I slide my hands to the apex of her thighs. "What do you mean?" she asks, her voice quiet.

"I strangled you."

"No one said this would be easy. Some days are going to be really hard, but at least we'll have each other."

Well, if hard days involve attempted murder on your other half, then okay. "What have I ever done to deserve someone as amazing as you?"

"Keep being romantic."

I huff and sit up. "I'm not romantic."

She giggles and grabs me, bringing our lips together. "You are. Now kiss me until we forget our own names."

I inhale smoke into my lungs and watch my team patrolling the perimeter. The crowd is still circling the manor, but the police helicopter is now gone, and two drones bypass my balcony.

"Chokehold" by Sleep Token is playing from somewhere out on the grounds. Or maybe it's the crowd. They're always playing music or chanting.

My phone is still off, the battery dead, so I've not heard anything else, nor do I know the damage I did to the underworld. Beyond killing someone live, I've really put my foot in it with the elite and leaders of the dark side of crime. It's just a matter of time before it all bites me in the ass, but I'll make sure I'm ready. If the police can be held at bay for a few more days, then I'll put an end to all of this.

I don't have Bernadette holding my family over my head anymore, and I don't need to worry about my dad's position in the institution or him being a target, so she has no idea what the fuck is coming to her.

Her failsafe is gone – everything destabilised.

She created me; the havoc that runs wild in my head, and I'll unleash it all on her.

Arms wrap around me from behind, and Stacey presses a kiss to my back then between my shoulder blades, and rests her cheek against my bare skin. "You have a lot of new tattoos."

"So do you," I say, offering her the cigarette.

She takes it and yelps when I drag her down on the seat with me. We're both naked – my cum is leaking out of her, but when I use my fingers to shove it back into her, she slaps my arm. "Stop that. You covered up all the tattoos you got for me. I feel like 'accidentally' kneeing you in the balls."

I chuckle and lace our fingers together, filling my lungs with nicotine when she passes the cigarette back. "I kept one."

I show her our initials in the exact same design she has on her back. She kisses there too and grins up at me. "Your balls are safe."

Stacey stands, and I look up at her like she's my own guardian angel. "Put your phone on charge so we can turn it on. We should really know the damage that's been done."

I huff. "If there's only a report to bring me in for questioning, then I should be more worried about being assassinated in my home. Will you go to the safe house?"

I know the answer, but she crosses her arms and gives me a deadly look, so I opt for dragging her back to bed and hearing her moan my name as I drive my cock into her again, and again, and again.

36

STACEY

Waking to an empty bed has my heart stopping. I panic until I see Kade's cigarettes and motorbike key on the bedside unit, his phone charging next to the digital clock. It's just after three in the morning.

I pull the duvet off and check the bathroom, bare feet slapping on the floor as I open the balcony doors and glance down at the grounds, only seeing security. The pool house is dark, and I can hear the water of the loch crashing into the small pier in the rain.

Dressed in Kade's boxers and top, I slip out of the room and down the spiral steps, stopping when I see two guards. The young one moves in front of me.

"Where are you going?"

For a second, I'm confused. I point my thumb over my shoulder. "Kade wasn't in bed."

"Boss had an urgent meeting, though I think it's over now."

"Where is he then?"

"I don't know, but I'll escort you." He lowers his head and gestures with his hand for me to continue, following me and leaving the other guard. "Mr Mitchell has instructed us to ensure the safety of all members of the household. We're... not allowed to let you walk around alone."

I screw my nose up, but I walk anyway. I get it. The manor and everything within its walls are at high risk, and he's only doing his job.

He's tall, blonde and wears a fitted black suit, a gun strapped to his chest. He walks beside me as I hunt the manor for Kade. His earpiece keeps falling out, he yawns twice and he looks like he hasn't slept in days.

To make conversation, I ask, "How long have you worked for Kade?"

He thinks for a second as we take the main stairs. "He wouldn't let me work for him until I was old enough, so only a few months. I'm shadowing the other guards just now."

"How did you meet him?" I ask. The more I look at him, the more I see a kid holding a gun.

"I was taken from my family and forced into a camp when I was eleven. Mr Mitchell raided the place and saved me when I was sixteen. He slaughtered everyone involved when he found out about the training regime."

I blanch, unblinking. "Oh."

"At least I know how to shoot." His shoulder rises. "My parents keep asking to meet him and thank him, but he's not one for being praised."

So he looks like a kid but probably has more experience with that gun than most. "How old are you now?"

"I just turned eighteen. There are five of us here from the same camp – same age. He saved us all. Him and Barry. But we aren't allowed to fight until we've had more training." He taps his gun. "This is for show. I'm only to use it if absolutely necessary."

I smile at him, and he visibly relaxes.

Even when going through hell, he still tried to help others.

Could I love Kade Mitchell more?

For it being the middle of the night, the manor is quite busy. Preparations are being made for the arrival of Base and his army. Aria has been on a roll with her workers, setting up all the spare rooms, even now, with Ewan handing out food to the crowd at the gate. Some of them are in tents, some sleeping in their cars, but loads of them are drinking around a huge fire and playing music.

Kade is grateful, but I know having to ensure the safety of them all is coming with a lot of extra stress.

Social media has been terrifying. My followers have risen, messages have been flooding my inbox and reporters have reached out to do exclusive interviews with *the love of Kade Mitchell's life.*

He laughed at that one.

I turned my notifications off last night, and the thought of looking again now makes my stomach twist.

But on the plus side, the outpouring of love and support for Kade has been insane. Everyone knows his story; everyone knows what he went through and what he did, yet they stand by him. They understand why he killed Archie and the countless others. They want Bernadette to be next, and even set up another petition for him to live-stream her death as well.

The world loves Kade.

Maybe that's why the police still haven't forced their way through the blockade.

Base's wedding has also been all over the news. He's yet another victim of Bernadette and the underworld's abuse, and his family isn't the slightest bit happy.

Luciella is nervous to see him, and as much as she held in her tears when she learned Base is now married, I can tell it's ripping her apart. Between that, and losing Jason and her father, I'm not quite sure how much more my best friend can take before she flips. She holds a lot in and can sometimes seem emotionless, but she really does have a heart of gold.

One that's slowly shattering.

We discover Kade is working out, and as the young man walks me to the basement, he tells me he'll stand at the top of the steps and stay on guard.

"Change" by Deftones plays from the home gym, only growing louder the closer I get. The corridor is barely lit, but I have no idea where the light is, and I can hear metal clanking from his weights.

The basement is huge. It spans nearly the entire length of the manor. I pass by a wine cellar, the walk-in freezer that makes me shiver at the thought of Archie's remains stored inside and the studio.

To the left of the studio, one of the doors is ajar, a beam of light illuminating the dust in the corridor. I push open the door, and the intense drum and guitars fill my ears, metal banging on metal as Kade lies on a weight bench, pushing a bar above his chest.

Freezing in the doorway, I openly gawk at my boyfriend as if I've never checked him out before.

His muscles tense up with each rep, sweat glistening on his skin, his hair wet. The tattoos and scars make him look terrifying as he clanks down the bar and sits up, intense blue eyes clashing with mine in the mirror.

His face is red from exercising, and I drag my gaze from his face, all the way down his body. He's been working hard the last few weeks and is already building his muscles.

He only has shorts on.

I gulp. "You weren't there when I woke up." I hug myself. "I got worried."

He wipes his face and hair with a towel and tosses it aside then turns the music low. "I had a meeting and needed to clear my head after it." He's breathless, his voice strained from his workout. "I should have told you."

Going by how swollen his muscles are, he's been working out for hours.

"It's fine. I'm just paranoid these days." I drop my hands to my sides. "Are you okay?"

Apart from the murmur of the music, there's a long silence. Kade flattens his lips, elbows on his knees as he looks for his words. "I don't know how to answer that, in all honesty."

I close the door behind me and walk to him, and when I stop near him, he takes my hand and pulls me closer, so I'm standing between his legs. My hands rest on his shoulders, and I massage the tension away with my fingers and give him a warm smile.

He looks up at me, sweat coating his face, his dark brows and long lashes making his eyes more defined.

My fingers slide up and brush through his wet hair. "What's going on in here?" I ask, tapping his temple. "Tell me, so you aren't doing this alone."

He shakes his head. "You don't need to know. We should move on from the past."

My voice lowers to a whisper. "I don't think either of us is ready to move on."

He sighs and presses his forehead to my stomach, holding behind my knees. "My head's just fucked. I'm trying to figure out how to save everyone at the same time as staying alive. I'm starting to run out of plans. Bernadette is better protected than royalty, and I have a huge bounty on me. It's only a matter of time before they come for me."

"You haven't been arrested yet either."

"No," he says. "I'm starting to believe I won't be."

I should be relieved, but that means there's going to be a war soon.

"Are you okay?" he asks me, looking up when I take a few moments to think of my reply.

"I don't think I will be for a while. It's been… constant. As much as we're in danger now, this is probably the first time I haven't had to look over my shoulder or worry about Chris coming for me. Even when I was in America, I could never be sure he wouldn't just show up one day."

"Did he always come for you?"

I tilt my head. "Mostly, yeah. Every time I went out, I'd come home to some sort of punishment. It only got worse after we got together and I started coming home later, my neck full of hickeys and all your texts on my phone."

Groaning, Kade presses his forehead to my stomach again. He has no reason to feel guilty, but I know he will. "What else did he do?" he asks, his voice muffled.

"He beat me up. Like, a lot." I gulp, trying to ignore the memories. "He forced me to go to these messed-up parties with him. He'd make me drink, take pills and sometimes—" I stop, a tear sliding down my cheek. "After he found out I had a boyfriend, he got more violent. I was terrified he was going to start raping me every night. I didn't know at the time he already was."

Kade's grip tightens behind my knees. "I wish you'd told me."

I stifle a sob lodged in my throat, and my lip trembles. "I wish I did too. I was so scared of what he'd do to you. He would've gotten even worse."

"Worse than killing our kid?" Then he winces. "Sorry, I didn't mean it to come out like that."

"You're right though. I was worried about him getting worse, but all the while he was already getting worse. He was sick. Mentally. He deluded himself into believing he loved me. I think he had this idea that he'd be able to Stockholm syndrome me."

He looks up at my face, his brows knitting together, and there's rage in his eyes. "I would have killed him sooner. If you'd told me, I would've never let you go back to that house, and I would have strangled him to death. Or kept him alive but incapacitated, so he could watch me fuck the woman he tormented, watch her marry me and give birth to my kids. I'd make him watch every fucking second that you loved me."

I have no idea why, but I smile. "I think the nails in his eyes were better. Your dad hit Barry with his foot."

He huffs out a laugh. "I knew they'd get along."

"They did. Sort of." I lower my voice. "Anyway, I've learned from my mistakes. From now on, no secrets. I promise to do better. I'll be better for you."

He kisses my hip through the material of his top. "You're everything I need and want. Don't ever change. Got it?"

I smile down at him. "Even when I complain?"

"Not everyone is perfect."

Giggling, I lean down, take his face in my hands and kiss him on the lips. It's a chaste kiss, short, but it holds so much meaning. "I love you."

Kade grins against my mouth. "You know, when you say it every hour, those three words lose their meaning."

I shake my head. "I didn't get to say them for years. They'll never lose their meaning."

"When I started working for Bernadette, I thought you hated me. I kept telling myself you did so I wouldn't approach you and put you in danger. I wanted you off her radar. But I kind of fucked that up when I picked you up from that house."

My fingers brush through his hair again. "How did you end up working for her anyway?"

"You already know the story."

"Tell me the full version, not the watered-down one. If we're going to talk about this, then please, tell me everything."

He sighs and pulls me into his lap. "Don't think any differently of me."

"Never."

As Kade tells me from the very beginning, I feel bile rising up my throat. The terror he went through is unimaginable. Bernadette lured him in, saying she wanted to help, only to groom him, turn him into a monster, and force him to kill and fuck and be their lapdog.

Tears flow down my cheeks when he tells how, one time, he was late for an assignment and Archie drugged him up so badly, he didn't wake for days, and when he did, he just knew the man had violated his teenage body.

He's shaking beneath me as he keeps going, telling me story after story. Bounty after bounty. How many people he tortured – how he tried to save as many as possible – and the number of people he had to perform for.

His words are spoken against my skin, his head buried in my shoulder, as if he's too ashamed to look me in the eye.

"How many clients did you have?" I ask, because by the sounds of it, there were loads.

"Please don't hate me," he says, lifting his head. "I don't know. Way over a hundred. You should know, she made me do shit with Base too. You might see the photos. It was only, maybe, five times."

I've already seen the proof, but I didn't want to ask him about it in case he was triggered by the memories. The amount of torture he went through, I didn't want to bring any of it up.

"You and Base are okay though?"

"Yeah." He nods. "If anything, it made us closer. We knew we had to play along to make sure you and Luciella were safe. We didn't have full sex, but he did stuff to me while I..." He pauses. "Sorry. I really don't want you to hate me."

"I could never hate you for that." Despite Kade being forced into that line of work, I have so much respect for sex workers. I've had many students who trained with me so they could apply to clubs, or webcam or gain confidence for lingerie modelling. "Did any of them ever hurt you?"

He laughs. "Yeah. I think Bernadette chose them for that exact reason. Someone actually stabbed me when I was—" He stops and groans. "I'm sorry. I know you don't want to hear any of this."

"It's okay; stop apologising. Is it helping? You talking to me about it?"

"Yeah," he replies, sighing and massaging his thumbs into my sides. "But I don't want to make you uncomfortable."

"I'm not," I say truthfully. "I want to help."

"You did help. The memories of us kept me going. I was always in subspace, reliving the times we had while stuff was happening to me. I never stopped loving you, Stacey, even when I was a dick to you. I've always been yours."

I sniff, my eyes burning. "And I'm yours." I wipe my cheeks. "What age were you when you had your first client?"

He grimaces. "Nineteen. Like a month after we split up."

"I didn't think it was possible to hate Bernadette more than I do," I hiss, raking my fingers through his hair, not bringing up the scars on his scalp. "I think I might help you kill her."

Kade laughs and snakes his arms around the small of my back, resting his forehead against my own. "Not a chance. As soon as I sort this shit with the police and find out if I'm actually getting charged, and Base arrives with his army of Russians, you're going to the safe house and taking the dogs with you."

I frown. "No. I already said I'm staying with you."

Sighing, Kade easily stands with me wrapped around him, like I'm a featherweight. "I have no idea how to explain this more clearly to you. According to Barry, I have fifty million on my head. *Fifty*. Do you know how many people are probably rounding up to attack the manor? If the other underworld assholes aren't already on their way. You staying here is out of the question."

I fold my arms, and he holds me up. "Why are you changing your mind? You were agreeing with me earlier."

"I was blinded by your pussy on my cock. I would have agreed to anything."

My eyes narrow. "That's irresponsible."

Kade turns, lowering us onto the weight bench and pushing me to lie back. "No. What's irresponsible is how many times I've been inside you while you're not on birth control. For that fact alone, you're going to the safe house."

"You're sending me away so you don't fuck me again?"

It annoys me that he's grinning, but my annoyance is extinguished as he settles on top of me, causing his top to ride up my body.

"No. I'm sending you away because if I've knocked you up, I'm not losing the two of you when they eventually come for me." He lowers his mouth to mine, softly kissing the corner of my lips and trailing down my jaw. "But seeing you dripping with my cum, knowing the probability of you falling pregnant, makes me fucking hard." He punctuates the last word by grinding against me once, and I gasp. "Even thinking about it makes me want to fuck you."

Breathless, I slide my hands up his naked chest. "Yeah?"

"Yeah. Can I fuck you now?"

I slap his chest, and he chuckles. "If you keep finishing in me, then—" I stop, my eyes widening. "Oh no. I forgot to tell your mum to get the nurse in."

Kade shrugs.

"As much as having a baby with you would be perfect, the timing is not. Can we call the nurse once you're done here?"

He sighs, rolling his eyes. "Fine, but I'm still fucking you."

As his mouth drops on mine, he turns the music up again, and Deftones echo around the home gym once more.

Kade takes his time as he strips me, and he kicks aside his own shorts until we're both naked on the weight bench. Then he drops to his knees and dives between my legs without hesitating, devouring my pussy like a starved man.

I tug at his hair as his tongue delves through my entrance, licking, tasting, sucking on my clit so hard, I moan louder than the music.

"Forever my addiction," he mutters. "I'm obsessed with everything about you." The suction on my clit grows more intense as he shoves two fingers inside and fucks me with them. "But your pussy is my fucking drug."

My body convulses under his mouth when he makes me unravel, then he climbs up my body and kisses me. I taste myself as I suck on his tongue, fisting his cock and making him whimper into my mouth as I stroke the length of him.

I'm still tender from all the sex we've been having, yet I need more – I want him inside me. Filling me.

He parts my legs wide, hooking his arm under one and hiking it to my shoulder, then slams into me so hard, the bench scrapes on the ground. His thick cock fills me, stretching me with each inch until I adjust to his length, like I haven't had him inside me repeatedly over the last couple of days.

I cry out as he relentlessly fucks me, the warmth of his body radiating against mine as his mouth sucks at my throat, right over my pulse.

His tongue swipes at my earlobe, pulling it between his teeth. "I can never get enough of you, Stacey. Even when I'm dead, I'll be haunting you, inside you while you lie in our bed, remembering all the ways I've rocked your fucking world with my cock inside this pussy."

I smile as I moan, throwing my head back as he hits a sweet spot that has my eyes rolling. He hooks his arm under my other leg, hiking both up to give him a deeper angle.

Breathlessly, I grab his chin and kiss him. "We need to be quick. Lu has been going to the studio through the night and she might walk in. She's quite sad."

Kade lets my legs drop and straightens his arms, halting the deep strokes of his cock. "I'm inside you, and you're talking about my sister being sad."

I bite my lip and try not to laugh. "Sorry."

Shaking his head, he hides his grin and dives into my throat, sucking on my skin while going slow and deep, his hands on my hips as "Cities" by Toby Mai (featuring Two Feet) begins.

"Fuck, Stacey." He pulls back to look between us as his thickness slowly pushes in and pulls out to the tip. "Your pussy sucks my cock so fucking good."

He thrusts harder. "Taking it so well," he breathes.

My legs wrap around him, and I hook my ankles under his ass to drag him deeper as his name rolls off my tongue like a lyric. "*Kade.*"

He lowers his mouth to my ear, his breaths heavy against my skin, his cock thickening as my inner walls tighten around him through another wave of euphoria.

"Is my good girl going to take every drop of my cum? Are you going to swell up with my kid and give me everything we've ever wanted? I'm going to keep fucking you until we get our miracle. Every day, every night, I'll be inside you. I want to see you fucking *dripping*, only so I can shove it back into you, my fingers deep inside your cunt."

I open my mouth to reply but only a scream comes out as I tense everywhere, my heart racing and my vision blurring as my orgasm rips through me, pulsing around his cock. He fucks me faster until he stills on a tense groan, filling me while his fingers bruise my hips.

When he collapses on top of me, my hands reach into his hair, stroking the dark strands as he pants in my ear.

"Fuck," he gasps. "Did I hurt you?"

I shake my head, unable to speak as I try to fill my lungs. Sweat clings to our skin; we're naked on the weight bench, the music still playing as the mirrors steam up.

He slides out of me, watching between my legs as he licks his lips. "I think you're making me crazy. I'll need to tell my therapist I've had the sudden urge to impregnate you."

I laugh. "He'd be mortified," I say, wincing as Kade grabs a towel and cleans up my thighs. "Does the therapist help?"

"Yeah. He's due to arrive today so we can work together in person, if he can get past the crowds outside the gate. He's been teaching me these mentally stimulating exercises and how to compartmentalise my trauma. When things get dark, I'm learning to work my mind away from the disconnection. I've been seeing him since I was young, so I trust him."

Being so focused on Kade and his downward spiral, I've barely spared a second to think about everything that happened to me. Everything I went through was packed into a little box and stowed away, waiting to be opened when the time was right. But it's really a shattering hourglass, the grains of sand representing everything we've been through, and it's close to cracking.

If talking to someone, a professional, makes Kade feel even a smidge better, then I should do the same. Maybe the weight on my shoulders will vanish – the hollow pit in my stomach threatening to break me.

Chris is dead. He can't hurt me anymore. Kade brutalised him, leaving him on the edge of death, but it was me who slit his throat. I killed my abuser. So why do I feel like he's about to pop out of the shadows and pull me under?

"Can... can I see your therapist too?"

Kade takes my hand and helps me off the bench, wrapping his arms around me with a warm smile, so our naked bodies are pressed together. "Of course. Anything you want."

"Yeah. I think I'm ready to properly talk about everything." I gulp and lace my fingers behind his neck. "I kept so many secrets, and I'm scared they're going to drown me if I don't actually... talk."

Not with him. Not with my best friends or Aria, or even Kyle, who's been calling constantly and insists on helping with whatever he can. Nora has apparently cut all ties with me, but I don't care.

I can hold my hands up and finally have my voice – be heard without the fear of rejection or backlash.

Kade kisses the tip of my nose. "I'm proud of you. I don't know if I've ever said it, but I am. You're so strong, Stacey. You've been strong enough for the both of us. Thank you."

I tilt my head. "Why are you thanking me?"

He kisses me softly. "I was an asshole, yet here you are."

Laughing, I pull away and grab my clothes, and we dress. "We have years. Let's make it up to each other until we're old."

Kade takes my hand and presses his lips to the top of it. "Years."

37

STACEY

"When did it start?"

I tilt my head, looking down at my leg, which is folded over the other, my fingers fidgeting. "When I was fourteen. My mother died, and my dad married a woman called Nora. She had two sons."

Kade's therapist hums and tips his glasses up his nose. "Had?"

"One is dead."

"And I assume that is Mr Mitchell's doing?"

My eyes flicker to the side; I'm unsure how much he knows and how corrupt he might be. "What do you mean?"

"Was he murdered?" he asks.

"Yes."

"Kade inherited many attributes from his father, but most of his *skills* were trained into him. I'm aware of these. I've been treating him since he was a boy and noticed a dramatic change in him when he was leaving his teenage years. He loves you, and has for a long time, but he had no idea how to control how he felt and sometimes it made him angry. But nowhere near the way he gets now. I know his aggression, and how deep he can fall into his own mind."

There's a pause, and he lowers his notebook. "If your abuser was the dead stepbrother, then I don't need to do the maths to know who took care of him."

For some reason, I feel comfortable talking to this man. Even though I don't know him, I blurt, "Both of us."

"Excuse me?"

"Both of us took care of him. Kade did the most, but I ended it. I had to end it."

"You should be proud of yourself then. It can take a long time for someone in your position to fight back." He notes down what we're saying. "Do you feel lost?"

I shake my head. "Even when he was here, I wasn't lost. I was scared of him, put up with his violence, but I never let him break me." I gulp down the water. "You'd think with everything he put me through, I'd be fragile and a shell, but I guess I got used to it."

For the next hour, we talk back and forth about my childhood, what school was like, when I met my friends, how I felt when I lost my parents, right up until Kade lost his brother and the terror that followed. He listens, and the more I talk, the more the words flow out my mouth. Unloading my emotions has never felt so... free.

"Do you still dance?"

"Yes, but not often for myself. I try to keep Luciella calm by dancing with her. I've been so focused on helping Kade too."

The man sets aside his notes and takes his ankle from his knee to lean forward. "You need to focus on yourself. Mr Mitchell has more than enough support. Help yourself. Love yourself. I want you to dance until you're in tears from the overload of emotions. I want you to *scream*. Write down your thoughts. Always, always put yourself first going forward. Do you understand, Miss Rhodes?"

I lower my eyes. "I'll try. I don't think I've ever put myself first, because I had no future that looked pretty. Chris robbed me of everything, and I've been zoned in on Kade to try to make sure he's okay."

"And do you have a future now?"

"Yes," I say without hesitation. "I can see us as a family, living in a house he's built, with our two dogs and children running wild in the garden. I can see myself performing during a dance show, and spending time with my two friends without feeling bad for always lying. I used to make up excuses when Chris would force me to come home."

He smiles. "I won't medicate you. I don't believe you need that kind of intervention, but I would like to see you regularly. Under the circumstances of the... manor being locked down, if I struggle to get past the crowds, then I can meet with you via video call."

"I'd like that."

"We can also do couples therapy. I think, although you are both working on your relationship, it could help."

I nod. "Anything."

"Thanks for having the courage to talk. It's the first step." He shakes my hand. "Before anyone else, love yourself, Miss Rhodes. You cannot give your all to someone if you aren't doing the same for yourself."

I nod again, trying to force down the lump in my throat. "Thank you."

When the therapist leaves, he's escorted to the gates by four guards. I watch the CCTV footage from the sitting room; the crowd moves aside to create a path for him to reach his car. I smile at all the new faces I can see.

The young man from earlier – who tells me his name is Malcolm – walks beside me as I go to the kitchen. My friends look like they've just woken, and Aria grins at me as she pulls pastries from the oven and sets them on the counter to cool.

"Dr Daniels is great. He was my therapist when I was pregnant with the twins. How did you find speaking with him?"

I slide into the seat at the breakfast bar beside Luciella and Tylar, who are eating cereal. "I felt strangely comfortable. I'm going to see him again."

Aria's eyes light up as she moves around the kitchen. This is what she's been like since we got back to the manor – constantly on the go, refusing to sit down and relax.

"How are you feeling?" I ask them. "Did you both sleep well?"

Ty nods and yawns.

Lu swallows her cereal. "I don't know. I don't think I'll know how I'm going to feel until Base is here. It's just..." Her eyes well up with tears, and she huffs. "Fucking hell. Every time I even think about him, I cry. It's annoying."

Aria rests her hand on her daughter's shoulder. "You're allowed to cry, sweetheart. You've been through a lot recently, and holding it in is worse than keeping it all bottled up."

"Thanks, Mum."

Aria dries her hands, and a guard escorts her out of the kitchen to go find Ewan. Luciella sighs and takes another mouthful of cereal, and Tylar yawns again, very audibly.

Ty leans her cheek in her palm, her face freckled from all the sun she got while travelling with Dez. "Out of curiosity, since we haven't broached the subject of anything since I got home, what the hell happened while I was gone?"

For some reason, Lu and I burst out laughing. "Where do we even start?" I say as Lu says, "Just the usual family drama."

Tylar snorts and glances at me. "You killed your brother?"

I bite my lip and nod. "I did."

"Yikes. I should say I'm shocked, but it's been a wild week. You didn't even tell us about him. I only knew about Kyle."

"You met him once. He was the guy at the studio you thought was my Tinder date."

"Oh, Jesus. I should have hit him in the nuts."

"Did I ever meet him?" Lu asks, her brow furrowing.

My eyes widen as I remember what Chris said to Tobias in the basement. "Oh, I think you actually had sex with him."

She pales, her eyes wide as Ty gasps. "What?"

I pull out my phone and click on his social-media page, zooming into the picture of him and Kyle and showing her it. "He said he slept with you. Or was he lying?"

She grimaces. "He was terrible in bed. He started crying when he came."

We all wince. "Ew."

Then we burst out in more laughter, and it only causes a chain reaction of leg slapping, snorting and us holding on to each other as tears roll down our cheeks.

"Wait, wait, wait," Ty says, and we all catch our breaths. "Were you fucking Base while telling us to stay away from your brother and his friends? That's so hypocritical!"

"No, no, no. I swear. We didn't sleep together until he came to Russia to get me. We... did do something before that. Two somethings."

We wait for her to elaborate.

She sighs. "They were in the moment, and even I'm mortified with myself." Luciella looks around then lowers her voice. "I had a threesome with Base, but we didn't touch, because I said it was off limits. He was inside the guy while the guy was inside me."

Well, that's...

Ty raises her hand. "Hold up. You had a threesome and didn't tell us? When?"

She hums. "A few years ago."

"What was the other thing?"

"We touched each other in my dorm room, and then he stormed out because I said it was a mistake."

"Shit," Tylar blurts. "I'm a little mad at you for pushing me away from Dez. But I forgive you. Can we all go watch a movie and wait on... What is Base now? I honestly feel like I've come home to a fairy tale."

Luciella wipes away her tears of laughter. "A billionaire crime lord basically. He made a deal to marry a mafia princess and take over from his grandfather. I think he was the Don or something. I can't be mad at him, because it was to save me. I just... miss him."

"And Kade runs his own organisation..."

"Yep," I reply.

Tylar shakes her head. "And Dez lives with his grandma. How come I landed the normal one?"

We all break into laughter again.

After we finish up breakfast, I text Kade to ask where he is, but the bodyguard by my side tells me he's in room four on the east wing.

The manor is a lot busier now that everyone is awake, and I smile at multiple staff as I make my way to the other side of the building. I go to open the door of room four and freeze when I see the plaque hanging from it.

It's Jason's room from when he was a kid. There's a superhero flying above his name and a "Keep Out" sign just below it.

I bite my lip and push the door open to see Kade sitting on the small sofa in front of the TV, his game paused. He doesn't look at me as I close the door or make my way towards him. He's staring at the screen, catatonic, not blinking – emotionless.

I sit down beside him, placing my hand over his, and let out a breath as his fingers curl into mine, his throat working on a deep swallow.

We stay like this for what feels like forever, a comfortable silence, as he slowly lets the controller slide from his other hand and drop to the floor.

"He used to sneak me in here when I was a kid. My mum sent me to bed for school, and Jason always made sure we spent the night gaming at least once a week. When I was grounded, he'd offer to babysit me while our parents went out, and we'd have this place filled with pillow forts and snacks. Luciella sometimes joined too."

I tighten my fingers around his hand as my heart twists in my chest. "He was a good brother."

"The best," he says, still not blinking. "He taught me how to drive. Took me skiing in France. Bought me the newest release of every game I liked. And he was the first person I told when I kissed you. He was hyping me up to kiss you again then celebrated when I told him you were my girlfriend. I told him before anyone else that you were pregnant too."

"You did?"

He nods and deeply exhales. "Fuck, I miss him, Stacey. I wish I'd had time to say I was sorry for kicking him out of my life. He was drinking himself to death and abusing drugs, and I wasn't there to help him."

"But you did apologise to him."

He looks at me, his eyes bloodshot. "When?"

"You ran away at the lodge, and we found you in the forest. Jason was the one who snapped you out of the spiral. You were apologising to him for everything. He forgave you."

Kade doesn't seem to remember that part; his brows are knitting together, but he no longer appears spaced out. "I... I didn't know that." He drops his face into his hand. "There's so much going on in my head. We can't track down my dad, and I'm starting to think he's actually dead. I'm just so fucking tired. I... There are detectives on their way here, and I've given them clearance to come through."

"You'll speak to them?"

He shrugs. "Yeah, I don't know what other choice I have. Barry said they just want to talk to me. There still aren't any charges on my record. He said it's squeaky clean. Even the offences from when I was younger have been scrubbed – Bernadette's erased every little detail."

There's a knock at the door, and a voice says, "Sir, Sebastian Prince is here."

38

KADE

My skin prickles with discomfort as Ewan and my mum follow behind me and Stacey with a few of my men in tow. Each step feels like I'm walking to my death, even though I'm just going outside to welcome my best friend and speak to detectives.

There's a riot in my head, and I have no idea how to make it stop.

Anxiety has always been an annoying factor in my life. Right now, my heart is racing, and I feel like I can't take a proper breath. I feel sick. My vision is hazy, and I'm certain I'm crushing Stacey's hand in mine. I want nothing more than to drag her to the bedroom and hide there. We could fuck and sleep then fuck some more. I might even cry into her lap just to get this fucking weird feeling out of my system.

It feels like Bernadette is sitting on my chest, laughing in my face as she crushes me, and no matter how much I silently scream at her to get off, she doesn't.

She's driving a knife into my heart and twisting. Any moment, she might appear and ruin my life even more. My therapist says that the fear of losing what I have is my trauma response, and instead of fighting my attacks, I need to breathe through them – not focus on my heartbeat or how harshly I'm breathing.

I count my steps instead. One, two, three, four. One, two, three, four. I even count Stacey's – hers are quicker as she tries to match my pace.

She's probably sore – all we've been doing is fucking recently. I have years to make up for, and making love to my girl, lying with her in my arms or even just having her look at me keeps me grounded.

My body's still alive from her interrupting my workout. I might even drag her into a room now and beg her to take my mind off the way I'm feeling by letting me drop to my knees and eat her pussy.

I make a mental note to smash Base in the balls for pulling me away from my safe place with Stacey, shut off from the world, and having me stand at the entrance of the manor while his red Aston Martin takes fucking years to drive up the cobbled path, followed by his army of Russian soldiers.

The dogs are waiting patiently too, sitting by my side.

I try not to look at the police car trailing behind. What if they're lying and the only reason there's no charges and nothing in my file is because this is all a ruse? They could easily put me in handcuffs and take me away from my unit.

How the fuck do I protect what's left of my family if they take me away? Fuck. Fuck, fuck, fuck.

I watch as the detectives climb out of the patrol car first in fitted suits, standing aside so the packed coaches and SUVs can park up. I knew Base had a lot of backup, but this many people? Where the fuck is my mother going to have them sleep?

The crowds are cheering, chanting my name in the distance as they all notice me, hand in hand with my girlfriend. As much as I appreciate the support, they need to leave. If anyone comes for me, they'll all be in danger.

There are teenagers out there, for fuck's sake.

"Are you okay?" Stacey whispers against my ear as she rises onto her tiptoes.

I'm guessing my worries are written all over my face. She can probably feel how sweaty my palm is. Even the dogs are fussing around me, nudging me with their noses.

I attempt a nod when Stacey stares at me, and she squeezes my hand. "I'm here."

"I know," I reply quietly, lifting her hand to kiss her knuckles, and the crowd squeals so loud Stacey blushes.

Someone wolf-whistles from afar, and I rein in my fierce possessiveness. I want them to stop looking at my girl. As beautiful and amazing as she is, she's mine – I'm the one she loves.

Fuck, my heart is hammering in my chest, and all I can think about is hiding, smoking a joint to take the edge off the pending panic attack clawing at my insides.

I can't control them. The frequency. The intensity. Sometimes I'll be sitting doing nothing and I'm hit with a wave of worry about something that shouldn't even concern me. It's fucking annoying. Stacey is asleep most of the time it happens. I'll sit on the balcony with my head between my legs and count down from fifty. Then I'll pace, smoke, punch something, and when it starts to fade, I'll wrap myself around Stacey and pray we make it out of all of this.

I've only had one seizure in the last few days.

I have a shot of happiness with Stacey. If I can survive the underworld's backlash, then I could have a happy ending with my girl, our dogs and any children I've already knocked her up with.

Feeling like I'm in control of my body now that I'm free from Bernadette's clutches is what I want. What I need. But all I have are a fuck tonne of unwanted thoughts and an impulsive need to *hurt* someone.

"You're shaking," Stacey says, stroking her thumb over my hand. Her voice is low enough that only I can hear, and as everyone starts to get out of the cars, she adds, "Name three of your favourite things."

My eyes flicker to her; I know what she's doing. My therapist gets me to do the exact same thing. I made Stacey do it after Crawley's warehouse. My dad even got me to name things once when I was freaking out on the phone about kissing Stacey.

My heart twists at the memory. I was such a dick to him instead of being a good son. Even when I told him to basically die, he still loved me. He escaped a highly secured institution to save me, to save Stacey when she failed to show up for her visitation.

And now I have no idea where the fuck he is or if he's still breathing.

"Three," Stacey pushes as Russians flood the driveway.

I gulp. "You."

She's smiling in my peripheral vision. "Two more?"

I look down at Hopper and Milo, both watching me with their tongues out, lightly panting. "The dogs," I say, picturing her dancing around the room with them, cuddling them in bed, her screaming as she was dragged across the wet, muddy grass when Milo ran for a rabbit.

"And my family." I glance at my mother and Ewan. My sister's probably hiding in the manor.

By not focusing on my breathing or my heartbeat, I realise they've calmed somewhat, and I don't feel like I'm slowly drowning. I sigh so deeply, my stepdad glances at me with a flat-lipped expression – a silent, *Are you okay?*

I nod.

Someone blows out a puff of air beside me. "Shit, that's a lot of people."

I turn to see Dez – Tylar holds on to his arm. My shoulders shake with a silent chuckle. "He always needs to make a dramatic entrance, doesn't he?"

Dez snorts. "I'm surprised there aren't any fireworks."

I guess Base marrying a mafia princess has some positives, considering he's pulling up to the manor with hundreds of Russian soldiers who look like they could rip your soul from your body with one glance. Units surround the manor's grounds, some outside in jeeps; others patrolling the crowd.

Bodyguards rush to the car as Base shoves open the door with more force than necessary. He's suited up and wearing sunglasses for some idiotic reason, but he immediately flips them off his face and grins at me. "Kade Mitchell," he says, slamming his door. "Who knew you'd ever be more famous than your fucking dad, right?"

I shake my head but fight a smile, some of the panic already easing off at the sight of him. Out of everyone, even Stacey, he understands what I went through the most. He was present. Took part. Affected. We kept each other semi-sane every time Bernadette summoned us to her room.

He grins at us. "I brought the party to you, oh famous one. Who the fuck are we killing?"

Even in the middle of a war, Base tries to lighten the mood. He can never be taken seriously.

"Fuckface," he greets Dez, patting his shoulder. "Been a while. You look shorter."

My mum places her hands on her hips at his bad language. She's probably gearing up to slap the back of his head and tell him she's going to wash his mouth out with a bar of soap. He winks at her, which makes her roll her eyes, but she's battling a laugh.

Good. She's been mired in grief since we returned to the manor, and I was starting to get really worried about her.

Luciella runs out of the front door and stops dead in her tracks, her wide eyes fixed on Base, who also freezes as he goes to walk around the front of the car.

His cheeks go bright red as he clears his throat. "Hi, princess."

She crosses her arms and chews her lip. "Hi," she replies softly, moving forward until she stops beside me. "Are you staying for a while?" she asks him, her tone full of hope.

A tall man comes up beside Base and speaks in quiet Russian. I faintly hear him give Base a warning, something about an introduction being more important, and I narrow my eyes.

Base stares at Luciella for a long second then swears under his breath and opens the passenger-side door.

I know who it is before the curly blonde hair comes into view, and I wish I could take my sister inside the house so she doesn't need to see this. The way her small hand clasps Base's, her stiletto-clad foot pressing into the cobbled path as she steps out of the car, seems comfortable, as if she's had plenty of practice touching him.

But the mafia princess is far too dressed up to be here, her earrings alone probably worth more than the manor.

Yeah, our house is huge and flashy, but can she not see we're in the middle of a shitstorm and not throwing a damn ball? If someone attacks, she's not going to get far with a long dress and heels on.

The impracticality of her even being here has me internally groaning. I bet her father forced Base to bring her – to show her off to the family he should have married into. I can't believe my best friend is fucking married.

Dez leans into me. "Who's the kid?"

Base holds his arm out for her, and she hooks hers into it.

"Fuck no. Tell me this is a joke. She's young."

Base plasters on a fake smile. "Everyone, I'd like to introduce you to Nikita." His voice is strained, his brown eyes flicking to the man who warned him. "My wife."

"What the fuck?" Dez mutters under his breath. "Luciella is a million times better."

I look at my sister – at the blood draining from her face and the way her lips are flattening to stop her tears from flowing – then back at my friend. "He didn't have a choice. He had to marry her."

I understand why he took the deal. I would do anything for Stacey. I'd even cut my own dick off to make sure she wasn't harmed in any way.

Despite the pain written all over her face, my twin steps forward. "Hi, I'm Luciella. Kade's sister."

Nikita glances at Base. "Oh." She takes Luciella's outstretched hand. "N-Nice to meet you. May I call you Ella? Your name. It is hard to... to pronounce."

The girl sounds nervous. Does she know about the deal? As far as I was aware, she just thought it was an arranged marriage.

Luciella blanches but nods and steps away, her eyes on Base for a split second. "You can call me whatever is easiest. I'll show you to your room. We have fresh bedding and robes set out. I assume you'll be staying together?"

"Of course," she replies then slips her arm from Base's and greets my mother, Ewan, Dez and Tylar. Then she stops in front of me, ignoring the dogs coming between us. "My father is very fond of you, Mr Mitchell. He wishes to work with you one day."

My eye twitches. "No thanks. Tell your father to stick his offer—"

Stacey grips my hand and smiles at Base's new wife. "I'm Stacey. You must be tired from your travels."

"I am. Kade is lucky man. You are more beautiful in real life." Her English isn't the best; her Russian accent is strong but understandable. "You could be model."

"You should sleep," Base says, raising his eyebrows at her and pushing his hands into his suit pockets. "You were falling asleep on me the entire drive."

"Who's fault is that?" Then she looks at me as if I give a fuck. "We were up all night consummating our marriage." She tuts and looks at my mother. "Newlyweds. Can you blame us?"

I grimace. Stacey looks at Luciella. Nikita giggles. The bodyguard beside Base nods, but I can see the twitch in his eye – the comment annoyed him. No one else makes a sound, but Luciella looks like she's about to burst into tears.

Milo and Hopper are growing uncomfortable. They're protective of my family and all these people have them agitated.

The detectives are waiting patiently, and I just want this day over with already.

Base coughs and asks one of his bodyguards in Russian to take their bags. Then he asks what I assume is the main guard if he can take Nikita, so he can catch up with his friends. The man's reply is whispered, his teeth gritted, his brows furrowing in annoyance.

I might sneak into his room tonight and put a bullet in his head for being a dick to my friend.

Luciella is temporarily frozen, so my mum and Ewan lead Nikita and her bodyguards inside, but when she rouses herself and makes to follow them, Base rushes for her and takes her arm.

"I didn't fuck her," he says quietly so the other Russians don't hear. "I swear I didn't. I told you I wouldn't touch her."

She doesn't look at him. Her lip trembles. "Please let me go."

"Not until you tell me you believe me. I didn't fuck her. Please."

"She's your wife. You can do what you want," Luciella replies, her eyes glassy. "Don't make this harder than it already is. I'm not mad, I promise. I know all of this is out of your control."

He releases her arm and shakes his head. "I tried to call the wedding off."

"I know."

He goes to take a step forward again but stops himself. "Please tell me you believe I didn't go near her."

"What I think doesn't change things, Sebastian. I'm not angry with you. I just... I need to go." Luciella glances at all of us, a tear slipping down her cheek. "I'm going to go to my room."

Stacey and Tylar let go of me and Dez, and for once, I'm okay with the temporary separation. Both walk with her into the manor, and Base watches my sister until she's out of view.

He turns to me and Dez. "I didn't fuck her."

Dez tilts his head. "Since when were you a cradle-robbing bastard? She looks fresh out of the womb."

"She's eighteen, you dickhead." Base groans and stares at his shoes.

The last of the guards are filtering into the manor, the detectives still standing beside their car, but I'm in no hurry. They can wait.

"She asked me to lie and say we slept together, and I obviously agreed."

Dez makes a sound of acknowledgment and pulls Base in for a hug, patting his back, and Base snakes his arms around him, looking like he really needs one as he buries his face in his shoulder.

"Shit, man," Base blurts. "Can we go back five years?"

"Why five?" I ask.

"You both had girlfriends and normal lives, and all I had to worry about was getting Luciella's attention for more than two minutes." He's still holding on to Dez. "Now we're all fucked."

"I'm pretty sound, in all honesty," Dez says. "I just have fucked-up brothers."

Brothers – meaning me and Base.

I stand and watch them, unsure if I should join or keep staring. I mean, I want to – at the same time, there are crowds pointing cameras at us, and I'm not really a hugger. Unless the person involved is a dancer with dark hair and freckles, with my initials tattooed on her.

Base doesn't give me a chance to decide; he grabs my shirt and yanks me to them, and the three of us hug it out. Dez says we're insane, Base says he's a boring pussy, and I shake my head at them and tell them I love them.

We became best friends in school. I was annoyingly popular because of who my dad was, and Base was cocky, even at the age of seven, while Dez was our sporty sidekick. I had no need for friends – or so I thought at the time. I could never have imagined how important they'd become. Our trio. The ones who got me into trouble with the law and gave me my first drag of a joint; who got me drunk and egged windows with me. Who crashed Base's car and left that heap of shit wrapped around a tree after attempting to teach me how to drive.

In the end, it was my brother who taught me. My friends were terrible teachers.

I pull away first and straighten my top then frown at Base. "Why the fuck are you crying?"

"I'm not," he says in a gruff voice and wipes his eyes. "I'm just tired."

"You missed us, didn't you?" Dez teases, and Base shoves him and puts him in a headlock.

I glance at the detectives and huff, telling my friends I'll get them at the pool house before I walk towards them.

"Coming at the same time as the Russians wasn't a good idea. Sorry that took so long."

I'm not sorry at all.

The main one, an older woman with grey hair and a form-fitting suit, lifts her chin. "This is urgent, Mr Mitchell. It can't wait."

39

KADE

The detectives follow me to my mother's office, and I feel itchy. I scratch my nape, and instead of sitting behind the desk I had Stacey bent over before blacking out, I sit on the edge of it and cross my ankles and arms. "Get it over with then. Did your chief talk through his ass? Are you charging me?"

"Not at this time, no," one says, then the other guy says, "As much as it would bring us great pleasure."

I scowl at him and commit his face to memory. "Hm. Then what the fuck do you want?"

The main woman speaks. "The file you sent, with all the locations of illegal activity... All those areas are now secure, and we would like to thank you for that. You saved a lot of lives with that information and reunited many families. We also gathered enough evidence from the file to make several arrests. Fifteen high profilers are detained. That doesn't include the hundreds all over the world that were arrested with no chance of being released anytime soon."

I rub my fingertips with my thumb obsessively. "Right..."

"As you're fully aware, Archie Sawyer's death was live-streamed to the world. It accumulated over three hundred million views. That video has now been deleted. All traces of it are gone and therefore cannot be used against you. Archie's wife, Bernadette Sawyer, has been struck from her position and a warrant has been issued for her arrest."

"Then go arrest her," I say, even though I'd rather kill her in a worse way than I did her husband. "I still don't know why you're here. You already thanked me and told me Bernadette would be dealt with."

The dickhead one leans forward with a smirk. "Are you aware that there's a very large price on your head?"

I nod once. "Here to chance your luck? You won't get far, you skinny prick. I'd snap your legs before you even got out of that chair and beat the shit out of you with them."

He goes pale. Did I just threaten a detective? Shit.

"We're not here for an argument, Mr Mitchell. Please refrain from threatening my colleague." The woman speaks with some authority, even with a spark in her eyes. "We're looking for Bernadette Sawyer and her acquaintances. Along with a handful of others who are extremely dangerous. We fear, based on what we're hearing from our intelligent sources, that there will be an attack on you soon."

I still don't understand why they're here.

She sighs and pulls out a folder containing two pieces of paper, handing me them. I scan the words, and the more I read, the deeper my frown becomes. When I look at her, she nods with a warm expression.

"We are providing you with protection. You and your family, your friends and your partner, Miss Rhodes. No one protected you before, Mr Mitchell, and we understand you went through a lot of traumatic situations and were let down by the system. You were attacked. Blackmailed. You were used as a weapon. And we want to do what we can to show our support."

"Is this a joke?"

"No," she says bluntly. "We aren't asking. Within the hour, enforcement officers will arrive at the manor with highly skilled firearms units. We'll have a helicopter overhead. Your team and Sebastian Prince's can stay if they want. But our officers are here for you."

The pieces of paper burn my fingertips as I read them again and again. I'm still reading long after the detectives leave. Barry calls, but I don't answer. I don't reply to any messages as I reread the papers a final time.

The crowds will be told to leave for safety reasons. They'll even be safely escorted back to their homes – their countries. The media will be kept out of it. And at the bottom of the page is a signed note from the new chief officer, offering me his condolences for all my losses.

Even when Stacey finds me sitting at the desk, my eyes glued to the words, I still don't believe any of this.

I was ruined by the head of Police Scotland. I was catapulted into the underworld by her when I was a teenager and violated in every way possible, and yet, here I sit with words offering me deep apologies and protection, thanking me, with Police Scotland stamped at the top.

They fired Bernadette, and she's now a wanted person. And I'm protected. Is this real?

Stacey lowers herself into my lap and kisses my temple. "I texted you hours ago. Your mum said the police are settling in to their roles."

I blink.

"You're sweating." A palm presses to my forehead. "Here, take your hoodie off."

I feel material pull over my head, and I want to thank her, but I can't speak.

I keep thinking my dad will pop up out of nowhere and surprise us. I keep thinking he'll walk through the manor doors and pull us all in for a family hug. That the police will call again and say he's been spotted somewhere far away. I thought, for a split second, the detective would mention him.

I think my dad is actually dead.

Mum probably thinks the same. She's worried; cries sometimes when my dad is brought up, and my sister can barely hold back tears whenever he's mentioned. But then again, she's been a bag of emotions lately. Even I've had to hold her for long periods of time. Like me, Luciella has a hard time registering certain emotions. But hers have always been more controlled, less angry, more silent. With Base being here with his wife, she must be losing her mind.

She doesn't see a therapist – Jason was the one she spoke to, until he vanished for two years. And now he's dead.

Base loves her regardless of how insanely controlling she is. And I know this marriage has been one of the worst things that's ever happened to him. He tried to get out of it. He tried to pay the girl to refuse the proposal and offered alternative men who would be more suitable. He even told the family that he would never love her, but a deal was a deal.

Now Base is trapped with a wife he doesn't want, in a family he hates, to protect the woman he loves. Their story has the potential to be more disastrous than my parents'.

"Kade, are you okay? Can you hear me?"

In all fairness, Dad did try to be good – the same way Base has been trying to win Luciella over since she turned eighteen, to be good enough, to show he's not just a fuckboy who wants another notch on his bedpost. When I was six, my dad got his diagnosis after years of professionals arguing for and against different spectrums. Mum fought and fought and fought even more to get him the help he needed.

Soft lips press to my temple again, but I'm trapped in my own mind as Stacey tries to take the life-changing paperwork from my grip. I can't let the pages go though, even if I try.

My vision is blurring, and there's a high-pitched ringing in my ears.

The doctors... The doctors... One argued Dad had a schizophrenia spectrum disorder. Another debated he had a schizotypal personality disorder that caused psychosis. He had autistic traits that didn't lead to a diagnosis because doctors refused screening, but he had even more traits that went against that diagnosis anyway.

"I'm going to walk you to our room, okay?"

Another stated that he could be a sociopath, or he had OCD. The last doctor said he was acting and was just trying to outsmart everyone, and he was simply obsessed with my mother to the point of becoming a danger to himself and everyone around him. But he showed signs of neurological behaviours way before he met her.

After medication, therapy and a lot of time in the institution, he fell into one personality – one dad, one human being – and his mind stopped playing games enough that he got his ASPD diagnosis, coexisting with anxiety, impulse control and depressive disorders.

Still, doctors strongly believed my father's mind was a lot more complex than that.

"Is he okay? What's that in his hand?"

"The letter about the protection order. He won't let it go. I think he's in shock, Aria."

"Oh, Ewan, darling, help Stacey get him to their room."

Someone tall snakes my arm over his shoulder.

My mum says, "Let's get him to bed. I think seeing so many people around him after everything that's happened has finally hit him. I'll make some tea and toast."

"Woah. Is he drunk?"

"No, Desmond. He's in shock," Mum says. "Sebastian, sweetie, take his other arm. He's losing consciousness."

I'm awake and I'm here, I want to tell them. *I can hear you all, but I can't talk.* I want to tell them that we're going to be safe. I want to tell my dad we'll all be okay.

My dad loved us.

"He's going to seize," someone says in the distance. "Get him on the floor."

Dad loved our family, despite struggling to understand the feeling.

Tobias Mitchell fell in love with Aria Miller, and no one will ever understand the level of obsession he had for her.

"Just breathe, sweetheart."

He's dead, so I guess no one will ever truly know how his mind worked.

40

KADE

Stacey's hand moves up and down my dick, and my head drops back against the wall of the broom cupboard in the kitchen. She's taking a breather from swallowing me deep into her throat by teasing my sensitive head and stroking my length.

Tears stain her cheeks from choking on it. The only tears I ever want to see on her. I wipe my thumb across her cheek and brush my fingers into her hair.

I worship every inch of her. The ground she walks on. The way she smiles and laughs and loves me.

We're trying to be quiet, unable to make it back to the bedroom before I dragged her in here and told her to get on her knees. I can't fuck her. She never lets me fuck her when she's on her period, as much as I'd love to.

I nearly did this morning when she was absently grinding her ass on me, but she ran for the bathroom when she properly woke up.

Her glazed, wet eyes are on me as she sucks again, hollowing her cheeks, and my fingers tighten in her hair. She pulls her mouth away, a string of saliva trailing from the head to her lips. She licks across them. "Am I being too loud?"

She means the gagging and slurping noises. I don't care if anyone can hear. Those noises are like heaven to my fucking ears. I remember the first time she did this to me in the dance studio; I had to slide down the wall and try not to pass out.

From the way she's slurping on my cock now, I think it might happen again.

I shake my head when she looks at me, my chest rising and falling. "No one can hear us. Keep going," I whisper. "If you stop again, I'll fuck your throat and make sure everyone knows what we're doing."

Her pupils dilate even more.

"I don't see that as a threat," she replies, and my balls tighten as she licks a bead of precum. She has me fucking leaking and begging to unload.

"You should," I warn.

When she takes me back into her mouth, she sucks me until my nerves are crackling, until I can barely contain the need to take control. My lips part with a deep moan as I throw my head back against the wall, feeling her caress my balls while taking me further into her mouth.

Heart hammering in my chest, I look down at her, my voice low. "You like sucking my cock, don't you?"

She tries to nod.

"You're going to be my perfect little slut and suck it for the rest of your life. Do you know why?"

She blinks, more trails of tears sliding down her cheeks.

"Because you're going to be my wife. You've already taken my heart, my body, and my butchered soul, so you'll take my fucking last name too."

Her response is a whimper around my thickness as she sucks

hard and moves her head up and down the length of me.

"Is that a yes?" I pant, carefully pulling her off my dick by the hair. "You'll marry me?"

I tense as she sweeps her tongue up my length. "I'm going to kill you."

I frown, a groan trapped in my throat as she pumps me in her palm. "Why?"

"You're seriously asking me to marry you while your dick is in my mouth?"

I blink, my voice a whisper. "Yeah?"

She shakes her head but smiles. "You're such an asshole." And then she takes me into her mouth and fucks me with her throat again.

Stacey didn't fucking answer me. Is that a yes or a no? Do I need to get down on one knee surrounded by roses with a violinist playing? Do I need to put a shirt on our future child that says, *Marry Daddy*? Get the dogs involved? Write the words on a dessert in chocolate in a fancy restaurant?

I'll ask again later. And I won't let her off without an answer.

I grab handfuls of her hair at each side of her head and start to take over, and she steadies herself on my thighs while I thrust into her mouth. She's gagging, saliva frothing at the corners of her mouth, and I knock over a bucket as I step forward and force her back to the wall and go faster.

My spine tingles, my vision blurs, and I press my forehead to the wall and grit my teeth. My muscles pull taut all over my body as a wave of euphoria smacks into me, pulsing through my orgasm. She drinks every drop of my cum, her throat contracting around my cock as I sink deeper, until she taps my leg and I pull out of her to let her breathe.

Stacey wipes the back of her hand across her mouth. "We were definitely loud there. You moaned!" she whisper-hisses.

Did I? Damn.

Tucking my dick back into my shorts, I grin down at her still on her knees, her eyes red, her cheeks wet, lips swollen. I pull out my phone, open the camera app and take a photo. "I'll put this in our locked folder." I turn the screen around. "Look how beautiful you are with my cum dripping down your chin."

I've grabbed some recordings and pictures of us. After getting her agreement obviously. I wanted her to experience something different from what her piece-of-shit stepbrother did to her, replacing the memory of that with images and clips of us. Me on her, her riding me, me bending her over and her sucking my dick while I eat her out. We even have videos of us kissing, her smiling at me and sleeping in each other's arms.

The boys would call me a pussy if they saw those ones, but anything for my girlfriend.

She rolls her eyes and takes my hand to get to her feet. "If anyone ever sees what's in that folder, I'll kill you."

That's twice she's threatened my life in the space of ten minutes.

"You didn't answer me," I say, pulling her to me. "Make my shitty life a little better by being Stacey Mitchell." I kiss the tip of her nose then her forehead. "Please? I'll wear a kilt to our wedding, and Kyle can walk you down the aisle."

Her cheeks go red. "And what if people ask how you proposed to me?"

I shrug. "Tell them the truth."

I haven't seen a future with Stacey at all, but the protection order gives us both hope. So fucking sue me if I want to marry Stacey and have a family, to grow old together – I have the chance to.

She laughs and slaps my chest.

It's been nearly nine weeks since the order was put in place, and all we've been doing is making up for lost time. I didn't think it was possible to fall *more* in love with her, but I certainly have.

When I'm not pounding her, I'm training my guys on the grounds. Armed officers, Russians and my own team have all united. They take turns in shifts. Guarding and on watch. Two helicopters circling the perimeter. One mine, the other belonging to Police Scotland. There's a rota for who patrols where and when, and when they aren't working, they're training, or resting.

Barry's still with his family in the safe house, but he's constantly in contact. He sent me a picture of his daughter yesterday, holding an ultrasound scan of Barry's next baby, due in six months.

Luciella, Tylar and Stacey are always in the new studio or doing girly shit in my sister's room. I've had to argue with my twin far too many times to let me see Stacey when I've been bored and the dogs give me no attention.

Nikita is always with her main bodyguard. She follows Base around like a puppy and plays the happy wife around everyone, but when it's just them, Base tells us that she cries and begs him to let her go back to Russia.

The bodyguard who keeps giving Base shit is Nikita's father's right-hand man. I want to rip his head off. But I think there's something going on between him and Nikita – I can tell by the way they look at each other.

Luciella has kept her distance completely. If she walks into a room and Base is there, she'll leave. She won't sit for dinner because his wife is there, and that usually means Stacey and Tylar eat in a different dining room with her. It's a pain in the ass, but I understand. I couldn't handle seeing Stacey married to someone else. And even if she was, I'd still fuck her, sneak into broom cupboards and kiss her until we can't breathe. I'd still be hers.

Dez has been trying to work with us, but he's useless, in the nicest way possible. He's too normal and careful and fucking sensitive. He can't hold a gun right or use a blade and has no idea how to follow orders.

Ewan, fuck, he's a tank for his age. I always knew he was fit and could fight. He's so far beaten everyone I've partnered him up with to a pulp with his fists. Losing Jason has changed him. He's angrier. I see it all over his face.

Stacey opens the closet door slightly and peeks out. "No one's here." She steps out and turns to me. "I'm going to sit with Luciella and Tylar and watch movies. My phone is in the bedroom. I'll see you at lunch?"

Tilting my head, I laugh. "Did you just use me again?"

She raises a brow. "You're the one who dragged me in there. Maybe you used me?"

I shake my head and close the distance between us, taking her jaw and swiping my thumb across her still-swollen lips. "I wanted to fuck you."

"A few more days," she replies, reaching up on her tiptoes to give me a chaste kiss. "Then I'm all yours."

"Can I fuck you tonight? It's only blood. I'll clean it up."

"No, Kade. We aren't having sex."

I groan, imagining all the positions I'll put her in when she's no longer bleeding. "Fine."

Considering the number of times I've not used a condom, I'm surprised she isn't pregnant. I think I've had her every night since Base arrived, except when she's been on her period. I've fingered her after I've cum inside her to shove it all back in and watched it drip down her thighs, and I think I'm becoming dangerously obsessed with the idea of putting a kid in her.

Maybe because I think there's still a chance I might die, and I want to leave a part of myself behind for her to love.

A mini version of myself I might never meet.

Stacey's hands rest on the sides of my face. "I know what you want, Kade. Trust me, so do I. But look at our situation." She gives me a warm smile. "Imagine bringing a baby into all this? We're only just getting back what we had, and neither of us is mentally stable enough for a baby. You're still seizing and blacking out, and I'm sometimes barely able to sleep from the nightmares."

"I haven't blacked out or had a seizure in over a month."

She sighs. "I know. I just... What if they found out I was pregnant and tried to hurt me or the baby? We should wait until we're in a safe and comfortable position with no enemies."

"But you said you wanted to..." I trail off, studying her face, her serious expression, and I deflate. "Shit. Am I pressuring you into this?"

"No. God, no." She kisses me again. "I want nothing more than to have your child. I just want to be safe and ready first. I can't lose another."

I nod, pulling her against my chest. "I'm sorry. We're so close to the end, Freckles. There are a few more arrests they need to make, then we just need to find Bernadette. It'll be over soon, I promise."

My team on the outside has slaughtered hundreds. Most of Bernadette's army is missing.

"You have nothing to apologise for, Kade. Besides..." She hesitates and checks our surroundings. "Luciella needs us now more than ever."

I frown, confused. "Why?"

"She's…" Stacey lowers her voice to a whisper. "She thinks she's pregnant, but she's too scared to ask for a nurse in case someone finds out. She's missed two periods."

I stare at her for too long before I blink. "What?"

"You can't tell Base."

"She thinks she's pregnant with *Base's* kid?" I ask, needing her to either clarify or elaborate.

"Yes," she replies. "That's why she keeps being sick and hiding from him. If Nikita's family finds out, they might—"

A door opens to our left, and Base walks in. "Ah, Rhodes. The very person I'm looking for. Fancy helping me out and forcing Ella to speak to me? Accidentally lock us in a room together? Tie her to a chair and text me the room number?"

Stacey pulls out of my arms. "She's just finding it hard to see you around Nikita. Give her time."

I'm still staring at Stacey, needing her to tell me more. When did she start to think this? It's impossible to get her to the safe house safely – what will happen if the manor is attacked and she's here?

What the fuck will happen when Base's new father-in-law finds out?

I drag my frown from her to Base as he huffs. "Does she know we don't share a bed? I sleep on the couch. I texted her weeks ago and told her none of it is real, and she blocked me."

"I don't think that makes a difference to her. You're stuck in your marriage, and she has no idea what to do. She knows it isn't your fault, but talking to you is too hard," Stacey replies. "I need to go." She glances at me. "Are you okay?"

Meaning, *Are you good with what I just said?* No, I'm not, but I'm annoyed at the situation, not with her. Base should fucking know. But I nod anyway. "See you at lunch."

I watch her leave then blow out a breath.

Base grabs an apple from the fruit bowl in the middle of the kitchen island and sits. "One thing I hate about all these authoritative cunts being here is that I can't get stoned peacefully."

"Did you get caught again?"

"Yeah. A fucking armed officer and his lapdog were patrolling the pool house and I had to sit on my joint because I had nowhere to put it."

"Burn yourself?"

"Yep. You want to put cream on my ass?"

I snort. "Fuck off."

Ewan and Dez walk in, both looking as tired as all of us.

"Your mother got a call that her patient just got married. Ivy Dermot? Tied the knot in Cyprus this morning."

"I didn't know she was getting married.

I met Ivy once when my mother won her tenth award for discovering treatments for rare genetic diseases. She's the reason my parents met. Dad was my mum's assistant on her case in America, and they both worked with her when she was a kid.

I guess that was before my dad went off the rails.

"The new treatment she's on is really helping with her mobility. Aria was invited to the wedding, but obviously with everything going on, she couldn't attend. Ivy's new husband read out a poem she wrote when she gained the ability to write at sixteen, and it was about your mum."

I feel bad she couldn't go. "She would have loved that."

"She cried. Then opened a bottle of wine, so I told her I'd give her some peace and see what needed to be done around the manor."

"I'll go see Mum later then," I say, leaning my elbows on the counter. "When's the next shift change?"

"In an hour," Base replies, glancing at his phone. "Then Dragon Breath Pavel will be breathing down my neck about Nikita's whereabouts. All she does is sit in the bedroom and watch her laptop. Can I accidentally shoot him?"

"Sure," I say seriously as Ewan says, "No."

"What's his deal anyway?" Dez asks, chewing on slices of orange. "He hates your guts."

"I think he's in love with her. He's the one that told her to pretend to sleep with me in front of everyone. If her father found out it's all fake, then it's her that'll get the biggest punishment."

If they find out Luciella is pregnant, they'll probably try to make her either abort or beat her until she miscarries – or worse, kill her.

My hands fist on the kitchen counter.

"Brutal," Dez replies, grimacing. "Does she have feelings for you?"

That makes Base laugh, but it's a bitter one. "I fucking hope not. I have nothing to offer her but a heart that belongs to someone who hates me."

"Luciella doesn't hate you; she's sad about it all." Ewan takes a glass and fills it with water.

"I just want to walk up to her, grab her and—"

Both me and Ewan glare at him.

"Fine. Fine. I was just going to say 'kiss her', you protective dickheads."

He really should know about his possible impending fatherhood. If Luciella is pregnant, she should be the one to tell him. But, fuck, I'm shit at this. I want to slap him across the face and tell him to go demand answers from her.

He's never spoken about having kids. I don't think he's even interacted with a child before. Dez wants two, and Tylar said as soon as she takes over the family business, she'll happily give them to him.

Me? I want whatever Stacey is willing to give me.

I rise from my seat and chew the inside of my cheek, needing something to take my mind off the turmoil of thoughts and impending panic. "You want to get stoned?" Ewan stares at me, and I shrug. "Old bastards like you can get baked. Up for it? I won't tell my mum."

Ewan rolls his eyes. "Little wanker."

Everyone, even my stepfather, eventually agrees. Dez claps once for dramatic effect. "Let's sneak a joint before they patrol around the pool house again."

Base jumps to his feet. "Thank fuck."

I shouldn't have smoked. I shouldn't have and I did. And now I'm stoned as fuck.

"Meet you at the Graveyard" by Cleffy plays from Base's phone while we sit around the coffee table. I try to sit up and fail, so I pull my phone out instead.

Me: *Might miss lunch.*

Me: *I can barely see.*

Me: *Also, marry me? I have four hundred million in my bank. I can use that for a ring? Would that be enough? I know you don't care about money but think of how fucking nice that diamond would be?*

Me: *Can you tell Luciella to talk to Base about all this pregnancy shit? He's a mopey prick and annoying me.*

Me: *I nearly sent my mum a picture of my joint. Maybe I should call it quits and go to bed.*

Me: *Might miss supper.*

Me: *If you don't get your phone from the bedroom and respond to me, I might just take your ass while you're asleep.*

Me: *That sounded bad. Sorry. But please let me fuck your ass again. It's very pretty, but it looks even better with my dick buried inside it. I'll go slow and very, veryyyyyy gentle.*

Me: *This conversation is awfully one-sided, Freckles. I'm a little offended.*

Ewan glances at my screen when I laugh at myself. "Oh, Jesus, Kade. I don't need to see that vulgar crap." He scoots away from me on the sofa. "You're definitely your father's son."

I screw my face up at him. "Don't look at my screen then."

"What was it?" Dez asks, taking a huge hit from the bong.

Ewan shakes his head. "You don't want to know." He looks at me. "You might not be my blood, but I raised you from birth and you're still my son. Please don't show me that again."

"You're the one who looked at my phone!" I say again, laughing. "How stoned are you?"

Base chuckles deeply and passes the bong to me. "Are you asking to fuck Stacey's ass again?"

I stop laughing and growl at him, packing the bowl of the bong and lighting it to take a hit. The rage I get when any of them mention her and something sexual is instant. Base read my texts to her last month, the same way Ewan absently did, and I got into an hour-long debate about giving and receiving, and he said I should definitely let Stacey peg me.

I punched him in the face for that one.

My haziness gets intense as I pass Ewan the bong, but he shakes his head and gives it to Dez. My phone dings, and I sigh in relief when I see Stacey's reply.

***Freckles:** You're cute. But you need to leave my ass alone. I couldn't sit for a week last time, so no. I'm in our room now. Luciella's with me. She's taking one of the tests we had under the sink.*

I gulp and look up at Base, slouched in his seat, ankle settled on his knee, elbow leaning on the armrest with his middle finger to his temple. He cut a line into his eyebrow the other day, and he weirdly suits it.

***Me:** And?*

Five minutes later, she replies.

***Freckles:** Positive. I've never seen her cry like this.*

***Me:** Hug her. But she needs to tell Base. He needs to be involved.*

***Freckles:** She's going to text him now. I miss you.*

Dez leans back in his chair. "Tylar loves it. Sometimes she prefers anal."

"So does—" Base pauses, looks at me and Ewan then shakes his head. "Never mind."

I grimace.

Ewan stands. "I'm leaving before I hit one of you."

He slams the door shut behind him, and maybe it's because we're all fucked up, but we burst out laughing until our sides hurt.

Dez nearly chokes on his smoke, and I drop my phone on the floor. "He's fucking scary," Base says through his sniggering. "He kicked me in the balls while we were sparring. He could have messed up my baby makers!"

"Do you want kids?" I ask, grabbing on to the subject.

"Fuck, no. No offence, because I know you two do, but I couldn't think of anything worse."

I chew the inside of my cheek. I nearly open my mouth to tell him he's knocked my sister up, but I refrain. It's Luciella's place to talk to him about it, and I think she's going to be even more heartbroken.

Dez rolls a joint and lights it. "I haven't said this before, but I'm sorry about what happened to you two." He blows smoke between us and hands it to me. "I wish I knew and could have at least tried to help. I didn't see the pictures and videos, but I heard..."

Base is staring at his screen, his brows furrowing. But then he looks up, hums and I already know his dark humour is about to make an appearance, especially with how stoned he is. It's his way of deflecting.

"I bet Kade takes a blowjob better than you do."

I drop my head. "Fucking hell."

Base grins at me. "Don't deny it. You came in my mouth. You

know I'm good. Tell him!"

Instead of slamming my fist into his face, maybe because I'm baked, I let out a laugh and nearly choke on the smoke again. My friends join in, and when I stub out the roach and stand, I yawn.

"I'm going to see my girl and go to sleep. Dez, I suggest you let Base blow you so you have an idea. I won't tell anyone. And, Base, you need to speak to my sister pronto."

Base stands too. "She asked to see me actually. Said it was urgent. I'll walk with you."

But before we can leave, there's a loud explosion outside that rocks the pool house, smashing in the windows and knocking us off our feet. The ground shakes, and the eruption in my ears has me wincing as things fall to the floor all around us, and alarms begin to sound as people shout orders.

Windows smash outside as another explosion goes off.

Stacey.

I rush to my feet and out of the pool house with my two friends behind me, warm liquid trickling down the side of my head. I must've been hit by something.

My heart sinks as I come to a halt, every drop of blood leaving my face as I stare at my side of the manor – obliterated and up in flames. My balcony is gone, and the entire top floor is non-existent.

No. No, no, no, fucking *no.* Stacey and Luciella were in my room. And it's gone.

"Fuck!" I yell and run towards the flames without giving it a second thought, but the ceiling of the entrance collapses and I stumble back, my eyes wide. I count to three in my head then run towards it with one end goal.

My skin heats from the flames nearly licking my body, my ears sensitive from the detonations. My friends are behind me, and we're forcing aside downed ceiling beams to get inside, covering our mouths with the collars of our shirts as we push through.

The fucking war is starting, but all I can focus on is sprinting through the burning manor, trying not to breathe in the toxic fumes to find my girlfriend and pregnant sister.

41

STACEY

My eyes ping open as a scream hits my ringing ears, everywhere hurting as I try to move and fail.

Confused and dazed, flat on my back, I will myself to stay awake. My head is aching from something dropping on me. I try to keep my eyes open in the darkness licked by flames, but they burn, just like my lungs do as I drag in erratic breaths.

A sharp pain in my legs has me wincing as I try to move, blinking as I cough on the thick smoke filling the corridor at the bottom of Kade's spiral staircase.

I tuck my chin in to see the glow of the fire on the wooden beam trapping my legs.

"Stacey..." The soft voice comes from my left, and I look over to see my best friend pushing herself to her feet.

Luciella looks at me, distraught, her face bleeding, her top ripped to shreds. One of her shoes is missing. She cradles herself, pressing her palm to where her baby is growing in her womb.

"Oh God," she cries quietly, limping towards me and taking in the demolished surroundings of her home. "What happened?"

So many memories burned away. Kade's room doesn't even exist anymore. The box I stored in his cupboard will be gone – the princess dress, the booties, the photographs and everything else he kept to remind him of us.

All gone.

I'm so weak that the gunshots I can hear from somewhere in the manor don't faze me. There's yelling, and something falls from the ceiling and causes embers to float towards us with a bang. There's crackling in my ears, and I don't know if it's from my head injury or the wood burning around us.

Luciella uses the shredded material of her top to cover her mouth. Pretty soon, the smoke will grow thicker, poisonous, and we'll probably die in here.

Every nerve in my body is aware of the pain I'm in, and everything burns from the polluted air. I pull my sweater up and over my mouth to try to filter some of the smoke filling my lungs.

I'm not sure how long I was knocked out, but one minute, Luciella and I were rehearsing how she'll tell Base she's pregnant, me hyping her up when she started to panic because he hates children, then the next, chaos. Something happened when we were walking down Kade's spiral staircase to go find Base and tell him the news. There was a bang, then we were catapulted down and everything turned black.

The smoke is getting thicker, and the flames are closer. I have sweat all over me, stinging the wounds on my skin. "Tylar," I say. "She went to your room. Can you phone her?"

Luciella pulls out her phone from her back pocket, but the screen is smashed. I have no idea where mine is.

My heart twists at the thought of whoever is attacking us getting to Kade, and I silently pray he's not too stoned to defend himself.

We freeze when gunshots sound louder at the end of Kade's corridor, two heavily armoured figures running past with gas masks on, torches attached to their guns and shining through the smoke. They're aiming and firing at someone.

We need to get out of here – and fast. Whoever attacked the manor is also storming the place.

Oh God. Where are the dogs? Kade? Tylar? Everyone?

My eyes sting from the smoke and pressure of the pain in my head, but I manage to push my palms into the floor beneath me and sit up. "I can feel my toes," I croak, coughing as relief courses through me – my legs aren't broken from being trapped under the beam. "Help me lift this off."

When she reaches forward, realisation hits, and I grab her wrist. "Wait. No. You can't lift it – you're pregnant."

"I'm helping you," she demands, freeing herself from my grip. "The fire is spreading, and I'm not leaving you here to either be shot or burned alive."

Three attempts, and we fail to move the beam trapping my legs. It sits just above my knees, but if I try to pull my legs out, my kneecaps feel like they're going to snap. I give up, coughing enough to make my throat hurt.

"You need to go, Luciella."

"Shut up. No."

"Lu, please. You're pregnant, and I'm stuck here. The smoke's getting worse." I take deep breaths that sting my throat. "Please go."

"No."

I go to groan, but the sight of two more figures pushing their way into the destroyed corridor has me pausing. Relief fills me as Kade snatches someone by the throat and repeatedly punches them in the face, so hard the gas mask drops to the ground. Base is strangling the other, a manic expression on his face.

"Motherfuckers chose the wrong family to fuck with," Base growls, kicking the person between the legs before they drop. "Pieces of shit."

Kade snaps the man's neck so easily, and I hear it popping.

They're both drenched in blood.

Kade's gaze clashes with mine, and I feel all the air vanish as he instantly runs to me, my name on his lips, Base just behind him, yelling for Luciella. They stop when another beam drops from the ceiling, missing them by an inch.

They bolt over the beam and run towards us, dodging debris. Kade reaches me first with wide eyes. "Fuck," he blurts, grabbing my face to check my injuries. Then he glances down at my trapped limbs.

He effortlessly lifts the beam, and I shuffle back to free my legs. He yanks me into his chest before I can say a word. His face buries into my shoulder as his hold tightens around me. "I can't ever lose you. I… I can't. Ever. I thought I lost you… I couldn't find you… couldn't fucking think straight."

I lean back and cup his stained cheek, his eyes wild. "It's okay. You found me."

"I killed a lot of people tonight," he admits, his eyes taking in all my cuts and bruises. "Don't hate me."

The knuckles on both his hands are burst open, his ear and eyebrow are bleeding, and there's a gash on his head – also bleeding.

"They deserved it." My chin wobbles. "The dogs?"

"They're outside with two of my guys. We found them at the bottom of the staircase. They aren't hurt, just spooked."

He doesn't take his eyes off me as Base speaks. "We'll need to jump into the bushes or try climbing down – the stairs are crawling, and this wing is about to collapse. We're out of fucking bullets."

Base is holding Luciella to him, shaking his head and muttering in Russian and English as he kisses all over her face. Then he adds, "Tylar is with Dez. She's safe."

Good. That's good.

"Where's my mum and Ewan?" Luciella asks. "And Nikita?"

"With her bodyguard. Ewan got Aria out too."

Kade lowers his forehead to my shoulder again. "I nearly lost you."

"You'll never lose me, Kade." I brush my fingers through his hair. "Get us out of here," I say, my lungs on fire, my eyes droopy. "I'm getting dizzy."

I stare down at my bloodied legs as Kade stands and slips a gun into the back of his waistband. He helps me to my feet, but the pressure on my knees has me buckling. The dizziness from being knocked out is starting to settle, replaced with panic and pain, making my heart race uncontrollably.

Kade holds me up. "Can you walk?"

I nod.

More gunshots go off as Kade pulls my arm over his shoulder for support, slouching down to my height. We only get halfway down the corridor before he's coughing and I'm falling. We get back to our feet, Kade pressing his hand to the wall for extra support.

"This room here," Base says, kicking the door open, and we follow him in. He jogs to the window and slides it open, looking down. "We can jump."

I glance at the steep drop and blanch.

Kade shakes his head. "Stacey's legs will snap. And there's not a chance in hell I'm letting my pregnant sister jump from that height."

Base pauses. "What?"

Everything goes silent. Luciella closes her eyes. Base doesn't blink, his brows furrowing. I internally cringe at the quietness. Kade crosses his arms and stares at them both like he didn't just drop a bomb.

"She's pregnant," Kade says, making it worse. "Congratulations, you're going to be a father – if we get out of this. Now, what's plan B?"

"Wait. Hold the fuck on. What?" He stands in front of Lu and tips her chin up, so she looks at him. "You're pregnant?"

"Can we talk about this later please?" she asks. "We're in the middle of a near-death experience, and this can be discussed later."

"They'll try to kill you. If Nikita's family finds out, they'll send orders for you to be killed." He looks at Kade. "Can you hide her?"

"I'm not hiding," she snaps before her twin can respond. "We don't need to say it's yours."

"It's definitely mine, right?"

Oh, he did not. I step forward with a tight jaw, but Kade beats me to it, grabbing Base by the scruff of his collar. "Watch your fucking mouth."

"Calm the fuck down!" Base snaps, shoving Kade away. "I know the kid is mine. Nikita's family will too! Do you understand how dangerous this is?"

"I can easily say it isn't yours! They won't find out."

"You think I'm going to go back there knowing you're carrying my kid?"

"We don't have time for this," Kade says, glaring at them both. "The smoke is coming through every goddamn crack. We need to get out of here."

Lu tenses her jaw, but before she can yell at him, the door bursts open, a large figure wearing a gas mask and riot gear filling the doorway, his gun pointing at us. "Jackpot," he says in an English accent. "I found Kade and Luciella Mitchell."

He speaks into his earpiece, but my view is blocked as Kade slides in front of me, giving me a full view of his blood-soaked back. Base pulls Lu behind him too.

"I want the four of you to put your hands above your heads and drop to your goddamn knees."

"This one is mine," Base mutters under his breath, but we can all hear. "I let you have the last one."

Kade lets out a breathy laugh and shakes his head. "You got your ass handed to you, and I had to step in."

When the man realises no one is listening, he radios to his team. "Send everyone to—"

The words stop, gurgling hits my ears then there's a thud. I look around Kade to see the man on his front, a blade in his skull. The murderer steps over him, the gas mask he's wearing drops to the floor and we all gasp.

"No time for dramatics," Tobias Mitchell says in a deep voice, standing above the dead body. He's wearing the same uniform as his victim. He nods to the door. "Let's go. The building's on fire, if you didn't notice."

"Dad?" Kade and Luciella say at the same time.

The former steps forward, hesitant. They don't believe their eyes. "How are you here?"

"Run now, talk later." His eyes fall on me. "Hello, little one." He looks at Base. "Sebastian."

"Shit," Base blurts. "I'm too scared to tell you to not call me that."

I grin at Tobias. "I knew you weren't dead."

"But I am," he says, smirking. "To the world, I am dead. Let's keep it that way."

"You're really here..." His son takes another step forward. Luciella is frozen in place, probably in shock.

Kade advances forward slowly and presses his hand on his dad's shoulder, who nods once, before his son lets out a sigh of relief and hugs him. And against his psychotic nature, Tobias hugs his son back, pulling Luciella in too when she finally runs at him.

Base is pale. Maybe from seeing a ghost – or the news that Luciella is carrying his child. It can't be all the people he killed tonight or the gaping wound in his shoulder.

"I thought you were dead," Kade chokes. "They identified your body."

Tobias pushes them back and nods. "Bernadette wanted them off my back. She faked my death. The stupid bitch only made things worse for herself."

Even her name makes me shiver.

The ceiling crackles as the flames eat at the wood, and Tobias kisses his daughter's head. "Stop crying, sweetheart. I'm okay. Look?" He pats his chest, over his heart. "I'm okay."

Kade pulls on the dead guy's uniform, and they both pretend to hustle us through the manor. Luciella keeps crying and whispering to her father that she loves him. He keeps telling her that he knows and begging her to shut up, so we don't get caught.

Kade holds my arm tightly to keep pressure off my legs, and I try to hold in my tears when I see the bodies lying everywhere. Russians. Officers. Kade's team. And others dressed in the same uniform as Kade and his dad.

The boy Kade saved, the one who wasn't allowed to work for him until he was eighteen, is lying in a pool of his own blood, a bullet between his eyes.

Kade pauses when he sees the boy's body then shoves me forward.

Whoever it is that attacked, their soldiers are swarming the place. Tobias mumbles in his worst English accent that he's taking us to the van and that Kade Mitchell was in the east wing trying to escape.

All of them sprint in that direction.

We veer into the kitchen where Kade kissed me that second

time, out onto the part of the grounds that leads to the pool house where we met, where we thankfully find the dogs cowering, and Tobias stops.

"Where's your mother? I couldn't find her."

"Ewan got her out," Kade replies as he bends down to comfort the dogs. "The police are surrounding the manor and trying to get everyone to safety. They think there are more bombs planted, so they won't come onto the grounds without their bomb disposal squad. What if they see you?"

"Don't worry about me. They think I'm dead, so I'm off their radar. All the bombs are disarmed. But I missed two," he says, gesturing to the havoc. "They snuck them in through the tunnels running under the manor."

Kade takes my hand. "We need to get the fuck away from here. We can take Ewan's boat."

"No," Tobias replies. "You all need to go to the gates."

"I'll take Luciella to Russia," Base says. "She's pregnant, and I'm not having her near any of this. My grandfather will keep her safe if he knows she's carrying his next heir."

"You fucking—" Tobias drops his gun and grabs Base by the throat, lifting him off his feet. "You better not have got my daughter pregnant. Are you trying to get her killed?"

Base kicks his legs, choking, until Tobias tuts and drops him.

"Fuck. Do you need to be so aggressive?" Base asks, rubbing his neck and turning pale. "We obviously didn't fucking plan it."

Tobias blinks and stares at his daughter. Something warm flashes in his eyes, but it quickly vanishes when we hear people yelling inside the manor and more gunshots firing. "Go to the manor gates and make sure you're all placed into protection."

His son frowns. "And leave you? No. I just got you back. Besides, Bernadette will be sending backup soon. We need to go. Now."

Kade turns in the direction of the boat, my palm firmly against his, our fingers locked together. I'm limping, barely managing two steps before Tobias says, "Stop."

We turn to look at him.

Tobias rubs the back of his head. "This is retaliation from one of the underworld leaders you angered. Don't worry, he's dead now."

He waves his hand towards the burning manor. "And that woman is in no state to cause this."

Kade frowns. "How do you know?"

An evil smile crosses Tobias's face. "Because, son," he says, raising both brows, "I have Bernadette Sawyer."

42

KADE

Before my dad was arrested, sentenced to life imprisonment and shipped to the institution to live out the rest of his days, he was an evil bastard who made my mother's life hell just by trying to love her the right way. It was a love he couldn't feel, so instead of giving her what she needed, he drove himself to insanity and destroyed himself, her and her life – everyone around her included.

To say he fell into obsession is an understatement. Dad didn't want to lose her and wanted her to feel like she had a functioning boyfriend who didn't rely on medication to survive who he is. So he did the one thing that broke him, causing a domino effect that made him spiral into someone else.

He stopped taking his medication. Stopped attending therapy. Never showed up for his support groups. He started drinking.

His obsession turned deadly.

The story ended right here, at the dog shelter I bought over not long ago and put in Barry's name – why are we here?

Stacey stirs in my lap, and I brush my fingers through her hair as the streetlights vanish and we're coated in darkness. "Where are we?" she asks in a rough voice.

"Somewhere safe," I reply then look at my dad through the mirror. "I'd love to know how you knew to come here."

"Does it matter?"

"You rose from the dead and are driving to *my* building," I add, my fingers still lazily brushing through Stacey's hair. "Yes, it matters."

Dad shrugs and keeps driving up the path. His eyes are sunken, probably from lack of sleep or from the stress of whatever the fuck he's been doing while pretending to be dead.

I was shocked when I saw that he was alive, but now, I'm starting to get pissed the fuck off. I mourned this motherfucker for months, and the whole time he's been shacking it up here, sleeping in one of the new beds, using the shower room and eating from the kitchen while I was losing my fucking mind thinking he was gone.

Jason is dead, and so was my dad, and all I can feel is rage towards him when I should be thankful – when I should still be hugging him and telling him how happy I am that he's here. I want to do that, but only deep down. I've watched my mother drink herself to sleep night after night because of how broken she was about his death; I can't just forget that.

I grit my teeth and look at Stacey, who shakes her head at me. "I know what you're thinking," she whispers, wincing a little when she tries to move her bruised legs. "He wouldn't have wanted to blow his cover by trying to reach out to you."

Her voice is quiet, but I know my dad can hear her.

"Let him explain his reasoning before you turn all dickheadish."

I snort weakly. "I don't believe that's a word." But Stacey has her own vocabulary, so I guess I'll give her that one.

I lower my hand to her thigh and caress the bruises lightly. "Where hurts?"

"It would be easier to ask where doesn't hurt. I feel like I've been hit by a bus."

"How do you know what it feels like to be hit by a bus?"

She scoffs. "I remember you said I sounded like a strangled cat when I sang and I asked you how you know what that sounds like. Copying me?"

I laugh quietly, leaning down and kissing the tip of her nose despite my face being covered in dry blood. "I have a room full of medical supplies in here. I'll clean you up, then we're showering and going to sleep."

"Demanding Kade is cute," she says with a smile.

Base tuts. "You both make me sick."

"After what I've witnessed since being your friend," I reply, "you can't say shit."

"Language," Dad scolds, cutting the engine.

Luciella yawns and lifts her head from Base's shoulder. "Where are we?"

"I think your dad is going to kill me for getting you pregnant and leave my body here."

"I hope he does," I add when Luciella looks confused.

He's been staring out the window, silent, probably thinking of ways to keep my sister safe from the Russian princess and her family. I doubt he's happy about any of this. He doesn't like kids. He'll be fully focused on keeping her away from his new family.

I could hide her, but I know how controlling Base is. He'll make sure she's safe. He even said his grandfather will help him now.

I hope he wasn't lying.

We climb out of my dad's stolen car, and the dogs follow behind us. I wrap my arm around the small of Stacey's back, taking most of her weight while we walk forward.

I pause and stare at the person leaning against the doorframe with his arms crossed.

"Why aren't you with your pregnant wife and daughter?"

Barry pushes himself forward and shoves his hands in his pockets. "I was dragged through hell watching what that woman did to you. If you think for a second I'm going to take a back seat now, you don't know me very well."

I narrow my eyes. "You're an idiot. Go home."

Dad shoulders past Barry, and they exchange glares. My assistant doesn't look the slightest bit shocked he's alive.

I feel myself growing more irritated. "You knew my dad was alive?"

A short nod, and he glances at my dad. "Security at the manor was breached, so getting that information to you would have been a risk. Instead, we've been working here for the last two months. We finished the renovations and the system operating room. Then, when Bernadette finally surfaced, we ambushed her transfer as it was going through Glasgow. She's been here for the last three weeks."

My nostrils flare. "Go home to your family."

Base pats my shoulder. "Let the kid stay."

"Kid?" Barry sneers, raising a brow. "Did you just call me a fucking kid?"

"You look like a kid. And watch your fucking language."

Dad takes the dogs inside with him then comes back and helps Stacey into the building while asking Luciella where her injuries are. After they vanish, I pinch the bridge of my nose as my assistant and my best friend fall into a verbal battle.

Base is smirking at Barry, and I'm too tired for this shit. I pull out my cigarettes and light one.

"I was Kade's best friend first," Base immaturely says, completely unfazed by the deep wound in his shoulder. "And I'll *stay* his best friend."

Barry is more than dumbfounded. "Is he serious?" he asks me.

"The kid needs to rein in his dirty mouth," Base retorts.

"He's not a kid; he's married with one kid and another on the way. He's also highly skilled in tech and combat, so I'd probably shut the fuck up if I were you. He could make your body vanish without a trace and have it look like an accident. Also, don't try to fuck with my staff."

"You're defending *him?*" Base asks. "Over me?"

I blow out my cheeks and take a draw of my smoke.

Base narrows his eyes at my silence. "But you like me better, right?"

I hand him the cigarette and don't give an answer as I leave them to it and head in to look for Stacey.

When I bought this place, it was a wreck. If it weren't for the foundation and bones of the building being intact and salvageable, I would've torn the entire place down and started from scratch.

We'd already replaced the roof and installed a security system and satellite signallers so we could still work. But with everything that's been going on, I thought work on this place would've come at a standstill; that all the labour put in would be for nothing.

But Barry wasn't kidding when he said he'd fixed it up.

The plastered walls smell of wet paint, there are new doors, and cameras installed for extra security, and five bedrooms with supplies in case of emergency. I can see a hole in one wall already though from someone punching it. My guess is that Barry and Dad got into a fight.

The hallway is dark, the spotlights only faintly lighting the route to the medical room. I pass by the office – my mother tried to kill my dad in there over twenty years ago, but she chickened out.

I pause for a second at the last door, wondering if I should go hunt for Bernadette instead, but then I hear Stacey's voice travelling through the door. She's hurt. I need to see her first before facing the reason for my demons growing stronger – the reason why the voices are louder.

Stacey is sitting on a chair while my dad rummages through one of our first aid kits, and Luciella is downing a glass of water and splashing it on her face beside her. Both of them are covered in remnants of debris, their skin stained from the smoke.

I open one of the cupboards and check if Barry brought in the oxygen stock I wanted. They'll need some to clear their lungs.

Relief fills me as I grab one and attach a nasal cannula, handing it to Luciella, who's coughing a lot more than Stacey. She gets it into place and closes her eyes while her head drops back. "I didn't know how bad my lungs were."

"We all inhaled a lot of smoke. You're pregnant, so you can use it first."

For the first time in years, Luciella, my pain-in-the-ass twin sister, smiles at me – a proper, full-on smile. "Thank you, Kade."

It throws me off. I nervously look around the room. "Yeah."

"You need that closed up," Dad says, pointing to the gash on the side of my skull.

I nod to the drawer beside him, where all the shit is for stitching up wounds. Again, for emergencies. If any of us got seriously injured, we couldn't go to a hospital.

Barry is, to some extent, trained, but I know my dad learned a lot from my mother and from intentionally harming himself in the institution only to heal himself again using only what he could make from objects in his surroundings. That was something his therapist fought hard to help him stop. The thin scars literally covering my dad's body are proof that his therapist had no idea how to stop him until ten years ago. He'd said the stinging helped the mental pain.

I stand silently, watching as the girls show my dad their injuries. Luciella passes the oxygen to Stacey and cries until Dad stops to cuddle her, and Stacey keeps looking at me and smiling.

She's tired. So am I. Of everything. I could sleep for years with her and just close off the world. Soon. I'll do that soon. I want to take her to the shower room so we can get cleaned up and go to bed.

"We don't have anything here to check on the baby, but Barry will get us an ultrasound machine."

Luciella nods, but then she falls apart again, and tears slide down her face. I've never witnessed my sister cry this much. It's... awkward. I just stare at her. So does my dad. Then Stacey takes her hand and squeezes.

"It's going to be okay."

"I'm scared. I'll be a terrible mother."

Dad shakes his head. "You are everything your mother is, and she's exceptional. It's a shame who the father is though."

Stacey takes my hand, and I sit down beside her and inspect her legs while Dad and Luciella keep talking. She's telling him how wonderful my best friend is, and how long he waited around until she gave in. Dad scoffs a few times – he doesn't really understand love outside of his own. Though I think he understands me and Stacey to an extent because of how much I struggled – just like he did.

"I'm still shocked as to why you let Sebastian of all people impregnate you," Dad says, and Luciella goes red with embarrassment. "But if you're happy, then so am I."

"I think I am," she says. "I only found out right before the explosion." She places her hand protectively over her stomach, and I look at Stacey, whose eyes are shining. We used to have that. "Even if I lose Base to the Russians, I still have a part of him."

She won't lose Base. He's an asshole, but he won't walk away from his own kid. He'll hide them and most likely himself. He'll step up.

He and Barry are obviously still arguing outside. He's borderline flirting. It's like it's built in to his personality that he can't have a conversation without picturing the person naked, and I should know – he's been flirting with me since we were fucking teenagers.

Once Dad picks out any debris from everyone's wounds, I kneel between Stacey's legs to help clean up the gashes on her skin. The bruises from where the beam trapped her are just above both knees. They're swollen and already turning a dark shade of purple.

"Are you okay?" she asks me, and I raise a brow in confusion. "The manor. Your dad being alive. And... everything that's been going on. It's a lot to deal with."

"I just need to stay focused," I reply, wiping dry blood from her ankles. "I want to deal with Bernadette and—" I stop, breathing slowly. "I'd like to move on from all of this."

It's been constant since I was nineteen. I'm still on edge, and I feel like something bad's going to happen. It always does.

"So do I, but I think we should sleep first."

"Where is Bernadette?" I ask Dad. "I need to see her with my own eyes."

"In the room you built for her. She's been drugged up for twenty-two days and locked in a cage."

I lean my elbows on my thighs, crouching in front of Stacey as I look at my dad. "A cage?"

He smirks. "You'll see when you go downstairs." Dad hands me a cloth for my own face. "Why did you buy this place anyway?" he asks me. "Of all the places, you buy this building."

It holds a lot of meaning. This was where all the chaos ended nearly twenty-five years ago. There's a little flowerbed and plaque outside for Aunt Gabriella.

"I already said it was so I had somewhere to take Archie and Bernadette when I eventually caught them. It's in Barry's name, so they can't track us here." Then I narrow my eyes at my dad. "But you already knew that, didn't you? You've been hiding here while we all thought you were dead."

Stacey places a hand on my wrist to calm me down, and I'm thankful for it. I shouldn't be mad at my dad – I just can't handle my emotions properly right now.

"I couldn't risk exposing myself. Barry couldn't either. He told you; the entire manor was bugged, and you had several rats in your team." He shrugs. "I killed them by the way. You're welcome."

"What about the people who attacked the manor?"

"I caught their boss in the tunnels and cut his head off. He had long, greasy hair, so I wrapped my hand around it..." He mimics the move with a cloth then swishes his arm. "I cracked about four bodyguards' faces in with it. Then I threw on their uniform and used the radio to track where everyone was."

"Jesus," Luciella blurts, screwing her face up. "I didn't need to picture that when I feel so sick already."

"Sorry, sweetheart."

I blow out a breath as I sit beside Stacey and start sorting through my own wounds. Nothing extreme, but I've burned my arm and I have a few cuts. Plus, I'm covered in other people's blood.

The door opens, and Base finally walks in with a bleeding lip. "Sorry, princess. I was in a football debate with the kid, and he decided to punch me. Kade, deal with your dog."

Despite everything going on, I huff out a laugh.

Barry rolls his eyes behind him. "I'm going to call Lisa and get some sleep. Everyone else should sleep too. We'll put together a strategy tomorrow on how to deal with Bernadette, then if all the threats are gone, we can all go home."

Unless we count my apartment in Stirling – though it's probably blown up as well – I have no home. I glance over at Stacey, and the thought vanishes.

Five minutes later, Base is gritting his teeth as Luciella and Dad try to fix the wound in his shoulder. There's a bullet lodged in it, and she's using forceps to try to pull it out carefully while Stacey wipes at the spilling blood with gauze.

I spot Dad pulling a box from under one of the units and tossing multiple tablets into his mouth, swallowing them dry. "You have your meds?"

He nods. "Barry got them for me. We didn't want to risk... you know. I need to keep my head."

That's good. There's less chance of him losing his marbles then. No one wants an unhinged Tobias Mitchell around Bernadette Sawyer. He'd kill her on the spot and ruin all the fun.

Then he'd hunt down Ewan, mutilate him and force my mum to marry him or some shit.

Dad tosses me another box, and I realise it's full of my meds. "Barry said you've been doing well on those. I tried similar ones for a while when I was a teenager, but they didn't work for me. I'm glad they work for you."

I should mentally smash myself in the dick for not even thinking about my own medication. My therapist is going to be fuming with me. That's if he doesn't believe I died in the manor's explosion along with everyone else.

"Mum is going to freak out," I say. "She'll be mad we didn't bring her with us. I'll reach out before bed and let her know we didn't burn to death."

"No," Dad snaps. "No one tells Aria I'm alive. It's better if she thinks I'm dead."

I tilt my head. "What?"

Stacey glances at Luciella, but it's Base who scoffs and speaks through his pain. "That's just fucking selfish. You want her to suffer, thinking you're still dead? I would've thought a psychopath like yourself would want all her attention."

Dad glares at him. "The world will think you all burned to death in the manor, so *you* are also dead, Sebastian. I'm more than happy to make that permanent. Just because you're the father of my future grandchild does not grant you immunity. If you ever talk to me like that again, I will fuck you up more than Bernadette Sawyer ever did."

Base audibly gulps. "Fuck. You are one scary bastard."

I sigh and shake my head. "We don't have time for this. I'm going down to the basement."

"Wait until you've slept," Stacey says. "You can barely stand straight."

I won't believe it until I see her. Trapped. No longer vying for me or threatening everyone I love. I want to see the bitch in her place, incapacitated and at our disposal.

Dad throws down his sandwich in annoyance. "Follow me."

The walk to the basement takes forever. We're all either limping, slow from exhaustion or Dad is stopping us every minute to show off his DIY work.

It's pitch-black in the short hallway leading through the basement. I can hear drops to my left as I hold Stacey's hand. She's leaning on me a little, limping, and I stroke my thumb over her hand when her hold tightens from the darkness and creaking wood.

We reach the metal door I designed, and Dad enters the code, followed by a beeping sound. The door opens, and I grimace, covering my mouth and nose at the strong smell of urine, unwashed skin and vomit.

The small light in the corner illuminates a thin Bernadette curled up into a ball inside a large animal cage sitting in the middle of the room. There are lines attached to her veins – the blush pink dress I've seen her wear loads of times is filthy, and she has an outgrowth of roots, dark against the wine-red hair she always had. She's pale, make-up non-existent, no expensive jewellery cradling her body.

The sight should make me feel some sort of relief, but the anxiety about her capabilities still rides my nerves into war. She could heal, manipulate one of us, get free and target everyone. She could kill Stacey, rip the unborn baby from my sister's womb and make sure my dad dies for real.

I let go of Stacey and inch forward. I almost don't recognise the she-devil as she lies unconscious before us all – the woman who singlehandedly ruined my life, destroyed me in ways I can't describe. The bitch who killed my brother.

Base comes forward too, but his reaction is totally different from mine.

He snorts out a loud laugh. "She looks like fucking Gollum in a wig."

43

STACEY

"I am *not* having sex with you in here."

Kade groans into my shoulder as the water from the shower pelts down on us, the washroom lined with six cubicles, white tiles and low lights so we aren't blinded. Our naked bodies are pressed together, his front to my back, and his hands are firmly on my hips as he starts dragging kisses across my shoulders and up the side of my throat.

My body hurts, but the warmth is helping a little – Kade giving me extra attention only relaxes me more, even though we definitely can't have sex only hours after everything that just happened – not to mention the fact I'm still on my period.

"I'm not trying to have sex with you. Am I not allowed to taste your skin without sinking my cock inside you?"

"Your dick says otherwise."

Kade cups my breasts and swipes his thumbs over my nipples, and the sensitiveness of them has me whimpering. "Because my girl is fucking beautiful and sexy, and I know how good she is when she's on her knees."

"I'm always good," I reply, giggling when he tightens his grip on my chest and drags his teeth lightly against my throat. "We can't do anything. We need to hurry up."

Kade shakes his head. "I see no reason to hurry up."

"Base has been waiting outside for five minutes already."

"So? Fuck him," he retorts then pauses. "No, fuck me. Or let me fuck you."

"So you *are* trying to have sex with me?"

"Yes."

"Not happening," I reply, and he lowers his head to my shoulder again, the water soaking his hair and making the dark strands fall over his forehead.

His cock twitches against my ass. "I'm going to die a born-again virgin."

I let out a sound of disbelief. "You are *so* dramatic. Are you spending too much time with Base?"

"Probably."

He groans again when I slap his hard-on away and hugs me to him. We stay under the water for a little while longer. I stroke my fingers down his arm, making sure I avoid the healing skin, then I turn in his arms to face him and brush my hands into his wet hair.

His eyes are sunken, and the colour in them is so dull. "You look like you could sleep for months."

"Not yet," he says, kissing my forehead. "I'll sleep for months once I deal with Bernadette."

I can't wait. We'll go somewhere with the dogs and just be together. Maybe one day there will be miniature versions of me and Kade too. But right now, in the middle of all this chaos, I'd rather only worry about Kade. No offence to Luciella, because I know her pregnancy wasn't planned, but I'd be far too paranoid not to go to Russia as Base suggested. He called his grandfather after we checked on Bernadette, and he agreed to hide her, but she refused; said doing so would take her away from Base. Tobias was right –

his wife thinks he's dead after heroically running into a burning building to save lives, so they have a chance to be together.

Then there's Kade's assistant.

"Barry's taking a huge risk being here. He could walk away and go live his life without anything biting him in the ass. What if Bernadette's people find out she's here?"

"They're all dead," Kade states. "Dad either freed them from her manipulation, or he shot them without hesitation. He kind of took out the underworld for me, and he's only one person."

Tobias, when triggered, is a machine. A maniac. And he doesn't care about death or fear it, which makes him even more dangerous. He's intelligent – *insanely* intelligent. He strategically took out everyone gunning for his son without being detected by the police.

Still, despite his capabilities, I think he's a goofball who gives the best hugs.

"Barry is still taking a risk."

Kade nods and hums. "He's loyal. Probably too loyal. But I know nothing I can say will change his mind. He hates Bernadette and everything she stands for. He… he witnessed me go through a lot, way before I forced myself back into your life."

"I know," I reply, sliding my arms around his neck and bringing our bodies together. "And you didn't force yourself back into my life. You were always there, and I never once stopped loving and wanting you."

"So you'll let me fuck you?"

I roll my eyes. "No. I'm still on my period."

He shrugs. "Shower. Water will wash away the blood while I pound into you. It's a win-win. Besides, you have three holes I can use."

For a second, I contemplate the other way, then I huff. "No."

He laughs a genuine laugh that shows his straight white teeth and shakes his chest. "You loved it the last time."

I know Kade is looking for comfort. When we're joined as one, he can let go and all his worries wash away until he finishes. Sex was Kade's punishment for so long, but with us, it's his sanctuary. To feel the love and the care and the way we fit so perfectly.

We once said we fit like the perfect puzzle – two frayed jigsaw pieces trying to stick together but being forced apart. Now I think we're fixed and solid in place, finally able to complete the beautiful, messy and magical picture of our life.

"You're touching my cock. The mixed signals are fucking with me, Freckles."

"Do you even have a condom?" There's sarcasm in my voice, because I know for a fact he doesn't, and we already agreed that falling pregnant right now would be irresponsible.

"No," he replies, narrowing his eyes. "Why would I wear one?"

Forget what I just said – he obviously wasn't listening when I said we should wait. I lightly tap the side of his shoulder. "No unprotected sex until this is over, got it?"

"I didn't exactly stock up on rubbers when I was renovating this place."

"Then no sex."

He looks mortified. "Fine." But then he pulls my mouth to his and kisses me hard. He's hard between my legs, his breathing is heavy, and I absently rock my hips into his, wanting so badly to hike my leg up and pull him into me.

"I'll have you know," I say, biting his bottom lip until it snaps back into place, "I have fantastic self-control."

He grins then walks me further into the shower, until my back presses to the cold tiles. He crowds me, kissing me so passionately, I feel like I might shatter.

Kade owns me, but that's okay, because he belongs to me too.

"If I could keep you hidden in this building for the rest of our lives, I would." He kisses me again. Possessively. "I have no idea what's going to happen next. Once I deal with Bernadette, everything is black in my head. It's like I know deep down, after what she made me do, I don't deserve a happy ending. I don't deserve to have you. I killed husbands, boyfriends, fathers, and there were a handful of wives who got in the way. I… I… Why should I be allowed to have you?"

"Because it's not up to anyone else. I *want* you. I *love* you. You were trapped and blackmailed. There's a huge difference between being forced to kill and doing it for fun."

Kade's head lowers, and so does his voice, his palm flat against the tiles next to my head. "But I enjoyed the killing part."

I stay silent, blinking as drops of water hit my eyelashes.

"When I knew the targets were bad people, I had no hesitation ending their lives. It was an adrenaline rush watching the light leave their eyes, knowing the world was safer without them. But, in the end, they were someone's partner or father or son, and I shouldn't be allowed to be one."

"Well – you are. The sooner you believe that, the better. You're my other half, and one day, you're going to be the best father in the world." I cup his cheek and stroke it. "One day at a time. You're not a bad person, Kade. You're everything to me."

I smile, and when he doesn't speak, I continue. "We should sleep and get rested enough for tomorrow. I assume you're going to make Bernadette's life hell when you wake."

"You'd be correct. She—" He pauses, hurt flashing across his face as he presses his cheek into my palm as if he's starved of my touch. "She killed Jason. I'm not going to grant her mercy by making it quick."

"Then make it hurt. Make it hurt for as long as you need."

It's morbid that we're even discussing this. Years ago, I would've been horrified to be standing in a shower, naked, holding Kade while someone was locked in a room just below us, covered in their own bodily fluids. But now? I'm not bothered. If anything, I want her to feel unimaginable pain for a long, long time. I want it to hurt. I want to hurt her.

She took what was mine. She warped Kade's mind and turned him into a... machine. She tried to destroy him, but as he places soft kisses over my face and helps me wash my hair, I realise the only thing she did was *try* and *fail* to do all those things. Because he's here, with me, loving me forever.

Kade is still that eighteen-year-old boy, nervous of touch, falling in love with his sister's best friend and not having a clue how to control his emotions.

Only now he's killed people. His future is balanced on a knife edge, and we have no idea if he'll fall off the blade unscathed or be cut open for the world to see the colour of his soul.

The police offered him aid, but I don't trust them. I don't trust that they're going to just let him get away with those crimes, despite him being manipulated and blackmailed into doing them.

"You can carry me to bed now," I say, rising on my toes to kiss him again. "I think Base has fallen asleep at the door."

He dries me then kisses the side of each knee before wrapping bandages around my clean skin. My body is sore, but Tobias gave me strong painkillers to dull the pain.

He lets me put cream on his burned arm, and when we open the shower room door wrapped in towels, we find Base is gone. Kade holds my hand all the way to our designated room like we're two high schoolers walking to class.

Our room is small and plain, but I love the fact the bed isn't huge. We'll get to be close, even when we sleep. Barry wasn't joking when he said he'd fully renovated this place. Even the wardrobe has spare clothes for me, and there's a drawer filled with new toiletries, a hairbrush and a small bag with tampons I definitely need.

Once I pull on cotton shorts and one of Kade's tops, I lie on the small bed, staring up at him rubbing a towel into his hair.

"What?" he asks, watching as my body curls around the duvet. "Are you still really sore?"

"No, the meds dulled the pain. But there's no heating in here and I'm certain my toes are falling off."

He chuckles deeply. "The manor was too hot; this building is too cold. Where do you meet in the middle?"

I roll my eyes. "When my supposed boyfriend takes the hint that I'm asking for cuddles."

He tosses down the towel, his dark, wavy hair basically dry. He needs a haircut, but I like getting a good fistful of the length it's currently at. "Maybe I don't want to cuddle you."

I laugh and lean my chin on my fist. "Says the clingy one."

Kade smirks, pulling aside the duvet and getting in beside me. I yelp as his warm hand grabs my cold thigh and hikes it over him, then he wraps his arms around me so the warmth of his body bleeds into mine.

He feels like home.

"Better?"

"Yeah, but your dick is still kind of hard," I state, sliding my hand over his growing bulge and making it twitch.

"Of course it is. I just spent half an hour watching you rub soap all over your naked body. Regardless of our situation and the monster of a woman downstairs, my body's going to react to seeing yours," he replies, groaning as I trail my fingertip down the length of him, feeling the faint ridges and veins. "You want to take my boxers off and tend to it or you going to keep teasing me?"

I lean my chin on his chest and look up at him. "I think my jaw might fall off if I blow you again. It's all we've been doing since I got my period."

"You aren't really bleeding much now though, are you? Can I fuck you?"

"Hm," I say, considering.

His eyes glint. "Please?"

There's a bang on the wall beside us. "The partition between us is thin. Don't you dare make me share a room with Barry."

"Sorry, Tobias!" I call out, feeling my face turning a deep shade of red. "Goodnight!"

Kade shakes his head, rolling onto his side and holding me to his chest. "Sleep, Freckles. I have a feeling tomorrow's going to be a long day."

"Goodnight," I whisper, watching his lashes fall as his eyes close. I nudge his nose gently with mine. "I love you."

But I don't get a response, because he's already fallen asleep.

Once Kade's arm goes heavy and his breathing turns shallow, I check to make sure he's definitely asleep by asking, "Do you want a drink of water?"

I wait for a beat. Two. Three. Nothing. Good.

I carefully slide away from him, tiptoe towards my shoes and pull them on before sneaking out of the bedroom. The door closes with a soft click, and I take a deep breath and lean against it.

Luciella and Base are in the room across from us, and going by the loud snoring, Base is fast asleep. How my best friend can sleep beside such a despicable noise will forever baffle me.

As I make my way down the corridor, another door opens, and I pause and glance behind me. Tobias is rubbing his eyes and leaning against the doorframe, wearing only a pair of cotton shorts.

"Where are you going, little one?"

For a long moment, I stare at him, this older version of Kade. "Um," I start, pointing my thumb in the direction I was going. "Water."

"The kitchen's that way," he says, gesturing in the opposite direction.

"Oh." I falter and straighten my spine, limping past him. "Sorry if I woke you."

"You didn't," he says, sighing and slipping back into his room before coming out in a black top that accentuates his build. "Are you hungry?"

"A little."

I follow him into the kitchen and sit at the table. He gives me a glass of water, and I watch while he rummages through the fridge and then opens the freezer.

My eyes widen. "Why does that look like a human head in the freezer?"

Tobias chuckles and lifts the plastic bag holding a man's head. "It's her driver. He tried to stop the ambush, so I cut his head off with a meat cleaver."

He did the same at the manor. "You have a thing for decapitating people, it seems."

He chuckles. "I had no idea, but I guess I do."

I'm speechless as he tosses the bag back into the freezer and slams it shut before filling a pot with water and sticking it on the stove. So domesticated. Like he hasn't spent over twenty years locked up and unable to cook for himself. Now he's boiling eggs and offering me a biscuit from a tub labelled "Do not touch". I guess Barry stole his cookies.

I have no idea why it makes me laugh, but it does, and Tobias looks at me like I have five heads. The man is a touch robotic with his movements as he shifts around the kitchen. He's still learning to do things himself, and it must be weird to even make boiled eggs for someone else.

"I missed you."

Tobias stops and turns to me. "What?"

"When we thought you were dead. You're like a dad to me.

And... and you were the first person to believe me. I told my own dad when Chris started abusing me, and he said I was just a hormonal teenager seeking attention. But you didn't even hesitate to offer me support. It took me so long to find my voice, and it was you who got that voice to work. Thank you. Truly. You saved a little bit of my sanity that day."

His cheeks go red, and he busies himself with the eggs again.

Socialising isn't his strong point. But then again, he's not wired like most people. If he has no response for someone, he'll simply ignore them. I don't find it rude – maybe because I spent every day with him for nearly a year and watched him fuss over baby Eva.

Sometimes Tobias will just stare into nothingness, still as a statue, hands on his lap. Like he's in a trance. Whenever I've seen it happen, he doesn't even blink, doesn't respond, doesn't snap out of it for ages. I remember Kade telling me about these episodes way before I met Tobias. He'd just come home from visiting him in America and told me the first time he noticed it was when he was seven. He was blank, unmoving, and they didn't visit him for eight months after that.

He loses his grip on reality during those moments, but thankfully, since being here, he's been focused.

"Can I ask you something?"

He sighs heavily, so like his son, slouches against the counter and replies, "If you must."

Leaning my elbows on the table, I balance my chin on my hands. "Why don't you want Aria to know you're alive?"

"It's easier that way," he replies without having to think. "She's spent the last twenty-five years worrying about me. Always visiting, calling, doing what she can to help me on my bad days." Tobias shrugs, but I can tell he's uncomfortable. "Me being dead will hurt her for a while, but then she'll be free of me."

"You'd just walk away from her after all those years she's spent devoted to you?"

"I escaped prison and am presumed dead. What benefits does she get from knowing I'm alive?"

"She'll benefit from knowing because she loves you."

Tobias looks away from me and stares at the wall. "Why were

you out of bed?"

Could he and Kade be any more alike? Subject-changing assholes.

"I told you, I needed a drink of water."

He turns his head and raises a brow. "Then why is your glass still full?"

I try not to blink.

Tobias scoffs. "You were going to see Bernadette."

I can't even lie to him now. It's written all over my face. "She and I are due to have a chat. I wanted to give her a piece of my mind while everyone was asleep."

Tobias laughs, nods then walks out of the kitchen without another word.

I stare at the empty doorway in total confusion.

A few minutes later, Tobias walks back in with a syringe to hand. I've still not touched my water. "Come on," he says, nodding behind him. "I'll take you down."

"Oh… Uh…" I frown. "You're taking me down?"

I fully expected him to drag me back to my room and tell Kade, not escort me.

Tobias twirls the syringe between his fingers. "I'll give her enough of this so she hears you, but I'm not leaving you alone with her. You were going to sneak down, so if I say no and take you back, you'll be a pain in my ass and try to go there anyway."

I blink. He's not wrong.

He shrugs and turns towards the door. "Move."

44

STACEY

As soon as Tobias inputs the code, the metal door to the dark room opens. The smell hits me worse than it did earlier, and I try not to gag. The outline of the cage sits in the middle – when the light turns on, I see the IV lines hooked up to some sort of machine I've only seen in hospitals.

I can hear heavy breathing, and part of me wishes she wasn't breathing at all.

"Can you give me a few minutes?" I ask Tobias. "She can't hurt me. I want to talk to her, just me and her."

He narrows his eyes. "Two minutes, and I'll be standing outside the door." He heads to the machine, messing around with wires and the syringe. "She'll wake, but she'll not be able to get near you. The cage is locked, and she's weak."

Tobias tugs at the cage door to double-check it's locked, then pats my shoulder as he leaves. He'll be right there, and with him being the way he is, I definitely only have two minutes.

For the longest moment, all I can do is study her and enjoy the sight despite my nose burning and my eyes watering. Everything she did comes to the forefront of my brain, and I wish I could just kill her. But I have no right. It should be Kade and Base who end her life.

Her entire team is dead – no one is looking for her. Dead husband, dead daughter, and pretty soon, she'll join them in hell.

Her skin is pale, red from the areas that have bathed in her mess, and she has saliva dripping from the corner of her mouth. In another life, I would probably feel sorry for her and want to help her escape. Maybe the happiness I feel seeing her this way means I'm spending too much time with people who ooze insanity.

She blinks, her head moving a little as whatever Tobias gave her works through her system. I wish she would wake up fully so I could slap her and she'd know it was me.

Her body flinches, then a muffled sound is ripped from her throat as she tries to lift her head to look at me.

"You look so pathetic," I sneer. "I wish I'd had front-row seats to see the look on your face when you realised you'd finally lost." I laugh. "You certainly did fuck with the wrong family, didn't you?"

Her eyes are dead when she opens them, and I don't think she even knows who I am, because she has no reaction to the sight of my face. Maybe she thinks she's hallucinating.

I smile at her anyway. "Hello, Bernadette."

Groggily, she shifts in the cage until she presses her back to the bars, facing me completely. She looks drunk or off her head on drugs. She blinks a few times, head lolling from side to side.

The humanity deep within me wants me to get her a glass of water, but I won't. Her mouth is probably dry, she's most likely starving to death and she could use a hosing down, but still, all I do is watch her trying to realign with reality.

The woman who watched Kade since he was a child. Ruined him.

Her slim hand raises slightly, shaking, but then drops to her lap.

This bitch raped my boyfriend when he was a teenager then

sold him to so many people. Turned him into a killer. A drug addict. Mentally and physically abused him. She did the same to Base, then sold me and Luciella at an auction. She took Tobias and who knows what she did to him, because he'll never talk about it.

She killed Jason.

I think even Chris's sickness pales in comparison to this horror of a woman.

"You must have thought you were some sort of queen. Having so many people bow down to you and kiss your shitty pedicure."

She would look good with the syringe sunken into her eyeball, like Kade did with Chris and the nails. But the thought of doing it makes me shiver, so I just keep taunting her.

"It was nothing but fake respect though. You had to blackmail everyone. You probably even blackmailed your mutilated husband to fuck you. The fact you let him have sex with your own daughter makes me sick. *You* make me sick."

Bernadette's eyes lift to me, and they darken a touch, but she doesn't talk – she doesn't seem to be in any state to respond.

I settle on my knees in front of the cage, watching the way her body tenses at my proximity. Her stench is making me feel sick, but I stay in place.

And I know I should be terrified that she could grab me through the cage, but she looks far too weak to do so. I want her to break out of the cage and fight me. I want to grab her by the hair and swing her around the room.

I always found Bernadette to be annoyingly beautiful. She had the hair, the perfect make-up, the style and figure, and she was extremely powerful. She didn't need Archie; he was just her shadow. But right now, she looks like a corpse: thin and sweaty and pale, her face drawn from lack of food. No make-up to hide her imperfections. No styled and dyed hair.

I still don't feel sorry for her.

I lower my voice and smile through my words. "I watched Kade put a bullet in your daughter's head. I heard the way her body dropped to the ground when it killed her instantly. I saw the light leave her eyes. She's better off dead. You can't hurt her anymore. You are by far the *worst* mother I've ever come across."

Bernadette just stares at me, shaking, but I can see the rage kindling in her eyes.

"It must be killing you inside. You tried everything you could to make Kade fall in love with you. You tried to trigger some sort of Stockholm syndrome. You abused a teenager, raped and drugged him, and turned him into a machine. You forced yourself on him and Base, turned them into property by allowing others to pay for them while threatening everyone they loved."

I pause, still glaring at her. "All that power and control you had over him and he still never fell for you. His heart always belonged to someone else. *Me.*" I point to my chest and hit the bars in anger. "Fuck you for trying to take him away from me. You failed. You'll always fail, because he'll always be mine."

I stand, looking down at her in disgust.

"Kade won't give you a quick death. He'll make it last as long as he can. And I'll be right there when he finally puts a bullet in your black heart and sends you straight to hell, where your equally sick husband will be waiting for you."

I keep seeing the way Jason's body went limp in front of me, and a tear slides down my cheek. It's an angry tear that represents so much heartbreak. It represents years of neglect for me and Kade. It's a tear that falls onto the dirty floor, representing how close our lives were to ending in that fire, how we're holding on for a future we might not get.

Because I have no idea what will happen next.

"No one will help you. No one will stop his wrath when he unleashes it. You're the one that made him this way. You're the reason he has so much going on in his head, and it's only right that he unleashes it all on you." I snort. "I'd be surprised if he didn't try to fuck me in front of you. How jealous would you get, huh? To see him actually enjoying it. I might suggest it."

My voice echoes in the cold room, and I can't seem to stop letting the words fall from my lips. Each one is angrier, gritted out through my teeth as I fist my hands at my sides.

"Kade will never love you. Do you know why?"

Bernadette is staring at me, her eyes rolling slightly, her head dropping to the side.

I'm not an angry person. I'm not a fighter. And I'm the last person you'd expect to wish death on someone. But I want her to die a horrifying death that's splashed across every news channel. I want the world to know she got what she deserved.

"I'm the one he loves. While you're lying in your own filth and wishing you were dead, I'll be in bed with him, wrapped in his protective arms and making promises we can keep. He'll make love to me – he'll whisper praises in my ear about how I'm made for him, how it drives him insane the way I fall apart beneath him." I laugh derisively. "I hope it kills you a little inside to know that Kade Mitchell will *always* choose me."

The metal door swings open to reveal Tobias. "Time's up."

I glance over my shoulder at her. "I want her to die, but I also want Kade to make it last as long as possible."

"He won't be able to move on until she's dead. I think dragging it out will be harmful," he says, turning off the light and closing the door. It beeps to indicate it's locked, and we walk along the corridor. "You okay?"

I nod and hug myself. "I just wanted to get it all out while I can. Kade and Base will be the ones to deal with her, so I wanted to get my piece in and out the way." I look up at him. "Thank you for letting me come down."

He shrugs. "She's incapacitated. I wouldn't let you in there if there were any risks she'd harm you."

Tobias walks me to my bedroom door, and when I limp too harshly, he takes my elbow. Exhaustion hits me then, and I yawn far too many times before saying goodnight.

The door clicks shut, and Kade groans and sits up, rubbing his eyes with his knuckles. "Stacey?"

I hug myself. "Sorry for sneaking away. I... I had to go see her."

He quickly gets to his feet and eats up the distance between us. "Did she hurt you?" he asks in panic, searching my body for any new injuries.

"No," I say, my voice cracking as my eyes burn with tears. I have no idea why I'm crying. "She wasn't in any state to even speak. I needed to tell her what I thought of her. I'm sorry. Your dad was standing outside the door. I was safe."

"And you're okay?" He carefully takes my face in his hands and wipes away my tears as I nod. When I start to shake, he pulls me against him and kisses the top of my head. "Don't go near her again without me there. She's unpredictable."

"I know." I sniff. "Your dad has a decapitated head in the freezer."

He laughs. "Sometimes I forget how psychotic he can be. Come on. Let's go back to bed, Freckles. It's cold without you."

45

KADE

I can't go down and see her. Does that make me weak?

When we first got here three weeks ago, I had to see with my own eyes that Bernadette was incapacitated. For peace of mind, knowing the army that followed her for years was dead and no one was looking for her, I needed to see her caged and no longer a threat to me and everyone I love.

But the thought of going down there, where she screams for help and calls my dad and Base every name under the sun at the top of her lungs, makes me physically ill.

Not that I'm scared or nervous to see her. I'm not. The torture she's going through right now brings me joy, but if I go down there, I'll strangle her so fucking tightly, I'll decapitate her and put *her* head in the freezer too.

The number of daydreams I've had, imagining myself ending

her pathetic life, should be questioned. Maybe I need stronger meds?

My anxiety has lessened. I don't black out anywhere near as much as I used to, and there's been no seizures, or dissociation that I'm aware of. Most of all, I've been getting more than enough sleep.

Stacey makes me go to bed at the most fucking ridiculous hours. Three in the afternoon and she wants to nap? I go with her. If she falls asleep on the sofa while we all watch TV, I carry her to bed and cuddle her until my eyes close. Once her legs healed, we started walking through the forest with the dogs, and one time, we fell asleep under a damn tree while talking about our future.

I've never slept so much in my life.

But still, I won't go down to that room and look at Bernadette. She's being fed but only scraps of what we don't eat, and she gets one glass of water a day – just enough to keep her alive but weak enough that she's out cold most of the time. The more weight she loses, the larger the cage looks.

I know this because Stacey goes down there a lot without telling me – I find out as soon as she gets back to our room. She'll sometimes just sit in front of the cage and not speak, enjoying the view of the woman who tried to take everything from us. Other times, Stacey tells her stories about us and watches the way Bernadette twists with jealousy. All Bernadette managed to say was, "You aren't good enough for Kade."

Asshole of a woman. Does she not realise Stacey is better than us all? Even if she did stab her in the foot then leave the blade in until the wound got infected. She hasn't gone back down since.

Barry's gone home several times. He had to take the tunnels so he wouldn't be spotted. Not that he's even in the limelight or known to the authorities, but he wasn't taking chances. He also brought the ultrasound machine so Luciella could hear the baby's heartbeat – which was strong and clear as day. Not that any of us knew how to fucking work the thing.

Base's eyes lit up in a way I've never seen.

I know he's nervous. Luciella has begged him to accept he's going to be a father, but he told me last night, while drunk off his ass, that he doesn't think he'll be a good parent. That he'll fuck it all up because he can barely control his own life.

But Dad told him he can't be more of a fuck-up than him – the only time he's spoken to my best friend without threatening him.

Despite what they both say about themselves, I know I'll be a damn good father. My kid will come first, forever and always. All I need to do is kill one last person and I'm done with that life. I'm getting my shit together for myself and Stacey.

Just to make things ten times better, Stacey is spending more time with my sister than she is with me, and Base is glued to my side. Whenever my dad tries to talk to me, Base attempts to fit into the conversation by being his usual talkative, hyperactive self, but Dad just glares at him until he shuts up.

Base acts like a devoted puppy that never knows where the line is drawn, but he's the opposite.

For starters, he's an animal in bed. We were forced into so many threesomes together, and the guy is into some primal shit that even made me baulk and wonder if he'd kill someone during it. He even stabbed a guy in the ribs once while... you know.

Despite his soft side, Base is a scary motherfucker. I'm extremely glad we don't need to do anything intimate anymore, because even though I never, ever, *ever* let him fuck me, I knew it was only a matter of time until Bernadette ordered it.

As much as it was forced upon us, we tried to keep ourselves together. We'd tell each other over and over that she wouldn't break us. When we were on each other, we'd promise not to let it ruin the friendship we'd built since we were kids.

I was always the receiver. Always. I think Bernadette liked it that way.

I would never have survived going through all of that without Base.

I watched him kill relentlessly, and when Bernadette first forced him to get into her bed, he chucked a vase at her head and got himself tied to the headboard for it. The entire time Bernadette had her mouth on him, he threw insults at her, drove his knee into her face and told her she was terrible at blowjobs. And when he refused to do as he was told, she made him fight with guards until he passed out from blood loss. Most of the time, I joined in when he grew weak and was losing, but then they started restraining me and making me watch him get beat up.

We went through the wringer with that woman, and she probably thought she'd break our friendship, but in all honesty, I trust Base with my life now more than ever. Even if he likes to occasionally embarrass me in front of my girl by asking her if I gyrate my hips with her like I did when he had his mouth on my cock. Or if I make a certain noise when I cum. If I kiss her as passionately as I kissed him.

Despite it being a trauma response for him to be brutally annoying about the subject, I punched him for that. An hour later, when Luciella found out I hit him, she barged into my room, threw a shoe at me and called me an asshole for giving him a black eye and swollen jaw.

Dad asked why we were fighting, but no one would tell him.

Base will never stop being Base. Because dark humour is his thing when he's mentally drowning.

He leans against a tree outside the building while we wait on the dogs doing their business and getting some fresh air. It's raining, both of us soaked through, but the silence is good.

"Is Tobester cooking steak?" he asks, ruining the mood.

I wince. "Please don't call him that. He'll chase you with an axe again."

Base bounces on his heels and inhales deeply. "He's making steak. I'm going for a bite."

I huff and whistle for the dogs to come as I follow my friend into the kitchen, stopping in my tracks when I see my dad wearing rubber gloves and a plastic apron. The dust mask only confirms what he's doing.

But regardless of the scene, Base walks straight over to the stove and looks down at the meat. "Where'd you pull that from?"

He reaches for a piece, but my dad snatches his wrist. "Unless you've decided to take up cannibalism, I highly suggest you keep your filthy paws off."

It takes Base a second to click, and then he backs away in disgust. "Oh, what the fuck? You're cooking bits of Archie?" He steps behind me as if I'm a shield. "Kade, your dad is more insane than I thought."

I pinch the bridge of my nose. "I have no idea why you're surprised. Why else do you think he took the time, during all the chaos, to go back for the buckets?"

"I don't fucking know! This is disgusting. Why are you acting so calm? Your dad is cooking body parts!"

Dad chuckles while flipping the meat in the frying pan. "There's normal food in the fridge."

Base inches forward. He's not domesticated in the slightest and never goes in there, so I lean against the wall and wait for it. I spotted earlier that Dad had moved Bernadette's driver's head out of the freezer to defrost. Maybe he's planning on feeding that to her as well.

As soon as he opens the fridge and sees the melting head inside, he gags, slams the fridge door and runs out the room yelling that we're all going to die.

"He's a little dramatic," Dad says, shaking his head. "You need better friends."

I shrug, glancing at Barry as he walks into the kitchen, unfazed by the sight before him. "How are Lisa and Eva?"

"Fine. She had some cramping, so we had her up at the hospital for an emergency ultrasound, but all good."

He crosses his arms, looking over at my dad. "Why are you cooking human meat?"

"You'll see. Can you bring Bernadette up?"

I flatten my lips as Barry huffs and goes to the basement. "You're going to feed her Archie's body parts, aren't you?"

"She won't know until after. A little surprise for her," he says, flipping over a chunk to fry the other side. "You can't say much. Look what you did to Christopher."

I hum in response.

"I called your mother."

My eyes widen as I drop my arms to my sides. "Are you insane? We said it was too risky to reach out to her."

"I didn't say anything. I just wanted to hear her voice."

"Still risking our location." Sighing, I sit down at the table. "Have you decided against not telling her you're alive then?"

"No," he replies instantly, staring down at the sizzling human flesh. "But she should know her children are alive. It's not fair that she believes she's lost you and Luciella too."

They're still searching the remains of the manor, hunting for evidence, but it's assumed that we're dead – consumed by the explosion or the fire. I feel terrible that my mum and Ewan will think that, and even Dez and Tylar, but we need to stay hidden until we deal with Bernadette the way she deserves. Then we'll come out of the dark. And only then will we get to move on and find peace in our fucked-up lives. I get to go build that house for Stacey and our future kids. I'll make a swing, build a tree house, and I'll be there every second of their lives.

"I told you, it's too risky," I say, glancing at Barry as he drags Bernadette by the arm along the floor. "She's in protection right now. Her phone might be traced. You calling her might have alerted the authorities that we're here and alive."

Barry drops Bernadette on the ground. She's groggy, smelly and her hair is matted at the back of her head. Good.

"She's in protection in Ireland with Ewan," my assistant says. "Tylar and Desmond are with them too. From what I can see on their reports, they're just being cautious. The protection is set to end shortly." Barry folds his arms and crosses his ankles. "The manor is gone. It collapsed completely a few hours after you escaped. The chances of them finding anything is low."

"Is Stacey still sleeping on the couch with Luciella?"

Barry shakes his head. "She's in the shower room. The dogs are sleeping outside the door." He looks over at my dad, then at the buckets, then to Bernadette and lets out a low sigh. "I thought you were joking."

"I don't joke," my dad replies. "Surely you know this by now?"

Barry only slightly shakes his head and raises his eyebrows at me. I pat his shoulder as I walk past and go get Base. He should be here when she realises she just ate her husband.

The dogs lift their heads when they see me making my way to his bedroom. Stacey's still showering. She usually takes an hour minimum when she's in there herself. I want to go in and kiss her against the tiles, but I stop a few doors away.

Base is being sick in the bathroom.

"Bernadette is in the kitchen," I say to him. "Come watch her eat Archie."

"Fuck," he replies, spitting into the toilet bowl. "I have a strong stomach, but fuck."

"Let's go," I reply, tossing him a face cloth to wipe his mouth. "We watch her suffer together."

I lean against the doorframe while he brushes his teeth and takes a few deep breaths, staring into the mirror. Then he pushes off the sink, shakes himself off and follows me to the kitchen.

We both pause in the doorway, seeing Barry lifting Bernadette into the chair, the cooked human meat on a plate in front of her. Her head lolls to the side as Tobias stabs her in the arm with a syringe and pushes the plunger to empty the contents into her system.

A few minutes later, Bernadette's eyes lift to me, and they widen a little. "K-Kade."

"Don't fucking talk to me."

"After everything I've done for you?" She's slurring her words, slobber down her chin. The adrenaline Dad gave her is kicking in. "You're going to allow them to treat me this way?" She sneers. "You're better than that."

Base blows out a breath and manages a laugh, and all I do is stare at her as if it will burn a hole in her face. Dad washes his hands in the sink, kicks aside the bucket then leans against the counter – silent. Deadly silent.

"Eat," Barry says. "This is the only courtesy we'll give you. You're growing weaker, and we aren't kind enough to let you die yet." He cuts a strip of meat from the chunk on the plate and lifts it to Bernadette's mouth. "Eat."

Her lips part, and Base grimaces and turns away. Her eyes are on me. Burning into me. Fucking watching me like I'm going to help her.

She chews and swallows. Then she takes another bite and another and another, until the chunk is gone. Barry tips water into her mouth, but only a little, pulling the glass away when she chases it.

Dad tilts his head. "How did he taste?"

She glares at him, weak, then glances down at the plate. Her eyes lift to me.

Base steps forward. "He asked you a motherfucking question, bitch. How did your husband taste?"

Her brows pull together in a confused frown, her bones shaking. "W-What?"

Base grins. "I think you ate a part of his leg."

"Yep," Dad says. "But we can't be sure since Kade blew him up with a grenade in his mouth."

She vomits all over the table and passes out.

For two days, Bernadette is forced to eat her husband until we decide what's next on our let's-torture-Bernadette-until-we're-bored plan.

Base came up with this next part. And I agree. Luciella and Stacey are inside helping Dad tidy up, Barry is sleeping and the dogs are playing in the shallow river in front of us.

"We're not here to talk," Base says, dropping Bernadette on the ground next to the river. "We're going to play a little game. We like games, don't we, Kade?"

"Yeah." I smirk and cross my arms. "You loved to play games too. Didn't you, Bernadette?"

She doesn't say a word, but her eyes are pleading with me. She's delusional if she thinks I'll help her. She's still in her dress. Still dirty as hell. So when Base told me his plan, I dived into it.

Base grabs her by the throat and lifts her off her feet. Then he walks into the river with her and smashes her into the surface, holding her under while her hands slap at his arms. Her body is so frail and weak; I'm used to her being a little curvy and tanned and always walking about in stilettos while issuing orders.

She looks so fucking pathetic.

Base pulls her from the water enough for her to choke and gasp. "We should've brought some soap. She's disgusting."

"I don't think that'll help."

"Nah," Base replies, shoving her back into the water. "Being rotten comes naturally to her. Do you want a shot?"

I shake my head. "I'll kill her if I go near her."

Base lifts her from the water, walks back out with her and drops her on the ground. "Beg for his forgiveness," he snaps, yanking her head up by grabbing her nested hair. "Tell him you're fucking sorry."

"K-Kade," she coughs. "Please."

Something snaps in my head, and I drive my foot into her face, bursting her nose and causing blood to piss down her mouth. I want to hit her again, but I fist my hands.

Base sees me struggling to keep it together and opens the bottle of vodka he had sitting to the side, crouches beside her and grabs her jaw to pry it open, then upends the bottle so she chokes on the strong spirit. He shoves the neck of the bottle as far as he can into her mouth, so she's deep-throating it. I can see her throat contracting around it as vodka spurts up, coming out her nose, puddling in her eyes.

Her pulse is racing in her neck. Her eyes are wide despite being filled with the strong spirit.

I move forward and wrap my fingers around her throat while Base keeps the bottle in place. I squeeze, and I can see the pressure building behind her eyes. "How does it feel to have your control taken away?" I ask, not really needing an answer. "You feel powerless as your lungs beg for fucking oxygen."

"You're going to kill her," Base says, pulling the bottle out of her throat, which only makes me tighten my grip. "If you don't want to yet, then stop."

I let go, stepping back, my heart racing in my chest with adrenaline. She gags and spits and coughs as much up as she can, vodka no doubt stinging her eyes and nose. The projectile vomit nearly hits Base. He flies back in revulsion.

Once she stops spewing, he steps forward, crouching in front of her. "Do you remember doing that to me? You made me stand still after forcing me to down *two* bottles, and if I stumbled, you used a taser on me."

My head snaps to him as he stands straight. "I didn't know that."

"There's a lot you don't know. You were in France working. I ended up in her little hospital wing for a week because of that night."

I knew other shit happened, but I always assumed it was the same stuff we always went through.

"Stand the fuck up," Base demands, and I can see the rage building in his eyes. He tosses the empty bottle into the water behind her while the dogs paddle around. "Stand. Up!"

Bernadette lets out a sob as she pushes to her knees, her body weakly doing as it's told as she gets to her feet, staggering to the side. She tries to grab Base's hand to help herself stay put, looking pathetic, but he slaps her arm away.

"Don't touch me. You'll never touch me again."

"You won't win," she says in a shaky voice, the alcohol starting to take control. She's looking right at me. "You won't break me. My team will find me, and you'll all be dead."

I scoff. "Funny. Your little minions are gone, and there isn't a competition to win. It's just us and you, and everything we have to do to you as payback."

Base comes up beside me. "Get into the water," he says, gesturing behind her. "I want you to drown yourself."

Somehow she manages to pale even further. "N-No."

Base sighs and shoves her so hard, I hear the air rush out of her lungs as she catapults backwards into the water. Her head hits a rock, and she struggles to keep herself up. It's shallow, about knee deep, but for some reason, she's unable to stand.

There's blood coming from her head too. Maybe she hit the rock too hard? I don't care.

Base chuckles beside me. "I won't let her actually drown," he says. "But check out how ridiculous she looks."

She does look ridiculous, desperately trying to stand up and failing, her lungs filling with water as she thrashes.

"She's not really trying anymore," Base says, tutting. "Right, let's get her back inside. She's making me cringe."

I shake my head, and we both grab an arm each, then he pulls her dress down over her bony ass. We drag her all the way into the building, the dogs following, then down into the basement before shoving her into the cage for her to shiver.

There's no heating down here, and she's soaked from the river.

"He belongs to me," she whispers to Base, her eyes going in all directions. "He w-was mine all those n-n-nights we spent together. You were n-never enough for him, Sebastian."

He scoffs. "Are you for real? Who the fuck was the one getting him off when you failed to?"

I roll my eyes, but he's not wrong.

"You tried and failed to ruin our friendship. He is mine. He's my best friend and the brother I never knew I needed. The only thing that's yours is your shame and your disgusting life – what little is left of it anyway."

Despite the pain and alcohol in her system, she laughs. "You have no idea what he needs."

Base turns to look at me. "I think even if I sucked you off in front of her, she'd still think the same."

I nod once and look away from him, staring at the sad excuse for a woman before us. She narrows her eyes at me. "Tell him I w-was enough. You... you don't need that whore either."

I grit my teeth. "Her name is—"

I glance up when I hear the door open. The beautiful woman in question is standing there in her PJs, her hair wet. "Oh, sorry. I was just seeing if you were down here."

I kick off the wall and approach my girl, turning to Bernie as I pull Stacey to my side. "You see how beautiful she is? I need her more than I need fucking air."

Base hums. "Did you know she thinks she's enough for him, Stacey?"

Stacey glances between us. "How silly."

My friend grabs Stacey's hand and places it right over my cock. "I think we should prove just how wrong she is," he says, and despite it being both their hands on me, my dick reacts. "We should prove that we're both enough for him."

46

STACEY

My heart stutters in my chest as Kade's gaze clashes with mine, but he doesn't move our hands. Neither do I.

Hesitation flashes across Kade's face then, his eyes flicking to his friend then back to me. As if he's silently asking if this is something we should really be doing. Probably not, but Bernadette forced these two together on so many occasions, and I think this is Base's way of battling his inner demons more than anything else. Because, as his fingers curl over mine, tightening our hold on Kade's thickness, he uses his body to back Kade into the wall, taking me with them.

"Tell him, Rhodes," Base says, his chest rising and falling as he starts moving our hands together, stroking, squeezing, watching as Kade looks down at our hands then at us. Base presses his forehead to Kade's shoulder and continues, "Tell him who he belongs to."

"Us," I reply. Then I reach up and grab Kade's jaw, making him look at me. "You belong to me. Not her." I glance over my shoulder as Bernadette slouches against the cage, barely conscious. "She's an irritant."

When I turn back, Kade's staring at me, his hand lifting so he can brush his fingertips through my hair, his thumb pressing to my bottom lip. His pupils are expanding, the black taking over the pale blue as Base and I stroke him.

When he draws my lips to his, Base lets out a deep, choked gasp as Kade snatches his throat, holding him back but not removing his hand from his cock.

His tongue pushes its way into my mouth, and I give him everything I can as I kiss him back, sucking on his bottom lip then grabbing his wrist and pulling his other hand to my throat.

He's not strangling me the way he's strangling Base, but he's showing dominance with the hold – showing that if he really wanted to, he could snap my neck without trying.

Not that he ever would.

Kade pulls his mouth away from mine, the back of his head hitting the wall as his cock throbs in our palms. He pulls Base to him and presses his forehead to his. "I know you need this, but I fucking can't."

Base fingers falter around mine, his movements slowing.

"I don't belong to you, and you don't belong to me." Kade lets go of his throat and grabs the back of Base's head. "I fucking love you, but you need to stop. You're with my sister."

Base freezes completely, his breaths stalling, then he releases my hand, pulling away from us. His hands run through his hair, and he looks erratically around the room. "Fuck."

Bernadette tries to chuckle. "S-See? No... No one w-wants you."

"Shut the fuck up," he spits. I think he's going to start mocking her more, but instead, he snaps, dragging her from the cage and punching her across the face, making her smash into the floor. "You did this to me!" He hits her again, but Kade grabs my attention by shifting us, so it's my back against the wall this time.

He slams his mouth to mine then, claiming me as his forever, thrusting into my hand while his best friend cries behind us. He's losing it as he yells in Bernadette's face that she tried to ruin his life and failed, before hitting her again. There are tears coursing down his face – it's the first time I've ever seen Base show this level of emotion.

He's too busy beating the living daylights out of Bernadette to notice us as Kade kisses me deeper, whispering possessive words against my lips as he yanks my body to his, wrapping my legs around his waist.

"Stop looking at me! Stop, stop, stop," he yells, punching her between words. "Fucking stop looking at me!"

Base drags a bloodied Bernadette to a chair and ties her to it while Kade sucks along my jaw and down my throat, marking the skin at my pulse.

He presses his rock-solid cock between my legs, and I moan and grab a handful of his hair, tugging his mouth back to mine. "We can't do this in front of him," I say breathlessly. "It's not right."

There's a horrifying scream that doesn't stop Kade from grinding against me, and I look over his shoulder as he goes back to kissing and biting my throat to see Base using a small blowtorch on Bernadette's face.

I look away before I can properly see the details of her eyes melting.

The smell is terrible, but all I can focus on is Kade's hands sliding down my sides, as if he's committing each inch of me to memory and not paying any attention to the gruesome torture going on behind him.

Base tosses aside the blowtorch and wipes his mouth with the back of his hand. "You need to force people to be with you, but me and Kade? We have people who love us. We love each other. And you tried and failed to screw with that. Every time you ordered me into your bed, you thought you were breaking me. But up here…?" He taps his temple. "Stronger than ever. I'm going to be a father, and I'll make sure I'm the best damn father that I can be."

Bernadette is shaking, her face destroyed. She's unrecognisable.

Kade grabs my jaw. "Do you want to go home?"

The glint in his eyes makes me smile despite the screaming

going on in the background. "My home is wherever you are."

He kisses the tip of my nose, lowering his voice. "I think I'm ready," he says quietly, and I've never heard him so… vulnerable. "You can go if you don't want to see this."

I swallow and kiss him. "Do what you need to do. Then we can live."

Base steps away from Bernadette, coming towards us. "I'm seconds from killing the bitch." He hands Kade the blowtorch. "Your turn."

He laughs and takes it but places it down. "I have a better idea," he says, staring down at how pathetic Bernadette looks, clawing at her melted face. "The first time she made me kill someone, I was forced to strangle them."

Base crosses his arms. "Me too."

Kade fists his hands then unclenches them, and Bernadette flinches as he grabs her by the hair and forces her to her knees. He's behind her, holding her up. "Wrap your fingers around her throat."

I move to the other side of the room so I can watch as Base cracks his neck from side to side and laughs like a maniac. "Bernadette, Bernadette. How weak you are, Bernadette." He grabs her by the throat with one hand. "Try to scream and beg for mercy – I dare you."

She bats at his hands, failing to get out of his hold.

"Press your thumb into her carotid artery," Kade says. "And tighten your grip. Make sure she can't breathe."

Base does just that, tightening his fingers around her throat. She's fighting but getting nowhere between his hold and Kade's fistful of her hair. She can't see them – can't see the look in their eyes as she slowly loses her battle of slapping at them.

I should leave, but I can't. The depraved part of me wants to watch this.

Her mouth is open, and I can see her tongue as she tries to gasp in air, desperate for that one bit of oxygen that may save her life. If her eyes weren't melted, I'd see the light slowly vanishing from them.

"That's it. The blood flowing to your head is reducing," Kade says, pulling a small blade from his pocket and pressing the sharp edge to her cheek, cutting into the skin while Base chuckles. He grits against her ear, "Your brain is being starved of oxygen and nutrients. Isn't it, Bernadette? Your skin is changing colour. Feel how we rob you of breath, of life." He lets go of her hair and holds her nape, pushing her into Base's hold. "Fucking die."

"Fucking whore," Base spits as they both press into her neck from the front and behind, and her legs give up, her body already unmoving, her arms straight and shaking from the pressure going to her head.

A tear slips down Base's cheek as he grits his teeth, his arms locked, shoving forward, and when he lets go, Kade snaps her neck with a rapid crack to the left. Her body drops to his feet, and he stares at her lifeless form.

"She's dead," Kade says, panting as they both stare down at her, as if it's not yet registered. "She's dead."

"Check her pulse."

"Can you not see the mangled neck?" Kade retorts. "Or did you miss the popping sound it made?"

Base leans down and presses two fingers against her pulse anyway then stands quickly, raking his hand through his hair. "Fuck, we killed her."

Kade nods. "Yep."

"She's dead."

"Uh-huh."

"Gone."

"She's fucking dead, Base."

I'm waiting for the relief, the smile, something to show he's glad this is done. That Bernadette being out of the picture is the beginning of everything for him and us and everyone.

Bernadette Sawyer, the woman who destroyed a part of him that Kade will never get back, is dead.

But no weight lifts from my shoulders.

Base grabs Kade and pulls him into him, and I try not to get involved as Base starts sobbing into his chest. Kade is emotionless, but he's comforting his friend.

"She fucked us up, man. So fucking much. I just... I can't fucking forget how much she messed with my head. How the fuck do we move on? How do we forget? How do we live normal lives after what we went through?"

Kade presses his forehead into his. "We do it proudly. We fucking live because we survived the Sawyers. You understand me? You go out there, get my sister, and you try to sort your shit out for her and your kid."

Base wipes his eyes and nods. "We survived."

"We did."

"Then why do I still feel dead inside?" he asks. "Why is it still hurting?"

Kade grabs him by the nape and pulls him back in for a hug, slapping his back a few times. "We'll be dead together. You die, I die, remember?"

"You die, I die," he repeats, sniffing and looking down at Bernadette. "How can she still look evil, even when she's dead?"

Kade kicks her aside, so she's face down. "Barry will clean this up. Go shower. You have burned flesh on your skin."

His gaze meets mine. "You okay?"

I chew my lip, looking down at the dead body, waiting for her to bounce up and shoot one of us. "It doesn't feel over."

"I don't think it ever will," he says, pulling me into his chest and kissing me. "Now, about that home. White picket fence or brown?"

I laugh and shake my head. "I would need to repaint the white more often than the brown."

Kade walks me until my back hits the wall. "You say that like you'd be the one painting when we both know I'll be doing it while you burn the house down with your terrible cooking."

Smiling, I whisper, "Kiss me, Kade."

He does. He smashes his lips to mine as his body presses me into the wall, his hands grabbing at my hips and sides and breasts, one hand sliding up to my throat, holding me there as he kisses to the corner of my mouth, along my jaw to my ear then pulls my lobe between his teeth.

"How does it feel?" he asks. "Having the hand on your throat that just killed Bernadette Sawyer."

"I want you to take me to bed."

He pulls his mouth away, his nose touching mine. "I can't

promise I won't try to fuck you on the way to our room. It's too far."

I grin, curling my fingers into his top and yanking him to me, so his mouth is hovering over mine. "I want you inside me. Now."

"Without a condom?"

I nod. "I want you, hard and fast, then I want you to fill me with every drop of cum you have."

Kade grabs my hand, pulling me towards the door. We step over Bernadette's body as he drags me out of the room that stinks of burning flesh, up the stairs and through the first door we come to – a storage cupboard.

It's dark, empty, and I get a second to look around before Kade snatches my jaw and walks me backwards, until I hit a wall. "Just to clarify, you want my cum in you. You're okay with that?"

"Yes."

Kade uses his free hand to unbutton my PJ shirt, exposing my breasts to the cold air, my nipples already tight. "Don't bullshit me, Stacey. You can't regret this."

I whimper as he pinches my nipple then caresses it with the pad of his thumb.

"I'll give you time to think."

I frown, but he drops to his knees and pulls one of my legs over his shoulder. A moan slips from my throat as he sinks his teeth into my inner thigh, my PJ shorts still covering me. My head falls back as he licks and bites and sucks the skin as far as he can to the apex, then kisses my core through the annoying fabric.

He looks up at me, his long, dark lashes accentuating the blue of his eyes. "I wanted to do this in front of her, but then again, I want to be the only person to see you this way." He curls his fingers into the waistband of my shorts and pulls them down, taking my underwear with them. He presses his thumb to my clit, and I tense. "You're all mine."

"Yours," I breathe.

He pockets my thong, and time stands still as he dives between my legs, pulling one back over his shoulder to open me up for him as he sucks on my clit, slipping his tongue inside and then around the sensitive area.

His fingers grip my thighs, and my spine tingles as heat spreads from my core all the way down to my toes. "Kade," I moan. "Oh fuck."

Tongue delving into me, he holds my gaze with his hooded one, taking my clit between his teeth. "This pussy is mine," he says, licking and kissing and trapping my clit between his teeth again. "This ass..." He grasps a handful and squeezes. "All of you belongs to me."

When my eyes flutter through the explosion rocketing through me, Kade shoves two fingers inside to maximise the orgasm, fingering me through it. I pulse around him, my legs barely holding me up as I scream into the empty room.

"Look at me."

I do. He pulls his fingers out and stands, holding my leg to his hip. I really look at him. The colour of his eyes, the shape of his lips, the feel of them against my fingertips as I trace them.

"I love you," I whisper.

"I love you too." He captures my mouth, kissing me softly. "Last chance, Freckles. If you don't want to fall pregnant yet, tell me now. We can wait if you want to. Anything you want, it's yours."

"All I've ever wanted was you. When we first met, when we were eighteen and falling in love, and every moment after."

Kade pushes inside me, and we both gasp, my lips parting and giving him full access to shove his tongue against my own, taking my breath away. He sinks to the hilt, and I grasp at his shoulders, adjusting to his size from this angle, my walls strangling his cock as he drags it slowly through my needy depths.

The kiss deepens. This time it's filled with desperation, like I'd disappear if we stopped. He cups the back of my head and pushes into me harder, picking up his pace. I whimper against his lips, and he sucks on my tongue, devouring me as passionately as he can while fucking me so hard, I think we might break the thin wall.

I don't think he'd even stop if we did.

"This is ours," he tells me, panting with each thrust.

I tighten around his cock, which is pummelling into me savagely. "Ours," I whimper.

I moan louder, and we hear voices on the other side of the

wall – Barry and Base arguing over something. But I can't handle holding in my noises, and since Kade still has his shorts on, shoved down only enough to free his cock, he's able to pull my thong out of his pocket.

"I'm asking… once more," he says, thrusting harshly between his words. "If I fill you with my cum, I won't regret it, but will you? Do you want me to stop?"

I answer him by digging my heel into his ass, sucking him deeper inside me. "Don't stop. Please don't ever stop, Kade."

"Open your mouth," he demands. "I don't want them to hear you."

He stuffs my thong into my mouth and presses his palm over it, hammering into me faster, shaking the partition behind us.

"We *can* hear you!" Base calls out. "I think the entire fucking building hears you."

Kade punches the wall beside my head, cracking the plaster so a glint of light streaks through, lighting up the dust. I don't flinch – if anything, his raging impatience makes me clutch his cock like a vice, a vicious building heat catching all my nerves and spreading like wildfire.

His palm and the underwear stop the sounds from escaping, and my eyes roll as Kade keeps going, a thin layer of sweat on his face. "You going to come for me? You going to fucking come?"

I clutch at his cock repeatedly through the orgasm that smacks into me like a car crash, my nails sinking into his shoulders, screaming around my thong as I screw my eyes shut.

"Eyes on me."

I listen, and he grins at me, biting his lip as he swells inside me, close to his own release. I know he can feel each pulse of my pussy, growing more intense as he keeps thrusting.

"You make me feel alive, Stacey. I've been dead for such a long fucking time."

When my high hits its pinnacle, Kade stills, filling me with everything he has. He removes his hand as he twitches and throbs inside me, then yanks my underwear out and kisses me like we might die tomorrow.

47

KADE

Embers from the fire heat my skin as Stacey lies between my legs. The crackling, the soft wind blowing around the trees, and the view of the hills and river at the break of dawn reminds me of a time me and Stacey went camping with my parents.

I was a nervous eighteen-year-old who couldn't stop obsessing over her. It seems nothing ever really changes because I'm still fucking obsessed. It feels like I've been in love with this girl since I was born.

I don't remember a time I didn't feel this way about her.

I do remember the butterflies I got when she snuck into my tent. I fucked her while my friends and brother slept beside us. I kept my hand over her mouth, a little like I've been doing the past two nights, since my dad's room is right next to ours.

What will it be like when it's just us two? No one else around, both lying in our bed, living in our house, planning our next day because we'll be able to.

Dad is arguing with Base about baby names. Barry is toasting a marshmallow that looks incinerated already. Luciella and Stacey are discussing the studio and songs to dance to when they eventually return. They talk as if my sister has that luxury – or maybe it's just hope – but I believe my best friend will do right by her, so I trust him to deal with this in a manner that means my sister stays unscathed, even if she is carrying his spawn.

Luciella glances over at me and smiles. "Are you okay?"

I nod slowly. "Has it sunk in yet? That you're going to be a mother?"

She shakes her head. "Has it sunk in yet that you're going to be Uncle Kade?"

My eyes crinkle at the corners as my grin widens. "Thank God our parents gave me a good name. Imagine being called Uncle Sebastian."

Base throws a twig at me. "Fuck you, asshole."

"I was the one who chose your names," Dad says. "If it was a girl, I wanted Luciella to be Lucy, and your mother wanted Gabriella incorporated in there somehow. If it was a boy, Kade was an easy choice between that and Aiden. We didn't know she was pregnant with twins at the time."

Grimacing, Luciella looks up at Base, whose arm is slung over her shoulders. "Twins would be hard if they end up like you."

He nods. "A nightmare. Especially if they're anything like you two."

I roll my eyes.

Then Base, doing his usual annoying shit, tilts his head at my dad. "Did you not kidnap Aria while she was pregnant and bring her here? Is that why you bought this place, Kade?"

I kick his shin. "Shut the fuck up."

Dad's eye twitches. "I was in a bad place at the time."

Milo and Hopper are lying on each side of us, the latter with his head on Stacey's lap, Hopper curled into a ball and pressed up against me. It's the calm I had no idea existed – I thought I'd lost everything, including my mind, yet here I am, smiling down at my girl, wondering what comes next.

The last two corrupt world leaders were arrested only a matter of minutes ago, and I've been able to breathe since. Even with the thick smoke from the fire, the incinerated marshmallows and the cigarette I inhale, I can breathe.

I lean down to whisper in Stacey's ear, "You want to go fuck before we leave?"

"We did it like an hour ago," she hisses back. "Your reload button needs to break."

Barry stands up, grabbing everyone's attention. "I think, going by the reports..." He zooms into something on his phone screen. "Yeah. They've got everyone now. It's really over."

He looks over at Base and Luciella. "I would suggest keeping Luciella hidden for now though."

"I was going to," Base snipes. "I'll go to my grandfather and demand a divorce and to keep Luciella in protection in Russia. He won't refuse me. I'm his only heir until my kid is born."

"What will you do?" Barry asks Dad. "You're technically dead. No one is searching for you, but I'd keep a low profile for now. I'll be able to keep your meds coming until I figure out something else."

For once, Dad doesn't argue with him or call him a dickhead. He just nods and warms his hands on the flames. "Does Aria know yet?"

"No," Barry replies. "But since the officers and investigators have closed all the reports and there's no active case, I think we're all safe to go home." He glances up at me. "Call your mother and let her know you're all alive."

"And then I need to leave?" Luciella asks.

"We'll stay here for now," Dad says to her. "Your plan better work, Sebastian."

"Give me a week," Base says. "I'll write down the address for where to meet me."

Stacey shifts between my legs, looking up at me. "We've waited years for this."

My head tilts. "For what?"

"The chance we deserve." She smiles. "I'm excited."

"What do you want to do first?" I ask, playing with her hair. "We can do anything you want."

She waggles her brows, lowering her voice to a whisper, so we can't be heard over the music that's playing. "I want us to go on dates, to live together and get married. You can fuck me every morning and night until I make you a daddy." Her lip traps between her teeth as my cock twitches. "How does that sound?"

I lean down and kiss her before we excuse ourselves – then I drag her back into the building, throw her on the bed and sink into her.

Luciella and Dad stand outside the building as we pack the car. The dogs jump into the back, and Barry shakes my dad's hand, tells Luciella to take care before getting into the driver's side.

"At least you didn't threaten each other," Stacey says to Dad. "Like I said before, there's a brewing bromance there."

"No," is all my dad replies. He looks at me. "I'm proud of you. I don't know if I've ever said it, but I am. You've gone through so much, endured so much pain that no person ever should, and you're still standing here, alive, and surviving it all."

The corner of my mouth twitches. "I take after my old man."

"Your mother sounded happy on the phone," he says. "I think it's still best if I remain dead to her. I'll reveal myself when the time is right."

Luciella tugs Stacey in for a hug, and they both start crying as if they're not going to see each other anytime soon. Me and Dad watch them, Base frowning at the ground, and when they pull away, I have the severe urge to wipe Stacey's tears and hold her against me and make sure she never cries like that again.

Stacey reaches up on her tiptoes and kisses my dad's cheek. "Thank you for saving me and being the dad I needed. Please stay safe."

He clears his throat and nods. "I'll see you soon, little one."

She heads to the car, and I pull my sister to me. "Don't stay away too long, brat."

She smacks my chest but sobs as she wraps her arms around me. My twin. My sister. She just cries harder, and I lean my head on top of hers.

When she steps back and wipes her cheeks, I give her a warm smile. "You're going to be an awesome mother. If Base doesn't keep you safe, I'll beat the shit out of him and break his legs."

He frowns and throws his arms out. "What the fuck?"

Dad pats my shoulder, and it's all we need, so I nod and walk to the car, hearing my sister break down as she says goodbye to Base for a week.

A week. Why are they acting like they're never seeing each other again?

I climb into the back seat, the dogs jumping forward to lick my face, and Stacey rests her head on my shoulder. "Where are we going to live?"

I shrug the shoulder she isn't leaning on. "I told you, I'll build us a house."

"In the meantime," she clarifies. "Where do we go in the meantime?"

"Ewan and Mum are back from Ireland and renting a house. We'll stay there until we figure out our next steps."

Barry turns in his seat. "I'm going to drop you all off and head home. Unless you need anything else from me?"

"You've done more than enough," I say. "I'll liquidate my company too. You're officially fired as my assistant."

He chuckles. "Thank fucking God for that. Don't even bother asking me to be your friend."

I snort. "I never want to see your face again."

We laugh, because we already know he's like a brother to me.

That makes me think of Jason, and my smile drops. So much loss, so many unsaid words – things I'll never have the chance to tell him. He sacrificed himself for my girlfriend, for my happiness, and I'm going to make him proud by being what he always wanted me to be.

Happy. I'm going to be fucking happy.

Base gets into the front, and we twist to wave at my dad and

Luciella while Barry drives us away from them, away from the building that has no trace of Bernadette.

Because Bernadette Sawyer doesn't exist.

The devil trapped me, but I got myself out of her hold. She's gone, and I'm fucking free.

Stacey falls asleep in my lap, and it reminds me of when I got her out of the States and away from Bernadette. I told her, while she slept in the same position, my fingers brushing through her hair, that she should have stayed out of my life, but she was always there. And that was true. No matter what I thought she did to break my trust, I was still in love with her.

The fifth rule never existed.

I'm even more in love with her now. My girl.

A couple of hours later, Barry pulls into the driveway of the house Mum and Ewan are renting. Dez and Tylar are sitting on the porch, and both stand up when they see us get out of the car.

They don't get a chance to come to us, because my mum and Ewan are bursting out of the front door and crashing right into me.

"Oh, son," Mum sobs, hugging me and kissing my head, wrapping her arms around me so tightly, I can barely breathe. Ewan is here too, his forehead to mine, both just standing with me while Stacey and Base go to see Tylar and Dez.

Barry gets the dogs out, and Mum still won't let go of me. "I thought I lost you too," she whimpers, her words broken. "I… I thought I lost all my babies."

"We were planning funerals with empty caskets until you called us," Ewan says, a tear slipping down his cheek. "We thought you'd died in the fire."

"I couldn't risk it," I say, pulling back from Mum. "If they'd tracked the call, they would've caught us, and I needed to deal with Bernadette."

"Did you? Did you deal with her?"

I glance up at Ewan and nod. "Me and Base strangled her, and Barry got rid of the body. Everyone's gone. All the threats. We couldn't show face until we knew every last person involved had been arrested."

Mum won't let go of my arm as I look over to see Base and Dez talking, Stacey and Tylar in each other's arms, and the dogs barking for attention.

Base and Barry agree to stay until morning, since it's the middle of the night. Barry looks like he's seconds from passing out too.

"Let's go inside," Ewan says, whistling to Milo and Hopper to follow us. "We made steak pie."

Of course Aria Miller has cooked a dinner big enough to feed an army at three in the morning. The table is covered with food, and Dez sits next to me so he can catch up on everything with me and Base.

Tylar and Stacey are in deep discussion about what we've been up to the last few weeks, and Mum won't take her eyes off me. "I wish your sister could be here."

Tylar nods in agreement. "I miss her." Her arm wraps around Stacey, and I imagine snapping it. "I'm so glad I got one of my besties back."

"She'll be home soon."

Mum finishes her water. "There are only four rooms. Sebastian will need to share with Barry, if that's okay?"

They glare at each other across the table. "I'll sleep on the floor," Barry says. "Or you can."

Base laughs. "Are you still pretending to hate me? Come on – we're practically friends."

Barry ignores him, and I try not to laugh at the outraged look on my friend's face.

Then Base mumbles through his bite of steak pie, "Tobes nearly fed me human food."

Mum's eyes widen, and Ewan tilts his head in confusion. "What? Tobias?"

I kick him, but he keeps talking. "Yeah. Mr Dead-Yet-Not-So-Dead. He was frying Archie's body parts like they were steak, and I nearly fucking became a cannibal, the asshole." He grimaces at his plate. "I've lost my appetite."

Mum pushes back from the table. "Where is he?" she asks, her eyes widening with every second. "Is... is he okay?"

"He's with Luciella. He's fine. He'll reach out when he's ready."

Standing, she wipes her mouth. "I need to go to him. Can you give me the address?"

I sigh, because I hate myself for this. "No. He doesn't want you to know he's alive yet. He isn't ready, and he's keeping Luciella safe."

Her eyes drop to the plate of food as she lowers to her seat once more. "Oh. But he's alive." Her eyes are watering. "Tobias is alive."

"Yeah. He needs to lie low for a bit."

She nods. "Okay." But that one word tells me she really isn't. Her hand shakes as she grabs her fork, and she misses the steak five times before Ewan places his hand over hers.

I get to my feet and go to her, crouching beside her seat and kissing her cheek. "He couldn't risk reaching out. He called you twice and didn't say a word. He just wanted to hear your voice. He's safe. He's alive, and once everything dies down, he'll reach out."

She forces a smile as a tear slides down her cheek. "I thought he died." She sniffles and blinks rapidly as more tears fall. "I… I thought I'd lost him."

I nod. "Me too. But he's as big a nuisance as ever."

Base scoffs. "Nuisance is an understatement. He fucking bullies me. Him and Barry. They don't even like each other!"

Stacey looks at me from across the table while Barry and Base go at each other. She smiles and mouths, *I love you.*

I go all warm inside. It's embarrassing how warm I get, and I think I'm fucking blushing. I smile back at her and press my shoe up against hers under the table like we're teenagers.

"We were thinking," Mum says, her eyes still wet. "Stay here for a few days before you contact the authorities and let them know you're okay and safe. The media interest will be intense, and the interviews are going to drain you all, so rest."

"I'm going to head to Russia tomorrow," Base replies. "I've got a shitload of grovelling to do and not a very long time to do it." He leans back on his chair. "Do you think I'd be a good dad, Aria?"

Her brows rise as she stabs a chunk of steak and dips it into gravy. "Is Nikita pregnant?"

"No," he replies. "Your daughter is."

Mum's fork pauses halfway to her mouth. Ewan's drops to his plate. "She's what?"

"Pregnant," Base repeats as if it's a given. "You didn't know?"

Mum and Ewan stare at each other, and I snort a laugh as her tears vanish – she covers her mouth and lets out a little squeal. "I need to call her! Oh, my, Sebastian dear, please grab me another glass of water."

Ewan flattens his lips. "Did you not say you hated children?"

"Don't you fucking start too." He shakes his head as he goes to the sink and pours Mum more water. "You, Barry and Tobes can stand in the corner while I become the best dad in the world."

"We need to bring her home," Mum says, giving Base a warm smile as he hands her the glass.

"Too dangerous," I say. "Base has an agreement with his grandfather's enemies, which is why he married Nikita. We told you this already. Luciella needs to stay dead until he fixes it."

Ewan narrows his eyes. "You've put my daughter into this mess."

Base smiles at him. "I'm not going to let you get to me. I just survived Tobes for weeks; you can't scare me. Not even Baz here can scare me. I'm a survivor of Tobias Mitchell, and I deserve a fucking medal."

"Language, Sebastian."

"Sorry, ma'am. You deserve a medal too."

I try not to laugh. "Baz?"

Base winks. "Suits it, doesn't he?"

"No," Barry retorts, clearly fed up. "I'll drive you to the airport in the morning, then I never want to see you again." Barry looks over at me. "Lisa and Eva are still at the safe house. I'll take them home."

Dez, who's been sitting silently for the past hour, eventually speaks, counting on his fingers each point. "So Tobias is alive. He fed Bernadette her own husband before you strangled her to death. Chris Fields is dead. The underworld you both were trapped in is destabilised. You both got away with hundreds of murders. And to top it all off, Luciella is pregnant with Base's spawn?"

Base raises a glass of water. "Spot on, Desmond."

"Did I miss anything?"

"I'm sure I'll text you if I remember anything. Since, you know, you were travelling the world with your girlfriend while we all fought for our lives. I think it's safe to say Kade loves me more than you."

"If one of you had told me, I would've helped."

Tylar leans her elbows on the table, looking at him. "You're terrified of harmless bugs, and you only drive small-engine cars because you don't like going fast. And you do the dishes with an apron on because the water splashes make you feel sick. When they were training at the manor, you pretended to be asleep half the time when Base came to the door because you didn't like fighting. What exactly would you have done?"

"Shameful," Base says with a repulsed expression. "Why are we friends with him, Kade?"

I shake my head. "Shut up, Base."

Once we finish eating and help clean up the mess, Mum shows me and Stacey our room. There's a king-sized bed, fresh sheets, fluffy pillows. I haven't slept like this in so long. I shower with Stacey glued to my back, and I lather her with soap while I kiss her.

She stands under the water while I wash her hair, then gasps as I drop to my knees until she unravels against my tongue. And when we climb out, I dry her hair then commit each inch of her to memory with delicate, chaste kisses against her skin as I slide her PJs on.

I kiss the tattoos I designed – the ones she got for me and never covered up the way I did mine. I kiss the initials on her back, then she falls asleep in my arms.

I don't sleep yet though – I stay with her against me, studying her face, playing with her hair while I silently go through every scenario in my head. Every scenario I've thought of that could ruin this moment.

None of them happen. Instead of the house blowing up or Bernadette rising from the pits of hell to take this away from me, I slip into a deep, peaceful slumber.

48

STACEY

Arms envelop me, keeping me safe as I stretch and yawn, the high sun glaring through the window making me wince and screw my eyes shut. For the first time in what feels like years, we slept until the middle of the day, peacefully dreaming of our future.

And what a great future it looks to be.

Base came in here at some point – he was fed up with Barry shouting at him for snoring. He's sleeping on the other side of Kade, and he's snoring so loud, I'm debating smothering him with a pillow and telling my boyfriend to hide his body. His flight isn't until ten tonight, but he'll leave in a few hours to go home and pack. Barry said he'll go with him, wait outside the Prince manor then take him to Edinburgh Airport.

Lisa and Eva are still at the safe house, and I can't wait to video call them again. I miss Eva – her smile and her little giggle.

I can hear movement downstairs – and voices. Aria is cooking – the smell wafts upstairs and under the door. My stomach growls, and I slide away from Kade's hold, sneak off the bed and tiptoe around it, careful not to wake him and Base as I leave the room.

Across the landing, I knock the door, and Tylar opens it. "Oh, hey!" she whisper-shouts. "Dez is still asleep," she says, opening the door enough for me to see him face down on the pillow.

"I was going to take the dogs around the garden for some fresh air. Come with me?"

She nods and pulls on Dez's hoodie, following me downstairs. Aria greets us as the dogs jump up on me, licking at my hands and wagging their tails. We don't put their leads on as we open the back door and walk.

"Are you okay?" Ty asks me when we circle the house twice in silence, the dogs running back and forth with a ball.

"I think so," I reply honestly. "I'm worried about Kade."

"But how are you? I'm worried about you."

I look up at her, hugging myself as the cold air nips at my skin. "I killed my stepbrother," I say. "And I wish I'd dragged it out and made it hurt more. Does that make me a bad person?"

She shakes her head. "He was a monster. As much as dragging it out would've felt good at the time, the end is still the same. You won."

"I won?"

"Who's the dead one and who's the one with her boyfriend in bed, waiting for more cuddles, and a life ahead of her?"

Me. That girl is me. I have my entire life ahead of me, and I get to spend it with Kade Mitchell. I get to love and be with Kade Mitchell, and there's nothing in our way.

I smile at my best friend. "I missed you. But I'm glad you weren't involved in any of this. It's been... intense to say the least. But let's talk about you – tell me how things have been since the manor exploded and what you're going to do now all this is over."

We circle the house four more times while catching up, and I feel lighter, as if some weight has been taken off my shoulders just by talking to Tylar. Even with everything that's been going on, she's been making happy memories with Dez, just like she was when we were all at our lowest, and that's a good thing. It's a sign that even when the world is in chaos, even when terror and havoc and death greet us at every turn, someone, somewhere, is having the best day of their life. It's beautiful yet tragic. It's hope of better things to come.

When we get back into the house, Tylar helps Aria with some chores while Ewan sits on the sofa with his laptop, doing some work. He's looking into the possibility of rebuilding the manor.

The dogs stay downstairs as I go see Kade. He and Base are still asleep, the latter's arm slung over Kade's chest. I smile at them, pull off my hoodie then slide back under the covers and lie down.

Kade automatically, possessively, pulls me against him, causing Base's arm to fall off him as he turns.

I rest my head on the pillow, staring at his beautiful face. I trace my fingers across his lips, down his scar to his chin then run my fingertips up the bridge of his nose to his thick, dark eyebrows.

He hasn't had a seizure a long time now, and his blackouts are few and far between. I can tell when he's lost in his mind. He stares at nothing the way his father does. He'll blink uncontrollably, and his eye will twitch when he's falling into his own reality. It exhausts him, and I know it makes him self-conscious of the way it makes him look.

But he looks like a survivor to me. He *is* a survivor.

"Stop staring at me," he mutters, reaching up to grab my hand and pull me into his chest. "Go back to sleep."

There's a shift behind him, and Base throws his arm over him again. Kade's eye pings open, and he frowns. "Can I kill him yet?"

I snort. "Wait until he helps Lu, then you can kill him."

Kade pushes Base off him and moves us further to my side of the bed, rolling me beneath him with his arms trapped under my back, his head buried into the crook of my shoulder.

"Why are you cold?" he asks quietly, his warm skin against me.

"I took the dogs out with Tylar," I whisper. "I didn't want to wake you."

He hums.

My fingers brush through his hair, and he falls back to sleep.

Soft, little snores fall from his mouth; nothing loud like Base's.

Base and Barry leave in a couple of hours. Tylar and Dez are going to head home too, and Ewan and Aria are going to sit down with us to properly go over everything that's happened. Aria's excited that her daughter is pregnant – though I think she's worried about the situation, and she's worried about Kade and the effect all of this will have on him.

Kade is doing okay. I can see that, deep inside, he can't quite believe it's over, but his therapist is good. He'll make sure he's okay. We'll go to couples therapy too, like we planned. We'll work on our relationship, live our lives and then, if he hasn't already knocked me up, we'll move on to the next stage of our relationship.

Having a family.

One day.

I shiver as he wakes again and kisses under my ear, and I can feel how hard he is against my thigh. "Is that morning wood?" I whisper, careful not to wake Base. My eyes flutter shut as he sucks on my pulse, his fingers digging into my hip, the other hand moving under my shirt, tracing my ribs.

"Maybe." He's kissing down my throat. "Maybe I need you. I always need you."

"Yeah?"

He nods against my throat, dragging soft kisses up to my jaw, taking my bottom lip between his teeth. "I always fucking need you," he breathes, rolling his hips into me. A tingling sensation is already twisting up my thighs to my core.

I glance over at Base, who's still snoring. Kade grabs my jaw, demanding my attention. "He's asleep."

I nibble my bottom lip, and he presses his thumb to pull it from between my teeth. He kisses me as his hand glides down to my throat, holding me there when his tongue slips into my mouth.

I let out a whimper, and he pulls back, the hand on my throat now clamped over my mouth. "I need you to be quiet, Freckles." He grinds between my thighs, the underside of his cock rubbing against my clit. Watching me as he dry-fucks me, he keeps his palm where it is and lowers his chest to mine, licking and sucking at my throat as he keeps grinding.

My eyes roll, and I mumble against his palm, begging him for more as I rock my hips up to meet his cock – so hard, so thick and long. I want all of him every day and every night.

His gaze shifts to Base again before he looks back at me, watching my eyes widen as he slips his hand down my side, under my waistband, making me tense so deliciously as he cups my bare pussy.

Mine, he mouths, pushing a finger inside me and making me moan into his hand. *All.* Another finger pushes in. *Mine.*

I rock my hips against his hand, and his fingers curl inside, pumping dangerously slowly, making me wetter and needier. I drop my hand between us and grab him through his shorts, stroking over the material while his fingers plunge in and out at a steady, rhythmical pace.

He kisses my throat, dragging his mouth down my chest while his fingers go deeper, then captures the material of my top between his teeth and drags it up and over my breast. I gasp as he sucks my nipple into his mouth. Every few seconds, he's looking over at his sleeping friend.

His fingers thrust, my hips move, and I eventually pull down his shorts and my own, positioning him between my legs. With my mouth still covered, I moan as Kade pushes the tip of his cock through my entrance, still a little delicate from all the sex we've had lately.

Each inch eases in, and Kade pays attention to my other nipple, capturing it between his teeth, marking me as his as he fully sheaths himself in my depths. "Fuck," he mumbles against my breast. "I'll never get used to this."

I arch my back, taking him even deeper. "Fuck," he breathes again, lifting his head and moving his hand to kiss me.

He hikes my knee to his hip and fucks me slowly, tenderly, making sure we don't wake—

"Is it too late for me to sneak out?"

I scream at Base's words and wince as Kade pulls out, thankful that the duvet covers us as he pushes his friend off the bed.

49

STACEY

Two hours later, after Kade and I finished what we started and showered, we stand in the driveaway and wave off Base and Barry. The latter will call us once he's dropped Base off, then he'll send pictures of his girls as soon as he gets home.

Tylar and Dez leave too, so it's just me, Kade, Ewan, Aria and the dogs in the sitting room.

Kade and Ewan are at the laptop. Ewan is still looking into how they might rebuild the manor, but Aria rather likes how much smaller this house is. She even asks Ewan if he'd be open to selling the grounds and buying a three-bedroom house.

"Oh, sweetheart," Aria says to Kade. "We were able to recover one thing from your room. I think maybe it was in the back of the cupboard." She rushes over to a large box and pulls out another smaller metal one – badly dented but intact – that has my eyes widening. "It's locked."

Kade's spine straightens as she rests it in his lap. "I thought it might be important."

Kade inputs the code, there's a faint beep and the lid pops open to reveal a damp sketch he did of me when we were eighteen. He lifts it, and I can see the emotion in his eyes. He won't want to fall apart in front of his parents, but the relief is there as I rub his back.

He sets aside all the drawings of me, the dogs and what he thought our daughter would've looked like, then lifts the princess dress with a shaky hand.

"I thought it was all gone," he says quietly. "Everything's here."

Aria lowers her head to Ewan's shoulder. "Your little girl will be proud of you," she says, and it stabs me right in the heart. "Both of you."

Kade's chin dimples as he holds in his emotions. His eyes go red, and he fights against the sound threatening to leave his throat before nodding and going through the rest of the box.

The Greatest Showman live theatre tickets – our first date that led to our first time; all the little pieces of memorabilia we collected – they're all here. And now we have time to fill it with more memories.

Kade takes my hand, curling his fingers around it, linking us. "We'll stay here for a few more days, like you suggested," he says to Aria, "then we'll need to tell everyone we're alive."

The world still thinks we're dead, and Nora hasn't once tried to arrange a funeral for me. It was Kade's family who was doing it all. Kyle was in contact with them too.

He knows I'm here – he's flying home in three days.

"There's something else you should know," Aria says, glancing at Ewan. "I think you should tell them."

He sighs and rubs his face. "Giana is pregnant."

Me and Kade frown before he asks, "What?"

Ewan nods, his eyes on the wall behind us. "She said it's Jason's, but we won't know until we get tests done. She swears there wasn't anyone else. I'll use my DNA and see if there's a match."

"Did Jason know?"

He shakes his head. "She found out the day after the funeral."

Jason told me they were trying to work on their relationship, but I had no idea they'd slept together.

Kade's hold on my hand tightens. "When is the baby due?"

"In four months," Ewan replies, getting to his feet. "She doesn't want it to get out because of how crazy things are though. The last thing she wants is the media bombarding them."

"But we're allowed to be in the kid's life?"

"Of course – once everything dies down anyway."

"Right," is all Kade replies. He's blinking, his right eye twitching, and I run my thumb over his hand.

Milo and Hopper nudge their noses against Kade's leg, and he pats them, scratching their ears, then turns to look at me. "Can we go back to bed?"

I nod. "Of course," I reply, knowing he needs to just lie and cuddle and talk. "We can put a movie on."

As we walk up the stairs, Kade's phone buzzes in his pocket. He takes it out and sees it's Barry. "Please tell me you haven't killed Base and he's safely on the flight?"

"We're surrounded," he says, and we both stop on the stairs. "They ambushed us on the way to Sebastian's manor." We can hear yelling in the background, faint sirens and Base swearing. "We're in the car. The police have us surrounded, and they're aiming right at Sebastian. I can see on their database right now. They have warrants out for your arrest, and Sebastian's, and details on your location. I suggest you run before they come for you."

We're frozen in place as we hear more yelling – Base telling the police to go fuck themselves – before Barry clears his throat. "I'm sorry, Boss."

The call cuts out just as we hear a door being thrown open and more yelling – they're being ordered to get out with their hands behind their heads.

Kade keeps the phone pressed to his ear, his eyes wide.

"What about the protection order?" I ask, panicked. "We need to leave."

Aria and Ewan run to the bottom of the stairs. "What's going on? Sebastian is on the news. They arrested him live on TV."

While I rush to the bedroom and pull out clothes for us both, I somehow repeat everything to Aria and Ewan. She cries and grabs Kade as he silently walks in, but he's still not speaking – expressionless.

I rush around while Kade thinks. I can see the gears turning in his head – I have to pack for him. My heart is in my throat that everything is going so badly. We need to run, *again*, and hide. Why does this keep happening to us?

"What about Luciella?" Aria asks, more to herself since no one has answers. "If Sebastian's been arrested, how can he help her?"

"We need a way to reach out to Tobias," Ewan says. "Which one of them has a phone?"

"I… I don't have his number. We couldn't risk saving it and reaching out in case it was tracked. He'd call us when he had to."

He'll see the news and run. He won't risk it.

Aria presses her hand to her chest. "Kade," she says, grabbing her son's face to make him look at her. He's still blank. "Run before they get here. Please," she says, shaking her head as she sobs. "This can't be happening."

"I can't breathe properly," I say, pressing my hand to my chest too, turning to Kade, who's watching me without a word. "We won't let them catch us; I promise. We'll go to the safe house and get Lisa and Eva. We can stay there until… until we figure it out."

My hands are shaking, and I fist them as I try to fill my lungs, my heart racing in my chest.

Aria and Ewan run to sort the dogs. We can't leave without them.

I walk past Kade and grab his phone charger, shoving it into the bag.

"Stacey."

"Do you know where I put my shoes?"

"Stacey, look at me."

I grab the dogs' harnesses. "Your mum and Ewan will be looking for these. Can you look for my shoes?"

Kade moves in front of me as I try to walk out the bedroom. "Think about this."

"What's there to think about? We don't have time to talk this out. Why aren't you getting ready?"

I don't wait for him to reply. I grab the door handle then run down the hallway and hand the harnesses to Ewan.

The dogs are barking, not understanding the panic as I run back into the room. Kade's sitting on the edge of the bed now. His elbows are on his knees, his hands clasped, his head bowed.

"Why are you just sitting there?"

Everything within me is close to shattering as he looks up at me, because I know what he's thinking. He's not doing this to me. He won't do this to me. He can't give up.

"No," I snap. "Don't say what I think you're going to say." I grab our bags and leave the bedroom, relieved when I hear his footsteps behind me, following me to the sitting room. For a second there, I thought Kade was going to—

"I'm not running."

I turn to him, my hair whipping my face. "What are you talking about?" I ask in unison with Aria.

He scrapes his stubble with his knuckles. "If I don't run, then you don't need to either."

I drop my bag. "What?"

"You're not in any trouble. If I stay and let them arrest me, then you don't need to hide. It'll be done. All of this will be over."

"No..." I step towards him, searching his face – he's serious. "Don't do this, Kade. Don't. They're going to arrest you for multiple murders. I'll be lucky to ever see you again as a free man."

I wordlessly move my mouth, glancing from Ewan to Aria. "Do something!"

Kade shakes his head. "I'm not running," he tells them. "What's the point? I'm not going to do that to Stacey. I'm not going to make us hide for the rest of our lives. This is what I deserve. I fucking deserve this."

He paces, grabbing his hair. "Fuck. I can't. I can't keep running from this. I was thinking about it the other day. If this bit me on the ass, I wouldn't drag you down with me."

I shake my head. "No." My face contorts with how much pain I'm in. I grab his top in a fist. "You can't leave me. Please just run. Just... come on. We have time to run. We can run to the car, drive and hide." I tug him. "Please."

"Having a normal life with you was all I ever wanted, but I don't have that luxury. I don't have time. All I have are the memories with you, and they'll keep me fucking going. But you need to let me do this. You need to."

I stare at Kade, at the seriousness on his face. "Please," I beg him, my free hand reaching up to cup his cheek, my jaw rattling. "Please don't. You're giving up. Please don't give up. Please, Kade. Please."

Ewan rushes to the window at the faint sound of sirens in the distance. "Fuck," he blurts. "They're coming."

My heart feels like it's splitting in two. I don't have enough time to change his mind. I'm the only one begging him to run. Why has everyone given up? Why is no one else yelling at him to get the hell out of the house while he has the chance?

"I'm not giving up. I'm giving in. I'm not innocent, Stacey. I've killed hundreds of people. Some of them were innocent. I'm tired. Exhausted even. I'm not going to allow you to ruin the rest of your life for me. I'm staying and surrendering. I'll accept the punishment. I'm not dragging you through all of this."

I let out a strangled cry, dropping my head to his chest. "Please don't leave me. Please, please, please. Run. Please. Run with me. I don't care about freedom as long as I'm with you."

"You need to let me do this, okay?" Kade kisses the top of my head, wrapping his arms around me. One last hug while he's in the outside world.

I sob into his chest. My own feels like it's cracking open. There's pressure behind my eyes and in my head, and I'm dizzy. "Please run with me."

Kade's chest shakes. "I'm so sorry, Stacey. I'm sorry for everything. For not seeing what was happening at home, for leaving you, for taking so long to get away from Bernadette. If I could go back to being eighteen and carefree with you, I would."

"I can't do this without you. You're all I have, Kade. Please."

Kade's shaking against me, his own tears wracking his body. "I love you, Stacey. So fucking much. I love you. I'll never stop."

I screw my eyes shut, a shock of pain in my heart, my head already aching from the pressure there. "I'll never stop loving you either."

I back away so Aria and Ewan can hug Kade. It's a long hug, and Kade trembles as they both tell him repeatedly that he's a good kid, that they're going to try to get him out and that he has a heart of gold.

Rage overtakes me as I hear tyres screeching outside, and I fist my hands, turning and running out the room and down the steps, throwing the front door open. I don't falter at the number of officers surrounding the house. All of them have guns – they're pointing them right at me as my footsteps carry me to the middle of the garden.

I throw my arms out to the sides. "How can you all do this?" I yell. "How dare you all stand there with your guns knowing what he's been through?"

"Hands behind your head!" one shouts at me.

"He's innocent! He was forced to do everything, and you all know it!"

The officers' aims shift to behind me, and I sob as Kade drags me behind him. He keeps me caged as he backs me away from the police, Aria and Ewan standing on the porch with tears streaming down their faces.

"I love you," he says, breathless from running after me. "I'll love you for the rest of my life. I love you more than fucking anything, but I need you to walk to the porch."

My head buries into his back as the officers yell at Kade to back away from me, to raise his hands, to kneel and put his hands behind his head. "I can't lose you," I cry.

"Let go and walk to my mother, Stacey," he demands, his throat cracking. "Please."

"I can't let go."

The dogs are barking inside, and more cars are speeding towards the house.

"I'm yours, and you're mine."

My jaw trembles. "Forever," I say shakily. "I love you."

He turns and smiles down at me, and I can see how tired he is as he wipes my tears with his thumb. I can see officers in my peripheral vision approaching. "So beautiful, even when you cry, my Freckles. You're amazing, do you know that? I was lucky to have you for even a short space of time. There aren't any threats left. No Chris, no Bernadette. You can dance and sing and live."

More tears fall down my cheeks, and I can't stop them. It's the strong connection between us. The love. The possessiveness of what we have. We've belonged to each other since we were fifteen, in a way. I've always wanted him, and now I'm about to lose him – the boy who sat at the pool, whose cigarette I stole; the innocence of him as he used to watch me, as I'd watched him throughout the years. Until that first kiss, and the second, and every kiss after. We fell harder than I thought possible. We lost. We fought. But after so many hurdles, we were so close.

"I was supposed to be your forever," I sob, and it's as if the world around us has slowed enough to let us have this last conversation. "You asked me on the beach in Greece if I'd be your forever, and I said yes."

We were going to get the happy ending we wanted. Where I'd give him children, marry him, build a home and grow old with him. I was going to fall asleep in his arms safely every night and wake to his, *Good morning, Freckles,* and laugh at his, *You are a terrible singer, Freckles.*

The dogs would have sat on the porch while I read, and Kade would have been building a tree house and attaching a swing for the kids. He'd be chasing them across the grass as their dark hair flopped in the wind, their tiny legs barely able to carry them away from their loving father.

We were supposed to have it all.

Kade and I stare at each other, holding tightly to one another, and he grabs my face and kisses me – a bruising kiss I hope to feel forever – before he's tackled away from me.

"No!" I scream, but it's no use. I'm outnumbered by at least twenty and dragged out of the way by Ewan as they pile on top of Kade like ants. One tasers him, even though he isn't fighting back, and I scream as I see the baton drop on his head.

I'm held back by three officers, as are Aria and Ewan. They're hitting him with their batons, and I can see blood splashing on one of their faces. Ewan gets tasered too, then Aria and I end up pinned to the grass when we try to get to Kade.

"He isn't resisting!" I scream, but they aren't listening.

An officer kicks Kade in the side, and I can taste dirt as the woman restraining me pushes my face further into the grass.

Through the sea of bodies, I notice an officer shoving his knee into Kade's back before handcuffing him and reading him his rights.

When Kade's yanked to his feet, he struggles against the four officers holding him, managing to turn and see me. "Get off her!" he yells, his face bloodied. "Get your dirty fucking hands off her!"

"Little bitch," the officer sneers in my ear as Kade vanishes from my vision.

I can't do anything but stay pinned to the ground, wincing as she pulls my hands back and cuffs me too. "Stacey Rhodes," she says, "you are under arrest for the kidnapping and murder of both Christopher Fields and Bernadette Sawyer. You do not have to say anything. But it may harm your defence if you do not mention when questioned something which you later rely on in court. Anything you do say may be given in evidence."

50

KADE

The clock on the wall doesn't work. I've been staring at it for what feels like hours, and the hands aren't moving. There's no ticking. What's the fucking point in having it hanging right in front of me, making me feel insane?

I tilt my head, the slight shift of my body's position making the cuffs chafe on my wrist. They're far tighter than they need to be. But I guess when you're being charged with multiple murders and kidnapping and whatever the fuck else they're slapping me with, keeping my hands and ankles restrained is a smart move.

The belt around my waist connects a chain to my cuffs too.

They've brought me to this room every day for the last week. Questioning me on everything, asking me to repeat what I disclosed on the live stream while killing Archie Sawyer. They've put over one hundred pictures in front of me and asked if I'm responsible for the disappearances of the people they show.

I mean, I am, but I'm not going to tell them anything.

I've not been allowed my call – I'm wearing scrubs because they won't give me the clothes I know for a fact my mother would've tried to hand in. Stacey has probably been at the front desk demanding information too, but as far as I'm aware, it's just radio silence.

It fucking hurts me to think of not seeing Milo and Hopper again. Sure, everyone else will be able to visit me, and I'll be able to talk on the phone to them, but seeing my dogs again? No chance.

The wanker who came to the manor with his boss to offer me the protection order months ago walks in. He's been the lead officer this time, and he hates my guts. Maybe threatening him every time he talks to me has been a bad idea, but I'm past caring anymore. I just want to speak to my girl, make sure Luciella's okay and that my dad hasn't been caught.

I don't care about myself.

"So," the dick starts, dropping a folder between us on the metal table. "Stacey Rhodes."

My spine straightens. "What about her?"

"Quite a while ago, she appeared at this station roughed up. She'd taken drugs and said her stepbrother had attacked her and killed someone. I so happen to be the big brother of his ex-girlfriend and knew her face. There was no evidence of this attack. He came to collect her, and I suggested therapy or to even section her."

My teeth grind together as I wait for him to continue.

He rubs his hand down his face. "I didn't know she was telling the truth. Three weeks ago, we discovered the remains of a man at the scene of where she said she was attacked. Forensics confirmed he died around the time she tried to report it."

"Stacey came to you for help and you pushed her back into the arms of her abuser?"

"That is a mistake I will never forgive myself for. Stacey is a victim. There's a video of her being sexually assaulted I'm sure you are well aware of. All her attackers are either dead or missing."

My lip twitches. "Shame."

"Stacey lost her mother when she was young. She also lost her father not long after losing her unborn child. It seems all she's had since is pain and heartbreak. She deserves a good shot at life, doesn't she?"

I narrow my eyes. "What are you getting at?"

His head tilts. "You don't know?"

"Know what?"

"Stacey Rhodes is being charged with the murder of Christopher Fields and the disappearance and kidnapping of Bernadette Sawyer."

I don't breathe or blink or move as I stare at him. "What did you just say?"

"Sebastian Prince has been charged with the same offences," he says, folding his arms. "Barry Lennox is being charged with kidnapping and being an accessory to murder."

"They didn't do anything."

"I was hoping you'd say that," he replies, grinning. "Do you know you're facing at least sixteen life sentences? You'll never see daylight again."

"I'm fully aware, asshole."

He scoffs and shakes his head. "You're just like your father."

I raise a brow – he's close to getting a fist in his face unless he gets to the point.

"We're willing to offer you a deal."

"Of course you are."

"You tell us what happened to Christopher Fields and Bernadette Sawyer, and we'll lift the charges from your three friends." He opens the folder between us. "We can also erase all of these names. You tell us what we want to know, and we can reduce all your sentences to ten years."

I bark out a laugh. "All of you are corrupt as fuck. Are there any genuine officers left?"

"You will also give us those names you left out in your original statement. We know there are detectives within Scotland Yard and the New York Police Department that have heavy involvement in the underworld. Those names, plus an admission of what happened to Christopher and Bernadette, and your friends and girlfriend are free."

"And I serve ten years?"

"We'll do what we can to get it as close to ten as possible. This is the only offer we'll make, Mr Mitchell. We know your circumstance and how you were blackmailed and coerced into your crimes. You can plead insanity too, like your father did, but I highly suggest taking this deal."

I gulp and look down at the folder, my eyes glued to the mugshot of Stacey. She's crying, and she has a bruise on her cheek.

"One more condition," I say, glaring at him.

"Fine. What do you want?"

As soon as the door opens three hours later, my heart accelerates, but the chain attached to the table stops me from getting up as Stacey is brought in, cuffed, wearing scrubs that match my own.

"Stacey." Her name drops from my lips.

Her chin trembles as she shakes – my girl is trying to hold it together.

Officer Dickhead unlocks the cuffs from my leather belt. "You have three minutes. Kyle Fields is waiting for her in the office."

Her good brother – he better look after her while I'm in here.

The door closes, and I go to her, taking her face in my hands and tracing the bruise on her cheek. "Are you okay?"

"What did you do?" she asks, her voice cracking as her face contorts. She slowly presses her forehead to my chest when I just stare at her. "Tell me what you did."

My restrained hands lift to brush through her hair. "You're everything to me, do you know that?" I take her face and tilt her chin, kissing her on the lips. "Everything."

"What did you do?"

I shrug. "You shouldn't be in here."

"Neither sh-should you." Her head drops again, and she grips at the fabric against my skin. "Tell me what you did."

I can't hug her because the cuffs are attached to the belt, so all I can do is cup the sides of her neck, stroking her pulse points with my thumbs. "I took a deal to get you, Base and Barry out."

Her body trembles as she sobs into my chest. "What kind of deal?"

"They'll try to reduce my sentence to ten years. I doubt they will since I'm facing sixteen life sentences, but my main reason for saying yes was to get you all out. None of you should be in here."

She shakes her head. "No."

"Yes." I pull back. "We don't have time to debate this. It's done. You're going to kiss me, then you're going to go to your brother and go live your life. You're going to dance. You're going to fall asleep next to the dogs every night, and you're going to be there for my sister and my niece or nephew. You're going to live, Stacey. Fucking live for me."

"I can't live without you."

"I love you. I'm so proud of you," I say, my eyes burning as I hold her against me. "So, so fucking proud."

"I love you too," she croaks. "Please don't make me do this without you. Please, Kade."

"You need to. Don't you dare waste the next ten years waiting for me. Like I said, it's unlikely they'll even reduce it."

Her voice is so quiet, like a beautiful calm as she pulls her head back to look up at me. "But I'm yours."

"And I'm yours." I press my lips to hers then run my thumb across her chin. "Just... promise me you won't pause your life for me?"

She smiles through her tears. "Kade Mitchell," she says, reaching up on her tiptoes and kissing me again. "Don't you get it? You are my life."

My voice cracks. "You're my life too."

The door opens once again, and my heart sinks. She doesn't fight as the officer pulls her away. "I'm going to wait for you," she tells me. "I'd wait forever for you."

I nod and let the first tear fall. "Forever, Freckles."

EPILOGUE 1

STACEY

FIVE YEARS LATER

One of my pet peeves is waiting.

Waiting on Tobias calling me to tell me how he's doing.

Waiting on Kyle proposing to his girlfriend after hyping him up for the past three years – he's nervous, but considering she's head over heels for him and already has their future planned out, she won't say no.

Waiting on Tylar's parents signing off on the sale of the studio and finalising the documents – it's to become the Rhodes Dance Academy for kids and adults.

Waiting on Aria and Ewan telling me we can finally meet Jason Junior – Giana hasn't let him have any involvement with the family so far, given how crazy the media attention remains.

Waiting on Kade walking through that door for our last ever

conjugal visitation – the clock says that he's two minutes late, and he's never late. It makes me nervous as I strum my fingers on the small table I've been bent over too many times to count.

I sit back on the chair and look around the room. It's almost identical to the one Tobias used to have me visit him in. There's a bed, a bookcase, a table and two chairs, and a box filled with board games.

We were offered a family room, but since we don't have any children, we accepted this one – a special circumstance, like everything else when it comes to Mitchells and the authorities.

There's a beep that draws my attention to the door, my frown turning to a full grin as it opens and Kade walks in. My boyfriend is as handsome as ever, his hair a black mop on his head, his eyes still the same beautiful shade of blue that drew me in all those years ago. Colour floods his cheeks when he sees me, and I take in the faded scar and the muscles he's been working on every day.

I'm the luckiest girl in the world.

He tries to hold in a smirk as the guard removes his cuffs and gives him the usual speech before closing the door.

Kade barely keeps his balance as I launch myself into his arms and slam my mouth on his. His back hits the wall, his hands holding me up and against him as I wrap my legs around him, devouring his mouth like I didn't just see him two days ago.

He spins us around then presses me into the wall and kisses along my jaw, snatching my earlobe between his teeth before letting his mouth travel my throat and sliding my dress up my body until it's wrapped around my waist.

"Sorry I'm late," he says as he rips my underwear and drops the material on the floor while I fumble with the string of his trousers then tug them down to free his cock.

We both gasp as he thrusts deep. It's not slow or sweet or careful – it's harsh and fast and mind-bending as he fucks me against the wall.

We don't use protection. A few times we were reckless, twice the condom broke, then for four weeks straight, we didn't use anything and I still didn't get pregnant. We haven't used birth control for months now.

Every test I've taken has been negative.

"You belong to me," Kade growls, pounding deeper so my back hits the wall with each thrust. "Ever since we met at the pool house at fifteen, you've belonged to me."

I smile against his mouth. "I was looking for you," I admit, hooking my heels into the back of his thighs to draw him in deeper. "I knew Luciella had a twin brother." I sink my teeth into his bottom lip. "I was intrigued and wanted to meet you."

His cock swells inside me as my inner walls clench around his thickness, my spine tingling and sending rushes of heat between my thighs. So close. I'm so, so close.

"I watched you from my balcony," he tells me, sucking on my tongue and swallowing my gasps. "Now you're fucking mine."

I let out a moan as he hits somewhere deep and sweet and euphoric, igniting a fire within that has my orgasm slamming into me so hard, I nearly pass out in his arms. He fucks me through it, telling me how beautiful and perfect I am, how soaked and tight I am, how I'm his and always will be.

He backs up to sit on the chair, me straddling his thighs, his cock still buried deep. He pulls my dress up and over my head, unclipping my bra so he can feast on my nipples while I fist his hair and continue riding him.

Kade's hands roam my body as I move – as his mouth leaves wet trails, kissing from my breasts to my throat, making my head drop back on a moan.

"So pretty," he mutters against my skin. "So pretty and mine."

Feeling his cock fill me with each drop of my hips, I tense around him some more, gripping his shoulder with one hand and fisting his hair tighter. "Yours," I breathe out harshly.

These types of visitations are over quick, so we make the most of them. There's usually no talking, unless we count him whispering dirty things in my ear while making me explode. When we aren't here, we're sitting at a table with twenty other inmates, everyone overhearing each other's conversations and hating life.

Kade usually stays silent and just listens to what life has been like for everyone since their last visit. His mum and Ewan chatter for the entire hour. Dez comes himself, and Base, if he's allowed to leave his castle in Russia, told Kade that talking to him for those sixty minutes is the only time he feels like he's still alive.

Kade was supposed to get six life sentences, though the officers told him if he took the fall and told them what happened to Chris and Bernadette, they'd free me, Barry and Base, and reduce his sentence to ten years.

They lied. He was given two life sentences with no hope of ever being a free man again. But I refused to let that happen, so Aria and I got to work right away on his appeal.

After five appeals and a worldwide debate on his sentencing, we managed to reduce it from two life sentences to fifty years. Then Aria got a new lawyer in, but the next appeal fell through, and then another, until a man from Australia with salt-and-pepper hair flew here and won the next one.

We got it down to ten years.

I was happy to wait – I would have waited until my last breath for Kade. But that was until petitions started gathering more attention, and mobs began standing outside the prison and courthouse, chanting for Kade to be released. Social media exploded when even more footage surfaced, proving that Kade had been forced and blackmailed into all the killings.

In one video, he was being forced to strangle a man and all we could hear was him repeatedly telling the victim that he was sorry. Witnesses came forward saying he'd saved them when their homes had been raided by Bernadette's team – so, so many witnesses – and the next appeal blew up the internet.

Ultimately, when his sentence was reduced one last time, we accepted it was time to stop fighting. Kade was ready to stop fighting as soon as he was told he'd never be free again, but the world refused to let him die in prison. It rallied for Kade, and now I get to stand outside the prison next week and run into his arms. I get to have Kade all to myself – no ties or blackmail or worrying about what will happen next.

We get to be happy.

"Fuck," he blurts. "Seven minutes."

I lean back, grinding against his cock as I smile at him. "That didn't stop you last time. You threw a chair at the guard while still inside me."

"Never again." His hold tightens on my hips. "I don't want anyone seeing me fucking you." He slides his hand up my chest and grabs my throat, using his hold to control me as he cuts off my air. "I want to feel your pussy strangling my cock while your eyes roll to the back of your pretty little head."

"I think I'll die if I come again," I gasp.

He yanks me to him by the throat and kisses me. "Then I guess we're both dying. Because there isn't a life for me without you."

We fall apart together – muttered words of praise and love and kisses to the forehead and shoulder. I stay straddling him, desperate to fill my lungs, sweat sticking to our skin as his hand strokes my back, tracing his fingers over each vertebra.

"Are you worried?" he asks, his fingers still playing on my spine.

"About what?"

"This has become routine. What if I don't fit into your life outside of here?"

"You fit into every aspect of my life, Kade. This isn't routine – this is us waiting for your freedom."

He takes a deep breath. "I'm nervous. What if I don't adjust? I've done all my therapy in here. I've worked on everything in here. What if I get out and the seizures and blackouts start again?"

Shaking my head, I wrap my arms around him and press my forehead to his. "Then we'll work on them like we have in here. Together."

He blinks at me, curling a strand of hair behind my ear. "Always fighting for me. I need to get out of here and make sure everyone knows you're mine."

"The entire world knows I'm yours," I say, rolling my eyes.

"I would still like to claim my girl on the outside."

I blush and stand, grabbing my bra and dress from the floor, and shoving my ripped underwear in my bag. "Can you still call me your girl even though I'm almost thirty now?"

"You'll always be my girl," he says.

I smile and sit on the table in front of him, leaning back on my palms. His hands slide up my thighs, kneading the muscles there. I've still been dancing and teaching. Luciella came back from

Russia two years ago, and I've spent a lot of time with her and the twins. I've had to hire more instructors in the studio so I'd have more time to help her.

The door beeps behind me, and I sigh.

Kade ignores the guard and stands, moving between my legs to tip my chin up and kiss me. "See you on the outside, Freckles."

We never planned on the media being here. We never planned on the entire world waiting patiently at the gates of the prison either. Crowds upon crowds, news stations set up, people with signs and whistles, all of them giving us space at the front of the crowd as we wait.

And wait, and wait, and wait.

Eden is hurting my arms with how heavy she is, and Anastasia is holding Luciella's hand. The Prince twins have been told not to try to speak to their daddy while in public – it's a sad necessity to keep them safe.

Luciella doesn't let her eyes slip to the father of her girls as he stands with all his bodyguards. His wife is on his right, her main bodyguard behind her, and she keeps looking at me.

A silent hello.

"Can I please go see Daddy?" Eden asks me, and I fix the nearly five-year-old in my arms as I tell her I'm sorry, but she can only see Daddy when he's by himself.

Anastasia is the well-behaved one. She stands with a stone-cold expression like she always does. Even when Base does manage to sneak away from his duties in the mafia, she doesn't pay much attention to her absent father.

It's not his fault. If the Russians find out the twins are his, they'll kill them and Luciella.

That's definitely a story for another day.

I look over my shoulder, my gaze clashing with Gianna's as a little boy the same age as the twins clutches her leg. It's not hard to tell that he's Jason's son. Jason Junior. He's his father's double.

She gives me a stiff smile – before she glances at the cameras and pulls Jason Junior's hood up. The fact she's here is the first step.

The mass of people starts screaming, and my head snaps back to the main gate as a group of guards walk out of the double doors, all of them crowding around one person, taller than most of them, his black hair a mess as he runs his hand through it.

I lower Eden to her feet, and Lu takes her hand. Aria is crying, because she's always crying; Ewan is beside her, his grey hair flapping in the wind; and on the other side, with a cap on, his hood up, wearing glasses and a short beard to hide his identity, Tobias waits for his son.

The gate slides open, and everyone stays put as I run. I don't even need to think about it – my feet carry me straight to Kade, and he catches me in his arms as everyone cheers. My legs hook around him as he keeps walking, further and further away from his cage, my head buried into his shoulder.

I sob into him, and he doesn't let me go, his hand at the back of my head, his chest shaking. "You waited for me," he says against my ear, kissing my temple. "I hope you're ready for the rest of our lives, Freckles."

"Uncle Kade!" the twins scream, and he settles me down just before they collide with him.

EPILOGUE 2

KADE

TWO YEARS LATER

"Pass me the flathead screwdriver."

Roman Tobias Michell, my eighteen-month-old son, stares at his grandfather while he holds up the instruction manual he just spilled juice all over. He throws the papers at my dad then runs away giggling as Milo follows him across the yard.

I laugh and shake my head as Dad scowls at the back of my son's head.

"I told you – you need to stop letting Roman near Barry's kids."

"He's one and has you wrapped around his finger."

He just grunts, because he knows I'm right. Barry and Dez are helping Ewan with the plastering inside the house I built for me, Stacey and our son while my dad and I build a tree house for all the kids to play in.

Stacey has nearly fifty picture frames of my sketches to hang up – as soon as I was in the right state of mind, I bought a new sketchbook and didn't stop until my hand hurt. My therapist is proud of me. He's encouraging me to keep walking the path I'm on. It's a path of accepting who I am, my past, my present, in order to claim my future.

And, man, my future is looking really fucking good.

Who knew Kade Mitchell would have a chance at happiness? I'm still coming to terms with it all.

Hopper, sadly, passed away six months ago. His heart just gave up in his sleep, and Milo hasn't been the same since. Fuck, I don't think me and Stacey have been the same since. If it wasn't for Roman, I think Milo would've died of a broken heart the same day. He's old – I don't think he has very long left, so we make the most of the time we do have with him.

He's my son's best friend.

We found out a week after my release that Stacey was pregnant – she was sick a lot, slept a lot and needed my cock a lot, and me being the doting partner I am, I gave her every inch.

We got married a year ago. We didn't want anything big and fancy – my family and Kyle all met up in Greece, and we got married on the same beach where I told her I was in love with her. Base carried Roman down the aisle with the rings. The twins were our flower girls, and Barry, Dez and Base were my best men while Tylar and Luciella stood beside Stacey.

She's always been beautiful, but seeing her walking towards me with her hand in my father's, a bright smile on her face, the mother of my child and my entire future, I knew I'd won at life.

I wanted my nephew to be there, but Gianna is still being strict. I've only met Jason Junior in person three times. Three. And one of those times was accidental. Me and Stacey bumped into them in the mall, and I could tell she was uncomfortable as I greeted my brother's son and tried not to break down.

He was nervous, and I didn't want him nervous, so we set up a video call with them a few days later. And since then, he's always calling me. And what makes it even better is that he's just like his dad. The missing part of me that was stolen in a smaller form.

I'll do everything to protect that kid, even if the visits will stay virtual until his mother feels comfortable enough for him to be fully in my life. It's still hectic. I refuse every interview, threaten to beat the shit out of people who try to stop us in the street and ask Stacey rude questions, and the social media experience has been extreme.

I'm never on my socials now. Ever.

Stacey uses her platform for charities and for her studios. They always do shows now in the theatres, and my girl even performed a fire dance before we found out she was pregnant with our second.

I toss my dad the screwdriver, and we watch Milo and Roman play on the grass in front of us. He only just started walking – but all he does is run. It gives me a fucking heart attack half the time.

He's got Stacey's eyes. These big green forests staring back at me every night while I read him his bedtime story and he falls asleep on my chest. His hair is as black as mine, and he loves my motorbike, even if he does startle when I start it up.

"The twins were fighting over who got to hold my hand again yesterday," Dad says. "Surprisingly, they seem to forget I have two hands."

He's still dead to the world – though I honestly think since he barely hides, they know and just leave him to it. He and Mum found their common ground when the twins were born. He still flirts with her, and she still rolls her eyes at him, but they're friends more than anything else now. Maybe they finally grew up and stopped thinking it was perfectly acceptable to fuck around when she's married.

But then again, they still love each other, so who knows.

"When do Desmond and Tylar leave?"

"Next month," I reply. "They travel the world more than anyone I know."

"I'd get bored."

I laugh, catching Roman as he rushes by me. He giggles as I tickle him and throw him into the air in a way I'm sure Stacey will find terrifying. "I think this one needs a change." I sniff him and arch my neck away. "Yep. Grandpa, it's your turn."

My dad wipes his hands off, lifts Roman, and starts baby-talking to him as he walks back to the house.

The ringing from my phone steals my attention, and I see it's Luciella. "Hello?" I answer.

"Don't freak out," she says, and I get to my feet quickly. "But Stacey's waters broke in the studio like two minutes ago, and she said the contractions are already coming."

Fuck. She isn't due till next month.

"Stacey's in labour!" I shout to my dad before he vanishes through the front door as I rush by the porch. Ewan and Dez appear and wish me and Stacey luck, but I'm already at my car in a panic of excitement and fear, remembering how exhausted Stacey was when Roman was born – she'd been in labour for nearly two days and had screamed until her throat went harsh.

I'm behind the wheel and backing out of the drive as I ask, "Where are you?"

"I'm driving us to the hospital now." There's a long groan in the background. "Oh, okay, just breathe. Yeah, she's definitely contracting, Kade. Please hurry. I'm nearly there."

I hang up the phone and fuck the law as I speed. I intentionally made sure we lived close to everything we needed. We have my parents two streets over in their new home, which is a lot smaller than the manor. I bought the plot of land and got to work on it as soon as we found out Stacey was pregnant with Roman.

It takes me fifteen minutes to reach the hospital, and I dodge multiple people as I run through the maternity ward while wiping my hands on my jeans. I push open the door to the stairs and take them two at a time until I'm on the floor I need.

"Stacey Mitchell," I say, breathless. "Where is she?"

"Delivery room five, sir. Are you the father?"

"Yes," I reply and hunt down the room.

I push open the door and see Stacey on the edge of the bed with her hands on her lower back while she does her breathing exercises. She turns her head in my direction and lets out a sigh of relief. "You made it."

I'm by her side in a second, taking her hands. "How do you feel?"

"Like my body is breaking from the inside."

I move a strand of hair from her face. "You've got this."

She grimaces through a contraction and drops her head to my shoulder, a groan following. "They're coming faster than with Roman," she cries. "Oh God. It hurts."

Luciella rises from her chair. "I'll go," she says. "You've got this, Stacey." Then her eyes land on me. "She might actually break your hand this time."

I huff a laugh as my twin sister leaves the room. The midwife talks to Stacey while filling in forms. Then they give me oils to rub on the bottom of her back while the contractions get stronger, until she's screaming in agony and gripping on to me for dear life.

I wish I could take this pain from her – I fucking hate seeing my girl hurting. She's crying and screaming as the contractions get closer together, until she tells the midwife she needs to lie on the bed.

We get her on it, and my heart is fucking racing as they keep checking our baby's heart rate and how dilated Stacey is.

"If you have the urge to push, then push. Just like last time."

Stacey grits her teeth as another contraction hits, and I stand by the bed as she grips my hand, kissing her forehead and temple, telling her how well she's doing, how fucking strong she is as she starts pushing.

My fingers are near breaking, but I'll happily let the bones shatter – it'll be miniscule compared to what she's going through right now.

"I can see the head!" the midwife says excitedly, but I don't dare go down and look, remembering Stacey nearly choked me for trying with Roman. I stay put, kissing her more and wiping her forehead and gritting my own teeth as her hold tightens.

"One big push!"

Stacey's body tenses everywhere as she holds her breath and pushes like she's never pushed before, and I think I might pass out.

"Okay now the shoulders. Another push, sweetheart."

Stacey pushes again, her face red and soaked in sweat, her hair sticking to her forehead as I move it behind her ears.

Then I hear the cries of our secondborn, and my heart grows a little in my chest when the midwife lifts the baby to Stacey's chest.

"A beautiful baby girl," she says. "With a full head of hair," she adds with a huge smile.

Stacey has tears in her eyes, and so do I as we fuss over our daughter. Another daughter. Our guardian angel is watching over us, protecting her siblings. Roman, and now a girl with dark hair who's wrapping her little fingers around my pinkie, and I melt into a puddle as I kiss Stacey. "Thank you," I say to her. "You did amazing."

She beams as the nurse works on her, her cheeks soaked, as if all the pain she was just in vanishes when she smiles down at our daughter.

Her bottom lip is trembling, and I know she's thinking of our baby girl we lost.

"I love you," I tell her. "I'm so proud of you. Thank you for giving me everything I've ever wanted. You. A son. A daughter. A life with you."

"I love you too," she replies, her voice breaking.

"Did you have a name picked out?" one of the nurses asks as she wheels over the baby scales and observation machine.

"Daisy Mitchell," Stacey says, sniffing and kissing her head, looking up at me. "She's our Daisy Mitchell."

EPILOGUE 3

KADE

FOUR YEARS LATER

Roman is on my right, Junior on my left as the lights in the theatre dim – red velvet curtains rise, revealing all the little dancers readying for their routine as "From Now On" from *The Greatest Showman* begins, and my eyes are already watering.

Daisy, Eden and Anastasia are among the dancers, and Stacey is kneeling to the side, guiding them through their steps. Base is recording, Luciella is crying already and our parents are behind us watching too.

I remember the first time I watched the movie with Stacey. I think her obsession with it matched mine, and I knew at that point I wanted to spend the rest of my life with her. And I am. We're in our mid-thirties now, with two kids, living in a house I promised to build, and Junior even comes to stay from time to time.

My sketches are all over the walls. The dogs we had, Milo and Hopper, have a portrait above our fireplace. There's a family portrait I did right next to it.

I even take Stacey on dates, and she still blushes when I say cute things to her. She also likes to drag me to bed when the kids are asleep and remind me what her mouth can do before I fuck her into the mattress.

The chorus hits, and I clap with everyone else to the beat. Daisy is so small on the stage, but she has the confidence of her mother, and she doesn't miss a step. My daughter is definitely a daddy's girl – even a grandpa's girl.

Stacey and I always place bets on which kid will come into our room first during the night. Most of the time it's Daisy, but recently, Roman has been sleeping on her floor when she gets afraid of the dark, and I don't have it in me to tell him not to because it reminds me of when Jason and I did that for Luciella.

Stacey is going nuts down there, and I watch her as she hypes her dancers up, following their steps, and as the little ones run off to the side, and the older dancers join in halfway through the song, so does Stacey. Four hoops lower from the ceiling, and she leads the rest of the routine, and I can't take my damn eyes off my wife.

She's breath-taking in every form.

Everyone gets to their feet, still clapping to the song as all the age groups join the stage, jumping up and down and singing along.

Stacey is crying, lifting Daisy into her arms and the twins wave at Base and Luciella. My best friend puts his arm around my sister and kisses her head as he keeps recording the stage.

The show ends, and Roman sighs in relief. "That was soooooo boring, Dad."

I laugh. "Don't say that in front of your sister."

He pinkie promises me, and we make our way out of the seating area, and my Daisy comes sprinting out of the side door, Stacey trying to catch up, and hurls herself right into my arms.

"Did you see me, Daddy?" she screams, her face red from jumping around.

"I did! You were so good, baby girl."

Everyone crowds around us. Dad and Mum say they're going to head home, Junior wants to come stay at my house, and Luciella holds her back and waddles towards us. She looks like she's close to popping, but she's only six months along.

"My little princesses! You were both great!" Base picks up his twins. "Are we going for pizza?"

"Shut up," I whisper-hiss at him so my daughter doesn't hear. "I already promised food and a movie with the kids at home."

He flattens his lips. "You're not going to subject your spawn to another viewing of the movie of the show you just watched here, right?"

"Hey!" Roman scolds. "I like that movie!"

Base shakes his head. "You would say that. You're just your father in a younger form."

My son scowls at him. He loves him really, but he's very protective of his little unit. Even if Base is technically a mafia leader.

Stacey grins and takes my hand, leading me towards the door. "We'll see you all at our place for Christmas?"

They all agree, and I smile at my girl as she looks over at me.

It all feels normal. We are normal.

We've never been normal before.

But now, since there's no Bernadette and no Chris forcing us to the edge of darkness, and we don't feel like we're in forbidden territory being together, Stacey and I can just... be.

Everyone knows she's mine. And everyone knows I'm hers. Everything has fallen into place for us, and now we have it all.

I don't regret letting myself get arrested all those years ago, because otherwise I wouldn't have this. I wouldn't have Stacey smiling at me as we walk our son, daughter and nephew to the car to head home and watch *The Greatest Showman* with bowls of junk food.

The fulfilling feeling of mattering to someone so much that they're still by my side even now, after everything – it's surreal. But Stacey's always been there. Through everything. She's been there.

Our broken puzzle pieces are finally firmly in place, and they'll never be torn apart again. Because we get to have this. We get to have everything we've ever wanted.

Kade Mitchell and Stacey Rhodes – the fifteen-year-olds who met by the pool twenty years ago – finally get to have their forever.

WHAT'S NEXT?

PSYCHOTIC OBSESSION

THE DARK AND DANGEROUS LOVE STORY

ARIA AND TOBIAS

ACKNOWLEDGEMENTS

How do I even start this? I'm far too emotional and my eyes are burning from crying too much. How can their story be done? How, after over three years of Kade and Stacey being so damn loud in my head and writing their rollercoaster of a story on Wattpad and then rewriting for publishing, can everything be over? I'm grieving them when I should be celebrating that they made it. We made it.

I would never have reached this point if it wasn't for my readers. Wattpad introduced me to writing. I started there in 2019, where Tobias and Aria's story sparked an excitement in me. They had a son named Kade, and my mind spiralled into The Edge of Darkness. With my weekly updates, the inline comments making me smile, and the messages about how excited readers were for the next chapter, I would never have had the confidence to publish this trilogy. Thank you to that little app and the readers within it, I found a career I love.

Thank you to my PA Tyla. I never knew I was missing a part of me until I met you. *Call me cheesy, I dare you.* Lauren, my ARC manager and hand holder, you kept me sane and on the right path. As a debut author, I was terrified my writing wasn't enough – Laura, my editor, made sure that wasn't the case. Shawna and my Kendras – you girls are my rocks!

To all my readers who fell in love with the characters and story, thank you for taking a chance on me.

And lastly, my amazing street team – could an author ask for a better group? Never.

ABOUT THE AUTHOR

Leigh Rivers is a Scottish Biomedical Scientist who has ventured into the world of writing dark, morally gray characters with rollercoaster storylines to drive her readers wild.

When she isn't reading, writing on her laptop, or gaming until ridiculous hours, she dances at the pole studio, goes to the gym, and walks her four dogs with her two sons and husband.

You can find Leigh on her socials:
Instagram - @authorleighrivers
Facebook - @authorleighrivers
TikTok - @authorleighrivers